THE ORPHAN CHILD

Catherine King

SPHERE

First published in Great Britain in 2010 by Sphere
This paperback edition published in 2011 by Sphere
Reprinted 2011, 2013

A CIP catalogue record for this book
is available from the British Library.

ISBN 978-0-7515-4386-5

Typeset in Bembo by Palimpsest Book Production Limited,
Falkirk, Stirlingshire
Printed and bound in Great Britain by
Clays Ltd, St Ives plc

Papers used by Sphere are from well-managed forests
and other responsible sources.

MIX
Paper from
responsible sources
FSC® C104740

Sphere
An imprint of
Little, Brown Book Group
100 Victoria Embankment
London EC4Y 0DY

An Hachette UK Company
www.hachette.co.uk

www.littlebrown.co.uk

Acknowledgements

I should like to thank my agent Judith Murdoch and the wonderful team at Sphere, especially Caroline Hogg, Louise Davies and Hannah Hargrave, for their encouragement, support and unfailing good humour during the writing and publication of this book. It is a pleasure to work with all of them.

PART ONE

Chapter 1

1829

Patterns of ice lingered on the outside of the scullery window at Meadow Hall and red berries set the holly bushes on fire. Across the cobbled yard the horses were restless; the ground was too frozen for their morning gallop. Steam streamed from their nostrils as devoted grooms clothed their backs in blankets and walked them through crisp snow that softened the clatter of hooves on stone. Inside the stables the master and his trainer watched silently as a brood mare wrestled with the birth of her foal. They sipped regularly from their hip flasks. This one was sure to be a winner.

Beyond the stables on the edge of the woods, a couple of young stable lads raced around throwing snowballs at each other; until one of them stopped abruptly and stared.

'What's that up there on the track?'

'I can't see from here. Let's have a closer look.'

'Not now. It's nearly dinner time. We'll get the whip if we're late today.'

'Well, don't tell anybody and we'll come back later.'

Indoors, the servants had finished their morning's work and coal fires were drawing well in the gracious bedchambers and reception rooms. They waited patiently in a cold passage until the housekeeper had completed her inspections. She sent three of them back to sweep hearths and dust wooden panelling; even a footman had to go off again and polish a knife in the dining room.

'The butler was happy enough,' he muttered; but not loud enough for her to hear.

'You'd think she was the mistress,' one of her maids whispered.

'Silence!' the housekeeper snapped and glared at them until they all stood perfectly still and expressionless as the draught chilled their ankles. 'Merry Christmas to you all,' she said without a smile. 'You may take your seats in the servants' hall.' She returned to the warmth and snugness of her sitting room, and her bottle of sherry wine.

At half past eleven a kitchen maid carried a roast leg of mutton to the servants' hall. There was roast goose for the master and his guests later, a dish also enjoyed by the housekeeper, butler and cook, who ate their dinner after everyone else, waited on by kitchen maids in clean aprons. When dinner was cleared, the pots washed up and put away, enough coal for the rest of the day carried to the master's fires and a cold supper left in the dining room, the servants were allowed to enjoy their Christmas. It was the only day of the year when they finished at three o'clock in the afternoon instead of nine or ten at night and a suppressed excitement bubbled. But they ate their mutton and greens quietly. The housekeeper frowned upon frivolity.

After steamed spiced pudding, the grooms hurried back to the stables and the maids to the kitchen and dining room. Mrs Watson, the cook, busied herself with ensuring the master's Christmas dinner was perfect. Meadow Hall was a silent place, if not a happy one, when the door from the scullery banged open and a rush of cold air swept into the kitchen.

'Look what we found on the track in the woods!' The stable lads carried a lifeless bundle, slung in a horse blanket, and placed it on the stone flags near to the fire.

'Take that thing out of here!' Mrs Watson yelled, 'and close the door!'

'Just have a look will you.' One of the lads unfolded the edge of the blanket to expose a pallid face surrounded by tangled wet hair. 'She must have been out in the snow all night. Stone cold, she is.'

Shocked, Mrs Watson turned around. 'Oh dear Heaven! Who is she?' She wiped her greasy fingers on her apron and tugged at the blanket. A mewling that developed into a wailing came from the bundle of rags. 'Lord help us, there's a baby!' The infant was wrapped in a torn flannel petticoat.

'Careful, missus,' one of the lads warned, 'there's a lot of blood.'

'I can see that.'

'Shall I fetch the midwife from the village?'

'It's too late for her now. Besides, the midwife won't thank me for spoiling her Christmas Day. You lads'd better clear off out o' here. This is women's work.'

The baby's wailing became the harsh repetitive cry of a newborn. 'Well, here's a fighter if ever I heard one. The little 'un hasn't given up even if her ma has.' Mrs Watson bent to pick up the screeching infant from its mother's flaccid arms. 'You must be made of tough stuff to survive last night's blizzard.' She lifted the mother's hand and let it fall. 'No wedding band, I see. On her way to the workhouse, I'll be bound, poor wretch.'

'*Mrs Watson!* What is all this noise?' The Hall housekeeper bustled out of her sitting room across the stone-flagged passage. 'Dear Lord! Who is that on the floor?' She stopped and took in the situation. 'Is that a baby?'

'Yes, ma'am. Its mother is in a deep faint and they're both freezing cold.'

The housekeeper's full black skirts swished across the kitchen and she peered at the pallid form in the fireside glow. She bent to finger the muddy, wet fabric of the mother's skirt. 'This was once a servant's gown.' She shook the material from her fingers and stated, 'The woman is a vagrant; one of the gypsies off the moor.'

'Shall I send for the workhouse cart to take them on their way, ma'am?'

'Not today. Give the warden and his wife a little respite.' The baby's screaming continued and its mother did not stir. The housekeeper frowned. 'Does the mother breathe?'

Mrs Watson leaned closer to the still form. 'I think so.'

'See if you can bring her round.'

'There's not much hope of that, if I may say so; look at her, just skin and bone. I'll try, though. I have a drop of brandy left over from the puddings.'

'See if you can quieten that infant, too. My head is splitting.'

Mrs Watson inspected the babe. 'It's a girl,' she commented. She placed a finger in the baby's mouth and watched her suck at it. 'She'll be wanting a wet nurse, ma'am.'

'One of the under-gardeners' wives lost her newborn just yesterday. Send a kitchen maid to find her.'

'Yes, ma'am.' Mrs Watson bobbed a curtsey.

But the child's mother did not recover from her deep faint and breathed her last even as cook tried to revive her. In contrast, the baby suckled greedily at her surrogate breast and quietened. Her foster-mother welcomed her task and the housekeeper waited until the Hall's Christmas guests had left before turning her attention to the child's future. She summoned Mrs Watson to her sitting room.

'I have spoken to the master and he has no concern for the infant. He is busy with his horses in foal and has more important affairs to occupy him. No one knows who her mother was. The vicar will make enquiries but he has already given her a pauper's burial in the churchyard.'

'Will the babe go to the workhouse, then?'

'No. She was a gift from Jesus on His birthday, so we shall keep her here. The under-gardener's wife will look after her until she's old enough to walk and then she will become a servant.'

'The master has agreed to that?'

'I have told you, he is not interested in vagrants or their

6

offspring. *I* have decided to keep her. A girl won't cost much to feed and clothe, you will see to that, Mrs Watson.'

'Me, ma'am?'

'You can have her in your kitchen as soon as her hands are big enough to hold a scrubbing brush.'

'Thank you, ma'am.'

'The master will have an extra maid without having to sign any indenture for her parents.' The housekeeper looked pleased with herself.

'What shall I call her?'

'Sarah. I think that is a fitting name for a servant, don't you? And Meadow; after the Hall that took her in.'

'Sarah Meadow she is, then, ma'am, born on Christmas Day.'

'She is a lucky child. She will have a half day holiday on her birthday every year.'

Chapter 2

Spring, 1844

'Have you made up the fireboxes?'

'Yes, Mrs Watson.' They were waiting in the scullery for the housemaids to light fires in the master's bedchamber, dressing room and dining salon. The other chambers were done later, after breakfast when the boot boy had carried in more buckets of coal.

'Start pumping your water, then.'

Sarah didn't need to be told what to do, but Mrs Watson liked to give orders in her kitchen. She went into the scullery and outside to the yard. The servant's supper crockery was stacked on the old dresser where she had left it after washing up last night, but now she saw bits of stale pastry and smears of pickle sauce all over her previously clean pots.

'Who's put these dirty plates in here?' she cried. It's those footmen again, she fumed silently. They went over to the stables after their work was finished to play cards and take strong drink with the grooms before coming back for a cold supper at the kitchen table.

'Mrs Watson!' she called. 'Somebody's been in here and left my clean pots all dirty.'

'Less of your lip, Meadow, or you'll feel my whip across your back. They're not *your* pots and you'll just have to wash them again, won't you?'

'Well, it's not fair!' Her thin arms and slender hands were already sore from too long in hot water and soda.

'Don't you answer me back or I'll send you to the workhouse and see how you like that! You'll know which side your bread is buttered then, my girl. You'll die of a fever in there just like your ma afore you!'

Sarah wished she'd had a mother instead of Mrs Watson. Her own mother would have been nicer to her. 'You told me my mother never went to the workhouse,' she said.

'No. She died before she got there. She were a gypsy, though, and that's what you'll be if you don't watch your step.'

'I won't!' she argued, 'I haven't got black hair like them.'

Auburn, one of the kinder maids called it; not as bright as that carrot-top jockey in the stables, but different none the less. She had wide hazel-brown eyes, a fair skin that freckled in the summer and, according to the master's valet, a pretty smile. But, he had added unkindly, she was too skinny by half for any lad to take an interest.

Mrs Watson didn't stand for any answering back and marched across the kitchen to hit Sarah across the head with the flat of her hand. 'Shut your mouth and get those pots cleaned up!'

Sarah pressed her lips together. Mrs Watson was a big woman and it hurt when she hit her. Sarah stalked off to clear up, muttering to herself, 'I'd rather they left their mess in the kitchen than all over my nice clean scullery.'

It was the only place she thought of as hers, and she took a pride in keeping it nice. It wasn't as though she hadn't enough work to do already this morning, and her resentment simmered as she pumped freezing cold water into a line of buckets until she ached. She carried them indoors, two at a time, emptied them into the copper in the corner of her scullery, and stoked the fire drawing underneath it.

As she swept up fallen ash from the brick floor she remem-
berd how, as a child, she had sat on a piece of sacking with a
blackened cooking pot, some soda and a scrubbing brush. She
had listened to the kitchen maids' chatter as they washed up at
the stone sink.

'Mrs Watson should have got another lass for in here.'

'One of the housemaids said they had a lot more servants in the old
housekeeper's day but she left when the master started spending all his
money on his gee-gees, and then his tradesmen stopped sending supplies.
Mrs Watson was only the cook then, you know.'

'Was she? She thinks she's Lady Muck now.'

They had giggled. 'It's better here than in the workhouse though and
that little 'un on the floor can do the scullery when she's big enough to
reach.'

And I did, Sarah thought. She remembered that she had needed
to stand on a milking stool to reach into the corners of the stone
sink. She was the youngest of all the servants, and therefore at
the end of the queue when beds and blankets were allocated.
She was the one who had to sleep in the draughts and be up
first, at daybreak, to light the fires in the kitchen range and under
the copper in the scullery. She was the one who was moaned at
when she woke the others as she went downstairs to get the
sticks and coal going.

The housemaids came into her scullery, bleary-eyed and
yawning, to pick up their waiting fireboxes. She smiled at them.
It wasn't their fault the footmen were unruly. 'Your kindling is
nice and dry,' she said, 'and I've put in a piece of greased rag to
start them off.' It gave off a bit of smoke but got the sticks going
nicely.

'Ta,' one of them replied.

'Don't let on about the grease, will you?' she warned.

They shook their heads and smiled back. Mrs Watson reigned
supreme over her female servants, as the housekeeper had done
before her, and they had all learned not to cross her. Sarah
blew out her cheeks, then stacked the smeared plates in the

sink and drew some water from the copper to wash them.

She knew more about Meadow Hall nowadays and had heard how it had been well provided for in the past; it had boasted first-rate stables and good bloodstock that fared well at the races. Its parkland was one of the finest in the South Riding, designed by a famous gentleman, and maintained by a band of gardeners.

But the master's wealth had dwindled. His butler had followed the housekeeper to a better position and the master had closed up most of the chambers – he had few guests now. He'd sold off much of his parkland and leased the remainder to a tenant farmer in order to keep his stables thriving. His valet took charge of those footmen who had stayed, and Mrs Watson, well, Mrs Watson had found special favour with the master. She took control of household affairs, growing round and florid in the process, and told the servants to do as she ordered.

'Meadow!' Sarah jumped. 'Get in here and do me boots for me.'

'Yes, Mrs Watson.' Sarah shook the greasy water from her reddened arms and wiped her hands on a sacking apron.

The older woman sprawled in her rocking chair by the kitchen range as Sarah knelt on the flagged floor. It was the only time she was grateful for her brown jute gown. The fabric was coarse and scratchy but it softened the stone under her skinny knees. Sarah eased the cold stiff leather over Mrs Watson's podgy stockinged feet, and her sore fingers wrestled with the hook as she pulled the tiny buttons through their eyelets.

Four times a day she did Mrs Watson's boots for her. She put them on in the morning, off again after dinner, put them back on for tea, and eased her smelly feet out of them last thing at night. And still her duties were not finished, not when the weather was bitter. She recalled one of those cold winter nights.

'Clean up the scullery and do the master's nightcap now,' Mrs Watson had ordered. 'And then get off to bed. No dawdling. It's a chilly one tonight.'

'Yes, Mrs Watson.'

11

Sarah had emptied the sink and threw two bucketfuls of cold greasy water outside. The sky was black but the stars were out and ice crackled underfoot. Across the yard a lamp glowed from an upstairs window in the stables and she heard girlish laughter.

'Meadow! Where's the master's tray?'

She had hurried back.

'You haven't fetched my carpet slippers yet.'

'Sorry, Mrs Watson.' They were warming by the kitchen range. Sarah eased the soft felt shoes onto the woman's swollen feet and put her boots in their place ready for morning.

'That's better. Upstairs with you now and warm my bed.'

'It's ever so cold tonight, Mrs Watson. Can I take a brick out of the oven? I'll wrap it well.'

'No you can't. I'm not having any grit in my bed sheets. What do you think I've got you for?'

Sarah took a candle, climbed four flights of backstairs and went through a small door in the dark wood panelling to the second-floor landing. Mrs Watson had moved into a guest chamber as soon as the master had given her the household keys. The room had a carved wooden bed and matching cupboard for hanging clothes and storing linen.

She took off her own boots and gown, placed Mrs Watson's folded nightdress carefully in a pillow sham and laid it on the soft mattress. The sheets were freezing and she wasn't allowed to curl up. She had to lie flat on her back with the nightgown underneath her until Mrs Watson came to bed. She lay awake listening to the squeals and grunts from the master's bedchamber below, where Mrs Watson had taken his nightcap and stayed to entertain him.

But she must have fallen asleep, for the next thing she knew she had been wakened by Mrs Watson, with her corsets in one hand and a guinea in the other, and ordered to get up and go to her own cold hard bed on the floor above. She had to creep around the attic in the dark, her bare feet freezing, because the older maids were asleep and they pinched and slapped her if she disturbed them. She had stuffed rags into the gaps around the window over her bed but the cold wind still rattled the windows, chilling Sarah to the bone.

This morning Sarah noticed Mrs Watson's ankles were getting puffier and her legs swelled over the tops of her boots. She was spending more and more time in the comfort of her rocking chair by the kitchen range and giving her orders from there. Sarah was fourteen and had had enough of being Mrs Watson's personal slave, as well as doing all the scullery work. She had considered running way; but not, she thought, until summer when the weather would be kinder.

'Chuck a bit more of coal on this fire,' Mrs Watson directed, 'then go and watch for the master's trainer.'

This was an important task for Sarah every morning. The master's trainer was in charge of the horses and he slept in the coach house, above the master's carriage. She stared out of the scullery window across the yard to the stables. 'He's on his way,' she called, as soon as he stepped outside, dressed in his plaid waistcoat, tweed jacket and smart leather riding boots. Mrs Watson rocked herself out of her chair and put a frying pan on to heat.

The master at Meadow Hall always took breakfast with his trainer and talked about his horses. This morning was different, though. Sarah was still in the scullery when she heard the head housemaid's cries in the passage leading to the front hall.

'Mrs Watson! Oh, come quick, the master's been murdered in his bed!'

'What's going on?' Sarah went into the kitchen in time to see Mrs Watson disappear down the passage.

The head housemaid came over to the range, her face as white as sun-bleached linen.

'You'd better sit down,' Sarah said. 'You look really poorly.'

The housemaid collapsed into the vacated rocking chair, clasping her firebox on her lap. 'Oh, it was horrible,' she cried. 'You should've seen him, his face was *purple*! His eyes were staring at me, wide open and fit to pop out of his head!'

Two kitchen maids stopped cleaning a basket of mushrooms and exchanged silent glances. The head housemaid never spoke to them as a rule, let alone took any notice of young Sarah.

'Has he been strangled?' Fear gripped Sarah's body. She had listened at mealtimes to the footmen talking about highway murder, and watched them frighten the maids with their antics as they acted out their tales. 'Do you think the murderer is still here?' She looked over her shoulder at the door to her scullery.

'Ooh, you shut up, Meadow. You're scaring me.'

'I don't mean to,' she responded. 'But I'll be the first he gets hold of if he comes in the back.'

The girls moved closer to the fire, and to each other, in a gesture of mutual support that was unusual in Mrs Watson's kitchen. Sarah picked up a heavy iron ladle and held it behind her back. They huddled together nervously until another housemaid clattered down the passage and into the kitchen.

'The master's valet wants you in the front hall.' She turned swiftly and the head housemaid followed her.

'Does he mean us an' all?' one of the kitchen maids asked.

'Don't know,' the other replied.

'I think he does,' Sarah decided. Even if he didn't, she didn't want to miss what he had to say. 'Anyway, I don't want to be left alone in here while a murderer is about.'

'What about the master's mushrooms?'

'Leave them,' Sarah replied. 'He won't be wanting no breakfast if he's dead, will he?' She put down her ladle and walked towards the passage. 'Come on, you two,' she called over her shoulder.

The footmen and boot boy were there, and all four housemaids were clustered around Mrs Watson. The master's valet was halfway down the stairs, talking to the trainer, who seemed very agitated. The valet, too, was unsteady on his feet and holding onto the dark wooden banister rail. 'Listen up, you lot,' he said. 'The master hasn't been murdered.'

A sigh of relief rippled through the gathering group. 'He's not dead, then?' a footman asked.

'Oh, aye, he's dead right enough. He had a purple fit in the night.'

'We're lucky it's after quarter day, then,' the boot boy muttered. 'At least we got our pay.'

'Hush up, you. Show some respect.'

'He never showed us any.'

The maids and footmen muttered among themselves, until the master's trainer walked slowly down the stairs. He was frowning and did not seem to notice the maids as they parted to allow him through. 'I'll tell the outdoor servants and send for his lawyer,' he murmured. 'This'll put the cat among the pigeons, right enough.'

Mrs Watson whispered, 'What does he mean by that?'

The valet shrugged. 'He's knows more about the master's affairs than I do.' He called after him, 'You'll take your breakfast with me, sir?' Then he addressed the servants. 'Get back to your work now. Carry on as normal. We'll be having callers, so make sure everything is done proper today.'

Mrs Watson turned to the green baize door at the back of the hall. 'Meadow! What are you doing here? In the kitchen with you and put another pan over the fire! I want two hot frying pans this morning.'

Sarah did as she was told and was followed by the rest of the servants. But things did not carry on as normal. The head housemaid who had discovered the body hovered uncertainly in the kitchen, still clutching her firebox.

Sarah took it from her gently. 'He won't be wanting a fire in his bedchamber this morning, will he?' she said.

The head housemaid looked surprised but didn't say anything. She sat down at the table with a pale face.

'I'll have all my fireboxes back, thank you,' Sarah continued, taking them from the other maids. She'd have enough dry sticks to get her copper going every morning for the rest of the week now. 'There's no point in lighting all those fires now, is there? It's bad enough doing all that work for just the one gentleman. No sense in doing it for nobody.'

Neither the footmen nor the maids disagreed and they loitered around the kitchen table, murmuring to each other and eating bread and dripping until Mrs Watson and the valet came in for their breakfast. The two most senior servants always took breakfast together after the master had been served. Mrs Watson cooked for the master, but she had Sarah to fry whatever she and the valet were having, and mash their tea.

'Right, you lot,' Mrs Watson said. 'Clear off out of here and keep yourselves busy until I know what's happening. Go on, then.' She rattled her chatelaine. 'Not you, Meadow. You can get our breakfast on.' She selected a key to unlock the larder, brought out a new flitch of bacon and carved thick slices for Sarah to put into the hot pans.

Sarah cleared one end of the huge deal table, cut more bread and made strong tea in a large brown teapot. She added slices of pig's liver to the bacon, then the mushrooms. When the master's trainer came into the kitchen she served up tasty platefuls to the three most important servants at Meadow Hall. She noticed that Mrs Watson had placed a slab of fresh butter on the table too.

'Put the flour and balm to warm for me, Meadow. Pour the tea first.'

'Yes, Mrs Watson.' As she moved quietly about the kitchen, Sarah listened to the conversation.

'What'll happen to us?' Mrs Watson asked.

'Don't rightly know yet,' the valet answered. 'But he's got no kin to inherit the Hall.'

'That's just as well,' the trainer added, 'Because he's got no money to leave 'em either.'

'None at all?'

'How do you know that?'

'He owes tradesman for tack and feed left, right and centre and the horses are not his any more.'

'What do mean, they're not his?'

'He sold his last one a few years ago.'

'Well, what about them in the stables?'

'That's what I'm saying. Other folk own them and leave 'em here so the master gets paid for livery and training and it keeps his stables going. I tell you, everything is in hock. I'm getting out of here as soon as I can and, if you take my advice, you'll do the same.'

Sarah listened as she carried the heavy earthenware bowl of flour to the hearth to warm.

'But he said he'd look after me,' Mrs Watson protested.

'He said that to keep you warming his bed of a night, old girl.' The valet smiled weakly.

Sarah saw that Mrs Watson looked cross. They thought she didn't know what they meant but the housemaids giggled and talked about Mrs Watson after they blew out the candle at night. One of the housemaids did what Mrs Watson did too, with a groom in the hayloft over the stables. Last summer, when Sarah didn't have to warm Mrs Watson's bed, she had listened from her attic bed as the housemaid whispered about it to her friend.

Three Christmases ago, on her eleventh birthday, they made fun of Sarah and told her that she was old enough to do it now if she wanted. She might have done, too, just to find out what it was like, but nobody asked her. Not even the stable lads were interested in Sarah Meadow; she was only the scullery maid, and a foundling at that.

During the next few weeks, life improved for the servants at Meadow Hall. There were no dining-room meals to carry down the passage and serve up on the best china, or huge fires to keep alight and clean up after. But Mrs Watson still roasted big joints of meat and made steamed puddings that the servants enjoyed instead of the master and his friends.

A succession of gaudily dressed gentlemen visited the trainer in the stables and they walked across the yard to take refreshment in the old housekeeper's sitting room, where Mrs Watson invited them to stay for dinner or tea. The spring weather was breezy and cold, but the valet held the cellar keys and he brought out brandy to warm them on their way.

One of the gentleman callers was more sombrely dressed in a long dark coat and tall hat. He came to the front door and spoke to the valet in the front hall. He did not linger for refreshment and what he said had a sobering effect on Mrs Watson; when he had gone she assembled the servants round her and held court from her rocking chair by the fire.

'Bailiffs will be in at the end of the week to put a value on the furniture,' she told them. 'The Hall and everything in it is to be sold off.'

'There'll be a new owner to keep us on, then?' The head housemaid sounded relieved.

Mrs Watson scowled. 'You all have to be gone. The sooner the better.'

The other housemaids looked alarmed and began talking at the same time.

'All of us!'

'Gone where?'

'But we've got nowhere to go!'

'Why can't we stay here with you, Mrs Watson?'

'Because I'm having to get out an' all,' she replied bitterly. 'It's a poor carry on, if you ask me. I've slaved my fingers to the bone these past few years for the master and I've nothing to show for it.'

Sarah blinked. All Mrs Watson did was stand in front of the range poking and prodding to see if things were done. Her two kitchen maids did the peeling, chopping, weighing and mixing and she did the washing up for all of them. 'Apart from the guineas he gave you for warming his bed,' she remarked before she could stop herself.

She thought Mrs Watson was going to hit her and she reckoned she would have done if she hadn't been too lazy to get up out of her rocking chair. Instead, the older woman's face darkened and she spat, 'You keep your tongue between your teeth,

Meadow, or you'll feel the back of my hand across your face.'

Sarah clamped her mouth shut. The kitchen maids looked frightened too; they knew what the back of Mrs Watson's hand felt like because they always got the blame when any of the cooking went wrong. One of them asked timidly, 'Where'll we go?'

'You two will have to go back to workhouse.'

They protested together. 'We can't! It's horrible in there!'

'It's meant to be. That way you work hard to stay outside.'

'Well, it's not their fault the master died!' Sarah commented. 'Why should they suffer because he spent all his money on horses?'

'I've told you to be quiet,' Mrs Watson snapped. 'You're growing into a right little madam, you are. Well, you'll be in the workhouse an' all. A spell in there will do you good. It'll teach you to know your place.'

Sarah swallowed her retaliation. Did Mrs Watson really think a scullery maid didn't know her place in the pecking order at Meadow Hall?

'Well, I'm not going there,' the head housemaid announced. 'I've got a mam and dad to go to.'

'And I've got an aunty who'll take me in,' another housemaid added.

'Aye,' Mrs Watson added, 'Them who 'as family will have to go home. But them who 'as not will be taken to the workhouse. The warden knows about you already and he'll call with his cart when the lawyer comes back to lock up.'

'Where will you go, Mrs Watson?'

She rocked her chair and stood up, taking off her big white apron. 'The master's valet has a sister with a lodging house in Sheffield.' She smoothed down her skirt and patted her hair. 'I'm just off to have a word with him.'

The housemaids collected their shawls and went outside to the stables where the footmen and outdoor servants were already talking about this new information. Sarah lingered by the fire with the kitchen maids.

'Is it really that bad in the workhouse?' Sarah asked.

'It's worse than here. At least we get plenty to eat here.'

'It's like being in prison.'

'How do you know that?' Sarah pressed. 'Have you been in a prison?'

'No, but some of the others had and they said it was.'

'You get all sorts in there. And you have to share a bed with an old woman who's likely to be dying.'

'Or loony.'

'Or both.'

'And you have to work even harder than here. The women do all the cleaning up.'

'And the washing; they do washing from all over the place.'

'Well, you two got out of it, didn't you?' Sarah parried.

'Aye, Mrs Watson took on both of us. The housemaids have allus looked down on us, though. They said the old housekeeper would never have had girls from the workhouse at Meadow Hall in her day.'

'But the workhouse will find us somewhere else, won't they?' Sarah asked.

'You'll not get a position easy because you've got that hair and a temper to match. Nobody will want you. That housemaid has the right idea.'

'Which one is that?' Sarah asked.

'The one who goes over to the stables at night; her sweetheart is leaving with the horses tomorrow and she's going with him.'

'Is he going to wed her, then?'

'She said so. Getting wed keeps you out of the workhouse.'

'Well, I'll just have to get wed then, shan't I?' Sarah stated.

'Who's going to wed you? You need a sweetheart first and you have to be bonny, like the housemaid, to get one o' them.'

'I'm as bonny as that housemaid, aren't I? Well, I would be if I wore a neat grey gown instead this old brown sack. And if I had a proper white cotton apron and a cap with lace on it, I'm sure I'd look as nice as her.'

'Hark at you, Meadow. You need a few more years on yer back before a lad'll even look at you.'

'Why's that, then?'

'Because you've got no bosoms, that's why!'

'Yes I have!' But she hadn't, not really; just a pair of bumps that were hardly noticeable under a chemise.

'Well, I can't see 'em! You don't even need a corset yet.'

Sarah frowned because the kitchen maid was right.

'It's the workhouse for us three,' the maid added. 'It'll be better than starving on the streets.'

Chapter 3

'How many shall I set for tea, Mrs Watson?'

Easter had come and gone and it was two months since the master had died. The footmen, boot boy and head housemaid had already packed their boxes and left. The grooms and stable lads were leaving with the last of the horses the following morning.

Sarah laid out clean plates and knives, fresh baked loaves and slabs of new butter in the servants' hall. Mrs Watson placed the remains of a large ham and a game pie on the table. 'A dozen I should say. Just like the last supper, eh? We'll all be on our way tomorrer. Fetch those stone jars of pickles in the pantry, and two more jugs of ale from the barrel for the lasses. We've got brandy from the cellar for the menfolk.'

Sarah and the kitchen maids sat on a bench, squashed together at the bottom end of the table. It was covered with food and drink that disappeared quickly and noisily as soon as the outdoor servants sat down. She watched in dismay as the wooden surface that she scrubbed every day became stained with red vinegar from pickled cabbage and beetroot, and littered with bread and pastry crusts and smears of butter. She wondered if Mrs Watson would make her scrub it with soda again before she went to bed even though there was no point any more.

'Meadow!' one of the housemaids called, 'Fetch more ale from the barrel. Look sharp, we're thirsty over here.'

'And while you're at it,' Mrs Watson added, 'bring a cloth to mop up this mess. Hurry up before it runs over me pinny.'

Sarah was up and down throughout the meal. When she tried to clear some of the worst debris, the men from the stables, who had been drinking steadily, pinched and slapped her backside, grabbed her mob cap and tossed it around. 'Stop them, Mrs Watson! It's always me they pick on!'

'Don't be such a little spoilsport. It's only a bit of fun and we'll all be gone tomorrow. You might be in the workhouse for a long time, my lass, so enjoy this while you can.' Mrs Watson swallowed more brandy and drew her chair nearer to the valet, who put his arm across the back of her shoulders.

Sarah went back to her place on the bench to find that a stable lad had followed the valet's example and was sitting between two kitchen maids with an arm around each one. They began to giggle as another lad topped up their mugs with more ale from the jug. He pulled one of the girls to her feet and said, 'You can't have two of them, this one's mine.' Sarah saw his hand creep around the kitchen maid's waist and she looked coy but did not protest. 'Why don't we go over to the stables and take this ale with us?' he suggested and the housemaids followed the stable lads into the night air.

Normally, Mrs Watson didn't allow antics like these in her kitchen because it made a lot of noise but tonight she did not seem to care. She was too intent on the brandy to notice what was going on. The valet picked up the bottle and got to his feet unsteadily. 'Come on, old girl,' he said to Mrs Watson, 'Let's be having you.'

Mrs Watson went with him out of the kitchen. Before she left she called over her shoulder, 'Meadow, see this place to rights before that lawyer gets here tomorrow morning. Don't forget that what I say to him about you will be passed on to

23

the workhouse master. You don't want to be going in there as a slattern, do you?'

Sarah was glad when she was left alone to sweep the floor and scrub the table. She pondered over what tomorrow would bring for her. None of the male servants were going to the workhouse. The stable lads were being taken away with the last of the horses to start a new life in Doncaster. If any one of them had shown the slightest bit of interest in her she'd have asked him to take her with them.

What was going to happen to her? Meadow Hall was her home, even if she was just the scullery maid. Her days were long and hard but she felt she belonged here. Although the other servants picked on her and made her cross, she would miss them as they were the only family she had. She stared at the table top and felt sad. Who would she be scrubbing for tomorrow? A shiver of apprehension ran down her spine. She didn't want to go to the workhouse and she was scared.

'They're off!'

The next morning Sarah joined the kitchen maids in the yard to watch the stable lads and horses leaving. 'Why aren't you going with them?' she queried.

'They never asked us. They only wanted slap and tickle and – you know.'

Yes, Sarah knew. 'Did you, then?'

'Course not! I might have had a babby.'

'Well, he'd have had to wed you then, wouldn't he?'

'That shows how much you know about lads, Meadow! You should allus get the ring on your finger first.'

The horses were led out in turn, strung together to be taken away. She saw one of the grooms crying. Sarah had never seen a grown man weep before and she watched him with interest. After that, the servants without new positions gathered up their bundles of possessions and set off to walk to their home villages in the Riding.

There were only three of them left with Mrs Watson and the valet when the black-coated lawyer came to inspect and lock up the Hall. Mrs Watson went to the front door to let him in. Sarah stood by her bundle in the kitchen listening to the other two kitchen maids snivelling.

'Don't cry,' she said. 'The workhouse won't be so bad; and it's not for long.'

'What do you know?'

'You've got each other. You just need to stick together.' Sarah wished she could be their friend as well. But they thought she was too young for them.

'They'll put us in the wash house,' one gulped.

Oh no, Sarah thought, not more hot water and soda. 'I don't want to do that,' she said.

'You have to go where they send you.'

Sarah stood in the cold kitchen and realised that once she was in the workhouse it would be true. 'I don't have to do anything,' she decided, picking up her bundle. 'Tell Mrs Watson I'm not coming with you.'

One of the kitchen maids stopped whining and looked up sharply. 'Where'll you go?'

Sarah's mind raced. She would have to say something. 'I'm following the horses.'

'But they've all gone.'

Mrs Watson's boots echoed on the stone flags in the passage. 'I've got somewhere to stay,' she added hastily. 'Tell her one of the stable lads has come back for me.'

'Really?'

'Yes. Tell her for me. Please.' She disappeared with her belongings into the scullery and stood with her back to the door, holding her breath.

'Just these two for the workhouse?' she heard the lawyer ask.

'There's a scullery maid somewhere,' Mrs Watson replied.

'Call her at once. The warden is waiting with his cart.'

'Meadow!' Mrs Watson yelled.

Sarah didn't move.

'Where is she? Well, you two, answer me.'

'One of the stable lads has taken her with him.' Sarah wasn't sure which one of the maids had eventually backed her story, but she was grateful to her.

'I didn't know she was friendly with any of 'em,' Mrs Watson muttered. 'She could be a real sly boots, that one could.'

'What about you, madam?' the gentleman asked.

'The valet and me'll travel in the workhouse cart to the cross-roads and take the carrier from there. We have a place to go.'

'Excellent. Give me your keys. I can see you all off the prem-ises, lock up the house and my business here will be finished. I'll start at the back.'

Sarah heard the jangling of Mrs Watson's chatelaine and her heart lurched as she remembered the large iron lock on the outside door. There was nowhere to hide and she would have to shift herself fast before the lawyer came in and found her.

She surveyed the scullery. This damp dark place was where she had spent most of her fourteen-and-a-bit years. She seemed to have been scrubbing cooking pots all her life.

She hated Meadow Hall and everything in it. She was glad to be leaving. Alone in her bed at night she had had occasional flashes of earlier times, an isolated cottage, the woman who had nursed her as an infant, she was told, and then nothing except this scullery and Mrs Watson's kitchen. Not even a proper mother to go and visit on Mothering Sunday.

She hadn't thought there was anywhere worse than this scullery until she had learned more about the workhouse and she guessed the unwritten rule was the same there as here; you had to look out for yourself because nobody else would do it for you. She took one last glance at the stone sink and ancient dresser, the wooden racks of pots and pans, and fled quietly out of the back door.

The yard was deserted; the stables, carriage house and upstairs chambers had been emptied and locked straight after the horses had left. She hid behind the low stone buildings and for a moment she really wished she had gone with the horses. But the stable lads tormented her whenever she went near them, teasing her and pulling at her long coppery hair. She thought, sometimes, it would have been better to be a boy as they seemed to be able to do what they liked and weren't shouted at as much as the maids; not at Meadow Hall anyway.

Sarah heard the workhouse cart rumble away in the distance and realised that she was totally alone. The Hall was now locked but she knew how the housemaid had climbed into the stable loft to meet her sweetheart at night so she decided to hide there while she thought about what to do. She stowed her bundle behind the mounting stone, clambered up onto a water butt, then stepped across to a wide, stone window ledge. Fortunately, the catch had not been mended. She pushed her fingers around the edge of the casement until it swung open, and scrambled into the chamber. The floorboards were bare apart from four sleeping pallets and an old wooden box. There was a fireplace, some logs, and a staircase in the corner that led down to a tack room.

'Is anyone here?'

Her voice echoed through the emptiness. She crossed to a door and opened it to reveal a dusty hayloft bereft of its contents. Horses, feed, servants; everything had gone. She sat on the wooden box for a few minutes then got up to look inside it. Someone had left an old horse blanket and a few garments. She took the blanket out and threw it on one of the pallets. The clothes were for a boy, probably left because they were outgrown, so she pushed them back and closed the lid.

Downstairs in the tack room she had better luck. A sack of oats and jar of molasses for the horses had been overlooked. She began to feel excited. She could live here until the weather got warmer and then – then what? She didn't know, but she couldn't stay for ever. When the new owners arrived she'd have to think of some other way of surviving. Sarah sat on the stairs enjoying the peace and quiet. For the first time in her life there was no one telling her what to do and she relished the freedom.

Chapter 4

Although Aidan Beckwith had expected his father's death it did not ease his grief and he wept. He sat on a log beside his camp fire and stared silently at the trees. He was totally alone and not yet eighteen. Fresh green leaves hailed a welcome spring, for it had been a long cold winter; one that his father had not felt as he drifted away on a cloud of laudanum. At least his agonising pain had ceased.

He heard a movement in the undergrowth and stood up, alert. Tall and broad, he had inherited his dark brown hair and grey eyes from his father, who had told him he had his mother's wits. 'Use them, son,' he had said, 'and you'll go far.' But right now he wanted to stay in the forest on a hillside above the empty mansion. He had walked by it on his way back from the village churchyard where he had buried his father. The vicar had told him there was no work there. Meadow Hall belonged to the bailiffs.

'Who's there?' he called. A few birds flapped away then silence returned. A fox or deer he thought, and went over to his wagon to secure its canvas covering. It was a perfect place to camp; secluded and sheltered with a nearby spring and brook tumbling from the hillside. His father's last days had been peaceful and Aidan welcomed the solitude to grieve. He missed his father so much. He missed his wise counsel and his conversation but most of all he just missed his presence, because he had always been there for him; always.

He heard the noise again and picked up a stout stick. He was strong and could take care of himself, but he had passed vagrants on the moor who had watched the slow progress of his wagon and old mare down the track to the forest and he was wary that they might seek him out.

'Show yourself,' he said, scanning the woodland. A scruffy lad wearing worn-out boots appeared between the tress. He had a battered old huntsman's bag slung across his chest. Aidan took in his grubby appearance quickly. The boy had a handsome enough face with startling blue eyes and a head of thick fair hair. But he was a few inches shorter than Aidan with narrow shoulders. 'Who are you?' Aidan asked, discarding his stick.

'My name's Danby.'

'What do you want?'

'Water. I was following the sounds of the stream.'

Aidan jerked his head. 'It's that way.'

'Ta. Shall I fetch you some?'

'I don't need any.'

Danby seemed reluctant to move on. 'Is this your wagon?' he asked.

The lad wanted to stay, Aidan thought. But Aidan didn't need any company right now; it was too soon and he felt too raw. 'The stream's that way,' he repeated and Danby hunched his thin shoulders and moved away.

Aidan surveyed his camp. His wagon needed a new front axle. He had a little money and had already sold their old mare to pay for his father's burial. But he had food stores and plenty of wood for fuel; also water and any game he could snare. And all summer to think about his future.

As he set about clearing saplings and undergrowth, he wondered about Danby. Where was he going? The track led onto the moor, where life was harsh for vagrants. Maybe he had kin there? Aidan's camp was well hidden from the track so Danby must have followed him to find it. Did he plan to return with others and rob him in the dead of night? Maybe it wasn't such good idea to stay here alone?

'I could give you a hand with that.'

Aidan straightened from his task. 'It's you again. I thought I'd seen the last of you.'

'You'll be glad you hadn't when you see what I've brought. Look at these.' Danby unfolded some large dock leaves to expose two glistening brown trout, sliced open and ready to fry. 'I left the heads and guts where the gamekeeper won't find them. Not before a fox does, anyway.'

'There is no gamekeeper. The vicar told me the mansion is closed up.'

'Have you got anything to eat with these?'

'I might have. How did you come by them? You've no fishing pole.'

'I don't need one. I catch 'em wi' me hands.'

'You know how to tickle trout?'

'I'll show you how if you like.'

Aidan liked fresh trout and they were tempting. But he was cautious. 'I've other things to do. Where are you from?'

'T'other side of the moor.'

'Are you going back there?'

'No fear. I'm heading for the South Riding towns. Look, I'm hungry, mister. If you let me fry these over your fire, you can have one. What do you say?'

Aidan walked over to the back of his wagon and reached in for a sack. He dug deep and took out the remains of a loaf wrapped in calico. He broke it in two, handing half to the newcomer.

'Ta ever so.' Danby's teeth tore at the crust savagely and he chewed noisily. When he stopped to breathe, he added, 'I can help with chopping wood, an' all.'

30

'Why?'

'I need somewhere to doss down for the night,' he answered through his chewing. 'I'm a hard worker. I know how to lay snares and skin rabbit.' He delved into his pocket and brought out a small wooden box with a lid that slid closed along a groove. 'I've got these, too.'

'What are they?'

'Lucifers. They're better than a tinderbox to start a fire.'

Aidan didn't ask how he came by them. He'd used them and knew they were dear to buy. 'There's a cave in the rocks up by the spring where you can shelter.'

Danby looked disappointed until Aidan added, 'You can fry the fish here and then be on your way.'

'I'll stack that brushwood for you first.'

He was determined, that's for sure, and used to labouring, Aidan thought as he watched Danby at work. He placed an iron plate to heat over the fire and fetched lard from the wagon.

Danby picked up the fish. 'What's your name?' he asked.

Aidan told him. 'Have you got another name?'

'Danby Jones. I don't like Jones.'

'Why not?'

Danby shrugged. 'It reminds me of when I was a nipper.'

'Did your parents call you Jones?'

'I never had no parents. I was brought up in the workhouse. I was Jones in there and Jones when I escaped.'

Aidan didn't know whether to pity him or be more wary. 'You're not on the run, are you?'

'Not any more. My ma was in the workhouse when I was born. She died and she'd got no one to take me in so I stayed there.'

Aidan decided he felt sorry for him. 'It's a tough life in there.'

'Oh, it wasn't so bad. I learned how to please folk.' Danby placed his trout carefully on the hot plate and it sizzled in the lard. 'They gave me lessons with the other orphans.'

'Can you read, then?'

'And write and do numbers. Can you?'

'My mother taught me.'

'Are you on your way to see her now?'

'What do you want to know for?'

'No reason,' Danby muttered. 'But are you?'

'She died five years ago.'

'Oh,' Danby looked more cross than sympathetic and said, 'Your dad, then? Have you got a house where you live with your dad?'

'I've just buried him.' Aidan's throat constricted and he swallowed.

Danby stopped what he was doing. 'It wasn't the cholera, was it?'

Aidan shook his head. 'He had a lump in his insides.'

'Good,' Danby answered and turned the fish deftly with a fork.

'No it's not,' Aidan snapped.

Danby seemed unconcerned and replied, 'You know what I mean. I never had no dad. Although when I was in the workhouse it felt like I had more than a dozen of 'em, shoving me about and telling me what to do.'

'Is that why you ran away?'

'I told you I didn't!' he protested. 'I'm not one of the vagrants off the moor, you know. I had a proper indenture on a farm.'

'So what happened?' Aidan pressed.

Danby looked uncomfortable and muttered, 'These are nearly ready to eat now.'

Aidan didn't know what to make of Danby Jones. He'd certainly made himself useful around the camp and he seemed honest enough. He wouldn't have made up his story about the workhouse because he didn't seem to be looking for sympathy. But he was looking for a home, Aidan decided, so he probably wouldn't hang about here anyway.

Danby licked the grease off his tin plate. 'I could eat that again, make no mistake.' It was dark now and the fire had fallen to red and grey embers.

'Tasty fish, that was.' Aidan agreed and swallowed a mouthful of water from his metal tankard.

'I'll catch some more tomorrow.' Danby stood up. 'Where did you say that cave was?'

'Follow the stream to the spring and you'll find it behind one of the boulders.'

'G'night then.'

Alone again, Aidan reflected on his decision to stay on this particular wooded hillside. Chance had brought him to the shelter of the trees with his damaged wagon. The rock-strewn moor had jiggered an already weak front axle. His father had hardly noticed as he neared the end. Regular sips of laudanum saw to that, and it broke Aidan's heart to see the emaciated frame of the man who was his hero.

They'd had to leave their cottage when the farmer had found a new blacksmith to take over from his father. Aidan could have stayed on and worked, but that would mean his father going to the workhouse as he would not be able to look after him. The farmer had given them an old wagon and they had filled it with their possessions and set off for the South Riding towns where Aidan could find work when – he choked back a sob as he remembered their conversation – when I'm gone, his father had said.

'One last journey,' Aidan had said as he placed his father's body carefully over the mare's back and set off to lead the gentle animal down the valley.

A church spire had guided him and he'd soon left behind the deserted mansion. He found the village rectory easily enough and explained his business to the housekeeper, who fetched the rector from his study straightaway.

'I should like to bury my father here, sir,' he had explained. 'I can sell my mare to pay for a coffin and a plot. She's old, but good-natured and gentle; suitable for children or a lady. Will you help me, sir?'

The rector had taken him to a carpenter who'd made the

33

burial arrangements and found him a bed for the night, and, eventually, a buyer for his mare. He had said his final goodbyes to his father, paid his dues and set off on foot back to his wagon.

Aidan stared into the cooling fire and remembered his father's last coherent words.

'I'm proud of you, son. You learn quickly and you're well grown. You can do a man's job now. Take lodgings with a respectable working family. Pay your dues and if they're decent folk, they'll look after you.'

He was not sure he wanted other folk feeling sorry for him and asking him questions, reminding him of the family he had lost. Neither was he sure that he wanted to be on his own for ever, and he would have to find work of some sort. But he was good with his hands and could work metal as well as any black-smith.

The empty mansion intrigued him. There was no steward, no dogs, no smoke from any of its chimneys. Everything would be locked away but he might find discarded horseshoes, cooking pots and broken tools he could repair and sell in the village, or even further afield in the town market. He needed a good fire. He'd start to build one tomorrow. Having a plan made Aidan feel better, and he gave in to sleep.

Aidan was searching for rocks by the stream when he noticed Danby. He hadn't moved on yet. He was sitting on a flat boulder in the morning sun and came over to Aidan as soon as he saw him.

'What d'you want those for?'

'I'm building a fire pit,' Aidan told him.

'Can I help you?'

'So you can cook your dinner over it again?'

'If you'll let me. I've set a rabbit snare.'

'So have I.'

'One of us might be lucky, then.' Danby grinned.

'Well there'll be no fire until we've built it today.'

'I can do dry stone walling. I learned it on the farm.'

'Very well,' Aidan agreed. 'Bring as many rocks as you can carry.'

They made several trips to the stream and by the end of the day had a raised circular fire pit big enough to roast a deer. Aidan shared the last of his cold bacon and bread with Danby and they had both snared a rabbit which they roasted as soon as the fire was hot enough.

'What do you need a fire as big as this for?' Danby asked as he chewed on hot meat.

'I can work metal and mend things.'

'Are you a tinker, then?'

'My father was a blacksmith. He could fix anything and he showed me how.'

'You'll need plenty of wood for that,' Danby commented, then added brightly, 'I could cut it for you.'

Aidan didn't answer.

'Have you got any bellows?' Danby pressed.

'I've got all my – my father's tools.' Aidan's voice wavered as he recalled his father's old workshop at the farm.

Danby didn't appear to notice and went on, 'Well, I'll be able to work them for you, won't I.'

'Aren't you heading for town?'

'I was, but the soles of me boots are worn clean through. You haven't got any to lend me have you?'

'I might have.'

'Can I stay, then?' Danby asked as they gnawed at the rabbit bones. 'I'll earn my keep and it's safer with two of us.'

'I know the arguments but I don't know you. How old are you?'

'Fifteen. What about you?'

'I'll be eighteen at the end of this summer.'

'I guessed you'd be older than me. You're big and you've got a proper beard growing.'

'If you had an indenture, why did you leave?'

Danby's face clouded. 'They think that they can treat you like a piece of dirt just because you're from the work-house.'

Aidan remembered having to leave his home because his father could not work and said, 'It's not just folk from the workhouse who get pushed around.' He looked up at the stars twinkling in a darkening sky. 'It'll be a cold one tonight. Have some of this.' He handed Danby a small stone flask of rum.

'Oh, ta. This'll keep out the frost.'

'How did you come to be on the road?'

Danby took a generous swig from the bottle. 'The workhouse farmed me out when I was ten but I tried to run away so the farmer sent me back. I was locked in the punishment cell for a whole week. It was pitch black in there, running with rats, and I only had bread and water for me dinner. Then when they let me out, I had to sit and pick hemp all day. It cuts your fingers to shreds that does.'

Aidan believed him. He had heard similar tales from itinerant farm labourers that lodged in the barn where his father had worked.

'I got away though; two or three years ago. They signed me out as an apprentice to another farmer when I was twelve and told him they never wanted to see me again.'

'Did he send you back as well?'

'He was a worse master than the ones I'd got away from. At least I was fed reg'lar and had a proper bed in the workhouse. I stuck it for over two years until he gave me a beating because –,' he hesitated, '– because his cow got sick. He said it was my fault. I cleared off after that.' Danby was still clutching the rum bottle. 'Can I have a drop more o' this.'

'Aye, but don't make yourself sick. What did you do to the cow?'

'Nowt, it were the dairymaid's fault. She was right pretty, she was.' Danby turned suddenly to face Aidan in the firelight. 'Have you ever had a woman?'

Aidan was surprised he asked but didn't show it. 'I think you've had enough of that rum. Give it back.'

Danby ignored his request and said, 'The men in the workhouse said I'd have one when I was fourteen.'

'I thought they kept the women separate in there.'

'They do. They said I'd soon have one when I got out.'

Aidan took the rum bottle from him and pushed in the cork. 'I'm turning in for the night.'

'Is there any chance of a bed for the night in your wagon?'

Aidan considered he'd worked hard enough to earn it and surveyed Danby's grimy appearance. 'Have you thought of giving yourself a wash in the stream?'

Danby looked aghast. 'But it's not summer yet. The water's like ice.'

'You're not coming in my wagon with all that filth on you. You can sleep underneath for tonight.'

'Can I? Ta.' Danby yawned. 'You haven't got a spare blanket, have you?'

Aidan lay awake a long time that night. He hadn't thought much about women while his father was sick. But Danby's question had set him thinking about them now and he reckoned he would like one. Not just any woman, like the tavern whores he'd seen. He wanted his own woman, living with him in his wagon. He wondered where he'd find her. He'd have to marry her first and his father had told him to wait until he was at least one and twenty for that.

He'd been annoyed with Danby's persistent intrusion at first, but had appreciated his company while they laboured. No one could ever replace his father but he had to think about a future without him. Danby was useful around the camp and willing enough, although Aidan knew it was because he wanted to stay. He decided he'd give him a chance. Danby had a restless nature and would probably move on soon anyway.

The next day Danby was up first and had the fire going and water heating by the time Aidan came back from washing. He noticed that Danby had a made an effort to clean up his hands and face.

'I'm going to take a look at that empty house,' Aidan said. 'There's bound to be scrap lying around.'

'D'you want me to come with you?'

'You stay and chop wood.'

Danby looked disappointed but Aidan had put on his good jacket just in case there was a keeper about. He didn't look scruffy and Danby did, despite his efforts to clean up. He carried his father's leather hunting bag with a sack folded inside.

As he approached the outbuildings his sharp eyes picked up a movement, a fleeting glimpse of a figure that shrank back into the darkness of the dovecote. The door swung closed. It could have been a gust of wind; or somebody who wanted to stay hidden. He wandered into the stable yard, peered through the grimy windows, then stood quite still and surveyed the area. He knew his size could be a threatening presence, especially with a good growth of dark beard that gave him a look of maturity beyond his years. Whoever was hiding in the dovecote had thought better of challenging him.

He systematically searched in corners and clumps of grass and weeds, picking up bits of metal until he had a sackful. Then he took one last look at the buildings and headed back to camp.

Danby was stacking logs. 'Any luck?' he asked.

Aidan jiggled his sack, which rattled pleasingly. 'Somebody is around though. He was hiding in the dovecote.'

'Maybe it was a bailiff?'

'He would have challenged me if he was. Some traveller, I expect. He'll be gone by tomorrow.'

'Did you see any doves? Pigeon meat is good. All we need is some grain and a net.'

'I've got those in the wagon. We'll go down tomorrow.'

'Show us what's in the sack, then?' Danby asked.

Aidan tipped out old nails and horseshoes, a leaky cooking

pot, a decent piece of harness with the broken buckle still attached and a collection of broken tools.

'They're not much use to anybody,' Danby commented.

'They will be,' said Aidan, pleased with his haul and anxious to get to work.

Chapter 5

Sarah hardly dared breathe and hid for a long time in the dove-cote after the big, dark-haired man had left. He was the only person she had seen since the house was closed up, and she had to resist a strong urge to run after him simply to say, 'Can I come with you, mister?' But even she knew that was a foolhardy thing for a young girl to do no matter how desperate she was for company.

She had enjoyed her solitude at first but now it had palled. She missed the liveliness of the other servants and Mrs Watson's scolding was better than another day of silence. She would have even welcomed teasing from the stable lads to relieve her lone-liness. She was hungry, too. Her diet of oats and molasses was dull and she craved meat. When she was sure the man had left, she picked up a large stone, threw down some oatmeal, and waited patiently for the birds to descend, hoping to catch one for her evening meal.

That evening Sarah noticed a plume of smoke rising from the trees on the slopes behind Meadow Hall. She sat on the wooden box in her makeshift bedchamber and thought. She was all alone and she couldn't stay here for ever. Some day new owners or tenants would arrive and she would have to leave. It was dangerous out on the road, especially if you were a girl. The housemaids had been frightened silly one night by the footmen telling tales of kidnap and evil doings. She didn't believe half of it, but if the fire was from that stranger and he was living rough in the woods, she had to be cautious. He definitely looked a capable sort that could and would take what he wanted. And he had had a good long look at the dovecote. He'd be back.

She went down to the tack room to search for a weapon; a knife that she could hone on a wet stone. It would be useful, too, for cutting up a pigeon if she eventually caught one. She found an old blade with no handle; it was better than nothing. She also found a tarnished tin whistle and blew on it tune-lessly. It created an awful sound but made her feel less lonely and gave her some comfort. It reminded her of Christmas, her birthday, when any servant with a talent would entertain the others after tea. But she couldn't play a tune like one of the little Irish jockeys could and, disheartened, she went back upstairs.

But it set her thinking. She stared at the wooden box then opened the lid. After further thought she took out a good shirt and a pair of old-fashioned moleskin knee-breeches, laid them on a pallet and stared. What if she wasn't a girl at all? What if she dressed up as a boy? She'd be so much safer on her own as a boy. But could she pass herself off as one; what would she look like in boy's clothes? Well, she thought, there's only one way to find out. Yet still she hesitated. Did she have the courage to do this?

A few minutes later she slowly unbuttoned her gown, removed it and tried on the clothes. The breeches nearly reached the top of her boots but she found enough leather strapping to knot around her waist and secure them. The shirt was also too big and she rummaged in the box for a woollen waistcoat she had noticed. It was thick and warm but even over the shirt it hung loosely on her thin body.

She missed the warm closeness of her bodice and in a flash of inspiration picked up the knife blade. She stopped suddenly. If she unpicked her gown and changed her mind, how would she sew it back? But she was beginning to feel excited about her new venture and looking forward to the freedom to move on. She attacked the waistline of her gown, severing the skirt and tossing it aside. She struggled into the bodice and, underneath the shirt, the familiar coarseness gave her warmth and bulk. She could do with a jacket, but that was only a dream. She had second thoughts about her skirt and retrieved it to take apart. The fabric might be useful and her calico petticoat would make good drying cloths.

Night had fallen. She lit a candle and gazed at her image in the darkened window. Her long, auburn hair spread in a straggly, matted mess over her shoulders. Her hair! She must be mad! Who on earth would believe she was a boy with all that hair? It dawned on her that she would have to cut it and she sat down on the box with a bump. She couldn't get rid of her hair, she just couldn't. But boys had short hair and if she wanted to be taken for a boy she had no choice. Her excitement turned to nervousness. Could she really get away with this?

She sawed at her thick locks with the knife, before any further misgivings. The blade blunted quickly and she stared at the single hank of hair in her hand. What was she doing to herself? Her lopsided image stared at her from the window. It was too late now; she had made up her mind and there was no going back. Picking up the candle she went down to the tack room and rummaged again in the jumble of old tools. Grooms used shears for trimming the horses' manes and tails; there must be a pair here somewhere. During her search she also found a spotted looking glass that the grooms had used for shaving on a Sunday morning. Satisfied, she climbed back upstairs and lit another candle, setting one either side of the looking glass on the box. She knelt on the floor in her moleskin breeches and took a deep breath to quell her nerves.

One by one, long auburn tresses fell to the floor, until she was left with a short shaggy mop. She combed it with her fingers then rolled her head around, feeling the light airiness about her neck. What had she done? Suddenly she didn't want to see her image in the looking glass and she blew out the candles. The shears clattered to the floor and, stiff with tension and exhausted by apprehension, she clambered onto her pallet and drew the horse blanket over her head as though to shut out what she had done. She couldn't sleep. She tried to anticipate her life as a boy and . . .

She sat bolt upright abruptly. What should she call herself? If anybody found her now she'd need a boy's name. She remembered other servants telling her that Sally or Sal was short for Sarah, because it was easier to say. Not Sal, she thought; Sam instead. Yes, Sam, Sam, Sam. Yes, tomorrow she would wake up as a boot boy called Sam, and at last she was able to sleep.

'Try this for size.' Aidan handed Danby one of his father's shirts. 'And give the one you're wearing a scrub when you wash yourself.'

'Do I have to?'

'You do if you want to sleep in my wagon. You can have a tot of the rum to warm you when you get back, and the food'll be ready by then.'

Aidan thought he and Danby had rubbed along well enough for the last week considering their different backgrounds. He was glad of the lad's help as work took his mind off his grief; he'd already been to the village to sell some repaired tools and brought back supplies for camp. He'd celebrated by buying a fowl that was simmering in an iron pot over the fire.

Danby came back shivering but several shades cleaner. He picked up the stone flask straightaway.

'Go easy on that,' Aidan commented.

'You've got plenty. I've seen the barrel in the wagon.'

It was the end of a long day and Aidan was tired so he didn't argue. 'Well, get some stew inside you. You'll soon warm up.'

They ate in silence as they were hungry, then stretched out by the fire in the fading light. 'You never did tell me why you left the farm,' Aidan asked.

'I did. It was the dairymaid's fault.'

'Was she the farmer's daughter?'

Danby shook his head and sipped at the rum. 'It was at the harvest supper last year,' he said. 'She kept catching my eye across the table, so I followed her to the barn afterwards.'

'Are you saying she encouraged you?'

'Well, she let me kiss her. I'm not lying! She wanted me to. She was all giggly but she didn't stop me and I was frantic for her.'

'I'll bet you were.'

'Wouldn't you be?' Danby challenged. 'I couldn't get me trousers down fast enough.'

'Didn't you think that was rushing things a bit?'

'Aye it was. She changed her mind while I trying to do it and started pushing me off. Then she started screaming so loud for me to stop that the farmer came and found us. We both got a right lathering for that. I was black and blue all over.'

'So you didn't go because his cow got sick?'

'Sort of. She never got milked the morning after. That beating was the last straw for me. He were a rotten bugger to me anyway. I decided to take my chances on the road and left one morning before daylight. Have you noticed any nice lasses in the village?'

Aidan laughed. 'Well, I wouldn't tell you if I had. Put the cork in the rum. You've had enough.'

Danby took another sip. 'But we could do with a lass about the place.'

'I said put the cork back.' Aidan sat up and took the flask from him. 'And I'll tell you one thing for nothing; if we did have a girl here I'd expect you to treat her with a bit more respect than you did that dairymaid. D'you hear me?'

'I'm only saying—'

'Well, don't. Get yourself off to bed. You can sleep in the wagon now you're clean. I'm going for a walk.' He calmed down as he strolled, wondering what his father would think of him taking up with a workhouse lad. But Danby wasn't all bad; he just hadn't had proper parents to guide him. It was only until the harvest started anyway. Danby said he would go for work on a farm then.

Aidan forgot about his concerns and started thinking about the following morning. Tomorrow they would set off together with a pouch of barley and a folded net to catch pigeons at that old dovecote. Might as well keep Danby busy if he was going to hang around.

Sarah was shocked by her appearance when she woke up the next day. She really did look like a boy; and, without her hair, even younger than she was. She rammed an old cap over her shaggy short crop and climbed out of the window for her morning search of the vegetable garden. Nothing had been sown or planted out this spring so she had to make do with the last of the winter greens and roots. But she knew how to light a fire and make a tasty stew, so, when she didn't worry about being caught, she enjoyed her freedom from scrubbing all day. Nobody shouted at her or pushed her around. She cooked and ate outdoors, in the lea of the garden wall. It was easy to fetch water from the pump and she had found an old iron pot that had been used to heat up mash for the horses.

The creak of a hinge on the dovecote door startled her. She picked up her makeshift knife and crept quietly to a gap in the wall. The stranger had returned and was intent on stealing the pigeons! They were *her* pigeons; the only meat she had to eat.

'Hey, you,' she called, without further thought. 'Get out of there!'

He looked up from inspecting the rotting door and she stood straight to show herself. At the same time another figure appeared in the doorway, another man, a younger man with bedraggled

45

fair hair and a net in his hand. Alarmed that there were two of them she turned and fled back into the garden, across to the gate on the other side and out into the scrubland beyond.

She hid there all day, in fear of her life. The lurid tales of the footmen haunted her and it was only when she was faint from hunger and thirst that she ventured back. She tried to think rationally. She was a boy now; the danger was less. Even so, she moved stealthily until she was sure they had gone. Her corner of the garden lay untouched except for − her eyes widened in disbelief − except for two pigeons, side by side, their necks broken and ready to be plucked. What kind of vagrants were they, who shared their spoils like this?

She watched the smoke rise from their camp in the trees for several days with mounting anxiety. They hadn't moved on and the big dark man had looked menacing, although the other one was less so. He was smaller and younger, she thought. They would be back for more pickings and she might not hear them approach. They knew she was here because they had left her the pigeons. But, at the same time, that wasn't the action of a vagrant. Surely it wasn't such a risk now she was a boy? There might even be a woman with them and then she'd really feel safe.

Oh, what was she to do? Go and find them or wait until they came back? And what if the new owners arrived and fetched the constable to lock her up? Finally, and fearfully, she made up her mind. She'd ask if she could throw in her lot with them. If they said no she'd be on the road alone. The latter didn't bear thinking about and she pushed it to the back of her mind.

Slowly, she rolled up her horse blanket, tied all her useful possessions onto it with bits of twine and old harness, dropped the bundle carefully out of the stable window and climbed down for the last time. She was uneasy of what lay before her and had to keep reminding herself that she was a boy now and had to act like one.

Her bundle was heavy, but Sarah was loath to leave anything, especially her cooking pot and the remainder of the oats and molasses. She fashioned two leather loops to hoist the burden onto her shoulders. Although slight in build, scullery work had made her strong, and she found her breeches much more comfortable and serviceable than the skirts she had discarded. Even so, it was a tough climb through the trees and their camp was well hidden and hard to find. Her burden became heavier with each step and she had to concentrate hard on putting one foot in front of the other.

Her slender body was bending under the strain and sweat was trickling down her forehead and into her eyes. It was difficult to straighten up and scan the track ahead of her. But suddenly he was there, standing in front of her, looking so much more menacing than before. She was frightened and exhausted and started to shake. What if he saw through her? But she had no puff left to run even if she wanted to.

'Looking for something?' he asked.

Terrified of what he might do, she tried to draw herself up to her full height. When in danger, the footmen used to say, attack was the best form of defence. 'My pigeons; you took my pigeons,' she challenged.

'We left you some.'

'Not many.' She sounded ungrateful. She had only herself to feed.

'Why did you run away?'

'There were two of you.'

'There are still two of us.'

She stared at him silently. Close up he was bigger than she remembered. His dark hair curled over his collar and he had broad shoulders. But it was his eyes that drew her. They were not brown as she'd expected; more like a stormy grey. In spite of her sweating she felt a shiver track down her spine.

He moved closer and inspected her pack. 'You have a good iron pot there, and some useful leather strapping. Who are you?'

'Sam,' she answered. Thank goodness she had thought of that.

'Where are you from?'

'I was boot boy at the Hall back there. The master died and it was sold so the workhouse came for us. I didn't want to go with them so I hid in the stables.'

He seemed to accept this and said, 'What else have you got?'

'Shears, old buckles, a looking glass.'

'Anything to eat?'

'Oats and molasses. Where are you heading?'

'We're not going anywhere until the harvest starts and we can get work.'

'Can I come with you?' she responded swiftly.

'You're a bit small.'

'I'm strong, though.'

'I can see that,' Aidan said, before adding, 'Do you want some water?'

Realising suddenly how thirsty she was. Sarah said, 'Yes. Is it far?'

'Follow me.'

He took her to the spring first, which fed a small brook that widened into a stream. She flopped down onto a smooth rock, easing the weight on her shoulders. 'Your camp must be near here,' she commented, looking around. 'Where do you sleep?'

'I've got a wagon.'

'A wagon?' Her spirits soared at the thought of proper shelter for the night.

'The axle's broken.' He picked up a substantial rock. 'It needs shoring up. Can you carry one of these for me?' He was selecting wide flat boulders and lining them up.

Sarah swallowed. It was all she could do to carry herself with this burden on her back. 'How much further?' she asked, struggling to her feet.

Thankfully, he gave her two of the smaller rocks and she clutched them to her waistcoat. She was a boy now and folk had different expectations of her. But her skinny legs were turning to jelly and she was shaking when they reached his wagon.

'Much obliged,' Aidan said. He put down the large stone he

had carried and took the others from her. 'You're stronger than you look. How old are you?'

'Old enough,' she answered, praying that he would not pry too deeply.

'Where are your folks?'

'I haven't got any. That's why they were sending me to the workhouse.'

'You don't want to go in there if you can help it.'

'I know. Can I fall in with you until harvest?'

'If you do you'll have to muck in.'

'What is there to do?'

'Collect water and firewood, keep the fire going.'

'I can do all that,' she replied confidently, adding as an after-thought, 'and polish your boots.' He laughed and she wondered how good she would be at being a boot boy. 'What's your name?' she asked

He told her. 'I mend tools and pots and sell them.'

She thought of the jumble of broken tools that she'd left in the tack room, and said, 'I know where there's some coal.'

'Where?'

'The coal house at the Hall back there.'

'I never saw it.'

'It's round the garden side. There's plenty of spilled stuff round and about. We could go down there. Have you got any sacks?'

She was rewarded with a broad smile that made her blink. His eyes crinkled and his face became kinder. He said, 'Get that pack off your back and give us a hand with the rocks. If I can make that axle secure you can sleep underneath it tonight.'

She had to sleep underneath? She was better off in the stable. She tried not to show her dismay. 'Thanks,' she answered. She hoped she sounded grateful. But she was thinking of how many woodland creatures there would be sharing her bed. She wondered if she would regret leaving the comfort of her stable loft. 'Where's the other fellow?'

'Danby? He's down at the stream catching fish.'

49

Sarah enjoyed eating fish and wondered if there would be one for her tonight. 'I'll cook them for you,' she volunteered brightly.

'Can you cook?' He sounded surprised.

She hesitated, her mind racing. 'The – the butler showed me. He often did late suppers for the racing gentlemen at the Hall.'

'He showed a boot boy?'

'I – I was learning to be a footman.'

'How come? Were you indentured?'

She was cornered. If you were indentured you had a bene-factor, a relative or even the workhouse, so why was she hiding in a stable instead of moving to another indentured position?

'I – I –' Her mind raced. 'I was a natural son of one of the servants. She was favoured and – and so was I.' I've told him I'm a bastard, she thought. It was probably true anyway.

'Was your father the master, then?'

Sarah's eyes rounded. She'd never thought of that, but she'd only been a scullery maid so she guessed not. 'I never knew my father.' She shrugged.

'Where's your mother now?'

'She died.' Well, that part was definitely true. She thought she saw a shadow of sadness pass across his features but it was soon gone and he set to work with the rocks and a heavy mallet to make her outdoor shelter steady and safe.

As she watched him work, her original opinion of him was reinforced. He was capable and quite brutal when he was attacking rocks. She wondered what he would be like if you got on the wrong side of him. He was sweating heavily and stopped to take a swig of water from a tin canteen suspended outside his wagon.

'Can you use a hammer?' he asked.

'Yes,' she answered untruthfully. She had never handled one but she had seen gardeners using them and it didn't look diffi-cult.

'I've got a piece of canvas for you. If you fix it round the base of the wagon before nightfall you'll keep the draughts out.'

And the fox, she hoped. 'Have you got nails?' she asked, bending

50

to survey her new home. Bracken had been pushing through the ground but it was already dying away. As a resting place, it was better than nothing and she could put rocks in the fire to heat up and dry out her natural bedding. She was searching for flat stones when Danby came back, his catch strung together with creeper stems.

'Who are you?' he demanded. 'Where's Aidan?'

'He's in the wagon. I'm Sam.'

'What are you doing here?'

'Are you Danby?' she responded. 'Are they for us to eat?'

'Us!' he exclaimed and yelled, 'Aidan! Where are you?'

Aidan clambered out of his wagon clutching an armful of heavy canvas. 'What's all this shouting about?' he parried.

'Who's this?'

'Sam. He's staying with us for a while.'

'Where? We've no room.'

'Underneath,' Sarah explained.

'We don't want nobody else,' Danby protested.

'We can always use an extra pair of hands.'

'But he's just a bairn!'

'No, I'm not!' Sarah protested.

'He's strong enough and he's nowhere else to go,' said Aidan. 'Besides, it's my wagon and I say who stays or goes.' He dropped the canvas at Sarah's feet. 'You'll have to pull your weight though,' he warned.

'I will.' She placed her own bundle by the folded canvas and checked it over to make sure she hadn't lost anything.

'Well, you're not having my bed,' Danby grumbled. He gazed at Sarah. 'What have you got in your pack?'

'That's none of your business.'

'Yes, it is. We share and share alike here. Don't we?' Danby looked to Aidan for support.

Aidan nodded. 'He's brought food. And that iron pot looks useful. Show us what else you've got.'

Outnumbered, Sarah displayed her salvage from the Hall stables.

Danby watched keenly, then suddenly dropped the fish on the ground and grabbed at her tin whistle.

Sarah tried to snatch it from him but he whisked it sharply above her head. 'Give that back!' she squealed. 'It's mine.'

Danby ignored her, examined the small instrument and put it to his lips, blowing as tunelessly as Sarah had. Angrily, she flung herself at him. 'I said give it back.'

He pushed her away with one hand as she desperately tried to recover her treasure. But she had watched the stable lads scuffling in the yard at Meadow Hall, and she ducked away from him, twisted round and landed him a kick up his backside.

He yelped, stopped blowing and turned on her, cuffing the side of her head. She'd had worse from Mrs Watson and snatched at her whistle trying to prise it from his fingers. He was bigger and stronger than her, but she wasn't going to let her most cherished possession go without a fight and kicked as hard as she could at his shins.

'You little rat!' Danby retaliated and gave her a forceful push.

She tottered back, lost her balance and landed with a thud on the forest floor.

'That's enough, you two!'

Sarah's eyes widened. Aidan's face was dark and angry. This was the side of him she feared. But he had marched across to Danby and forced the whistle out of his fingers.

Danby stared at Aidan belligerently. 'Why should you have it? I saw it first.'

'It's *my* whistle,' Sarah protested. She was beginning to think it was not a good idea to fall in with these two. 'Just because I'm the littlest doesn't mean you can take my things,' she added valiantly.

'Can you play it?' Aidan asked her.

Sarah shrugged, not wanting to admit that she couldn't. 'I found it.'

'Play it for us.'

'Go on, then. Play it.'

'I can't,' she admitted eventually.

Danby sneered at her. 'See? He can't play it, so it's not much use to him, is it?'

'I thought I might trade it for food,' Sarah argued.

'No,' Danby protested. 'I want to have a go at playing it.'

'You won't starve here,' Aidan said. 'Not with the three of us to find food and summer just round the corner.'

'Give it back, then,' Sarah demanded.

Aidan stood in the middle. Sarah frowned. He had the advantage of size and he knew it. He said, 'This is my home and my camp and I don't want any stealing or fighting.'

'Tell that to him, not me,' she said.

'I wasn't stealing it. And I didn't do any kicking,' Danby retaliated.

'Shut up, will you?' Aidan growled. 'We none of us want to be on our own, but you're not staying, neither of you, if you cause trouble. We have to be friends.'

Sarah saw the sense in that. That was why she had searched them out.

'What do you say, Danby?' Aidan pressed.

Danby kicked at a stone wedged in the ground. 'Give him back his whistle, then.'

Sarah gave a triumphant smile, stood up and walked over to collect it.

'And we have to share,' Aidan added, holding the whistle high so she could not reach it.

That's what Danby had said earlier on. But Sarah was not accustomed to sharing. She had never had anything that anybody else had wanted from her before. Sharing to her was being given what Mrs Watson said she could have. She stopped in her tracks. Aidan was not going to let her have it back. He was going to steal it from her. He was a bad as Danby. She glared at him and hissed, 'It's mine.'

He glared back at her but she didn't waver. He expected her to give in. Well, she wouldn't! It was her whistle, and she pushed out her bottom lip defiantly. 'You're not going to cry are you?' he asked. Hastily she shrugged her shoulders and looked at her feet. Boys didn't cry. 'You can have it back if you let Danby have a go at playing it,' he went on. 'What do you say, Sam?'

She glanced at Danby who beamed with the triumphant smile she had sported a few moments ago. 'He might break it. Or lose it,' she answered.

'No, I won't,' Danby said crossly.

'Is that yes or no, Sam?' Aidan pressed. 'Are you staying and sharing; or leaving?'

Sarah didn't really have a choice because she wanted to stay. She would have to be wary of crossing either of them, but she'd rather they were on her side than against her. 'I'm staying,' she muttered. 'He can lend my whistle if he wants.'

Aidan handed it back to her 'Good. Maybe Danby can give us a tune later.' Sarah tucked the whistle away in a pocket on the inside of her waistcoat and unrolled the heavy canvas to fix on the wagon. It was thick and stiff and hard for her to cope with its weight.

'What is this stuff?' she mumbled as she heaved on its length.

Aidan was working with Danby to build up the fire pit using the rocks he had collected, but he heard her. 'It came from a sailing ship. The farmer used it to keep the rain off his hayricks and he gave it to my father for the wagon.' He stopped as he remembered helping cover the hayricks as a lad, sometimes in a biting gale that had blown up without warning. He'd been bigger than Sam at twelve and the canvas had been a struggle for him then.

'We'll finish this later, Dan,' he said. 'Let's give Sam a hand first.'

It needed the three of them to hold and hammer the canvas in place and secure it to the ground. When they had finished, Sam was pleased with her new abode. It was small and dark, but snug and private; not as good as her bed above the stables, but at least she was no longer alone. She stowed her belongings and then went over to the fire pit with its surrounding stone wall.

'Why have you built such a big fire?' she asked.

'You'll see,' Danby said. 'I reckon with the bellows we'll build up enough heat for mending cooking pots.'

'I'll give it a try tomorrow,' Aidan added. 'But we need wood for now. Come on. We'll all go.'

They returned dragging heavy branches that exhausted all of them and Sarah was feeling weak with hunger. She stamped on some of the smaller branches and twisted off some dead twigs. 'I'll get the fire going for supper,' she volunteered.

'Sam reckons he can cook,' Aidan added, 'so let's see what he can do with the fish.'

'Well, don't let 'im burn 'em. It's all we've got,' Danby responded.

'He won't, will you, Sam?'

She shook her head, confident she knew what she was doing when cooking over a fire.

'I'm going to chop this lot for tomorrow. Danby, show Sam where the lard and salt is in the wagon then give me a hand. And hurry up. I'm starving.'

'Me too.'

United by their need for food, they concentrated on their allocated tasks.

Aidan had a thick metal plate for cooking on over the fire and three metal rods lashed together to make a tripod for hanging a cauldron. Sarah decided to use her own iron pot to make a porridge with her oats and molasses. Our pot, our oats and molasses, she corrected herself. It was give and take here and a new way of living for Sarah.

The fish was tasty and there was plenty to go round. They ate all the porridge too and finished off the water from all the water bottles on the wagon.

'With three of us we need a bucket and ladle for water,' Sarah suggested. She knew where there was one in the walled garden at the Hall.

'Give us a lend of your whistle then,' Danby suggested as they sat around the dying embers of their fire.

'You can't play it.'

'Neither can you so let me have a try.'

She took it out of her waistcoat pocket and handed it across to him. He put it to his lips and blew tunelessly. But after a few minutes he began to get the hang of it and the vestiges of a tune emerged. Aidan was lying on his back and looking at the patches of night sky visible through the trees. He sat up and listened.

Sarah, too, watched in surprise. He could play a tune! A proper tune, like the ones she'd heard from the stables at the Hall. She began to move her body to the rhythm and tap her hands on her breeches-clad knees. This tune had words as well, she recalled. The stable lads used to sing them raucously when they had taken ale. Aidan knew the words and began to sing. But he didn't know them all so he made them up about Dan the fisherman and Sam the little lost lamb, making Danby splutter with mirth and stop playing.

'I know what we'll do,' Danby said. 'We'll go round the fairs as entertainers. I'll play, Aidan can sing and you, Sam, you'll have to dance.'

'Dance? I can't dance.'

'Yes, you can. Everybody can dance. Dance us a jig. You must have seen 'em when you were at the Hall. Come on, give us a show, then.' He blew on the whistle again and Aidan added more words, so Sarah got up in the fading firelight and jigged about, stamping her feet and kicking her legs as she had seen the footmen do at Christmas time, until she ran out of puff.

Danby stopped playing. 'There,' he announced with satisfaction. 'He can dance. We can form a troupe of travelling players.'

'Don't be daft.' Aidan laughed. 'You have to be better than us for folk to pay.'

'I'll start practising,' he retaliated and tried a more complicated tune without success.

Sarah put her hands over her ears and screwed up her face. 'Give it a rest, Danby.'

He did, shaking his spit out of the whistle and stretching out his hand to give it back to her.

'No, you keep it,' she said. 'I could never play it like that.'

'You might if you practised,' Aidan suggested. 'You dance well enough. You have a sense of rhythm.'

'Do I?' She had no idea as she had only copied the footmen. But it was too dark to see whether Aidan was laughing at her or not.

'We'd better turn in for the night. The last of the fire should keep any fox away. Bang on the wagon floor if you're troubled, Sam.'

'I'll not disturb you. I've got used to being on my own,' she replied.

'You're not on your own now.'

But she knew she was. And it was a different kind of being alone now. She was a girl so she would always have to keep her distance from them. She could never dare say how frightened she was at night. Boys were supposed to be brave.

She hadn't thought beyond not being caught living in the Hall stables when she'd climbed the hill to join them. Well, she'd just have to learn from them how to behave as a boy. It was only until the harvest started, when they'd all go off to find work in the fields and she would move away from them. But where would she go, and what would she do?

She still had no idea.

Within a month Sarah had insinuated herself as a boy into their camp routine. Meadow Hall had given her a deal of insight into how young men behaved. But Aidan, she realised, thought of himself as a grown man and, to him, she was just a boy. He made fun of her sometimes but, on the whole, he treated her well because she kept out of his way. Danby caught fish and rabbit and helped Aidan with his metalwork. Sarah fetched water from the spring and cooked food. She journeyed back to the stables to search for anything that might be of use to them, keeping well out of sight as a tenant farmer continued to plough and plant nearby fields. Every visit she expected new owners to be there, but no one came to live in the Hall. She carried back broken tools for Aidan to repair, and herbs from the garden to flavour the meat and fish that she cooked.

She helped them build a shelter over the fire pit and the log pile so they could work and cook in the rain, and they found a secluded rock pool near the cave where they washed. But she never removed her clothes, even when she bathed alone. It was easier to wash them on her body anyway. On warm sunny days she stretched out on the hot rocks to dry out rather than stand steaming by the camp fire. If Aidan thought she was odd he didn't comment. She caught him frowning at her from time to time but, under his menacing exterior, he had a consideration and thoughtfulness that she hadn't experienced from anyone before and she liked him for it.

As summer approached, leaves covered the treetops giving welcome shade to Sarah, for her skin burned easily in the heat. June was sunny and the temperature climbed until one hot July day when the sky darkened early and a storm brewed. Sarah counted the seconds between flashes of lightening and claps of thunder. The time was getting shorter, and huge plops of rain began to spot the canvas over the wagon and the shelter.

'We'd better go inside until this passes,' Aidan suggested.

Inside the wagon it was dark and cramped but cosy, with a cleared bit of wooden floor in the middle where Aidan and Danby slept. The rest of the space was taken up by shelving, boxes and sacks for storage. They sat on boxes, watching for the lightening through the canvas and waiting for the clap of thunder. Once the rain started it seemed as if the heavens had opened.

The air became chilly and Aidan took out a bottle of rum that he said was for when it was wintry, but they swigged from it all the same. Danby took out the whistle and began to play.

Aidan joined in with his voice and Sarah got up to do her jig. She had improved over the weeks and quite enjoyed jumping around to a bit of music at the end of the day.

'Stay in the middle, Sam,' Aidan warned as her boots clunked on the floor and the suspended pots and tools rattled.

Danby got up to join her, stamping to the rhythm of his tune as he played and Sarah stretched out her arm towards Aidan. 'Come on,' she called. 'Have a go. Let's see what you can do.'

He laughed and unfolded his long body to make a threesome. But there was very little room for the all of them and Aidan had to duck and sway to avoid hitting his head against the suspended household items that jangled as the three of them shuffled around. Aidan lost his balance and fell against Sarah, grabbing at her clothes for stability. She leaned over to grasp one of the suspended pots and it was then that the sound of creaking wood overcame the noise of the music. The wagon moved and the floor listed drunkenly.

'Stop! Stop!' Aidan clutched at Sarah's waistcoat, his fist pushing against her chest. 'Don't move, either of you!' They looked at each other with wide eyes. The wagon was moving, very slowly, creaking and leaning. 'It's going over! Move to this side. Now!' He dragged her by the front of her shirt and pushed her against the canvas. 'Keep still. Both of you.'

Sarah held her body rigid as the creaking ceased and the wagon stopped moving. It was not the thought of injury that alarmed her; it was the knowledge that Aidan's knuckles had brushed against her swaddled breasts.

'What's happening, Aidan?' she asked.

'I don't know. We'll have to get out. Go on, Danby, you're nearest the back, you go first.'

'But it's pouring down out there.'

'Just get out, will you? Before the wagon goes over and kills us all!'

Danby obeyed and climbed down slowly. Aidan had let go of

Sarah's shirt and was using his weight in an attempt to balance the sloping floor.

'You next, Sam. Go careful now.'

She nodded wordlessly and obeyed. Aidan followed her cautiously and turned immediately to peer underneath at his shored-up axle. 'It's too dark. I can't see a thing. I should have remembered the lantern.' He sounded cross.

Danby ran over to the fire pit and sheltered under cover. 'I'll light a flare,' he offered.

'No, Danby,' Aidan called after him, 'Don't use a flare for looking underneath; it might catch light. I'll have to go back inside.'

'You're too heavy,' Sarah protested. 'You might tip it over and we'll never get it righted again.'

'What do you suggest then?' he demanded. 'If I can't see, I can't fix it.'

'I'll get the lantern. I'm the smallest. It's on a hook in the middle, isn't it?'

The rain continued to fall steadily in sheets, wetting them through.

'Yes, but if the wagon tips over, you'll get hurt.'

'You could wedge stones under the wheels to stop them moving.'

Aidan wiped the rain from his face. 'Very well. Go careful and keep to the middle.'

'I'll have to stand on a box to reach the hook.'

'You can't risk that. Perhaps I'd better go.'

But Sarah was already creeping carefully into the wagon, straining her ears for sounds of creaking wood. She shoved the bedrolls together and climbed precariously on them stretching for all she was worth until her fingers closed around the lamp base. One last push and the metal handle was free from its hook. She clutched it closely to her body and climbed out nervously.

'Watch your step. It's slippery. Pass me the lantern and then jump. I'll break your fall.' He stood with his arms outstretched and for a second she wanted nothing more than to fall into them but she dare not.

60

'No need.' She stretched over to hand him the lamp then tumbled from the back of the wagon, anxious to avoid Aidan's hands near her body again. She staggered over to the fire pit where Danby had rekindled the embers. Wet through, the three of them stood shivering while Aidan turned up the wick on the lantern and lit it with a glowing stick from the ashes.

'Get the fire going, you two. We'll be sleeping by it tonight.'

'There's not enough room for the three of us,' Danby complained.

'Oh, stop moaning, will you? At least we won't be crushed to death.' Aidan picked up the lantern and went to inspect his wagon.

'There's the woodpile as well,' Sarah said. It was away from the fire but it was under cover. 'I can sleep over there.'

'Good idea,' Danby replied. 'Go and fetch some logs so I can dry 'em out for the morning.'

Sarah had made two journeys in the slippery mud, each with an armful of damp wood, by the time Aidan came back with the lantern. He took the rum from his pocket and handed it round. 'The dancing's caused more splintering in the rotten axle.'

'It looked a decent piece o' timber to me,' Sarah said. 'It must be rotten in the middle.'

'The farmer my father worked for reckoned it was from a sea-going ship and had woodworm.'

In the firelight, Sarah saw Danby's eyes widen. 'Ship's timbers? They have worms as big as your cock in them,' he said.

Aidan let out a guffaw, and Danby cried, 'It's true, I swear it is.'

'Do they?' Sarah was alarmed that she had been sleeping underneath them. An image in her mind of a gross undulating maggot above her head as she slept made her gag and she disguised it as a choking cough.

'Oh aye; an' they're a lot bigger than yours, Sam,' Danby giggled.

She thought he was just frightening her, like the footmen used to at the Hall and demanded, 'How do you know?'

Danby, enjoying the joke, answered, 'Perhaps I followed you when you went to relieve yourself?'

He couldn't have done! She always walked twice as far as they did and was extra careful to be alone. Sarah felt herself blushing in the firelight and protested, 'I don't mean that! I mean how do you know about the worms?'

Now even Aidan found this funny and began to giggle help-lessly. Sarah, anxious not to be different, forced a laugh with them, though she didn't think a simple misunderstanding was that amusing.

But Danby thought it was, ignored her question and continued to taunt her. 'Shall we get 'em out and measure 'em? See who's got the biggest?'

Aidan snorted. 'I suppose that means you think you've got a big 'un, then. I'll measure up against you any day, Danby Jones.'

'Come on, then,' Danby laughed. 'Give us another snifter o' that rum and turn up the lamp. I say the little 'un shows us his first.'

Sarah was mortified. She had no idea what to do and could think of nothing to say. She sat on a boulder with a frozen grin on her face.

Aidan made an effort to quell his laughter. 'That's enough, Dan. Leave the lad alone.'

Danby sucked the spittle in his mouth. 'I can't help it. Look at him. He's scared out of his wits. Give him another sip of the rum.'

'I said leave it, Dan. He's only a lad.'

'Go on wi' you, I'm just having a bit o' fun,' Danby protested.

Aidan recovered from his laughter and answered, 'Aye, I know. But I'll have none of your workhouse ways here. We can at least try to keep a bit of decency.'

Relief flooded over Sarah and her face relaxed. She forced another grin to cover her embarrassment. She wouldn't be able to stay much longer. Sooner or later one of them would discover she was a girl and she had no idea how they would react. Would they laugh it off and forgive her for deceiving them? Or be angry and extract revenge? Suddenly she felt more alone than ever.

'Were you really in the workhouse, Dan?' she asked, anxious to change the subject.

'I was. That's how I know about the worms. An old sea dog told me.'

'Will the worms still be alive in the wood now?'

'No,' Aidan answered. 'But they've eaten half of it away and left some big holes inside.'

'What can we do?'

'Shore it up with more rocks. We'll start collecting 'em tomorrow. I can make it steady again.'

'I'd best move my bedding to the rear,' Sam added.

But Aidan was shaking his head. 'Don't sleep there again. Even when I've propped it up I wouldn't want you underneath. You'll have to come inside with us.'

'There's not room!' Danby protested.

'We'll have to make room. As soon as I get the wagon solid, we'll move the boxes to where Sam slept. I don't know why I didn't think of that before. Anyway, it's warm enough to sleep outside if the rain stops.'

'Not me,' Danby said. 'I had enough of that on the road.'

'Actually, it'll get too hot with all three of us in the wagon,' Aidan warned.

'Then I'll take all me clothes off. It's time they had a wash, anyroad.'

'I'll stay outside,' Sarah volunteered. 'I'm used to it now.'

'It looks like you'll be on your own in there, Dan.'

'Suits me,' he replied. He took another swig of the rum and passed it on to Sarah. 'Anyway, I've been thinking of moving on. The harvest'll be starting in a week or two and there'll be plenty of work.'

Aidan took the bottle from her after Sarah had taken a sip. 'So it'll be just the two of us, Sam.'

'Aren't we all going to the hiring fair?' she asked.

'I'm better off staying with my anvil. I've already sold tools and pots to the villagers. I want enough to take to the Michaelmas market when the harvest is over.'

'Oh.' Sarah realised that now was an opportunity for her to

leave, before either of them discovered she was a girl. Suddenly, she realised she didn't want to go, she was enjoying her summer in the forest, especially with Aidan. She really liked him. But she had noticed that he gave her strange looks from time to time and it worried her.

'I'll go with Dan, then,' she decided quickly.

As soon as she had said it she regretted her decision. But she had to be sensible and go.

Chapter 6

'The coal's hot enough now, Dan. Go and cool yourself off at the spring.'

Danby stopped working the bellows and sat back on his heels. 'I meant what I said last night. I'm leaving for the hiring fair tomorrow.'

Aidan's sooty face looked up from the fire. 'Sam wants to go with you.'

Sarah was gutting trout from the stream. She didn't particularly want to go with Danby, but she did need to move on and find work as a girl.

Aidan's hammer shattered the silence as he flattened the hot twisted metal into shape and then plunged the buckle into a pot of water, making it sizzle and steam. 'You don't have to go, Sam.'

'He can work the bellows for you when I'm gone,' Dan suggested.

'And learn how to work at my anvil.'

Sarah looked up from her task with a bloody knife in her hands. 'I'll try the hiring fair, thanks.'

Aidan wiped the sweat from his face with a grubby cloth. 'You're not big enough yet. Farmers take their pick of labourers and they'll only take a little 'un if he comes free with his father or his brother.'

'He's right,' Danby echoed. 'Stay here with Aidan for another couple of months until Michaelmas. You'll have filled out by then.'

'I can't help it if I'm small,' she argued.

'But I thought you liked it here?' Aidan sounded cross.

'I do. But you don't want me hanging around for ever.'

'I haven't said that,' Aidan protested. 'Honestly, sometimes, I don't know where you get your ideas from.'

'Me neither,' Danby echoed. 'But I don't want you tagging along. You'll slow me down.'

'No, I won't!'

It was clear to Sarah they didn't understand she had to leave with Danby; and why should they? She couldn't go on the road on her own but neither could she stay here much longer without discovery. They were staring at her, expecting her to agree and she felt trapped. She saw them exchange a glance and hated it when they conspired against her. She felt excluded and she supposed she was.

'What will you do for the winter?' Aidan asked Dan.

Dan shrugged. 'They say there's plenty of work in the manu-factories in the town. That goes on all year round.' He disappeared in the direction of the spring.

'What will you do, Sam?' Aidan queried.

'The same as Dan, I expect.'

'Have you ever been to the town?'

'No.'

'Well, I don't know about the town in this valley, but I've been to others in the Riding with my father. It's easy to get in with the wrong crowd.'

'I can take care of myself.'

'You're sturdy enough. But you're nowhere near as strong as Dan.'

'So?'

'Didn't you hear what I said to Dan? I've been to hiring fairs. No farmer or his steward will pick you from a hiring line and pay you a wage until you've grown a bit more.'

'I'll find something.'

'Well, if you don't, you can always come back here. Dan knows that, too. We get along well enough and it has to be better than being on the road and dossing in a workhouse, doesn't it?'

'I'm not going to no workhouse neither,' Sarah added defiantly.

'You'd better stick with one of us, then,'

She truly wished she could, but replied, 'I'll take my chances on my own.'

'Tough little fighter, aren't you?'

'I've had to be,' she muttered and brought her knife down sharply to cut off a fish head.

Aidan picked up his tongs holding the cooled metal. 'Well, if you think you're that strong you can work the bellows for me now. Let's see what you're really made of.'

She stabbed the knife point into the ground. 'I will. Any time you like.' It couldn't be harder than pumping and carrying water, she thought. Just hotter, and she was used to frying over a red-hot fire at the Hall.

'You might start to fill out a bit then,' Aidan commented.

Aidan checked the fastenings on Dan's backpack and waved him away. Danby was heading off alone, having steadfastly refused to take Sarah. Aidan had agreed with him and she was outnumbered. Half of her was angry, but the other half looked forward to staying with Aidan. When she looked at him she was aware of a bubbling nervousness within. As she watched him at his anvil she wished more than ever that she could tell him she was a girl.

She enjoyed being with him, more so now they were on their own. He didn't make fun of her as Danby had and he treated her well, even offering to let her sleep in the wagon. The thought of lying so close to him at night sent a thrill of excitement through her that she found bewildering. But it wasn't to be as, when she moved in, he took to sleeping under the stars and she had the wagon all to herself.

During the day the sun was high and Sarah was grateful for the leafy shade of the trees. She didn't mind the bellows but she hated the heat and her back sweated under all her layers of clothing.

'Come on, Sam. The fire's cooling. Get your backside over here.'

There was more work to do now that Dan had left. But it was nothing compared with the amount she'd had to do at the Hall. It's just that, these days, she didn't feel like doing any of it. She was irritated by everything.

'Oh, shut up!' she retaliated. 'Anybody'd think you were making the crown jewels.'

Aidan looked up from his anvil with an exasperated expression on his face. He worked in just his trousers and his grimy chest was sweating. It had a covering of dark hair that was flecked with sooty dust. But she didn't grimace at the dirt; rather, she felt strong urge to run the palms of her hands over it, and over his shoulders to feel the muscles on his arms.

'Are you missing Dan?' he asked. 'You've been a right pain since he left.'

She blinked and pulled herself together. 'Well, he was fun. All you do is work.'

'No, I don't. I just want to take as much as I can to sell at the Michaelmas Fair and it's less than two months away now. If you put your back into it now, we can enjoy ourselves afterwards. We might meet up with Dan in town.'

Sarah dragged herself over to the fire pit. She had been feeling like this for days now. Her stomach felt like a lump of lead and she had no energy to pump the bellows. It must be the heat, unless – unless she was sickening for something.

'Your face is red before you start. Why don't you take off your shirt?'

'Stop telling me what to do,' she snapped.

Aidan gave an impatient sigh and muttered. 'Please yourself.'

She pumped as hard as she could. But her stomach was hurting and her back was aching.

'Can't you do better than that?' Aidan demanded.

'No, I can't,' she barked.

'Well, it's not hot enough.'

She was roasting with her bodice under the shirt and felt ill. She wondered if she had caught some dreadful disease that was about to strike her dead. If that was the case, the last thing she needed was high-and-mighty Aidan pushing her about. He was as bad as Mrs Watson for giving orders.

'Do it yourself, then,' she said and got up to walk away.

Who did he think he was? Just because it was his wagon he thought he could tell her what to do and she wasn't having it. She took the path to the spring. The ice-cold water might cool her down. She heard metal against metal as Aidan finished the harness buckles, and then silence until fallen twigs cracked under foot behind her.

'Come back, Sam. Tell me what's troubling you.' He was wiping his brow with a dirty rag.

'Nothing!'

'Yes, there is. You've never been like this before. Something's wrong.'

She stopped and sat on a boulder. It was warm to touch and the sun was high. All she wanted to do was lie down with her eyes shut. 'Leave me alone, can't you?'

'No. I think you're sickening for something. Go back to the wagon and I'll bring you some cold spring water.'

She took his advice without a further word and rolled out her bedding on the floor space. She felt better when she was lying on her stomach; it seemed to take the strain off her aching back.

Aidan brought water in a metal tankard, and a tot of his father's rum in a tiny thick glass which he put by her head. 'Drink that and try to sleep it off.'

She swallowed the rum, closed her eyes and drifted away. When she awoke she thought she wanted the privy as she felt a stickiness between her legs. She pushed her hand down the front of her trousers and inside her drawers. A few seconds later she realised what it was. Was that all that was wrong with her? She should have known. The maids at Meadow Hall were always talking about it.

She had started her courses. She closed her eyes and groaned, not knowing whether to be happy or sad. Her secret was becoming too difficult to keep. She'd have to leave now. She shuffled about to find her bundle of rags. Perhaps she could feign illness and go into town to see an apothecary?

The canvas moved and a shaft of light flooded into the wagon. 'I heard you moving about.'

'Go away!'

'I just want to know how you are.'

'I've caught too much sun. It's given me a fever.'

'You look as though you might have. You can't take it with your colouring. You'd better stay inside.'

'No, it's too hot in here. I'll walk down to the stream and cool my feet.'

'Do you want me to come with you?'

'No! No, thank you.'

'Don't be long or I'll come looking for you.'

Alone in the wagon, she shoved rags torn from her old calico petticoat down her drawers and between her legs, pulling her breeches up tight to keep them in place. She decided she'd tell Aidan she was going to the stream every day to get her fever down. That night when Aidan was sleeping under the trees, she took off her bodice and replaced it with calico strips that she bound tightly around chest, squashing her growing breasts against her ribcage. Without the long sleeves, the freedom for her arms was bliss. After a couple of days her bleeding slowed and she felt better; quite a lot better in fact.

Aidan noticed. 'Your fever's gone,' he commented.

She had rehearsed her explanation. 'I just got overheated by the fire.'

'Well, I did suggest you take your shirt off.'

'I'm not like you. I burn up when I'm in the sun.'

He grinned. 'Aye, I've noticed you're a freckle-face. It goes with the hair, I suppose. The sun has brought out the copper in it. You don't often see that colour.'

It had grown since she'd joined the camp and she fingered the ends. 'Do you like it?' she asked.

His eyes widened and then he frowned at her. 'What sort of a question is that?'

The sort of question a girl might ask a boy that she liked. She didn't know what to say and felt herself blush.

He was staring at her with narrowed eyes.

She tried to laugh it off. 'I must have had too much sun again. Maybe this open air life isn't for me.'

'Maybe not,' he agreed readily. 'You should find yourself a position somewhere.'

She felt cut to the quick. 'Do you want to be rid of me?'

Her question seemed to irritate and confuse him. 'I don't know. Do you want to go?'

No, she thought, never. But she said, 'I told you I would and it's not long until the hiring fair now.'

'Very well.' He hesitated then added. 'You can always come back here if nobody takes you.'

She stifled an urge to put her arms round him and instead simply replied, 'Thank you.'

'You'll have to keep that temper of yours in check, though. You're too quick to fight all the time.'

I've had to be, she thought and said, 'Not everybody's been as decent to me as you have, Aidan.'

'Is that so? Well, shift yourself over here because we've got to buff up this lot to get the best price for it. And you'll have to carry some of it as well as your bundle when we go to market.'

* * *

The harvest was in and the days were growing shorter as Michaelmas approached. Sarah was aware that Aidan frequently looked at her with a serious expression on his face but he never said anything. It was becoming more and more difficult to keep up her pretence. She wanted to hire herself out as a maid but didn't see how she could without Aidan finding out the truth. They secured the camp as best they could and set off to the fair burdened with artefacts to sell.

It was a long walk to town, past the smoking chimneys of Meadow Hall, which now had new owners. They stopped off in the village to visit the churchyard and shed their cumbersome backpacks for half an hour.

'My father's buried here,' Aidan explained.

'So's my mother.' At least that's what Mrs Watson had told her once.

'Oh? Where? We'll tidy her grave as well.'

'I don't know.'

'Well, look for a Meadow on the headstones.'

'She wasn't called Meadow. I don't know her name.'

He frowned. 'Don't you ever wonder—?'

She shook her head. 'She's in a pauper's grave with no head-stone. She wasn't a favoured maid like I told you. They said at the Hall she was a vagrant and couldn't do anything to help me. So I've just got on with my life without her.' She gave a bright smile. 'I'll pick some flowers for your father's grave, if you like.'

He looked at her in that thoughtful way of his and simply replied, 'Thanks, Sam.'

When he had weeded and cut the grass, she laid the flowers and then left him alone with his memories. She wished she had some. No one should die alone like her mother had. As Aidan walked towards her she wished, again, that she did not have to leave. But the longer she deceived him the more she regretted doing so. No more lies, she thought. The sooner she could start afresh the better.

They were soon on their way towards the navigation and the

towpath that led them past furnaces and forges into town. It was a steep climb to the noisy, crowded market square and Sarah was astounded by the number of people and the racket they were making. It was worse than Meadow Hall stables after a race day. She shed her backpack gratefully and helped Aidan to lay out his wares for sale.

When they had finished, she said. 'I'll be off to the hiring line then.'

'You don't have to do this, Sam,' he responded. 'You can stay with me.'

I want to, she thought, but I daren't. She respected him too much to go on taking advantage of his good nature. I've lied to him and when he finds out he won't want any more to do with me, she thought, but said, 'Don't fret about me. I'll find something.'

'But what? And who will you be working for?'

'I'll survive.'

'You deserve better.'

Dear Lord, she had to go before she threw her arms around him and kissed him! 'Better get over there now,' she answered brightly.

He gave her a coin to buy a pie for dinner. 'Come and tell me where you're going before you leave.'

She nodded wordlessly. Her throat seemed to close up. Nearby, a fiddler put down his collecting bowl and struck up a jaunty tune that attracted a crowd jostling to see who he was. Suddenly, inexplicably, she felt tears welling in her eyes and turned away so Aidan couldn't see them. She knew she had to leave him but she didn't want to and could only make a croaking sound in reply.

He raised his voice against the noise. 'What was that you said?'

She tried again to speak and couldn't so she simply waved her arm and walked away.

'Good luck,' he called after her.

She took a few deep breaths, squared her shoulders and headed for a straggle of men and women seeking work. Perhaps if she confided in one of the women they might help her? She felt a sharp poke in her back.

'Over that side for thee, lad.'

The shove propelled her in the direction of the men. Farm labourers jostled each other for the best positions and she was pushed to the back. Some of them were very rough and talked in profanities that made her wince. This was more risky than she realised. As the morning wore on Sarah realised that Aidan had been right about her size. A few men were taken on by a rough-speaking overseer from a manufactory. But, although he inspected all of them, he turned away from most with a sneer on his face. She looked across at the women. They had fared better and their numbers had already dwindled. She thought of joining them when an older man with a sooty face approached the line and singled her out. He wore a jacket and hat and gave her a broad smile. 'Looking for work, little 'un?'

She thought he was a coal miner and answered, 'I might be.'

'You wouldn't be here if you weren't. You'll do for me while my lad's leg mends.'

Suddenly she was frightened and wished Aidan was there beside her. Who was this man and where did he come from? 'What'll I have to do?' she asked.

'Clean chimneys, lad, that's what. Climb up and sweep out the soot. I'll give you bed and board over my stable and sixpence a week.'

A chimney sweep! She remembered them from her time at the Hall. Every two or three months the fires were not lit and the nippers were sent up the flues to clean them out, they came down looking like devils from Hell. They always complained about the one in the kitchen because Mrs Watson never let the fire out early enough to cool down in time and the lad's hands got burnt. Sarah could still remember the smell of his singed boots.

'I'm not doing that!' she exclaimed.

The other men started to shout at her and push her about.

'Hark at you!' they called out. 'You'd rather beg on the streets, would you, until the constable carts you off to the workhouse?'

I can't do this, she thought. What am I doing here? This is a dirty, dangerous place and I hate it!

They were all bigger than she was. They looked down on her and yelled, 'Folk want their chimneys swept, lad, and beggars can't be choosers.'

Was that was she was now? A beggar? This is hopeless, she thought. Nobody is interested in a skinny little boy. She looked again at the women's line. The mine and manufactory owners weren't interested in them. But another girl was being taken on as she watched. Men dressed in decent clothing were choosing lasses in neat gowns and clean cotton caps for domestic service. She could be one of them if only she had the right clothes!

'What's all the commotion, Sam?' Aidan's voice came from behind. 'I heard it from the High Street.'

'Aidan? Is that you?' Tears were threatening. She blinked them away and swallowed before turning round. 'It's nothing,' she said. 'These men are a loud-mouthed lot, though.' A few more had been chosen by a railway company and were moving away.

'You really shouldn't be here,' Aidan sighed, 'You'll get yourself hurt. Why must you be so stubborn? Have you had anything to eat yet?'

He sounded angry with her. She shook her head silently.

'Here, have my pie. I'll get another.'

'Thanks.' She bit into it hungrily. It was delicious; golden pastry full of juicy pork, flavoured with onions and sage. 'Have you sold anything?'

'I've done well today, so I'm off to get supplies. Want to come with me?'

Yes, she thought but said, 'I'll stay a while longer.'

Two hours later her feet had gone quite cold and the sun was sinking in the sky. The remains of the hiring line had wandered off and she scanned the dwindling crowds for a sight of Aidan. What if she never saw him again, she thought miserably. She couldn't bear the heartache. She didn't want to go on deceiving him but he would hate her for it if she told him now. She had nowhere to sleep tonight, and only the coins he had given her. When, eventually, he reappeared, she was so pleased the see him she had to stop herself running across the square. He was pushing a handcart.

'Is that yours?' Sarah gazed at it in awe.

Aidan stood beside it proudly. 'I got shot of everything I'd made and could have sold more. This town has so many folk in it!'

Sarah peered inside. It contained coal, a few bricks, bar iron and food supplies. 'Is that a piece of bacon in the cloth?'

'I've bought potatoes as well.'

'It'll be heavy to push it up the hill,' she commented.

'You'll have to come back with me, then, and help me lift it over the boulders.'

'Can I?'

'I said so, didn't I; unless you really are determined to go on with this?' Aidan raised his eyebrows.

She guessed he meant the hiring line, so she shook her head and chewed on her lip. 'But I have to start earning my own living sometime.'

'You'll be taken on after next Easter when you've grown some more. Besides, I still need somebody to work my bellows. A joiner bought all my wrought-iron coffin handles and says he'll take as many as I can make.'

'Is that what the bar iron is for?'

'You learn fast, Sam. Perhaps I'll make a blacksmith of you yet.' He grinned.

She took one of the cart handles as they set off together, grateful that he didn't say 'I told you so'. 'I'll never be as big and strong as you,' she answered as she put her back into pushing the cart.

It was a long walk and it was dark by the time they were through Meadow Hall village. 'You know,' he commented. 'One or two folk here know about my wagon up in the woods there and nobody's been to throw me off the land yet. I was thinking of coming down to church on a Sunday.'

'I'd like that. When I was at the Hall, if there were no visitors for Sunday dinner, Mrs Watson let me go with the housemaids.'

'With the housemaids?'

'And the footmen,' she added hastily, and returned her attention to pushing. He didn't say any more but he kept staring at her and when she caught his eye, he looked away quickly. They were both tired and hungry when they reached the wagon.

'Get the fire going, Sam, while I unload the cart.'

'What are they for?' she asked as he stacked the bricks carefully on the ground.

'I want a deeper fire pit.'

'You'll have a proper forge up here soon.'

'Don't worry yourself. I was joking about teaching you to be a smithy.'

'But I'll have to do something for my keep.'

'Do what you're good at; you can snare rabbits and catch fish, and cook them.'

'And clean your boots.'

He laughed. 'Yes, Meadow Hall trained you well.' They carried the rest of their supplies up to the cave near the rock pool. 'I've decided to sleep up here to keep an eye on these,' he said.

'But nobody hardly ever comes up here!'

'I prefer the outdoors.'

'Even in winter?'

'I'll keep a fire going when it gets really cold. You can have the wagon to yourself.'

'Really? Oh thank you,' she replied quickly. It certainly suited her, although she fretted about her lies and thought that now was the time to stop her deception. But she didn't know how to. She could not think of the words. Besides, he might be angry with her and she didn't want that. She preferred him when he was kind to her and didn't make fun of her puniness. Pushing the unwelcome thoughts crowding her head to one side, she pumped on the bellows and soon she was frying slices of bacon and potato on the iron plate over the fire. She would tell him as soon as the time was right

Chapter 7

As October and November passed, the days became shorter and colder and Sarah expected Aidan to change his mind about sleeping in the cave. But he didn't. He worked hard at his anvil, taking his wrought-iron coffin handles and door furniture to the joiner in his handcart and coming back with more coal and iron to work. It was nearing Christmas and she'd had such a wonderful time living with him in the woods, but she was alarmed at how her body was filling out. Her breeches felt snug around her rear and she had to bind her breasts really tight to get into her bodice.

On Christmas Eve snow clouds threatened. Aidan gave Sarah coins to buy milk, eggs and a collar of bacon to boil in the pot. As she returned to the wagon with her heavy basket she heard two men talking. She recognised Aidan. The other voice was Danby.

'Oh, no,' she thought with a sinking heart. She remembered how excluded she had felt in the past and didn't want him coming back and spoiling everything between her and Aidan.

'I thought we'd seen the last of you when you didn't come back after the harvest,' Aidan said. He had finished at his anvil and Sarah slowed down, staying in the trees to listen from a distance.

'Aye, well, I wanted Christmas Day with my friends, didn't I?'

'It's good to see you anyway. Are you staying?'

'I thought I might.' He took a small glass bottle from his pocket and drew the cork with his teeth. 'Want a sip?'

'Save it for later. Sam'll be back soon with eggs for tea.'

'Is he still here?'

'Why shouldn't he be?'

Danby shrugged. 'He's a funny lad, I thought. Not man enough for my liking.'

'Don't go on at him, Dan.'

'I don't know why you haven't sent him on his way.'

'I couldn't do that. He'd have starved on the road. Besides, he pulls his weight. See those lumps of clay? They've got potatoes inside for tea. Put them on the coals, while I go and wash off this soot.'

Danby sat on a boulder and took a swig of his brandy.

Sarah hung back in the shadows feeling disappointed. She had been expecting to go with Aidan to the village church for the Christmas Eve service and prepare a Christmas feast tomorrow for them both. He had suggested walking up the hill to the moor afterwards and she knew he had been looking forward to a day away from his anvil. She had even thought of telling him the truth and had rehearsed the words. Now Danby would be there too, taking up Aidan's time and attention with tales of his endeavours, and she found his intrusion irritating. From what he had just said, he found her tiresome too.

But the evening was fun. The potatoes cooked and Sarah fried eggs on the iron plate. They had hot chestnuts, too, warmed in the cooling embers at the edge of the fire, with nips of Danby's brandy to keep out the cold.

'Look what I've still got,' Danby said, and took out Sarah's tin whistle. He played much better than before and had learned more tunes; they sang and danced around, laughing in the firelight, before flopping down, warmed and exhausted. The weather was clear and frosty and they could see hundreds of stars through the leafless trees.

'I could live here for ever,' Aidan sighed as he stared up at the light sky.

Sarah gazed at him and thought she could too; with him.

Danby shook his head. 'Not me. I like the hustle and bustle of town.'

'And a proper house to sleep in, no doubt,' Aidan quipped. 'Well, you can have my bedroll in the cave tonight, Dan. I'll sleep under the stars.'

'You'll freeze!' Sarah exclaimed.

'Not if you lend me your horse blanket.'

'You're a hardy soul, Aidan. I'll say that for you. What's wrong with sleeping in the wagon?' Danby asked.

'It's rotten right through and can't take any more weight than Sam.'

'Go on with you, it was only the front axle that was eaten away. It'll take me, won't it?'

'Have you gone soft while you've been on a farm living off the fat of the land? You slept rough for months before you joined up with me.'

'That was only because I had no choice. Like Sam here. Give me the wagon any day.'

'I wish I could, Dan. It's the cave or nothing for you to-night.'

Sarah detected a firmness in Aidan's tone and she guessed that Danby had too, for he took another swallow of his brandy and muttered, 'Maybe I'll sit up all night with this bottle for company then.'

'And me,' Aidan said. 'I bet you've a few tales to tell.'

'About what?'

Aidan winked at him. 'About what you've been up to this summer.'

Sarah brightened. Danby made her laugh when he got talking. But Aidan said, 'You get off to bed then, Sam.'

Sarah wasn't included in their late night tale-telling. She knew it and they knew it. Disheartened, she realised there was no point in arguing with the two of them. She stood up, stretched and yawned. 'I'm all in, anyway.'

Danby stared at her. He watched her climb into the wagon and toss out her horse blanket. Sarah took off her boots and unrolled her bed, straining her ears to listen to their fireside conversation. But their low voices were muffled by the canvas. The brandy took hold of her and she drifted off to sleep.

Outside, Aidan added wood to the dying fire. 'The wagon is draughty compared with my cave. I've built a log windbreak round the entrance.'

'But the ground is icy this time of year.'

'You'll be warm enough in my bedroll.'

Danby shrugged his shoulders. 'If you say so.' He jerked his head in the direction of the wagon. 'He hasn't filled out much, has he? How old did he say he was?'

'I don't think he ever said.'

'In fact,' continued Danby, 'I think he's lied about one or two things. I'm sure I was never like him, even as a nipper.'

'Maybe his dad was a jockey. They're only little fellows.'

Danby shook his head and sneered. 'There's something not quite right about him. He moves more like a lass than a lad and did you see the way he—'

'We don't want to be talking about him,' Aidan interrupted. 'It's Christmas. Give us a drop more brandy and tell me about this farm you found.'

Danby grinned. 'They treated me real well. I worked right through the harvest and stayed on for the shooting.'

Aidan nodded, encouraging Danby to go on and the two settled down next to the fire, taking it in turns to swig brandy from the bottle.

Sarah awoke with a start. The wagon rocked and creaked as someone climbed in. She guessed it was Danby, for Aidan would have whispered that it was only him so as not to frighten her. Danby's movements were slow and deliberate as he unrolled his bed at the side of hers. She opened her eyes a fraction and watched him. He took off his jacket and shirt and she noticed how his shoulders had broadened and how muscled he had become. He was not as tall as Aidan, but he was definitely more manly than he had been in the spring and she was fascinated by the way he moved. He sat on the floor and splayed his knees to unlace his boots. Then he stretched himself out on his blanket and put his hands behinds his head. He kept his eyes wide open.

In the darkness, she was staring. It was not pitch black; the moon was bright in a cloudless sky and a little of it penetrated the gaps in the canvas. Suddenly, Danby turned his head sharply to her and said, 'What are you looking at, Sam?'

She didn't answer for a long time, nor did he move his eyes from her. Finally, she said, 'You.'

'Well, don't, not like that.'

'Like what?'

'Like a lovesick dog.'

She turned over hurriedly and hunched her back against him.

'Do you want to know what we've been talking about out there?' Danby asked.

She stayed silent until he pressed, 'You do, don't you?'

'Yes,' she muttered.

'Aidan wants me to help him build a shelter outside the cave for me and him to sleep in so you can have this all to yourself. Why would he do that, Sam?'

Danby sounded angry. Sarah had always thought he was jealous of the favours she received as the smallest and weakest of the group. 'I don't know,' she muttered.

'Yes, you do. He thinks I don't know why, and I didn't at first, but he's been looking at you like I have. The same as you've just been looking at me.'

'We're friends, aren't we?'

'I think you've become more than that with Aidan while I've been away. I thought you were a bit different and now I know why.' He leaned over and placed his hands on her shoulder, gripping

83

it hard and rolling her back towards him. 'You're a girl, aren't you?' He began to pull her shirt out of the waistband of her breeches.

'No! Stop it!' she whispered.

'Don't lie!' He pushed his hands roughly underneath her shirt and felt along the bindings over her breasts.

'Leave me alone,' she protested.

'Yes, that's what you've always said and now I know why!'

'Well, you should be sleeping in the cave tonight! I'll yell out and wake Aidan!'

'No, you won't; not tonight, because I saw to it that he had too much of my brandy.'

'Well, don't tell him about me. I don't want him to know.'

'You mean he doesn't already? You haven't been – y'know.'

'Been what?'

'Been doing it together?'

'No!'

'You know what I'm talking about though?'

'Yes.'

'So if you weren't a boot boy, what were you?' Danby persisted.

Sarah gave in, it was almost a relief to finally tell someone 'I was a scullery maid.'

Danby laughed softly. 'And we both believed you.' He was sitting up now and looking at her with interest. He reached over and stroked her chin with his finger. 'Baby-faced Sam with the squeaky voice, who took us in right and proper. No wonder you never wanted to take your shirt off. I thought it was because you had such puny little arms and a chest to match.' He laughed again, lowered his voice and raised his eyebrows. 'What have you got under that shirt?'

'Nothing.'

He didn't move and she noticed his breathing slow. His finger moved down her throat slowly, making her skin tingle, and she held her breath. His hand slid down under the shirt until he reached the binding and the small calico bow she had tied at the front.

'Don't,' she whispered.

'Why not? It's not a secret any more; not between us, anyway.'

As soon as he pulled on the bow the binding loosened and she inhaled deeply. It was such a relief to release the constraint.

'Is that better?' He pushed the fabric down and ran his palms over her small breasts, moving from one to the other and back again and then fingering their delicate tips.

Her tiny nipples hardened and she felt a peculiar yearning sensation. She began to squirm a little and whispered, 'Stop it, Danby.'

'Don't you like it?'

'I – I don't know.' The sensation was new to her; it was a strange feeling and it made her nervous in a way that frightened her. 'You mustn't do that,' she squeaked ineffectually.

'Why not? It's nice, isn't it?'

'Yes,' she answered in a small voice.

'Come on then, give us a kiss.'

'A kiss?'

'Aye. A proper kiss on the lips.'

It starts with a kiss. She remembered the maids' chatter and answered, 'No, Danby.'

But he ignored her and leaned over to cover her mouth with his. He forced his tongue between her pursed lips, pushed it against hers. She tried to pull her head away from him but he was on top of her, his heavy weight pinning her to the wagon floor. His hands roamed over her back and waist then slid inside her breeches, *inside her drawers,* and grasped the flesh of her bottom. He hugged her body towards his and rammed her hard against him.

'You mustn't do that,' she breathed again. But her fear was tinged with something else, because although she knew she must stop him, an unusual excitement tingled through her. A part of her wanted him to go on holding her tight and feeling his hands exploring her developing curves. It was all so new to her; exciting and frightening at the same time.

He sighed in his throat, it was more like a groan, and he shifted his weight to press against her. It was then that she felt his hardness. The thing the maid had giggled about in their attic dormitory. It was what men did it with; that something they did to you and you had to like it. The maid had said it wasn't all it was supposed to be but when you were married you had to do it all the time. It was really only for married people, because if you weren't married it was fornication and fornication was wicked; that much Sarah did know from the few church sermons she had heard. Danby must have known it was wicked too, for he rolled away from her and cold air rushed between them.

Then he sat up and whispered, 'Get your breeches down,' and then he pulled off his trousers and kicked them away in some agitation.

Now she was scared by him. She didn't want to do it with him. She didn't want to do it with anybody because the maid had said it had hurt the first time and she didn't want Danby to hurt her. 'No, I won't,' she said. 'Leave me alone.'

He did not seem to hear her and when he rolled back over her his hardness was exposed and he was rooting feverishly at her body. She squeezed her legs together as tightly as she could and tried to push him off, but he took both her hands in one of his fists and held them over her head while he pushed down the waistband of her breeches with the other. 'I said, take these off,' he hissed.

'No! You can't make me.'

'Yes, I can,' he muttered as he pulled them towards her knees. He shoved his hand between her legs and probed around with his fingers. 'You want this as much as I do.'

Confused and scared by the strange new sensations taking over her body, she tried to yank her arms free. 'No, don't! I don't like it!'

'All the girls say that. But they don't mean it. You'll like it the same as all the others.'

'I won't! I'm not going to let you do it to me.'

'Yes, you are.' He grasped both her hands again and added, 'I can't stop now.'

Now she was really frightened by Danby's strength. He was holding her wrists so tight that they hurt and one of his knees was pushing hers apart and she felt his hardness on the flesh of her thigh. He was rutting on top of her like an animal, hardly listening to her protests. He seemed to be losing all control, and the wagon was creaking with his movements and the suspended pots were rattling on their hooks.

His thing was jabbing at her between her legs and she was horrified. She didn't want it to go inside her. She squeezed her bottom against the floor to get away from him, and cried, 'Stop it, Danby!'

He didn't hear and he seemed to forget it was her because he was breathing heavily and groaning, 'Come on, you little polecat, come on.'

Her muscles were beginning to scream with the strain of resisting him and she wondered how much longer she could hold him off. He kept pushing his thing harder and further between her legs and his weight on her was hurting. She felt tears spring to her eyes. She couldn't stop him. He was too heavy and strong for her, and she was terrified it was going to happen. Danby was supposed to be her friend but if she had had a knife at that moment she would have stabbed him.

'Get off me, Danby,' she begged repeatedly. 'Please.'

Oh! He must have heard her at last! He must have, for suddenly he stopped. It was over and he hadn't done it to her; he was sliding away from her, and – and being dragged backwards by his feet.

'What the—' Danby released Sarah's wrists and grappled with the air as he disappeared out of the back of the wagon.

Sarah listened to the scuffling then, after pulling up her breeches, scrambled to her feet and pushed her head through the canvas flaps. Danby was on his knees as Aidan towered over him and demanded, 'What do you think you are doing?'

Rising to his full height Danby squared up to Aidan angrily. 'Well, only what you've been doing through the summer. How long have you known Sam's a girl?'

'Since Michaelmas, after we went to the hiring fair; and I stayed well clear of her, just as you should have done.'

He'd known for nearly three months? Sarah didn't believe what she had just heard. Aidan had known about me all that time, when I could have behaved normally, she thought angrily. He should have said he knew and everything would have been different between them!

'Don't give me that,' Danby shouted. 'The two of you all alone and him – her – tempting you like she did me. Quite a little tease, isn't she?'

It was then that Aidan hit Danby. His fists had been clenching and unclenching by his side and now he raised his right arm and connected heavily with Danby's jaw. 'Shut your filthy mouth!'

Danby did not waste his breath on a reply. He reeled, recovered quickly and hit back with vigour, catching Aidan on his cheekbone. Aidan retaliated with two blows to Danby's body that winded him. The younger man continued to lash out and was repaid in kind. Fist after fist, both of them hit out with all their strength, until they began to stagger and sway with the effort. Aidan, taller and heavier, had the advantage but Danby was a more cunning street fighter making them equal opponents in their struggle.

Speechless, Sarah watched this awful sight. She had seen men fight before. The footmen and grooms at the Hall were always squabbling over something. But they were not hefty solid fellows like these two, who could both give as good as they got, and neither, it seemed, was prepared to ease up. Horrified, she wondered if they would carry on punching and thumping until they killed each.

'Stop it! Stop fighting!' She jumped down from the wagon and ran with her head down, directly at them, pushing herself in the way of their fists and catching a blow or two before either realised she was there.

'Get out of the way, Sam,' Aidan spat at her. 'This is between us.'

'But I'm one of us as well,' she shouted. 'I am!'

Surprised that she did not move from her stand between them, they stopped their fighting.

'I am,' she repeated as she pushed them apart. She glared at Aidan angrily. 'If you knew about me why didn't you say something?'

'I've been waiting for you to own up,' Aidan retaliated. 'And don't look at me like that!' He resumed his angry exchange with Danby. 'You had no right to force yourself on her like that.'

'She wanted it,' said Danby scornfully, and slouched off in the direction of the stream.

Aidan was breathing heavily and there was blood on his face. She would have fetched water to bathe his cuts if she wasn't so angry with him. Finally, he looked directly at her and stated, 'This is no place for a girl.'

'It was fine before *he* came back!' she protested.

'No, it wasn't! Why do you think I was sleeping in the cave?'

She stared at him. 'You – you would've have tried to – to take me, as Danby did?'

'I wanted to. The way you were growing out of those clothes and the way you moved . . .' His voice trailed away.

She was shocked at first and then, as the realisation dawned, her heart began to beat faster. He wanted her as a man wants a woman! She took a step closer to him. 'You – you wanted me?' She was startled by his response.

'Stay away from me.'

'But I don't want to.'

'You're leaving, Sam,' he stated firmly.

Sarah was devastated. He didn't want her after all; he wanted rid of her. She felt as though he had punched her in the stomach and almost choked on a sob. 'Don't send me away. Not now.'

She saw him hesitate and his fists, hanging clenched by his sides, twitched. He took a deep breath then asked, 'What's your real name?'

She told him, adding, 'I was a scullery maid.'

'And how old are you?'

'Is it Christmas Day, yet? I'm fifteen on Christmas day.'

'Fifteen? Dear God,' he breathed, 'you should be living with other women, like you were at the Hall.'

'They were horrid to me!' she wailed. 'They pushed me about and gave me orders all the time. The boot boy had a better time of it than I did. I'm not going anywhere like that ever again.' She looked appealingly at him.

'Don't look at me like that! This is as tough for me as is it for you.'

'Then don't do it!'

'I have to.'

'No, you don't! You don't care what happens to me!'

'Don't you understand? It's because I care about you that you have to go. I've made my decision and that's final.'

Chapter 8

Aidan straightened his cap and attempted to tidy Sarah's shaggy hair as the cottage door opened. 'Good day, madam. The joiner in the village sent us. He said you wanted help in the house.'

The housewife struggled with a fretting babe in her arms and two whining children tugging at her skirts. 'That's right, I do. But I'm seeking a girl.'

He placed his hand lightly on Sarah's shoulder. 'This is my sister.'

The woman began to close the door. 'Don't waste my time. That's a boy.'

'No, I'm not,' Sarah protested. She felt Aidan's fingers grip her more tightly and, mindful of his earlier instructions, shut her mouth.

'She was lately at Meadow Hall, ma'am, as a scullery maid.'

'Oh, aye, that were a while ago now. Where's her uniform then?'

Neither could answer and Sarah kept her eyes on the ground as Aidan had told her to.

'Ee, you must think I was born yesterday,' the woman went on. 'I'm not taking any scruffy little urchin off the streets into my house dressed like that. You'd be off as soon as I've kitted you out and I'd be the laughing stock of the village; now clear off, the pair of you.' She closed the door firmly in their faces.

Sarah tried not to show how pleased she was. This was the fourth place they had called at to find her a position. Aidan would have to take her back to the wagon. They had walked a long way from the village to this woodman's cottage and it was her last chance.

'Come on, let's go home,' she said brightly and set off down the woodland track.

Aidan followed at a slower pace, deep in thought. When he caught up with her he said, 'You will need a gown and new boots. A bonnet would help, too. It would cover your short hair and make you would look more like a girl. Otherwise you'll never get a place.'

Her heart lifted as she realised there was nothing in the wagon that remotely resembled a gown. 'That's that, then,' she remarked, jumping over a log. 'There's no hope of me getting a position. I'll have to go back with you.'

He wasn't listening to her. 'We'll go into town next market day and see what we can find for you.'

'What? Get me a position with a town family? It's too far away.'

'I was thinking more of buying you some ladies' clothes at the market.'

'I don't want any. I like what I've got on.'

'Yes, I know. That's what's wrong with you. You have to act more, well, more ladylike in the way you go about things. Can't you remember how the other maids behaved at Meadow Hall?'

Yes, she could. They ignored her most of the time. But she guessed he didn't mean that. He meant looking clean and tidy, being seen and not heard and curtseying neatly when required. She remembered coveting a housemaid's uniform because she thought she might look bonny in it. Yet she hadn't needed it for Danby to think she was bonny because he'd wanted her in the way that housemaid's sweetheart had wanted her.

Danby had frightened her that night and she was glad Aidan had rescued her. But she remembered the thrill of it as well and the way her body had felt, wanting him to carry on but knowing it was wrong because he wasn't her sweetheart and that would have made it fornication. She recalled the conversation at the Hall about sweethearts and thought that she would be pleased to have one. She wondered if Danby had thought of her as a sweetheart. But, she decided, if she was going to have a sweetheart she would rather it were Aidan. She had believed Danby was more fun but now she wasn't so sure.

'And I don't want to work in town. I won't see you and Danby again.'

'I don't think that's a bad thing. Not after the way both of us behaved on Christmas night.'

'It was the brandy. That's what Mrs Watson used to say about the footmen when they mucked about in her kitchen at night. She used to shout at the valet for letting them drink it.'

'It's no excuse.'

He sounded like the old butler at the Hall, who everyone said had a broomstick up his backside. 'Danby said it was only a bit of fun,' she said.

'Bit of fun?' He stopped and took her by the shoulders giving them a gentle shake. 'Listen to me, Sarah. You should hate him for what he tried to do to you.'

She frowned. 'He's our friend.'

'Yes, for most of the time. He has this wild streak about him, though. Can't you see that?'

Perplexed, Sarah answered, 'But he makes us laugh.'

'You weren't laughing on Christmas night, were you?'

'Well, no. He frightened me.'

'Decent men don't take advantage like that. If he tries it again, I'll kill him.'

Shocked at his tone she retaliated quickly, 'But he wouldn't, would he?'

'Oh, Sarah, you don't understand. You need somebody like my mother to show you how to carry on, otherwise God only knows what will happen to you.'

She chewed on her lip, thinking of her last night at Meadow Hall, when the kitchen maids had gone off with the stable lads and she had been disappointed that no one wanted her. It was different now, she thought.

'Do you think I'm bonny,' she asked suddenly.

Aidan didn't answer at first. Then he shrugged. 'I don't know.'

'I'm not, am I? I know why,' she added. 'It's because I've got no bosoms or bottom.'

'Yes, you have,' he muttered.

'Really? The kitchen maids said I needed them before any lad would be interested in me. I'll ask Danby when we get home.'

'No,' he said firmly. 'Don't do that.'

'Why not?'

He raised his voice. 'Because I say not!'

She stopped and he almost knocked her over as he walked into her, grabbing at her to prevent her falling. She allowed herself to be pulled towards him and relished the feeling of his firm chest against her back. His hands slid down to hers and crossed them in front of her. For a brief second she felt that she was in heaven, surrounded by Aidan's strong, muscular arms. She was safe with him. She never wanted to leave him. She liked him because he was kind to her. A sweetheart was kind to you and gave you a keepsake to put under your pillow so that you would dream about him. She wondered if Aidan might do that one day.

'I liked it in the summer with just the two of us,' she said.

'So did I.'

She liked it, too, when he put his arms around her and she thought he did as well. But after a brief, blissful few seconds, he pushed her away and said, 'The sooner you are in a place with a respectable woman to guide you, the better.' Perhaps he didn't like her after all, otherwise, why was he sending her away? It was all very confusing.

'Can't you make Danby go instead of me?'

He covered his face with his hands. 'Haven't you heard a word I've said?'

'Yes, but—'

'There are no "buts". I'm taking you to the market on Lady Day. There'll be a hiring fair. We'll say you're my sister and our mother and father are dead, and no more arguments, Sarah.'

It was frosty as they set off, loaded down with wrought-iron coffin handles and door hinges, enough for the joiner's needs and samples for a shop in town. Aidan and Danby had worked hard over the fire to make them. Sarah had cleaned up their clothes and polished their boots. She had even washed herself and her underclothing in the ice-cold rock pool, because Aidan told her she must. Danby, too, looked as well turned out as Aidan today.

'I'll buy you the best gown I can afford, so you can get a proper position. The joiner in the village has given me the name of a shop owner whose family need help in the house.'

They found a market stall with neat piles of clothes that the stall holder tried to keep in order as customers inspected her goods. Sarah saw Aidan take the woman to one side and talk in a low voice for several minutes. Then he showed her the contents of his backpack and passed her some coins.

'This woman will see you properly clothed,' he explained to Sarah. 'Wait here for me and Danby when she's done.'

'Where will you be?'

'I don't know yet but I'll come back for you when I've sold everything.'

'Will you bring me something to eat?'

'Of course I shall, just as soon as I've sold this lot. Now pay attention, Sarah. This woman knows what you need so you listen to what she says.'

Her friends disappeared through a moving throng of Riding folk intent on their marketing.

The woman had a canvas screen strung up against the wall

behind her stall, guarded by a small assistant. 'Come over here then, lass.' With a frown on her face, she ran her hands up and down Sarah's body.

'What's wrong, missus?' Sarah asked.

'Nothing. I'm just getting the size of you. My name's Annie. How old are you?'

Sarah told her.

'High time you were out of those farming togs, my lass. Have you not got a corset?'

Sarah shook her head.

'Any chemise or drawers?'

'Under my shirt and breeches.'

'Well, tek everything off except them and I'll see what I've got.' Annie jerked her head at her small assistant. 'Watch the stall.' She gave Sarah a broad smile, and pushed her behind the screen where she had a handcart. She flipped away a canvas cover and selected some garments.

Sarah shivered in her underclothes and stockings. 'Hurry up. It's freezing.'

'Hold up your bosoms.' Annie wrapped the corset around Sarah's middle, laced up the front deftly and pulled on the strings with strong fingers. 'Get this on now,' Annie ordered, dropping a flannel petticoat over Sarah's head.

'Biddy, hand me that grey stripe,' Annie called to her assistant and a small pair of hands pushed a pile of fabric round the edge of the canvas. 'Quality this is, my lass,' she said. 'It came from a big house in Derbyshire. Feel that.' She fingered the woollen garment fondly.

Sarah did too. It was softer than anything she had known at Meadow Hall; even softer than Mrs Watson's skirts.

'Lift your arms for me.'

The gown settled over her like a warm cloud and the woman did up the buttons at the front. It felt beautiful and she wriggled her shoulders and hips inside it.

'It's too big for me,' Sarah commented.

'Aye, but only a little bit and I reckon you'll grow into it soon enough. How does it feel?'

'It's lovely; so soft and snug. I've never had nothing like this before.'

'You can take it in down the back for now if you want.'

'How do I do that?'

'Don't you know? You'll have to ask the missus when you get your position.'

'You mean if I do.'

'You will by the time I've finished with you. I'll give you a cotton cap to cover that hair. Keep it on at all times. If your missus sees that mop, tell her you caught it in a mangle and you had to be cut free.'

Sarah reached for her waistcoat. 'Can I put this back on now?'

'Nay, lass. I'm tekking that and your other things in part exchange. Besides, you're a lady now. I've a nice wool shawl for you to keep the cold out. Oh, and you'll need a straw bonnet for church.' Annie disappeared to her stall, returned to finish dressing Sarah and then stepped back. 'My, you look a picture, even if I do say so messen. Them brothers o' yours'll be right proud of you.'

Sarah ran her hands over the bodice of her gown and then back up again to her neck. 'Am I pretty, Annie?'

'Ee, lass, you're beautiful. Hasn't nobody told you that?'

'I really have got bosoms, haven't I? I mean proper ones.'

'Oh, aye. You've bit o' room in there for 'em to grow an' all.'

'Do you think they will?'

The woman laughed. 'Wait til you've had bairns, my lass, then you'll know what bosoms are. Now, come and wait at the side o' me out there til your brothers get back with the rest of the money.'

Sarah fastened her bonnet ribbons under her chin and wrapped the warm shawl around her shoulders. She looked down at her full skirts with a smile on her face. She was bonny at last! 'Thank you, Annie,' she said. She was as pretty as those stuck up housemaids any day, and she lifted her head proudly to scan the crowds for sight of Aidan and Danby.

She grew hungry. She was also bored, standing still and waiting for Aidan to come back with the shillings she owed, and her dinner. She scowled at Annie's small assistant, who stuck her tongue out at her. Sarah grinned and asked, 'What's your name?'

'Biddy.'

'Is Annie your mam?'

Biddy nodded.

'You're lucky. I never had no mam.'

'Everybody has a mam,' Biddy answered.

'I know,' Sarah answered wistfully. She would have liked Annie to be her mam. Annie was rough and ready and brisk in her ways but she'd made Sarah look really lovely. She knew she had because people were smiling kindly at her and nodding as they walked by.

'Biddy,' Annie called. 'Come and sort these ribbons and when you've done that you can fetch us some dinner from the pieman.' She turned to Sarah and added, 'I hope your brother has sold his iron wares. He showed me some of what he's made and it was worth a bob or two right enough. Oh, there's one of them over there, thank the Lord. He better have the money.'

Sarah searched the folk milling around the market stalls and spotted Danby weaving through the crowds. She waved her arms. He was eating a pie in one hand and carrying another which she reckoned was for her. He stopped chewing, stared at her and she dashed out from the stall towards him.

'Hey, come back here, you,' Annie called. 'That's not paid for yet.'

'I'm not running off,' she answered. 'He's got my dinner.'

'All the same, lass, stay where you're put for now.'

Annie's strong hands pulled her back behind the stall and kept a firm grip on her arm. 'Five shillings, young man,' she said as Danby approached the stall.

'Sarah?' Danby breathed. He seemed lost for words and unable to take his eyes off her.

She grabbed at the pie and bit into it hungrily.

'Watch the crumbs down your front,' Annie said and prompted, 'the money, sir.'

'I've got it,' he muttered. He wiped his hand on his trousers and dug into the pocket. 'It's only three.'

'What about the rest?'

'Aidan – my – my brother'll be along with it soon.'

'Well, he'd better, because she's not leaving until he does,' Annie said.

Sarah swallowed another mouthful of pork and pastry. 'Where's Aidan?'

'He's gone to one of the High Street shops. The shopkeeper's looking for a girl.' He seemed to have forgotten his pie. 'Sarah, you look like a proper lady.'

'I feel like one,' she mumbled as she pushed the last of the pie into her mouth.

'Ee, lass, you don't look like one to me, not when you're stuffing your face,' Annie said with a grimace. 'And don't wipe your hands down the skirt.'

Sarah stood with her hands in the air, not sure what to do next. Last time she was dressed as a girl her hands were always clean from scrubbing. Annie tossed Sarah a grubby cloth and she rubbed her greasy fingers on it. 'Clean round your mouth an' all.' The older woman shook her head. 'Whoever takes you on has got a job on her hands.'

She frowned and stuck out her lower lip, wondering if her new mistress would be like Mrs Watson. 'Can I work for you, Annie?'

'I've already got my Biddy, lass. Besides, with a scowl like that you'd frighten off me customers. You ought to try smiling a bit more.'

'Why?'

'You're even lovelier when you smile.'

'Am I? Honest?' Sarah pasted a false smile on her face.

'Aye, but only when you mean it, like when you're happy about summat.'

Sarah wasn't very happy and her features sagged. Oh, she was pleased with her gown and being a girl again, but she didn't want to go into service and leave Aidan and Danby, and she thought it was mean of them to make her. She turned her large sad eyes and pouting mouth on Danby who continued to stare at her. 'I want to go back to the wagon,' she said in a small voice.

He didn't say anything. He was looking at her strangely and her frown deepened.

'Nay, lass. We all have to work for a living,' Annie said briskly. 'You'll be fine when you're settled. You'll get somewhere nice dressed up like that as long as you remember to keep your gob shut.'

'What's up with you, Danby?' Sarah asked.

He gave a crooked grin. 'Nowt.'

'Will Aidan be long?'

'He's trying to find you somewhere. He was given the name of this shopkeeper.'

'Oh aye?' Annie queried. 'Who's that, then?'

'Mr Smith, he deals in hardware.'

'Him? If he's who I think he is, he's a widower with a whole tribe o' bairns. The big 'uns are growing up now and that eldest lass of his'll keep you in line. But he's worth a bob or two so you won't want for owt.'

Sarah turned down the corners of her mouth. She felt grown up in her corset and gown but she didn't want to go back to scrubbing floors and being shouted at. She'd enjoyed being a boy and living in the woods and didn't want to stay in town in a shopkeeper's house. 'Oh, do I have to?' she whined.

'No, you don't,' Danby replied. 'Not if you don't want to.'

Her eyes widened with delight. She smiled happily at him. She saw his eyes darken and his mouth twitch. 'You're not laughing at me, are you?' But she could see that he wasn't. He was deadly serious and he had a strange searching look about him.

He shook his head. 'I'll never laugh at you again. Listen, Sarah.

Don't say anything to Aidan when he comes back. Let me do the talking.'

'Why? What are you going to say to him?'

'Wait and see. He's been giving the pair of us orders for too long. It's my turn now.'

She stared at him. Danby? He was going to tell Aidan she could go home with them? He was going to take her side against Aidan?

Annie was getting restless. 'Where is that brother of yours with my money? If he doesn't get here soon, I'll be having that gown off yer back, lass.'

'Oh, don't do that! He'll be here, I promise you. He always does what he says.' Sarah hugged her arms around the bodice. 'I won't let you have it. It's so lovely and I've never been dressed as nice as this before. Not ever.'

'Aye. You do look handsome. There's plenty of women 'ere who've been giving you the green eye.'

'What's the green eye?'

Annie laughed and turned to attend to another customer.

'What does she mean, Danby?'

Danby sucked in his cheeks and moved closer to her. He put his arm around her shoulder and drew her towards him. But he wasn't looking at her. He had a gleam in his eye and was watching the towns folk walking by; he wore the kind of expression he had when he'd won an argument with Aidan. 'She means you've got something they want,' he said. He squeezed the top of her arm and murmured. 'That must be me. You stick with me Sarah and remember what I told you when Aidan gets here.'

Sarah saw Aidan's head above the throng as he weaved his way towards them. 'He's here, Annie! I knew he would be.'

Danby pinched her shoulder 'Be quiet, like I said.'

She flinched and frowned. But more than anything she wanted to stay with her friends and now, it seemed, so did Danby.

Aidan looked at Sarah, standing close to Danby, with a shocked expression on his face until Annie placed herself between them with an outstretched hand. 'I'll have the other two shillings, if you don't mind.'

At first Aidan seemed surprised by Sarah's appearance, which pleased her no end, but he pulled himself together quickly as Annie shoved her hand in front of his face. 'Yes. Yes, here it is. You've done a splendid job with her, ma'am. Thank you.'

Annie replied, 'Well, you can all clear off now and give me some space for my other customers.'

'Sarah,' Aidan breathed, 'you look great.'

'Do you think so? I feel beautiful.' She pushed herself away from Danby, spun round, and did a few dance steps.

Aidan seemed lost for words. He looked stunned and was clenching and unclenching his fists by his side. She twirled again and he said, 'Dear Lord, you really are grown up. You're a – a proper woman.'

She smiled, moved closer and looked up at his serious face. 'Let me come back to the wagon with you. Please,' she beseeched.

His eyes darkened and she couldn't guess what he was thinking. He opened his mouth to speak, then shivered slightly as he seemed to recollect his thoughts. His face took on a troubled frown. 'Stop this, Sarah. You're not coming back with me.'

The smile faded from her face. He didn't want her, not even when she looked as lovely as this. What was she doing wrong? The more she thought she would please him, the more he pushed her away.

Before she could say anything, Danby took hold of her arm and said, 'Are you thirsty? I am so we'll go and find the Wellgate spring. The say it's the best water in the Riding.'

There was a crowd around the spring. The three of them had to wait their turn as folk filled buckets and tubs to carry away to their homes. The water was good; ice cold and crystal clear. Sarah drank thirstily, using her hands as a cup and stretching her neck as far as she could to keep her gown dry.

'Let's sit over there,' Aidan suggested, 'and decide what to do.

The shopkeeper was already suited so I'll have to find somewhere else.'

'I don't want somewhere else. I don't want to go back to pumping water and scrubbing pots all day.'

As she followed him to a low stone wall, she felt Danby's hand slide around her waist and give her a brief squeeze. 'Remember what I said,' he murmured. When she turned her head quickly, he put his finger to his lips. She nodded silently.

'You won't have to stand in the hiring line,' Aidan began, 'if I can get you into a respectable family. You'll have a proper home and a few shillings of your own.'

'She doesn't want that,' Danby said. 'She's coming with me instead.'

Aidan's eyes widened. 'What?'

'I'm not going back to the wagon,' Danby added.

'But where will you stay?'

'I'll find somewhere.'

'And what will you live on?'

'I've got money from my farm labouring.'

'That won't last until the next harvest, you know it. Are you going down the pit?'

'I'll get bed and board at an inn by entertaining travellers with my tunes. Sarah can dance for me and we might even join the travelling players when they come through town.'

'Oh, Danby, how exciting.' Sarah smiled and was immediately silenced by a glare from him.

'Well, you're not taking Sarah,' Aidan responded.

'Yes, I am. She doesn't want to be a scullery maid again. She wants to come with me.'

'No, she doesn't,' Aidan stated. 'You're the last thing she wants, prancing about taverns with all the riff-raff of the town.'

'I'll look after her.'

'You'll ruin her.'

'I'll marry her. She's old enough.'

'Oh, it's always that on your mind, isn't it? You can't keep it in your trousers. What happens to Sarah when another pretty girl crosses your path?'

'What's up? Are you jealous because she prefers me to you? At least she knows I'll give her what she wants! Because we both know she does. Ripe and ready for it she is, and has been for months.'

'Don't be such a foul-mouthed brat! You've no respect, that's your trouble. I'll not let you marry her! D'you hear me?'

'What's it got to do with you? You're not her father. She does what she wants to and she wants a bit more fun in life than what you have lined up for her. She coming with me and that's final.'

Sarah was astounded by this exchange. Danby was going to marry her? He hadn't even asked her if she wanted to wed him, but if she did she wouldn't have to go as a maid to any shop-keeper's house in town. Working in taverns sounded exciting and fun to Sarah, and she would have her very own sweetheart. But she wasn't at all sure she wanted Danby as her sweetheart. He had hurt her when he pinched and poked her to keep quiet. And something that Aidan had said echoed around her head.

Another pretty girl. When another pretty girl comes along. Didn't that mean Aidan thought she was pretty? It did. She was sure it did. Aidan did think she was lovely after all.

As Danby and Aidan spat and squabbled with each other about where she should go, she dreaded that they would start fighting again. Why, oh why couldn't they all be friends together?

But it seemed that Aidan and Danby were intent on being enemies and she was beginning to think it was all her fault. When they disagreed about other things they usually laughed it off in the end. But when they argued about her it just got worse and worse and she was fed up with it. She couldn't stand it any more and she stood up to say so.

She was too late.

'You are not having her!' Aidan shouted.

'Who's gonna stop me?'

'I am.' Aidan's fists struck out and Danby retaliated with vigour.

'Stop it, you two, stop it!' she pleaded. 'I'm so tired of all this. You neither of you listen to me, to what I want. You both think you know best. Well, you don't!' But she realised how right she was about them not listening. Neither heard her as they slugged it out, landing blows that bruised and drew blood. She raised her voice to a shout. 'I hate you both and I don't want anything to do with either of you any more.'

When they continued with their grappling and overbalanced to roll on the muddy ground by the spring she closed her mouth, turned sharply on her heel and marched away, straight down the road that led into the centre of town. She meant what she said. She'd survived on her own before and she would do it again.

She did not notice a man in a long jacket and tall hat push himself away from a wall in the shadows and follow her.

Chapter 9

'What are you doing back here?'

'Oh, Annie, can you help me? I don't want to live in town.'

'Well, you'll just have to go home with your brothers then, won't you?'

Sarah chewed on her lip. 'I can't do that. You see – they're not my brothers. Aidan – he's the big one – he took me in when I was destitute but he says I shouldn't be living with them any more, not now I'm growing up.'

'Did he now? He seems a sensible fellow that one.'

'But I've nowhere else to go. Can't I work for you on your stall?'

'No, you can't. I told you, I've got Biddy and besides you'll get yourself into a worse scrape than if you stayed with those two lads. Anyway, I thought you had a position at Mr Smith's.'

'He's already got somebody and I'm glad!'

'Don't be foolish, lass. You've nowhere to live.'

'Well?' She'd lived rough and could do it again.

'Well, you'll have to go to the workhouse.'

'I'm not going there!' Not after all she'd done to avoid it before, she thought.

'You'll not have a choice if you're found wandering the streets. You can be put in prison for vagrancy, you know. The workhouse is better. One of the church ladies'll take you there.'

'Church ladies? Who are they?'

'They're the town's gentlewomen. You won't find 'em buying off my stall. They have their fine gowns sewn by a dressmaker and paid for by their rich husbands.' Annie laughed. 'You'll have to behave yourself if one of them gets a hold of you.'

'Maybe they would give me a position?' On balance, she thought, being a servant again would be better than the workhouse.

'Not you, me ducks. They want maids from respectable families who can afford the uniform.'

Sarah turned down the corners of her mouth. 'I'm a hard worker, Annie, honest I am.'

'Your best bet is to go to the Mission House up Sheep Hill. You'll find the ladies meeting there and they'll be able to help. You must tell them the truth, though.'

'Won't they take me to the workhouse?'

'They might. But they might know a family in one of the villages round and about who would take you in.'

That sounded a suitable option to Sarah. 'The Mission House, you say?'

'You can't miss it. Good luck, lass.'

Sarah set off up the hill but before she reached the top, a man and a woman fell into step beside her. She glanced at them, taking in their smart dress. The man wore a long jacket and top hat while the woman wore a bonnet that was trimmed with the same colour ribbon as on her gown. She had shiny buttoned boots on too, and Sarah wondered if she was one of the gentlewomen come to take her to the workhouse.

'I see you are all on your own,' the woman said. 'You shouldn't be alone in town on market day, my dear, it isn't safe.'

'Are you a gentlewoman?' Sarah asked.

The woman smiled at her. 'I am; and this gentleman is my husband. Where are you going?'

'To the Mission.'

'What do you want with them?'

'I'm looking for work. Do you know of any?'

'Well, it just so happens that I do, my dear, in a nice house too. Why don't you come with me and see?'

'Is it far?'

The gentleman smiled at her benignly. 'I have a carriage. Look, it's over there.'

A horse and carriage! She had never been in a carriage before. She walked between them with wide eyes and climbed inside in awe. She, Sarah Meadow, was riding in a gentleman's carriage with these kind folk. What a piece of luck for her!

'What is your name, dear?' the gentlewoman asked as she settled her skirts over the plush seat.

'Sarah Meadow.' She copied the woman's actions and smoothed her own gown with her hands.

The woman smiled and said, 'You may call me Madam and my husband Sir.'

As they drove way, Sarah began to feel a little uneasy about these people. She didn't know where she was going, but at least they were gentry. However, her anxiety was nothing compared with the deepening unhappiness she felt at parting from Aidan. Their friendship had splintered, she could see that now, and he was determined for them to separate. Perhaps it was time for her to go her own way. She had survived well enough as a servant at Meadow Hall, and she was older and wiser now. Aidan had said she needed to grow up in the company of other women. Well, perhaps this as an opportunity for her to do just that. She smiled at the woman, who smiled back at her. This was her chance to show Aidan how she could look after herself and find her own employment. She couldn't wait to see the surprise on his face when she told him!

They were riding out of town, to an area where forges and manufactories belched out smoke from their huge chimneys. She felt excited at the prospect of her new position.

'What shall I be doing, Madam?' she queried.

The gentlewoman smiled again. This time Sarah noticed that although her mouth widened, her eyes did not change. They glittered coldly making the smile seem more like a sneer. Sarah shivered and her companion unfolded a small blanket so that it fell across her knees. 'We shall see what you can do first,' she replied.

The house, when they arrived, was not as big as Sarah had hoped and its stonework was blackened by soot. The gentleman had driven the carriage himself, so they obviously didn't have a lot of servants, which probably explained why it was so quiet. The gentleman took them around the back and, after climbing down from the carriage, they went indoors though the kitchen, but there was still no sign of any servants. It was the middle of the afternoon, the fire was out and the table was littered with pots and food debris. Sarah's heart sank. She was to be a scullery maid again.

'Well, now, this is a serviceable gown you have on, but the neckline is too high and it covers your arms.'

'I'll roll 'em up, Madam,' Sarah volunteered.

'No, that will never do. Not here.'

'But if I am to clear up this lot . . .'

'Clear up? Whatever gave you that idea?'

'Am I not to be a scullery maid, Madam?'

The woman gazed at her with a serious expression on her face. 'You will be in the parlour, my dear girl, and the bed-chamber.'

Sarah's heart lifted. She would be a housemaid, a proper housemaid, like the older girls who had ignored her at Meadow Hall. She glanced at the dirt and debris around her. This was not Meadow Hall, though, and she might be the only maid they had. 'Will there be a girl for in here?' she asked.

Madam ignored her and Sarah felt uneasy. She was nothing like Mrs Watson, or Annie. She was distant and cold and Sarah didn't like her at all.

'What colour is your hair?' Madam put her hand on Sarah's cap to remove it.

'No!' Both of Sarah's hands held onto the cotton.

'Let go,' Madam ordered, and with growing horror Sarah realised that Madam was no gentlewoman for she kicked Sarah on the back of her legs, making her knees buckle. Sarah grasped the table to stop herself falling as the woman tossed her cap aside.

'Hell and damnation,' Madam cursed. 'It'll be a year before you can show that off.'

Sarah fingered her shaggy mop. 'I – I caught it in . . .'

'Shut up. You'll have to wear a wig. Wait there. If you move I'll kick you again.'

Sarah stood up straight, trying to look taller than she was because it made her feel braver. Mrs Watson used to hit her but she had never kicked her and Madam's boots had hurt. Sarah was left alone in the cold dark kitchen, straining her ears for household sounds. There were none and she wondered where everybody was.

This didn't seem to be a respectable family at all and she thought better of staying here. She tried to get out of the back door but it was locked and there was no key. They were a long way out of town and she had no money but if she could escape she would. She was used to surviving outdoors overnight. But she had not been on her own for months now and she felt uneasy. Even though she was so angry with them, she wished Aidan and Danby were here to help. It was their fault she was alone! If they hadn't started fighting again she would not have been so angry with them and walked off.

Her leg hurt where Madam had kicked her and she bent to rub it with her hand. She lifted the bottom edge of her gown and petticoat, and turned to the window to look for a bruise. She heard Sir come in from stabling the horse and dropped her skirts immediately.

He appeared surprised at her appearance and she guessed it was due to her hair.

'Do that again,' he demanded.

'What, Sir?'

'Lift one side of your gown.'

She didn't think she should when Madam wasn't here and did not move.

'*Do as I say!*' He slapped his gloves against the dresser.

Reluctantly she bent to lift the edges of her skirts.

'Higher.'

Frightened, she pulled them towards her thighs until the bottom of her drawers was visible.

'Now look at me.'

She swallowed and raised her chin, wondering what he was going to ask her to do next.

'A frightened little street urchin.' He nodded. 'Perfect.'

Madam was standing in the open doorway with a carrot-coloured wig in her hand. 'I think you're right,' she added. 'She doesn't need this.' She placed the wig carefully on the dresser. 'She needs a few rips in the gown.' Madam rummaged in a drawer, pulled out a pair of scissors with long blades and walked over to Sarah.

'No, please don't cut my gown. I've never had a gown as beautiful as this before. Please don't spoil it.'

But Madam simply laughed and said, 'Stand still or I'll cut you.' She knelt down and hacked away at Sarah's skirts then snipped off most of the tiny buttons from the bodice fastening so that the front gaped open, exposing the top of her corset and her swelling bosoms.

Sarah's lip trembled as she watched her beautiful, beautiful gown reduced to tatters. Why? Didn't they want her to look nice when she was in their parlour? She had a choking feeling in her throat and felt hot tears spring to her eyes. Why would someone be so destructive? If she did manage to run away, where could she go dressed like this? She wished she had her boy's clothes back again. In fact she was beginning to wish she was a boy again.

Sir went to the pantry and drew a tankard of ale from the barrel. 'Take her upstairs until later. We'll announce that we have just found her, wandering the streets.'

Madam grasped Sarah's arm firmly and half dragged her to the bottom of a narrow winding staircase. 'Don't make a noise. My other girls are sleeping.' She poked her fingers in Sarah's back and pushed her up the stairs.

On the top landing they passed a girl who seemed to be only half awake. She wore a mob cap and was tying on a kitchen apron. She was yawning widely, showing her small blackened teeth. When she saw Madam she shut her mouth and bobbed a curtsy.

'Meg, this is a new girl and she'll be in with you to start with.'

'Yes, Madam.' The girl suppressed another yawn and went on her way.

Madam pushed Sarah into a small attic room with sloping ceilings and a tiny window in the end gable. It smelt of the chamber pot that was standing unemptied beside the untidy bed.

'You'll stay here and not utter a sound until I fetch you.' Then she left her alone, closing the attic door behind her. Sarah heard the key turn in the lock.

Neither Aidan nor Danby had heard Sarah's pleas to stop fighting. Nor did they know that she had left them. Their fists and faces were bruised and sore before they were pulled apart by a hefty fellow who shouted, 'That's enough, you two. Take your fighting somewhere else.' When they resumed their squabble he threatened to fetch the constable to have them thrown in prison for the night.

Aidan dropped his fists and looked around. 'Where is she?' He raised his voice and called her name.

'She'll be hiding from you and the servant's life you've got lined up for her,' Danby sneered. He was rubbing his knuckles with his fingers.

'Where has she gone?' Aidan grabbed at a passer-by who had

stopped to watch the spectacle. 'Did you see a young woman in a grey dress? She's very pretty and wearing a white servant's cap.' The man shook his head and Aidan dashed to a young couple, arm in arm. 'Did you see her? You must have done. She was standing just here, on her own.'

The woman said, 'We passed a girl going in the opposite direction. Pretty, you say? This one was; she had really big hazel eyes, the sort that melt your heart.'

'That's her! Did you see which way she went?'

The woman tugged at her sweetheart's arm. 'You turned round to watch her. I saw you.'

The man looked sheepish. 'Not for long. Aye, she were pretty enough, but she were talking to, you know, them folk from that alehouse in Mosbrough. I thought she were, like one of their lot.'

Aidan's alarm grew. 'What do you mean, "their lot"?'

The man glanced at the woman beside him. 'It were Jack Jackson and his missus. They have, you know . . .' he could hardly get the word out, '. . . girls.'

'What do you know about them?' his companion demanded, dropping her arm from his.

'Only what the men at work tell me. Honest. I've never been there messen.'

'I should hope not neither, else you can find another lass to walk out with!'

'Don't take on like that. I'm trying to help this fellow here. Is the girl your sweetheart?'

Aidan didn't answer. He felt a cold hand grip his heart and his breath caught in his throat. 'Did you see her go off with them?'

'I can't say I did. It doesn't do to be too nosey about Jack Jackson's business.'

A small group of onlookers had gathered around them to listen, interested in this exchange. 'I saw her,' one said. 'Fair skinned and real bonny. Aye, she went off with the Jacksons in their carriage.

113

Looked as pleased as punch she did, climbing in beside her lady-ship.' His last two words were said with a sneer.

'Where is this – this alehouse?' Aidan demanded. He was aware that Danby had wandered over and was standing quietly by his side, their fight forgotten.

'I told you. It's past the big ironworks in Mosbrough, over where they're building the new railway.'

'We've got to find her, Aidan,' Danby said, 'before she gets in with a wrong crowd.'

'We're already too late for that. She's still a maid and doesn't know about these things. Dear Lord, that's the trouble; I wanted to get her into a decent family before anything like this happened to her. This is all your fault, Danby, filling her head with ideas about inns and taverns and stuff.'

'Don't blame me. If you had listened a bit more to what she wanted, and weren't so stuffy about us all living together this would never have happened.'

The man interrupted them both. 'I should get over there sharpish if I were you and fetch her out before it's too late. But be careful, lads. Jackson's a nasty piece of work.'

'How far is it,' Danby asked.

But Aidan was already on his way and he called over his shoulder. 'I'll find it. Hurry up if you're coming with me, Dan.'

They hurried down into town, past the Chapel on the Bridge, across the navigation and on towards Mosbrough. Aidan stopped twice to ask the way. It seemed that all the working men in the area knew about Jackson's place.

They finally found the house and catching their breath, hung around outside for a while, watching a few men go in.

'They're not miners and ironworkers, are they?' Aidan observed.

'Looks more like them in charge to me. I suppose they have more money to spend.'

'How much have you got?'

Danby patted his jacket. 'My harvest wages are still in here.'

'And I've done well at the market today. We'll go in and see what we can find out.'

'What if she's not there?'

Aidan passed his palm over his eyes. 'I don't know, Dan. I don't know.' He squared his shoulders. 'Come on. Let's go inside.'

It was bigger than other alehouses, thought Aidan. There was a good fire and a few wooden tables and chairs but no wooden counter. A large, dark-skinned man wearing a white apron stood in front of the ale barrels. Aidan thought he appeared to be guarding something rather than serving the ale.

'He looks like one o' them foreign pugilists,' Danby whispered.

Aidan agreed and answered, 'I'll get the ale. You go and sit by the fire.' He walked boldly up to the man and took out some coins and nodded. 'Good evening to you. Two glasses, if you please.'

'I've not seen you around these parts before. Where are you from?'

'The other side of the moor. I – I have business with the railway company.'

'And the other one?'

'The same.' He took the glasses of dark ale across to Danby and sat down.

'I don't see her; or any girls at all in here,' Danby said in a low voice. 'Perhaps she's gone. Y'know, run off to look for us.'

'Lord, I don't know whether that's good or bad. We'll sit and watch for a while; see what goes on.'

'I don't think that fella in town was right about here. Them sort o' women are usually hanging about, talking to men who have money to spend.'

'You know about these things, do you?'

Danby shrugged. 'There were one or two during the harvest.'

'You paid for a woman?' Aidan was surprised.

'Why not? You should try it. They've learned what to do, these women have, and—'

'Shut up, Danby. I don't want to hear about it, now.'

Danby smirked and swallowed a mouthful of ale. Eventually he got up and fetched another two glasses. The room was becoming noisy and crowded, with groups of older men talking about business. There were not many in that were as young as Aidan and Danby.

'Have you seen that door at the back?' Danby asked. 'Every now and then, someone goes through there. I reckon that's where the women are.'

'I noticed that as well,' Aidan answered. 'Let's go and see, then. I hope we're not too late.' Aidan's face took on a haunted look. He couldn't bear the thought of anyone hurting Sarah, or even touching her, not in that way, not like this. She was too young and it wasn't right. 'Come on, Dan. Follow me.'

Aidan sauntered over to the barrels with an empty glass in his hand.

'Another one?' the large man said.

'No, thanks. I heard you've got more to offer here.' He looked directly into the man's eyes and knew he'd understood what he meant.

The man said, 'Both of you?'

Aidan nodded.

'A guinea each, then.' He held out his hand.

Aidan heard a choking sound from Danby and kicked his foot. They each found a guinea and the man nodded towards the door. 'Through there.'

Danby whispered, 'I don't fancy getting past him in a hurry.'

'There must a way out of the back. If she's here, keep calm until I've got the measure of the place.'

The back room contrasted sharply with the dim front parlour. There were plenty of oil lamps so the light was good. It was furnished with comfortable sofas and chairs where the women were sitting, displaying their finery. Aidan stared at them and he noticed Danby did too, making an appreciative noise in his throat. The women were all handsome, with their hair done up in coils and curls and dressed with ornaments. They wore tight-fitting gowns with low necklines showing off their ample bosoms. He understood why it cost a guinea.

Danby whispered, 'Do you reckon we can have one o' these for our money?'

Aidan ignored him. A portly gentleman was sitting beside one of the women, talking and holding her hand. She stood up and led him to the staircase in the corner of the room. Then his view was blocked by another man and a woman who appeared in front of both of them. This woman was dressed differently, elegantly, Aidan thought, as was the man by her side. He held out his hand and Aidan found himself shaking it as though they were friends. He tried not to show his distaste.

'Welcome, sir,' the man said. 'My name is Jackson. This is your first visit, is it not?'

Aidan nodded silently.

'Well. You can see what I have to offer. If you have any special requirements, talk to Madam.' He inclined his head sideways to indicate the woman at his side. 'She knows my girls.'

Madam gave a cold smile and her eyes glittered in the lamplight.

'That dark one in the red . . .' Danby began.

Aidan elbowed him and Danby closed his mouth and shrugged.

Aidan was scanning the room indifferently. 'These are all too old for my liking.' He leaned back in his chair and stretched out his legs, trying to look bored. 'Is this all you've got?'

The woman's eyes narrowed. 'Have you been talking to Jonah out there?'

Aidan's eyes glittered back at hers and he raised his eyebrows.

'She's not ready yet. You'll have to come back tomorrow.'

'Aye, and then you'll tell me to come back the next day. What sort of whorehouse is this?'

'Keep you voice down, sir. You can see her along with everybody else later but she's not working tonight.'

'Not even for an extra guinea?'

'No.'

Madam went to join Jackson in front of a door at the back of the room. Danby joined the woman in red on a sofa and Aidan's heart sank. A gentleman crossed the room and sat beside him. 'Is it your first time here?'

'Does it show?'

'No, but I'm a regular and I haven't seen you here before; just visiting town, are you?'

'I'll be staying as soon as I'm fixed up.'

The gentleman chuckled. 'They'll fix you up here well enough. I remember how hard it was to make up my mind when I first arrived!'

'You're not from round here yourself, then?'

'No, and we don't ask each other too many questions, son.'

Aidan shrugged. 'Madam said she had a new girl coming down later.'

'Aye. When there's a few more customers here. It'll be a show to get us interested in her. Izzy told me. That's her in the blue. She's my favourite. I can recommend her. She's what you might call – adventurous.' He grinned and winked.

'I'll wait to see the new one.'

'Don't waste your time. Izzy said she only arrived this afternoon and Jackson never lets 'em loose on his customers until he's sure they'll give good service.'

Aidan felt sick. It must be Sarah. He had to get her out of here tonight. He tried to catch Danby's eye without drawing too much attention to himself. But Danby had decided to get his guinea's worth from the black-haired woman. Aidan's blood was as red as Danby's when it came to women, but he couldn't even think about going with any of them while Sarah was in danger. Now Danby was distracted from their task he didn't seem worried about Sarah at all and Aidan despised Danby for risking not being here when Sarah came down. Yet he was irritatingly grateful to him for at least behaving like a regular visitor to whorehouses. Dear Lord, even when they got Sarah out of here there was no way he was going to let her go off with Danby!

Jackson came over to him again. 'Have we no one to please you tonight, sir?'

'Maybe. I hear there's a show later on.'

'Just the one girl, sir.'

'I'll wait to see her.'

'Why not try one of my other tempting beauties?'

Aidan curled his lip.

'It's your guinea,' Jackson replied and turned away. Aidan sat back and waited.

The room was crowded; word had got round that Madam was bringing in the new girl and there was jostling for a good view. Jackson turned the lamps down and then opened the door at the back of the room.

There was a gasp and general murmuring as Madam appeared with Sarah in tow who was clothed in – in . . . Aidan could not believe what he saw. Sarah's new gown had been torn into tatters. No, not torn, he realised; it had been cut and slashed deliberately, exposing her undergarments and flesh. Danby, to one side of him, moved closer and whispered, 'What have they done to her?'

'We've got to get her out of here,' Aidan answered.

Jackson raised his arms to ask for quiet. 'Gentlemen, look at this poor wretched child. My good lady found her begging for food in the market. Such a vision of loveliness and so reduced in circumstances. But we have rescued her from the gutter and we present her now to plea for her survival.' He paused while Madam circled round Sarah so that Sarah was obliged to turn with her.

She caught sight of Aidan and Danby in the middle of the room and her eyes widened. There were tears in them, Aidan was sure. He put his fingers to his lips and tried to reassure her with a smile.

Jackson continued, 'Who will want her like this? None of you I am sure. But dressed in silk and lace? Who will offer ten guineas

119

to clothe her? And,' he lowered his voice, 'be the first to taste her delicious body.'

Aidan felt a trickle of saliva gather in his mouth. He wanted to step forward and punch this Jackson fellow in his filthy mouth. He had to do something before Madam took Sarah away again. The onlookers around him were shocked at the price. Ten guineas was a lot of money even for these men. One of them rebuked, 'Ten guineas for a street urchin? I can get one for a tanner down by the cut.'

'Then you go and do that, sir. But will she be wearing a silk gown with pearls around her throat? Gentlemen, I give you my guarantee. If you are not satisfied with my good lady's ministrations on this poor waif, you may have every penny of your money back. Now, who has ten guineas for this privilege?'

Aidan thought he was going to choke with hatred for this man. If he had a pocketful of sovereigns he would throw them at his face. But he knew he could not raise ten guineas even with Dan's harvest wages. He glanced at Dan, who was already moving, and put out a hand to slow him.

He was too late. 'Me,' Danby said, 'I have.' He dashed forward and tried to prise Sarah's wrist from Madam's hand. The older woman was strong and would not let go. 'You can't do this to her,' he cried. 'She's not like the others, she's still a maid.'

'Danby, you idiot!' Aidan shouted, but it was too late now. Aidan darted to Danby's side and managed to grab hold of Sarah's arm before he was dragged away. Within seconds the scuffle had ceased. Dan's arms were firmly pinned behind him by a big stocky man and moments later Aidan felt the same happen to him. Where had these strong men come from? They were smartly dressed; they were customers of the Jacksons. Or rather, they were not. In his employ, no doubt, and placed to deal with trouble-makers.

Aidan struggled with his captor until a heavy blow aimed at his middle winded him and he sagged. He recovered quickly and would have struggled again but he glimpsed a knife. Its blade glinted in the lamplight, sharp and curved, and he did not doubt these men would use it.

'We're going,' he said and yelled, 'Leave it, Dan, he's got a knife.' Neither of them were any use to Sarah if they were dead.

He was bundled into the parlour and out though the front door. Dan tumbled out after him onto the muddy road.

'What are you giving up for?' Danby wheezed. 'She's still in there.'

'They'll kill us as soon as look at us if we don't clear off. Did you see that blade?' Aidan was angry. The man had caught him squarely in his stomach and it hurt. 'You should have kept your mouth shut,' he breathed.

Dan was nursing his groin. 'They fight dirty too,' he moaned. 'What'll we do?'

'Stay out of their way. They're evil.'

'You mean leave her in there?'

'No. We'll wait until it's quiet.'

'They won't sleep until daybreak, I bet.'

'It – it might be too late by then. I'm off to look round the back.'

'How do you know where'll she'll be?'

'I don't!' Aidan shouted. Then more quietly he repeated what he'd said but added, 'Not yet anyway.'

Chapter 10

Sarah was terrified. Madam had kept her locked in the attic room all evening, until well after dark, without even giving her a drink of water. She heard people going up and down the wooden stairs and women's voices but the scullery maid didn't come back and she had no idea what was happening.

She sat on the bed, the only furniture in the room, and felt like weeping. Her beautiful woollen gown was in tatters and she feared what Madam would do to her next. How had she got herself into this scrape? This was Aidan's fault. If he hadn't argued with Dan about her she would never have run off and met up with Madam! But she had run off; her lovely new outfit was ruined and she was a prisoner in this pokey little attic.

When Madam finally unlocked the door to take her downstairs, Sarah was hungry as well as thirsty. Her hunger was made worse by the smells of fried bacon wafting up the stairs.

'I want something to eat,' she said boldly.

Madam hit her across the head, just as Mrs Watson used to. 'Speak when you're spoken to and do as you're told,' she snapped. Sarah knew how to keep quiet when she had to.

The fire in the range was lit and the kitchen was tidier than before. It was not much cleaner, she thought, but she heard sounds of pots being washed in the scullery. Madam ruffled her hair, tugged at the rips in her gown to make them worse and pulled the neckline away to show the swell of her bosoms. Then she encircled Sarah's wrist with fingers that felt like iron bands and took her through a wooden door and a plush red curtain.

At first, Sarah was overwhelmed by the heat and sweaty smell in the room. Her large eyes brimmed with tears and her lip trembled as she stood in the midst of all these strangers. But when she saw Aidan her heart lifted and she wanted to run over to him, desperate to feel the comfort of his strong arms around her. She would be safe now he was here, she thought, and attempted a smile at him. But he signalled silence to her and her features fell again. Danby was there, though. He wouldn't let them keep her a prisoner either. He was going to take her away and make her laugh again. She turned her beseeching eyes on him and then – then he made a lunge for her, and Madam yanked her away as the room broke into chaos.

Furniture was toppled and there was shouting and struggling and when a space cleared and she searched for Aidan and Danby they were being thrown out like buckets of rubbish. Her tears threatened again. If this was being a girl she didn't like it all. She wanted to go home, to go back to the wagon and pretend to be a boy again.

Madam tugged at her arm and made her walk around the room again. Aidan and Danby didn't come back. Instead, drunken men with florid faces and greedy eyes ogled and pawed at her with their sweaty palms until eventually she was ushered back through the plush curtain and the wide door to the kitchen.

Madam shouted for the servant girl and she brought Sarah some cold mutton and ale. Despite her ordeal Sarah devoured the meat hungrily and was wiping her mouth with the back of her hand when Sir came in. He looked very pleased with himself.

'So you're still a maid, eh? Is that what you tell the lads on the street? We must try that one again. I had them all clamouring for first bite of this particular cherry.'

'You don't believe it's true, do you?' Madam said.

He tossed his head to indicate the door behind him. 'They do and that's all that matters.' He chinked the coins in his hand and gave a sovereign to Madam. 'Fit her out like a bride tomorrer. Make her look special. This one's gonna be the goose that lays the golden egg for us. What did you say her name was?'

'Sarah.'

'Sarah,' he repeated. 'Look at me, Sarah.'

She did, taking in his jowly, raddled features and glassy eyes.

'Is it true what that lad said about you? You're still a maid?'

She stared at him until Madam prodded her in the back. 'Answer Sir when he asks you a question.'

'Yes,' she said.

'Oh no,' he mocked, 'so much more work for me to do tonight.'

'Well, don't enjoy it too much,' Madam snapped.

'What's up with you? You're not jealous, are you?'

'Of that thing?' she sneered.

Sir laughed scornfully. 'You watch the other girls with her an' all. They won't be happy about a young 'un taking all our best customers. And she will, so you make sure we don't have no cat fights. Understand?' He went back through the curtained door.

As soon as he'd gone, Madam shouted, 'Meg, can you hear me? You're sleeping down here on the pallet tonight.' Then she dragged Sarah all the way back up the stairs to the attic.

'Take off that rag and I'll burn it,' she demanded. 'You can sleep if yer want. Sir'll wake you when he's ready for you.'

'Where do you suppose she is?' Danby whispered.

'How should I know? I'll just have to search for her,' Aidan replied.

'Aye, and before they find you with their knife.'

'Do you think I don't know that! Say something useful or keep quiet.'

'Don't go on at me. It's as much your fault as mine that she's in there.'

The lights had gone out at the front of the house and Aidan had found a way to the rear of the house. It was surrounded by a high brick wall; a solid wooden gate was the only way in. The gate was securely locked and probably barred as well. Aidan stood back and looked up at the house. It was a tall building, three floors at least and, like most big houses, the domestic quarters jutted out into a yard at the rear. Fortunately there was no moon and Aidan chose the darkest corner to scale the wall. It wasn't difficult, using Danby's back as a step up. Aidan straddled the wall and leaned down to hoist Danby up too.

'We're in luck,' Aidan breathed. 'It'll be easier coming back.'

The garden was neglected, overgrown and littered with discarded beer barrels and splintered wooden crates. Lamps glowed in the ground-floor room and he could make out people moving around. He could smell cooking too. That was in his favour. If they drank and ate well they might sleep heavily and not easily be wakened if he had to break glass to get in.

'You stay here, Dan, and use those barrels to build an easy climb up the wall, one that I can knock over when we're done.'

'I want to go in with you and get her.'

'I'll be quieter on my own. Besides, I might have to fight off that burly fellow, so if I can get Sarah to you here, you can escape with her. That's what you have to do. Get her away from here.'

'What about you?'

'I can take care of myself.'

'How are you going to get inside?'

'I don't know. But I'll find a way. Remember, don't make a sound or we're done for.' Aidan slid noiselessly down the rough brick, landed with a soft thud on the ground and crept silently towards the light.

From the shadows he saw Jackson and his madam, the burly guard, and two of his whores. They were sitting around the kitchen table drinking and finishing the remains of roast fowl and potatoes. A kitchen girl poured ale from a pitcher and then placed it on the table. But Jackson drank from a bottle of spirits by his elbow. The girl disappeared and Aidan realised there must be a windowless scullery at the end of the building. And a back door, he thought.

He watched for a while longer. One of the whores appeared to fall sleep with her head on the table and the burly man hoisted her to her feet. He took the arm of the other one as well and ushered them away; to bed presumably. Jackson and his madam continued drinking spirits and talking. He wished he could hear what they were saying.

He went around to the other side of the kitchen and was faced with a line of outhouses built against the high wall. Wash house, coal house and, judging by the smell, a privy. A door opened and a girl threw a bowl of water on the ground. The light from the scullery door was dim. Aidan moved quickly and before she closed the door behind her his foot was on the threshold. He felt the door push again at his foot before the girl looked down at the obstacle.

She dropped the metal bowl with a clatter on the brick floor and opened her mouth. Aidan moved forward and put a hand firmly over it, holding his breath. No one came to investigate. Aidan fished in his pocket for a shilling and offered it to her, putting his finger to his lips. Her eyes widened but she nodded and he removed his hand. There was only one candle in the scullery and that was already burning low.

'What are you after?' she whispered, picking up her bowl.

'I'm looking for the new girl. Where is she?'

'Who wants to know?'

'I'm her friend. She doesn't have to do this.'

'Well, she didn't look as though she wanted to, not to me, anyway. I thought she was frightened.'

'She doesn't know what she's got herself into. Can you tell me where she is?'

'Oh aye, she's upstairs, waiting for his lordship.'

The way she said 'his lordship' made Aidan think she had little respect for Jackson. 'Has he harmed her in any way?'

'Not yet, but he has ways of persuading his girls to do what he wants.'

'I have to get her out of there. Will you help me?'

'You'll be lucky. He'll kill you if he finds you, and then he'll whip me for letting you in.'

'He won't know it's you. I'll break the kitchen window lock and leave it open.'

The girl looked steadily at him in the candlelight. 'Why should I help you?'

'Because you don't like Jackson and his madam any more than I do.'

'Aye, you might be right. I'm not pretty enough for the front parlour but he pays me well, or else I wouldn't stay. Who would?'

'How much do you want?'

'He asks a guinea for his girls.'

Aidan gave her the last of his money and hoped Danby had some left.

She took the coins and hoisted her skirt to secrete them into a pouch tied to her drawer tapes. Aidan was surprised she didn't even turn way from him to do this, but he supposed there was no modesty for anyone in a whore house. His heart began to beat anxiously. He must get to Sarah before Jackson did. 'Show me where she is.'

'I can't do that because he's still in the kitchen. But there's a door to the back stairs from the kitchen and she's in a small attic on your right when you get to the top. When he's ready he'll come out to the privy. Then he goes upstairs to learn his girls.'

'Learn them?'

'He shows 'em what to do. That's what he says, anyroad.'

'Who else is up there?'

'Three other girls are across the landing. They're still learning an' all. So he says.'

'What about the madam and the others?'

'They sleep up top in the front and they'll be off to bed soon. Nobody stays awake after four o'clock. Then he'll go up to his new girl. Madam has put her in my bed for tonight.'

'What about you?'

'I sleep in the kitchen when we have a new girl in.'

Aidan felt sick again. His heart was thumping so hard he thought his chest would burst. He knew he had no choice. 'I'll wait outside for Jackson. Don't say a word to him; nothing. Do you hear me?'

'None o' my business.' She shrugged, biting on the coin. She looked excited as she added, 'What are you gonna do?'

He didn't know but said, 'Leave the scullery door open and the door to the attic stairs.' He went outside into the darkness. Everywhere was still. Danby had moved some barrels to the wall and was quietly heaving another on top of them. Aidan watched him for a few moments and then searched the darkness for something, anything, he could use as a weapon.

He selected a heavy, solid piece of wood and hid in the shadows by the wash house. He held his breath when Jackson finally came out smoking a cigar. Jackson walked right by him without noticing he was there, but Aidan waited until he was inside the privy. He inhaled shakily. He had to do this. Sarah's virtue depended on it, but even so, it was wicked and alien to him. His mother would turn in her grave. Don't hesitate. Do it. Do it now. Hit him. Hit him hard.

Jackson had left the privy door open and Aidan crept up behind him. He lifted the wood above his head with both his hands and brought it down heavily on the back of Jackson's head. Oh God! Oh God! For a second, he panicked.

Jackson crumpled and groaned, lashing out with his arms to save himself. Aidan hit him again. This time it was harder. He had to be out cold. Aidan stood over him wanting to bring the wood down again and again until he was dead. But he didn't. He was not a murderer. He needed Jackson senseless; that was all. He bent over him to check that he was out cold and he was.

He threw down the wood as though it was red hot and hurried indoors, past the wide-eyed girl.

'Get the key,' she squeaked.

Oh Lord, what key? Of course, the key to the attic room; why hadn't he thought of that before? 'Where is it?'

'Madam will have given it to him. It'll be in his waistcoat pocket.'

He went back to Jackson and rolled him over. Jackson groaned but fell back into a faint. Aidan didn't know whether he was pleased or not. At least he hadn't killed him, but how long would he have before Jackson came round?

Aidan found the key easily and retraced his steps. His boots thumped on the stairs but he reasoned that anyone who heard would think it was Jackson. His hands shook as he tried to force the key into the lock. It didn't fit! It was the wrong one! He panicked again until it turned smoothly and released the door.

Everywhere was so dark in this house, but he made out a figure in the far corner of the room, huddled in a heap. 'Sarah,' he whispered loudly. 'It's me,'

'Aidan? Oh Aidan, get me away from here. Please.' She flung herself at him and wrapped her arms tightly around his middle.

He clasped her meagrely clothed body to his and allowed himself a few brief indulgent seconds of bliss. But she was not safe yet and there was no time to waste. He took her hand and breathed, 'Be as quiet as you can.'

They stole down the stairs to the kitchen. A single candle stub burned low beside a makeshift bed on the floor. The girl was motionless as they crept by. He guessed she was feigning sleep. 'What's your name?' he asked softly. She opened one eye and said, 'Meg.'

'Thank you, Meg,' he said and she closed her eye again.

Jackson was sitting up and rubbing the back of his head when Aidan and Sarah came out of the scullery door. 'Hey, you,' he shouted and drunkenly attempted to scramble to his feet.

Aidan dragged Sarah past him towards the barrels, but Jackson was already staggering towards them. 'Jonah!' he shouted. 'Get down here!' He threw a punch but Aidan easily ducked out of range. 'Meg!' Jackson yelled. 'Get Jonah. Now.' He knew Meg had to obey and wondered where Jonah slept.

'Hurry, Sarah.' He lifted her onto the barrels and pushed her upwards. 'Danby,' he called. 'Lean down and grab her arms.' The barrels rocked. Sarah was not quite tall enough to reach Danby's hands. 'Jump, Sarah,' he ordered, and she did, rocking the barrels. Aidan clambered up beside her and lifted her again until Danby had a firm hold and was able to hoist her to safety. The barrels tipped precariously and Aidan felt himself going over with them.

He landed, shaken, on his behind. 'Take her and run, Danby,' he cried. 'Get her away from here. Head for the bridge into town.'

Jackson was on his feet and swaggering towards him. Aidan had not much time before Jonah would appear with his knife. Aidan aimed the toe of his boot at Jackson's groin and wished he had done it earlier. Hastily he righted the biggest of the barrels and climbed on it, stretching for the top of the wall.

He heard a door bang and Jackson's strained voice calling, 'Over here, Jonah. Get him.'

Aidan bent his knees and leapt, his fingers clutching the top of the wall. His pushed his feet against the wall and jack-knifed upwards to give himself a firmer hold. He made it! He scrambled over, dropping like a stone on the other side, and took a few more precious seconds to recover. His heart was going nineteen to the dozen but at least Sarah was safe; for the present, anyway. He staggered to his feet and set off at a jog to catch up with her.

The three of them headed for the spring to drink and clean themselves up. It was daybreak and milkmaids were already at work as they passed one of the town dairies. They stared at Sarah clothed in Aidan's jacket over her chemise, drawers and corset.

'How much money do you have left, Dan?' Aidan asked.

'None. I gave the last to that . . .' He glanced at Sarah and lowered his voice. 'She was, you know, very obliging.'

'Dear Lord, Dan, couldn't you have said no? We've got nothing now.'

'What about your money?'

'I gave my last sovereign to the scullery maid back there.'

'Why? Did she—?'

Aidan sighed impatiently. 'She helped me get Sarah out. I hope Jackson doesn't beat her for it.'

'Well, if we have no money, we can't stay in town.'

Sarah, who was walking ahead of them, heard and said over her shoulder, 'Oh, can we go back to the wagon? Can we be like we were before?'

'No, Sarah, we can't,' Aidan replied and elbowed Danby, who added, 'He's right. There's too many like Jackson and his missus about. You – you want a decent mistress who'll look after you proper.'

'And you need another gown.'

'You can lend me a shirt and some trousers,' she suggested.

'Oh no; they're too big for you. You'll never get a place, unless . . .'

'Unless what?'

'There might be a way; somewhere that'll clothe Sarah and keep her safe until – well, until I can earn more money.'

'Oh aye? Where's that then?' Danby scorned. 'She'll just have to try the hiring fair again.'

Sarah stopped suddenly and turned, shaking her head. 'I'm not standing in another hiring line!' she said. 'That's what it was like in that house. I was paraded around and stared at the same as I was at the hiring fair, and then sold off like a prize cow. I'm not doing it again.'

'That's out then.' Aidan sighed. He had already resigned himself to the only solution left. Neither Sarah nor Dan would thank him for it but it was the only one he could think of that would ensure she was safe. 'Let's walk up to the dispensary,' he suggested. 'They might give us some wych hazel for these cuts.'

Danby yawned. 'What if Jackson comes after us?'

Aidan frowned. Jackson was a thug who wouldn't let anyone get away with stealing a prized possession. Aidan was a marked man and had to get out of town quickly. But that was the least of his worries. He had to make sure that Sarah was safely lodged first. He couldn't risk her falling into Jackson's clutches again. 'Sarah, come back here and walk between us,' Aidan called.

Thankfully, she did as he asked and even Danby thought it was a good idea to keep Sarah closer to them. They each linked arms with her and set off up the hill to the dispensary. It was still closed when they reached it so they sat with their backs against a stone wall and dozed in the early morning sun's meagre warmth. Sarah, exhausted and shielded by a solid body each side of her, fell asleep.

'Those thugs know who we are,' Danby said. 'I'm getting out of here today. I'll take Sarah. She'll be safe with me.'

'No, she won't. If you'd had any respect for her, you wouldn't have tried to bed her at Christmas, so show some now. You can clear off, but you leave her alone. I know what I've got to do.'

'Aye, I bet you do! You knew you were doing wrong with her in the woods but it didn't stop you.'

'You were the one who did wrong,' said Aidan angrily.

'She wanted me and I could have had her if you hadn't poked your nose in!'

'Aye, you would have taken her for your own satisfaction without any concern for *her*.'

'She likes a bit o' fun as much as I do,' Danby argued.

'Not that kind of fun! You were only thinking of your own interests as usual. Admit it.'

'Well, I've had enough misery in my life so far! I'm not hanging about if I can't get what I want. I like girls.'

'So do I.' Aidan glared at him

'I can't help myself sometimes. Maybe Sarah's the same. There are some like that, you know.'

'Well Sarah isn't!' Aidan retaliated. 'She's frightened underneath all that talk of hers. She's not going with you. If I have to fight you again, I will. I'm bigger than you, Dan.'

'Have it your way, then! I'm moving on with or without her.'

'Well, you'll soon find another lass to ruin.'

Danby bent down, placed a kiss on Sarah's forehead and added, 'Sorry, Sam. We could've had some fun together.' Then he walked away from Sarah and Aidan without a backward glance.

Sarah felt cold when she woke up. She tugged Aidan's jacket closer about her shoulders and yawned. 'Is the dispensary open yet?'

Aidan pulled her to her feet. 'We can't wait any longer. Come on, Sarah, we've got to go. There's nothing else for it.'

'Where are we going?' Sarah was puzzled by Aidan's determination but followed him anyway. She was relieved to be back with him and guessed he had sent Danby off to find food. She trusted Aidan.

They turned off the main track, walked alongside a high stone wall and stopped outside a small door next to a pair of large wooden gates. There was lettering on the gates but Sarah could not read it. 'Is this the Mission House?' she asked.

Aidan thumped on the door before he could change his mind. 'It's the workhouse, Sarah. Don't be angry. They'll look after you in here.'

'But I don't want to go there!' She turned to run away and was stopped by Aidan's firm grip on her hand. 'Let me go!' She shouted.

'It won't be for long; just until I can find the money to get you out.'

Sarah was filled with horror, and the stories she had heard from the kitchen maids at Meadow Hall came flooding back. 'But don't you realise what I've done to stay out of here? Hiding in the stables, pretending to be a boy, joining up with you and Danby, it was all to avoid being sent here.' She looked around. 'Where is Danby anyway?'

133

'He's – he's gone.'

'I thought he was my friend.'

'I'm your friend.'

'Then why have you brought me here?' she snapped.

'I'll come back for you as soon as I can. I promise.' Aidan's heart felt heavy as he looked at Sarah's frightened face.

'When?' she demanded, trying to shake off his hand.

He couldn't answer that.

'See? You don't know,' she went on. 'I could have gone with Danby.'

'Cavorting round the taverns? You might just as well have stayed with Jackson.'

'You sent him away, didn't you? You've betrayed me! Traitor!' She spat out the words and tears welled in her eyes.

'Don't look at me like that. I don't want this either.'

'Then don't do it to me! Take me back to the wagon!'

'You know we can't live like that any more.'

'You want rid of me, don't you? I'm a burden to you.'

'No! You know that's not true. But you need proper looking after or you'll end up – well, you know how you'll end up. You'll be ruined and I can't let that happen to you.' His face was a picture of pain.

'Then please don't leave me here,' she begged.

'It's not for ever and you'll learn to read and write. This is best for you.'

'No, it isn't! It's best for you! So you can go your own way without me to worry about.' Too late Sarah realised the door had opened and Aidan pushed her in front of him until they were inside a small lobby. She reached round to escape but the door swung closed with a click, and a large woman with a chatelaine of jangling keys barred Sarah's exit and locked the door.

'No!' Sarah protested. 'Let me out!' Sarah had never felt worse. How could he do this to her? 'You've put me in a prison, Aidan,' she added. 'I thought you cared about me.'

'I do! I'll be living in town so I can visit you.' But as he said it, he wondered how he would avoid Jackson and his men. He tried to reassure her. 'I won't be far away.'

'I don't believe you. You're the same as everybody else. You don't care about me at all. Well, I don't care about you either. From now on, I'm the only one I care about. So you go off like Danby and forget about me. I can survive without you. I did before and I'll do it again.'

'Don't be bitter, Sarah.'

'Why not? You've got me off your hands so you can do what you want. But it's not what I want! It's not!' She pressed her lips together and scowled at him with steely eyes. 'I'll never forgive you for this, Aidan. Never! This is the finish of us.'

Aidan lingered outside the high stone walls watching the sky grow lighter. His heart felt heavy. He should have heeded his father's advice earlier; obtained work and lodgings with a respectable family instead of spending his summer in the woods. Then he would have been able to take care of Sarah without deserting her like this. No wonder she hated him.

If only she knew how hard it was for him to leave her here. But it was the only place he knew she would be safe until he could come back for her. If she would have him, he anguished. She was so angry with him and had turned away from him to face the wall without saying goodbye when he'd left.

The woman with the keys had given him his jacket, which Sarah had been wearing, and told him to leave.

'When can I come and see her?' he'd asked.

'Oh no, sir, I wouldn't advise that. You look a decent sort of working man to me and you don't want to be associating with a moral defective.'

'Oh she isn't – that is, it wasn't her fault.'

'Is that what she told you? I've been matron here long enough to know you can't believe anything her sort tells you. They are all the same these street women. The town doesn't want them. Well, you've done your duty, sir. I'll see you safely outside and you can forget all about her. You can be sure we'll learn her better ways in here.'

Reluctantly he'd left, wondering when he would see Sarah again. But what else could he have done to ensure she was safe from harm? Let her go with Danby to sing and dance lewdly as he played his tin whistle outside taverns? He would soon be offered more than coppers for her favours and he wondered how hungry Danby would have to be before he persuaded her to accept. She would end up no better than if they hadn't rescued her from Jackson. At least the workhouse protected her from that.

If only he had a proper home to give her, and a proper wage so that he could look after her and offer her marriage. He could admit it now she was no longer with him – he wanted her to be his, without question, to cherish. Dear Lord, how long would it be before he was in a position to come back for her? Leaving her alone in this prison of a place was the biggest wrench of his life. He could not drag himself away from the austere stone building. He did not know where to go or what to do. Perhaps he should have gone in with her? But what good would that do? Men and women were kept separate and at least if he was outside he could earn money. He was strong, had wits and could work iron. This was an iron town . . . as long as he kept away from Jackson's patch near the railway . . . he could not think clearly as fatigue overtook him. He walked around the high forbidding walls of the workhouse. There was a smaller walled enclosure nearby and he sat with his back to the stone. He could see branches of fruit trees spreading over the top of wall. No longer able to fight his exhaustion, he finally gave in to a troubled sleep.

Chapter 11

Inside, the matron pulled at Sarah's hair as she peered at the roots, then poked her knuckles painfully into Sarah's back. 'Get a move on. We'll soon get these mucky rags off your back and burnt.' She gave Sarah a contemptuous stare, unlocked another door and ordered, 'Follow me.'

Sarah found herself in a large room containing a chair, a plain couch and a tin bath. There was one small window high up in the lime-washed stone wall.

'Wait here.' Matron went out of another door that opened onto a yard.

A few minutes later another woman came in with two buckets of water which she tipped into the bath. Sarah sat on the chair, watching wordlessly. When the woman came back with more water, Sarah asked, 'Who are you?'

The woman did not look at her but said, 'Matron will be in to see to you.'

'See to me?'

'Aye, see to you,' Matron echoed as she came back, rattling her keys. 'Get them things off and get into the bath. Look sharp because the doctor is here and he wants to see you when he's had his breakfast. Can't think why any fine gentleman like the doctor would be interested in a little trollop like you. He doesn't even know you. But he answers to his betters just as we all do.' Matron shook her arm roughly. 'And that's something you'll have to learn now you're in here. I'm supposed to make a silk purse out of a sow's ear, so you think on that.' She stopped and took a long hard look at Sarah's exhausted, bedraggled appearance. 'You look more like a sow's backside, if you ask me.' She gave Sarah another shove towards the buckets and went out to the yard, locking the door behind her.

'But I don't need a doctor. I'm not poorly,' Sarah said to an empty room.

She bent down and put a finger in one of the buckets. The water was cool but not freezing like the spring. In the bath was a small brick of soap and a scrubbing brush. She tipped all the buckets of water into the bath and took off her corset, boots and stockings. Her feet were filthy. She climbed over the side wearing her chemise and drawers. The water felt cold but she soon got used to it. She sat down and rubbed the piece of soap quickly all over then leaned forward to wash her feet with soapy hands. She was making patterns in the floating bubbles when she heard the door open and looked round. Matron came in carrying a pile of linen and a pair of boots. She was followed by a gentleman; a fine gentleman, Sarah thought. He was dressed in dark trousers, a long jacket with shiny buttons and a waistcoat.

'Is this her?' he said loudly. 'She isn't ready for me, Matron. Really, you cannot waste my time like this. I have patients waiting in town.'

'Oh, I am so sorry, sir,' Matron replied. Sarah was surprised at her simpering tone, especially when she turned on her and barked. 'Get out of there at once, Meadow, and stand by the bath.' She took a towel from the couch over to her. 'On your feet, girl,' she snapped, giving her another sharp stab with her finger.

Sarah clambered out and stood dripping wet on the cold stone. She reached for the towel to dry her feet.

Matron look horrified. 'Dear Heaven! I said take all your things off.'

No, you didn't, Sarah thought, but Matron was already apologising again to the doctor. She tugged at Sarah's drawers until she stepped out of them.

'Now the chemise. You wear our clothes in here.' She went back to the couch, leaving Sarah standing by the bath. The chemise clung wetly to her body and she took hold of the bottom edge to wring it out, watching the water make dark splashes on the flagstones. When she looked up the doctor was staring at her. It was the same sort of stare she had seen from the gentlemen in that Jackson place and she scowled at him.

'I said, take it off,' Matron repeated. She sounded annoyed with her.

'Not while he's there,' Sarah responded.

'He's the doctor and he hasn't got all day so you'll do as you're told.'

'Tell him to turn round then.'

Matron lost her patience. 'Oh, really. Who do you think you are?' She took a firm hold on each side of the chemise and yanked it over Sarah's head, then handed her a garment that looked like a flour sack with slits in the sides for her arms. 'Put that on and go and stand by the couch.' She went to a shelf and took down a ledger with a pencil attached by string.

The doctor walked slowly towards Sarah. 'Has she been here before?' he asked Matron.

'No, sir.'

'I do not recall her, either. But someone must have shaved her head at sometime.'

'I've checked for lice and they've gone.' The matron opened her ledger. 'She's a vagrant, sir, and been living on the streets. A working man brought her; one of the Methodists, I expect.'

'I see. Any sign of disease?'

'She's strong and seems healthy to me, sir. No cough or spots. Well, none that I can see.'

There was a short silence then the doctor asked, 'Where did this man find her?'

'He didn't say.'

'But he brought her in from the streets?'

'Yes, sir.'

The doctor's face became very serious. 'I shall question her myself, ma'am.'

Matron looked surprised. 'Oh, you do not have to trouble yourself for this one, sir.'

'I have my duty, ma'am.'

Sarah thought that the matron seemed unsettled by this but appeared to compose herself quickly and answer, 'Yes, sir.'

'Stand by the couch where I can see you,' the doctor said to Sarah.

'Do as the good doctor tells you,' matron added.

Sarah obeyed. She had never met a doctor before but remembered when one had visited Meadow Hall. She had not seen him herself but his presence was revered, even Mrs Watson had stopped what she was doing to get anything the doctor wanted. A bit like the matron, she thought. The doctor wasn't master of the house at Meadow Hall, but when he visited he was treated as such.

Sarah walked over to the couch.

The doctor waved his hand at the pile of clothing on the seat. 'Remove these.'

Matron scurried to shift them to the chair.

'Who was the man who brought you here?'

Sarah pursed her lips. She hated Aidan for doing this to her. She wished now that she had run away with Danby when she had the chance.

'Answer the doctor's questions,' Matron snapped.

'Nobody.'

'Nobody brought you here?' The doctor's expression was severe.

'He – he found me.'

Matron glowered at her. 'Tell the truth, Meadow.'

'I was in this house. It was like the hiring fair,' Sarah added quickly. 'Only they were all gentlemen.'

'How do you know they were gentleman?'

'They wore fancy waistcoats and were smoking cigars.'

Matron made a small disapproving gulp in her throat. 'She was in a – a disorderly house!'

'No, I wasn't! I wasn't living there, I lived with my – my—' She was going to say 'friend' but Aidan was no longer her friend.

'You were living with a man; the man who brought you here?'

'Not just him on his own,' Sarah added. 'There were two of them.'

'You were living with two men?' The doctor had taken a step closer to her and was staring at her intently.

'They used to be my friends.' Sarah sighed.

'Were you not related to them in any way?'

She shook her head. 'We just lived in this wagon.'

Matron seemed shocked and choked on her words. 'But you lived together, all three of you?'

The doctor appeared to be growing hot. He ran his fingers around the inside of his high collar. 'You must tell me what you did together.'

'Did?' She looked from the doctor to Matron. 'We did lots of things together.'

The doctor took in a deep breath. 'Matron, I have left my bag in the master's office. Would you fetch it for me?'

Matron stared at him. 'Surely there is no need to prolong this, sir. I think we know the life she has been leading.'

'She may be diseased.'

'Of course, sir.' The matron bobbed a curtsey and left, gathering up Sarah's underclothing and boots to take with her.

Sarah was glad to see the back of her. She was as bad as Mrs Watson with her domineering ways. But now she was left alone with the doctor and his probing questions. 'I haven't got no disease,' she said.

'Climb on the couch and lie down.'

Sarah hesitated for a moment and then obeyed. Her coarse workhouse chemise had ridden up above her knees. He stood beside the couch and placed a hand on her exposed thigh. His eyes closed for a moment and when he opened them they were glittery.

'Tell me what they did to you?' This time his voice was softer. 'Tell me, child. What did they do with their members? Where did they put them?'

He was whispering in a breathy way that alarmed her. Oh, she could guess what he meant by their members; he meant their cocks. What did he want to know that for? He might be a high-and-mighty doctor but he was behaving in a really loony way. You did get loonies in the workhouse. Did that mean the folk who worked here were loonies as well as the inmates?

She didn't answer and began to think what she could do if he kept moving his hand up her leg. She'd have to run. But the door was locked. She'd noticed that right from the start. Every door was locked so there was nowhere to run in the workhouse. It was a prison. The kitchen maids at Meadow Hall had said as much.

His hand was stroking at the skin of her thigh and moving upwards and underneath her chemise. 'Did you take one in your mouth? Tell me, child.' His hand travelled under her chemise to her belly and then her breasts. He was stroking each one in turn. He might be a doctor but this wasn't right and Sarah reckoned he knew that, otherwise he wouldn't have sent away Matron. She put both her small fists over his knuckles to stop him and said, 'Get off me.'

He didn't seem to hear her. He didn't want to. She could see that. He was as bad as the gentleman in the Jackson house, leering and pawing at her. He towered over her and easily lifted both her fists away with one hand and placed them firmly over her head. She inhaled sharply and held her body rigid, frightened of what he would do next.

He continued to draw the fingers of his other hand back and forth over her breasts and breathed, 'Tell me what the other man was doing. Where was his member?'

She laid there motionless, her anger seething, feeling like a prisoner and wondering what to do. If she tried to get off the couch, he could easily stop her and then he might beat her. His eyes were closed and there were beads of perspiration on his lined forehead. His hand left her breasts and returned to her belly and then her thighs.

'Where did he put it? Was it in here?' His large fingers slid between her legs and prodded her most private area.

She pushed her bottom into the couch as hard as she could and squealed. 'Stop it! You can't do that to me!' She didn't care who he was, doctor or no, she wasn't poorly and he had no right to be mauling her in this way. She tugged at her imprisoned hands and tried to roll of the couch.

He leaned his considerable weight over her, pinning her to the solid surface and continued his fondling. 'Shall I put my member in there? Do you want that?' His eyes were closed and his face so near to hers that his sweat smeared her cheek.

She was terrified of him and had no idea what to do. Scream for Matron? She was out in the yard and wouldn't hear her. Bite him? Yes, bite at his revolting whiskery face. Her mouth turned down in disgust at this but she would have sunk her teeth in his cheek if the rattling of a chatelaine outside the door had not brought him to his senses. Or so it seemed to Sarah.

He let go of her hands and his tone changed so suddenly Sarah thought she must have imagined his onslaught. 'Ah, there you are at last Matron,' he said in a strong voice, 'I need your assistance.'

'I am here to help you, sir,' Matron replied in her grateful tones.

'Look at this child! Red-faced and wild-eyed, I have an alley cat on my hands. I fear she has never been examined by a doctor before and believes I am to kill her.'

'I don't!' Sarah retaliated. 'You tried to do things to me. Things you shouldn't.'

'See how she rejects my civilised ministrations? She does not know how lucky she is to be in my care, Matron. She is, without doubt, a moral defective but she denies it most strongly; so strongly that I must confirm her lies myself.'

'I don't understand, sir.' Matron frowned.

'She protests that she has her virtue. I must satisfy myself that it is so.'

'Oh!' Matron stood quietly by his side for a moment and then asked, 'How will you do that, sir?'

'My dear Matron, it is well known in medical circles that the gentry request such assurances from a physician when ladies are betrothed. You will assist me and I shall soon determine if she tells the truth. Stay where you are child.' He turned to take his bag from Matron and opened it, taking out his shiny steel instruments and holding them up to the window light.

Horrified, Sarah stared at the tiny sharp blades and pointed probes and tongs as he slowly returned them to his bag. Even Matron looked alarmed and did not move.

'Come now, Matron,' he smiled. 'I have done this before.'

'The old doctor never did such a thing, sir.'

'I am not he. I have knowledge from consulting rooms in London, no less. Do you question my ways, Matron?'

'Of course I do not, sir. But who will pay your fee for such ministrations? I am not so sure the guardians will approve of the expense.'

The doctor clicked his tongue impatiently. 'That is not your concern. You do not wish me to complain to the master of your disobedience, do you? You will hold her steady for me.'

'Yes, sir.'

'Look to it, then. I haven't got all day.'

'Meadow! You will do as the doctor says or I shall punish you myself,' Matron ordered, adding, 'we have tamed wilder cats than you in here.' She moved to the head of the couch where she took hold of Sarah's wrists and held on to them firmly. Her knuckles dug painfully into Sarah's flesh. She leaned her mouth close to Sarah's ear and whispered, 'Keep still or I'll tie you down with buckled straps.'

The doctor stared at Sarah and gave her a weak smile that sent a shiver down her back. 'Raise your knees,' he ordered.

She didn't move until Matron barked, 'Do as you're told.'

Slowly, Sarah drew up her knees. When she did, the doctor pushed her legs wide apart, exposing her private area to a rush of cool air. She slapped her thighs together again but Matron dug her fingers painfully into her wrists and growled, 'Meadow.'

The doctor parted her legs again. Saliva gathered in her mouth and she had to try really hard not to spit in the doctor's face. He kept a weak slobbery smile on his loose features as he took out a couple of shiny steel instruments. Fear leapt into Sarah's eyes. She was terrified of what he was going to do to her. 'Please don't hurt me,' she said in a tiny voice.

'Be quiet,' Matron snapped.

'Thank you, Matron. The workhouse has a duty to reform moral defectives so they learn to obey their betters.'

He stroked the cold metal along Sarah's inner thighs. She felt its heavy chill push aside her soft flesh and held her breath in terror. What was he going to do? Would he have to cut her to do his dreadful deed? But no, he put aside the metal; she felt it resting against her skin, and, oh dear Lord, stop him, his fingers soft and warm by comparison, pushed aside her flesh and stroked her, slowly back and forth. She quelled a protest of disgust that rose in her throat. What was he doing to her? She pressed her lips together to stop herself from crying out and looked pleadingly at Matron. But Matron did not care to watch what he was doing, she was concentrating on the high window and her grip on Sarah's arms was firm.

Sarah, her eyes filling with tears, turned to look at the doctor. His eyes were closed and a small, triumphant smile played around his lips as he continued to paw at her private area. At that moment she hated him with such a passion that she wanted to stab him with one of his own knives. She tried so hard to suppress her cries but a frantic squeak escaped her throat and her bottom was pressed so hard against the couch she thought her back would break.

His eyes opened suddenly and his evil smile widened a second before he lifted the edge of her workhouse chemise and lowered his head to look at her. Sarah thought she would die of shame. Is this what doctors did? Is this what well-off folk paid good money for? Now he was using both hands to push aside her thighs and then her intimate flesh. Again she pulled herself back into the couch, holding every muscle rigid. She wanted to kick out and scream and her legs ached with the effort of keeping them still. But she was pathetically grateful that he did not use any of those dreadful steel knives and things and her tears spilled out onto her cheeks. She looked up again at Matron but could not see her expression. Matron's face was turned away from the doctor and his instruments and she was staring out of the window with an expression of distaste on her lined face.

Suddenly he prodded more firmly and she felt a twinge. She squealed and jerked, pushing her feet along the couch. He looked up and glared at her, breathing heavily. Her bottom lip throbbed where she had been biting it so tightly. Then he stopped, straightened and took up a cloth to wipe his fingers. His face still held a small sneering smile and she noticed a tiny lick of spittle at the corner of his mouth.

'I have no doubt that she has lied about her virtue, Matron. She is not a maid and most definitely a moral defective. You must take great care that she does not corrupt others. I know that in your charge she will learn humility. See that she is never allowed near to any of the men, not even the master,' he paused, 'except, of course, myself. I am equipped by my vocation to rebuff the most tainted of her harlot's ways.'

'Very well, doctor. I – I am sorry she has treated you with such disrespect, sir. It will not happen again for I shall not spare the rod.'

The doctor smiled benignly at Matron. 'Excellent. I shall make it my duty to monitor her progress personally when I visit. The Board of Guardians will be most interested to hear of your success with the rectification of a moral defective.'

'Do you think I shall have success with this one? She is very wilful.'

'Of course you will, my dear Matron, with my help.'

'Oh, doctor,' Matron burbled. Her gratitude seemed to be overwhelming her. 'The master will be so pleased.'

'Yes, yes,' he muttered, taking his timepiece from his waistcoat pocket. It was gold, Sarah noticed. His smile lingered and she scowled at him but he did not notice. 'Good day, Matron.' He shut his black leather bag and hurried outside.

Matron threw a bundle of coarse-textured clothing at her and said, 'It's the wash house for you, my girl. And if I catch you as much as looking at any of the men over the wall in the yard you'll be in the punishment cell with your head shaved again. Now get dressed and looked sharp about it. You've wasted enough of my time already.'

Sarah struggled into her workhouse uniform. Her drawers were as coarse as the flour-sack chemise and the gown was fashioned of fabric that she had used for aprons at Meadow Hall. She thought miserably of the lovely soft gown she had worn only yesterday, and of the cruel woman who had ripped it to shreds. But she knew that she had had a narrow escape. That woman would have dressed her in silks and satins and painted her face like the others in her house, so that horrible old gentlemen, like the doctor, would pay to paw at her body.

Well, thought Sarah, if that was the price to pay for wearing a pretty gown, she'd rather have this workhouse garb any day. Except that it seemed to be no guarantee that so-called gentlemen would not take liberties with her body. The despicable, revolting doctor had done it for free. Danby had tried, too, she realised sadly. Were all men like that?

No, they weren't. From the way he looked at her, she knew Aidan had wanted her as well. But he hadn't tried to maul her; instead, he had betrayed her by bringing her here, and she would never forgive him for that. She felt depressed. She wanted to be back living in the woods again, pretending to be a boy. She'd felt safe there. Now she was a prisoner behind these high stone walls and judged to be a moral defective. It wasn't fair! Somehow she had to get out of here; she just had to.

Chapter 12

'Get a move on,' the washerwoman grumbled. 'It's cold out here.'

A gusty breeze blew around Sarah's ears. She had hoped to work up a warming sweat by pumping water, but the wintry weather kept her hands and feet chilled to the bone. Her nose felt as cold as ice. She had been set to the pump as soon as the doctor had left and she realised, with a heavy heart, that it was to be her daily task; all day and every day.

'I'm going as fast as I can,' she answered.

The pump was in the yard at the rear of the workhouse and she had a good view of the austere building that was now her home. Four rows of blank windows stared darkly at her as she laboured. A rear extension jutted out into the yard and linked with a high brick wall, separating the men from the women. She could hear the men at work on their side, breaking rocks and chopping wood. The single-storey wash house was built across the back of the yard, and smoke rose from its chimney stack.

'Well, it's not fast enough,' the washerwoman snapped.

Between the wash house and the pump, lines of washing were strung out between poles set in the clay ground. Dowdy inmates trudged in and out with buckets of water and baskets of wet sheets. Matron had told her that her first task in the morning and again after dinner was to pump the water needed to keep the workhouse going all day. A succession of silent women came out from the wash house to collect endless buckets full of icy water and take them indoors. Sarah's aching arms were trembling and she was hungry. Breakfast had been finished by the time the doctor had left and Matron hadn't offered her so much as a crust of bread before setting her to work.

'Do it yourself, then,' she retaliated, straightening up to stretch her back. She didn't know who she was speaking to except that it wasn't Matron. The women in here all looked the same to her, in their coarse ill-fitting gowns and dingy caps. Their faces were the same grey colour as their garb.

'Shut your mouth.' The washerwoman picked up a full bucket and tipped it over Sarah's feet. The freezing water splashed the edge of her skirt and seeped through the worn stitching and lacing of her workhouse boots, soaking already chilled feet. Her toes would never warm up now and she wondered how long it was to dinner time.

The next woman added her empty buckets to the line waiting to be filled. 'You're new, aren't you?'

'Who wants to know?' Sarah said without looking up.

'It won't do you any good being like that in here, ducks. There's a pecking order and you're at the bottom of it.'

Just like Meadow Hall, she thought. Only it was worse here, for her empty tummy rumbled.

'Anyway, you can slow down for me. I don't mind waiting.'

Sarah heaved a full bucket aside and shoved an empty one under the pump. 'You're the only one that does, then.'

'No, I'm not. There's others who want to see their bairns.'

'Why? Do they come out here?'

'No. The schoolroom is up in that middle bit on the third floor and my bairns look for me through the window.'

Sarah stopped pumping and gazed upwards. 'Whereabouts?'

The woman pointed. 'There. See?'

A small face appeared at the glass and a tiny hand waved. The woman raised both her arms to wave back and within seconds a cluster of tiny faces crowded against the glass. The woman called indoors and others rushed out to join her at the pump and gaze upwards at the schoolroom window, calling the names of their children.

A minute later the washerwoman who had tipped water over Sarah's feet came out and shouted, 'Get inside you lot or I'll fetch Matron.' At the same time an adult appeared in the schoolroom and the tiny faces melted away. The bleak wash house yard became quiet as quickly as it had come alive.

The woman who was waiting for her bucket stood quite still with tears in her eyes.

Sarah didn't resume her pumping. 'You'll see them at dinner time,' she said kindly.

The woman choked on a sob. 'No, I won't. They've taken them off me, all four of my little ones. That's what they do when you come in here. Your bairns aren't your own any more. They belong to the workhouse.'

'That can't be right.' Sarah had never known a family of her own but it seemed to be one of the best things you could have, because you could look out for each other. At one time she had thought Aidan and Danby had been a family to her and she had liked that. To have your family taken away from you by strangers didn't seem very nice at all. 'You're their mother. What about their father? Doesn't he have a say?'

'He died. That's why I had to come here. Matron says if I can't look after them I can't have them.'

'But they're your children!'

She shook her head. 'Not here. The guardians own them now.' Tears trickled down her face.

Sarah didn't know what to say. She put her arm around the woman's shoulders. 'You won't be here for ever.' But she wondered how anyone could get out of the workhouse if they had no family and no money. The woman leaned against her, trying to stifle her sobs. 'What's your name?' Sarah asked.

'Maggie.'

'Don't cry, Maggie. You don't want your children to see you crying.'

Maggie raised her head. 'Are they at the window again?'

'I can't see them now. You look worn out. Shall I carry your buckets for you?'

'Oh no, Matron gets cross if we don't pull our weight.'

'She's not here to see.'

'Someone might tell her and you'll get into trouble.'

Sarah picked up two buckets full of water. 'Come on, Matron doesn't like me anyway.'

Maggie wiped the tears from her face. 'She doesn't like any of us. She doesn't like this place. I don't think she even likes the master and he's her husband.'

'She seems partial to the doctor.'

Maggie managed a smile. 'Dear Lord, yes! You'd think he was Prince Albert himself the way she fusses and fawns around him. I can't stand him meself. He makes my skin crawl. I wish we still had the old apothecary to see to us. Has this new 'un been to see you, then? You haven't got something nasty, have you?'

'No, I haven't! He was already here and she asked him to look at me.' Sarah decided not to tell Maggie what he had really done to her. 'But he thought I'd brought in the plague or something.'

'If the doctor was already here, somebody must be badly. One of the old 'uns, I expect.'

'Are they the loonies?'

'They're not loony. Loonies go to the asylum. One of the men has the falling sickness but the old folk here are just, well, just old. What's your name?'

'Sarah.'

'Watch that sour-faced washerwoman, the one who tipped water over you.'

'Who is she?'

'Mrs Turnbull.'

Sarah grinned. 'She would too.'

'Would what?'

'Turn a bull around. One look at her and he'd run for his life.'

'Be careful you don't make an enemy of her, me ducks. She reports everything to Matron.' Maggie picked up her filled buckets. 'Thanks for carrying these for me, Sarah. You have a kind heart.'

'It's nothing. I have a younger back,' Sarah responded. 'What time's dinner?'

'Half past eleven. We'll all come out and cross the yard so just join the queue.'

Sarah went back outside to the pump and picked up another empty bucket from the line. When she had finished, Matron took her through a dark passage in the main building to a smaller yard at the front of the workhouse. Another line of buckets, this time slop buckets from the chamber pots, was standing by the privy in the corner of the yard. The front yard was smaller than the back and where the women took their recreation, when they were allowed. Matron barked orders and left her to it. The master watched from his bay window on the first floor. He could see into the men's and women's front yards from there.

She finished her task and was about to use the privy herself when a stream of children led by a neatly dressed woman in a plain grey gown with white collar and cuffs came clattering across the yard for the privy.

'Let the children go first,' the woman commanded loudly.

Sarah stood back to allow them to crowd in front of her and one or two began pushing in the queue and squabbling. 'Wait your turn,' she muttered, putting a steadying hand on the shoulder of one the larger girls. 'Let the little ones go first.'

'Why?' the girl demanded.

'Because they might wet themselves if you don't. Can't you remember what it was like to be little?'

The woman in charge clapped her hands. 'Stop talking at the front. Who are you? What are you doing here at this time of day? Women's recreation is after dinner.'

Sarah explained and the woman's tense features softened. She had an olive skin with brown eyes and a plain face made more severe by the dark plaits worn around her head.

'I see. Very well, Meadow.'

Sarah stood back silently and the sound of the boys in the next yard drifted over the wall. She noticed one of the little girls struggling to hitch up her skirts as she waited in line. Her tiny hands were too small to hold the bunched petticoat and it kept falling down at the back. She bent down and helped by tying loose knots in the coarse material to keep it out of the way.

'Will you do mine, miss?' another asked and a small group collected around her. Sarah was flattered by being addressed as 'miss'. She felt important even though she knew she wasn't. She was aware that the woman was watching her but she didn't tell her to stop. As the little girls came out, Sarah undid the knots and smoothed down their skirts. 'Is she your teacher?' Sarah whispered. A little girl nodded and an older one added, 'She's Miss Green.'

Sarah smiled at Miss Green, who stared back and said, 'You can help me with the little ones on the stairs. They take so long to climb them.'

Sarah wasn't surprised. The stairs were too steep for the tiniest legs to span the risers so she took to holding the smaller girls by their arms and swinging them up. The bigger ones counted the steps and made a game of it. Sarah could count up to twenty; she had learned how to at Meadow Hall, but these children could count higher than that, for the schoolroom was three floors up, which meant six flights of narrow stone steps. Sarah stood in the doorway as the children sat quietly on benches and their teacher gave out slates and chalk. Miss Green looked at her and said. 'That will be all, Meadow. Run and find Matron now.'

Sarah was reluctant to leave. She wanted to join them in the schoolroom even though they were all much younger than she was. There were so many children and she wondered which ones were Maggie's bairns.

'Thank you, Meadow,' Miss Green said pointedly. 'You'll find Matron in the master's office down the corridor.'

Sarah tried to dispel her disappointment. She felt the same way that she had about the housemaids at Meadow Hall when they wore their neat afternoon dresses with lace trim, like Miss Green's, and their pretty white aprons and caps. But it wasn't Miss Green's appearance that she coveted; it was the children in the schoolroom. She envied their learning and wished she could better herself – perhaps then she could leave this horrible place.

Chapter 13

'You and you. The rest of you can go.'

Aidan stood in line on the canal wharf with other hopefuls seeking work. He was head and shoulders above the others and this worked in his favour. He sympathised with the men who were turned away, but a day's work meant a day's pay and, if he found favour with the overseer, more to come.

The man in charge had the physique of a blacksmith, and had driven two shires pulling an empty coal cart. He beckoned Aidan over. 'You. Yes, you, the new boy.'

Aidan didn't think he was a boy, but he was clearly the youngest of the three. 'Yes, sir,' he responded.

'My name's Thorpe and this is Jed. He's in charge and you follow his orders, he knows what to do.'

'Yes, sir.'

The canal brought in coal from local mines to the town's forges and manufactories, which were strung out along the banks of the sludgy waterway. Aidan would have preferred to be further away from town but this was where the labour was needed. Iron-smelting and glass-blowing furnaces were hungry for coal and a barge-load was waiting to be unloaded.

'Get yourself onto the barge and start shovelling, lad.'

Aidan took off his jacket, folded it on top of his backpack and rolled up his sleeves, exposing his forearms, strong and sinewy from working at his anvil.

Jed looked at them with approval. 'Have you done this before?'

'No, sir.'

'You don't have to call me "sir". I'm not the one who gives the orders. Mr Thorpe is.' Jed inclined his head towards Thorpe's receding figure. 'He makes crucible steel.'

'I've heard of that. It's supposed to be the best there is.'

'It is. You'll see some if you come back tomorrow when we bring the ingots down for loading.'

Aidan's spirits lifted at the prospect of more work tomorrow. 'Where do they go?'

'Sheffield. We'll be sending them there on the railway soon. Have you seen it?'

'Not yet. Will the coal come in that way too?'

'I doubt it. Our coal comes from local pits. We've no railways planned for them yet 'cos we've got the navigation. Let's get this lot off the water. I hope your back's as strong as your arms. You keep filling the buckets and hook them on the crane. I'll crank the winch and yon fella'll unload onto the cart.'

'Right, Jed.'

After two hours, Aidan's back was screaming. Coal dust lined his mouth and stung his eyes. He felt weak from hunger and thirst but he had made inroads into the mountain of coal on the barge. 'I need some water,' he called. 'There's a canteen in my pack.'

Jed threw it over to him and he emptied it in one go.

'You can slow down,' Jed said. 'You'll not last the day going at it like that.'

Aidan nodded and took the advice. His hunger receded and he developed an easier working rhythm that seemed to satisfy Jed. As the morning wore on he noticed a line of women gathering outside the gates of a big ironworks yard. They wore shawls around their heads or shoulders and carried baskets over their arms. He heard a loud clanging from a bell inside the yard and a stream of working men appeared, ruddy faced and covered in smuts.

'Dinner,' Jed called, and left off turning the crank handle.

Aidan clambered over the remaining coals in the barge and straddled the gap between the barge and the wharf. He had nothing to eat in his pack and his canteen was empty. His mouth watered at the smell of hot soup and pies that wafted over from the women's baskets as their menfolk devoured their dinners, sitting on the ground with their backs against the high ironworks wall. He thought of the workhouse wall and Sarah and how much he wanted to see her, imagine her bringing him his dinner in the middle of his working day.

'Over here, Mrs Thorpe,' Jed called, waving his arm at an older woman with a young girl carrying a basket. 'Have you got any money?' he asked Aidan.

'Not until I get paid.'

'I'll lend you the price of your dinner, then, and take it from your pay at the end of this shift. What have you got today, Mrs Thorpe?'

'I've made mutton patties with leeks, and bread pudding.'

'Will that do you?'

Aidan nodded hungrily and raised his empty canteen. 'Where can I fill this?'

Mrs Thorpe answered. 'There's a pump over there, up by the glassworks, but I wouldn't drink from it. Wellgate spring is the best water round here.'

Aidan knew where that was and it was a long walk.

Jed said, 'You can share my canteen for now.'

Mrs Thorpe handed two warm patties to Aidan. 'What's your name?'

'Aidan Beckwith, ma'am.'

'Where are you from?'

'My folks came from the East Riding but there's more work to be had here.'

'Aye, you're right about that. My daughter'll fill your canteen for you if you'll let her.'

'Thank you. I'm much obliged to you, ma'am.'

The young girl scampered off to the spring. 'She won't be long.' Her mother smiled.

'I need lodgings for the night if you know of any, Mrs Thorpe.'

'Well, not at my house, I'm afraid. I've an ailing husband and a little 'un to look after, as well as my baking. But there's plenty'll take you in if you clean some of that pit dust off before you ask. You can use the pump for that.'

'Thanks.'

Mrs Thorpe picked up her basket of hot food and continued on her way.

'I'll give you a couple of addresses,' Jed volunteered as they ate their dinner.

'Will you have me back here tomorrow?'

'That's up to Mr Thorpe. Look, he's here. He's brought another empty cart and he'll take away the full one.'

'Is he related to Mrs Thorpe? They have the same eyes.'

'He's her son. Done well for hessen, he has. He runs the Bowes Iron and Steel Works.'

'Whereabouts is that?'

'You go up the alley and into town. That's why we need carts for the coal.'

'He got some fine horse blood pulling 'em,' Aidan commented.

'Aye. He looks after 'em well. He's one o' the good 'uns, is Mr Thorpe.'

Aidan nodded in unconscious agreement. He wiped his mouth with the back of his gritty hand and bit into his patty feeling better already. If he had paid work and a roof over his head he'd soon get Sarah out of the workhouse. It would take time to get regular labouring and lodgings decent enough for her to live in but this was a start. 'Do the coal barges come in every day?' he asked.

Jed laughed. 'Have you seen the size o' them furnaces over

yon wall? You want to go and have a look. Coal-eating ogres, they are.'

When he had eaten and drank, Aidan wandered over to the open gates where the men were drifting back to work. The furnaces were giant brick chimneys chucking out smut and smoke that drifted right across town. So this is how the iron was made, he reflected. Most of it went for the new railways and some was made into steel that was good for knives and wood-fashioning tools. Aidan preferred iron. He was fascinated by what he could do with it when it was hot enough to bend and hammer into the shapes that filled his imagination. It gave him an itch to get back to an anvil. That was his dream; to have his own smithy and make more interesting artefacts than hinges and coffin handles.

This town had big houses with rich folk that had a need to show off their wealth with fancy iron and brass on their doors and boundaries. He gazed up the high wood-and-iron gates of the ironworks. They were substantial enough; serviceable but not beautiful. He could make beautiful wrought-iron gates with brass knobs on if he had his own anvil. He didn't know if he would ever achieve his dream, but he'd give it his best, his very, very best.

The bell clanged again as the last man let go of his wife's hand and returned to the furnace yard, closing the heavy gate behind him. Aidan climbed back onto the barge and picked up his shovel. As he laboured and sweated in the bottom of the barge, he dreamed of the life he would have as a smithy with Sarah by his side, and hardly noticed the afternoon go by. He chewed his lip as he thought of her in the workhouse. He hated that he'd been forced to put her there, but at least he knew she was safe from Jackson and the like until he could look after her properly.

Daylight was fading when the bell went again, this time signalling the end of the working day. Mr Thorpe came down on foot to drive the final cartload of coal away. He was a tall, handsome fellow with dark brown hair; he was wearing what seemed to Aidan to be Sunday best clothes but he didn't seem to mind a bit of coal dust on them. Thorpe jumped down from the driver's seat. 'Good work, Jed. Hold the horses for me while I pay off the men.'

Aidan took the coins. There were more than he expected. 'Thank you, sir.' Close up, he didn't look old enough to be an ironmaster; thirty maybe.

'What's your name, fellow?' Thorpe asked Aidan.

Aidan told him.

'I've been watching you work. Have you somewhere to stay the night?'

'Jed's got an address for me.'

'Good. There's another day's work for you tomorrow. It's an early start, mind.'

'Yes, sir. I'll be here.'

Mr Thorpe raised his head. 'Come on, Jed. I want this unloaded before the end of the late shift.'

Jed clambered into the cart brandishing a scrap of writing paper at Aidan. 'I've put the lodging houses on here but I never thought to ask if you could read.'

'Yes, I can. Where are they?'

'Mosbrough way, where the new railway is. Watch your back after dark over there. Get yourself cleaned up and indoors for the night as soon as you can and I'll see you here at daybreak.'

'Right, Jed.' He clicked the coins in his palm. 'Thank you, sir.' He hurried towards the pump. He had a piece of soap and a drying cloth in his backpack but neither had much effect on the coal dust, which stuck steadfastly to his skin. He did the best he could and set off to find some food and a bed for the night. There were several workmen like himself at the pump but he did not notice two well-dressed men watching him from the shadows of an alley. If he had, he might have recognised them.

He was nearing his destination when he heard a familiar sound coming from an alehouse. Above the voices and laughter he recognised the lively, high-pitched sound of a whistle. The tunes reminded him of recent happier times when he'd listened often

161

enough to Danby practising them. They hadn't parted friends but a pint of ale would slake his thirst and he was curious to see if it was Danby in the alehouse – he doubted Danby had gone far. He changed direction to find out.

The front saloon was crowded with working men and at first he couldn't see who was playing. The tunes came from a corner by the counter that separated the barrels from their customers. A short and very round man was filling tankards and lining them up on the counter. Over the drinkers' heads Aidan saw the dancer, a pretty, dark-haired lass holding her skirts above her ankles so the audience could see the frilled edges of her petticoats as she danced a jig to the music. When she moved he could see that it *was* Danby playing, sitting behind her, his eyes following the dancing girl as she moved about.

The dancer's boots clicked and clattered on the stone-flagged floor. Her gown had a bodice cut so low that her bosoms nearly bounced out of it. Danby finished playing and a workman grabbed hold of the dancer and attempted to kiss her. She squealed and protested but Danby made no move to protect her. Instead the man behind the counter picked up a long stout rod and thwacked the workman across his back shouting, 'Get your hands off my daughter!'

The man released her, and the dancer smiled saucily at Danby, who smiled back at her. She moved to stand next to him and Aidan noticed Danby's hand creep up the back of her skirt where, out of sight of her father, he guessed Danby was squeezing her ample rear. It hadn't taken Danby long to find a woman! How right he had been not to let Sarah go off with him.

Aidan thought perhaps this alehouse lass suited Danby and decided against showing himself. He left as silently as he had arrived and resumed his journey. It was quite dark now and the only light that fell across his path came from candlelit windows in the brick terraces that formed the streets of Mosbrough. Two men emerged from the shadows where they had been waiting and fell into step either side of him.

162

Surprised, he turned to speak. His mouth opened but no sound came out. He did not need to see the man's face. The man's size and shape was distinctive. It was Jackson's burly barman and Aidan's heart began to thump with fear.

'Where is she?' He turned to his other side to see Jackson.

'Who?' he prevaricated.

The burly man punched Aidan hard in his middle, taking his breath away and making his knees buckle. 'Answer the man,' he said.

'I – I –' Aidan struggled to form the words. 'She's gone,' he breathed hoarsely. 'She – she took the carrier out of here.'

The man hit him again, this time in his back making him wince with pain and cry out.

'Tell us where she is and we'll let you live.'

This was no idle threat. He had no doubt they would kill him if he didn't tell them. His only chance was to run. He groaned and whispered hoarsely, 'Let me get my breath.'

In the seconds that followed his mind raced. He didn't know the area so he would have to trust to luck. Best retrace his steps to the pump where others might help him. He inhaled, ignored the pain searing through his body and ducked, twisting on his heel. He ran like the wind into the darkness.

He thought he'd shaken them off. They knew the terrain but he was faster on his feet. He slithered through muddy, gritty streets lined with small brick houses. Would anyone take him in if he pounded on a door? He'd lose precious seconds by asking and only involve an innocent family in Jackson's terror. Where was that pump? It was near the canal and this way surely? He was lost and he was tiring. The men pursuing him with such determination had not shovelled coal all day on the wharf. His legs were turning to jelly and his breath came in painful rasps. Keep going; don't give up; don't let them catch you.

Suddenly he was faced with a brick wall, high and wide, but he'd passed an alley and he darted back and disappeared down it, losing a few more precious seconds. There were long gardens either side of him and in front the canal glistened with a still, oily sheen in the blackness. He clambered over a garden fence half falling into the young crops and staggered towards the back door, beating it with his fists. Hurry, hurry up and let me in. Please.

He heard Jackson pound down the alley after him and saw the glimmer of a candle through the cottage's kitchen window. A frightened face, ghoulish in the dimness, stared at him as the two men bore down on him. The face disappeared and with it his last vestige of hope.

'I don't know where she is,' he croaked wearily, sinking to his knees.

But it did not help him and he knew it wouldn't. He had crossed Jackson and he would likely kill him anyway, even if he did tell him. They took hold of his arms, one each, and dragged him down the path through the gate and onto the towpath. He was exhausted, his reserves of energy spent, but this couldn't be the end, he wouldn't let it, and he struggled. He kicked and punched when he could, but there were two of them. They punched and kicked him back until he welcomed the senseless, painless oblivion of death, the crimson of his own blood in his eyes turned darker and darker until all was blackness and then – and then nothing.

It was dark, there was no blue sky or fluffy white clouds so he must be in hell. But hell was hot and this was cold and wet, very cold and very wet, seeping everywhere – in his ears, up his nose and filling his mouth. Aidan tried to move his lips and couldn't. He tried to open his eyes and couldn't. Something heavy was tugging on his legs and pulling him down, down into the cold wetness of this special hell. The chill revived his reason. He didn't deserve hell, and like a dog he fought to claw his way up. His arms moved and he heard a splash. He inhaled and took in water, oily cold water that made him splutter and cough, and pain seared through his chest. He didn't know where he was or why he was here but he was sinking, drowning, dying. He made a feeble effort to swim but his legs would not do as he wanted and his arms were as weak as a child's. He must, somehow, keep his head up. Why were his feet such dead weights on the end of his legs? His hands were numb and his mind was drifting. No, he was drifting. He was on his back and – and yes, he was in the canal. Hell was the canal. He mustn't sink, he mustn't drown, he mustn't . . .

His consciousness returned slowly. He realised that he couldn't feel his feet and it was his boots that were dragging him down. Where he wasn't numb with cold, he hurt. His head wanted to burst and every breath he took filled his lungs with pain, but he knew he was alive and he had to stay alive. As he drifted he used his weakened arms to paddle his useless body to the side of the canal. He felt the cold, rough iron sides and inched his way along, willing his tortured muscles to move. He didn't even know if he was floating in the right direction but eventually he felt and gripped a rope, a thick mooring rope, trailing in the water, and clung to it for life itself.

He wrapped it round his body, pulling it as tight as his ebbing strength allowed and tied a clumsy knot across his chest. If only he could pull himself out! But he was too weak and in too much pain. He must stay conscious and hold onto the rope until morning. But his injuries were too severe and his remaining strength was going. His mind drifted again. Perhaps this was the end after all. 'I'm sorry I let you down,' he breathed, 'I am so, so sorry . . .' He saw a pair of serious hazel eyes staring at him from beneath a shaggy crop of auburn hair. He didn't want to go, he didn't want to die. He placed his hands over the knot on his chest as the blackness engulfed him.

'Do I get a bed for the night or not?' Danby asked the landlord. He knew that Rose had taken a fancy to him but he studiously avoided looking at her. He addressed her corpulent father who was counting his night's takings at the alehouse counter.

'Aye. I've never seen so many in here when it's not been a Saturday. They stayed longer an' all.'

'A tune or two cheers folk up.'

'Where are you from, lad?'

'Around these parts.'

'You're a South Riding man, then?'

'Aye.'

'Will you take a drink with me?'

'Don't mind if I do. Playing always give me a thirst.'

'Draw a couple of tankards, Rose, and fetch us summat to eat from the back.'

Danby watched Rose's swaying hips as she obeyed.

Her father locked his takings away in a metal box and placed it on the counter in front of Danby. 'You can bed down in here for the night. I've an iron bar across the door to the back so don't go getting any ideas about this.' He rattled the box and added, 'Or her.'

Danby's face stayed serious. 'I noticed how you saw off one of the drinkers earlier. Is she spoken for?'

'Eh you, mind your own business. I said you could stay the night for bringing in more customers, that's all.'

'Well, I could clean up for you in the morning,' Danby suggested.

'Rose does that.'

'You could do with help shifting the barrels, Father,' Rose volunteered as she set down two heavy stoneware plates of cold pork pie and pickled vegetables.

'Just you keep your tongue between your teeth,' her father barked. 'You're as bad as your ma were.' He sank his teeth into a solid piece of cold pie, chewed and swallowed greedily and followed it with a large onion.

'Nice pie,' Danby commented as he copied the landlord. 'Aren't you having any, Rose?'

'Mine's in the back.'

'I told you to keep quiet. Fetch a pallet and blanket for the lad and then get yourself off to bed,' her father ordered.

'Oh.' She seemed disappointed. She dragged in the wooden bed base for Danby, wiggling her ample bottom as she bent over to place it in the middle of the room. 'I'll say goodnight, then, Father.'

Her father grunted a response and took another mouthful of food. Danby used this distraction to look at Rose, smile and wink. She grinned back at him and disappeared through the door to the back.

'Does your daughter sing as well as she dances? This is a big room you've got here. You've space for a bit of singing, like. That'll bring in your customers.'

The landlord was interested. He finished his large helping of food and, as Rose had given Danby far too much to eat, he scoffed his as well, then belched loudly. 'We'll see how a regular Saturday night goes first.'

'Just a Saturday? I – I was looking for more than that and – and, well I need lodgings an' all.'

'Aye, well, I could do with a bit of young muscle around here. But I'll not 'ave you in the back.'

Danby took that as an offer of work and didn't push for more answers. The landlord was a prickly individual and easily crossed. No wonder folk had stopped drinking at his alehouse. But it wasn't the work that had attracted Danby to this place. It was Rose, and she knew it.

He was asleep when a noise woke him. The fire had burned out but it wasn't cold. Overhead he heard deep vibrating snores from the landlord. The door to the back opened slowly and he smiled to himself. He'd taken off his boots and trousers in anticipation. A moment later he was lifting the blanket as an invitation for Rose to join him. She placed her candle on a chair and slipped off her felt shoes.

'Your father'll kill me,' Danby whispered. He really believed he might and the excitement fired his passion.

'He won't know. Listen to him.' She raised her eyes towards

the vibrations above. 'He sleeps like the dead after a skinful of ale.'

Danby propped himself up on one elbow and gazed at her as she snuggled down beside him. She looked so virginal in her long white nightgown that he hesitated for a second. Virgins could turn funny on you afterwards. But he reckoned that Rose was no virgin despite her father's domineering ways.

'Blow out the candle,' she said.

'No. I want to look at you.'

She smiled at him and ran her fingers through her long black hair curling over her shoulders. He was aching for her already and pushed down his under-drawers. She lifted her long night-gown, bunched it around her waist and spread her legs for him. Oh, he couldn't wait! He'd do his best to make it last for her, but she was so luscious he didn't know if he could. He kissed her briefly, but his hunger for her body pulled him. He pushed the nightgown further up then covered her breasts with his hands. He squeezed and kneaded them, then bent his head to let his tongue search for her nipples, allowing his burgeoning erection to brush the side of her thigh.

A shaky half laugh rattled in her throat. His hands followed the contours of her curves, up and down, as he nibbled and toyed with her breasts; and then her soft secret areas, moist and ready for him. She groaned contentedly and her back arched, thrusting herself at him, knees splayed to welcome him.

Every time he did it he marvelled at the thrill of it. God wouldn't have made it so exciting if He hadn't meant him to do it a lot. Sometimes he felt he couldn't get enough of it; he was always on the lookout for a willing lass so he didn't have to pay a whore. He couldn't go without; it wasn't in his nature. And Rose seemed to like it as much as he did. He drove into her, raising himself on his hands to get deeper inside her, and listened to her appreciative whimpers as he did.

She loved it. He knew she would; some were like that and they were the ones for him. She raised her knees until they were nearly under her chin and held them there with her hands, crying more loudly, so noisily that he lifted a hand and placed it over her mouth. What if her father heard them? He couldn't stop now, and neither, he realised, could Rose. He pumped away at her and gave himself up to his own enjoyment. Oh, it was good with her. Better than the farmer's wife he'd had during the harvest and that was saying something.

He lay flaccidly on top of Rose's softly rounded body, sweating slightly. She had crossed her ankles over his strong back so he couldn't withdraw and they lay entwined in a warm wet comfort until their breathing had subsided. He was smiling to himself in the dark. Rose knew what she was doing. He'd felt it inside her, like he had in the farmer's wife and she'd told him what it was. A vinegar sponge to stop the bairns coming, and he recognised the sharp acid smell mixed up with the more familiar welcoming scent of a woman on heat. He inhaled sharply through his nose.

'You've done this before, haven't you?' he asked.

'Once or twice,' she answered.

'Liar,' he responded.

'Do you mind?'

He glanced at her smooth throat and her ample curves, free of restricting corsets. She was so luscious, he thought, like a ripe plum, soft and squashy, with her plump breasts and round bottom that was a pleasure to hold and squeeze. How could I mind, he thought?

'Not as long as you have no more while I'm around.'

'You'll have no fear of that,' she answered and reached up to kiss his lips, turning to allow her drooping breasts to brush lightly across his smooth muscled chest.

But fear excited Danby. It fired his blood and the knowledge that Rose's belligerent father was sleeping a few feet above him magnified his thrill. The snoring faltered and the bedstead creaked. Then all went quiet until the heavy breathing grew louder and settled into a familiar wheezing snort.

'Do it again,' Rose whispered in his ear.

'Give us a minute or two first,' he answered.

He always took longer the second time but he knew Rose would like that. She didn't get bored like some did, telling him to hurry up and finish. Rose was perfect for him. Perfect. Her father's alehouse was in a convenient place amongst the iron- and glassworks' furnaces. He and Rose'd bring in more trade of a Saturday night and he'd soon make a few useful friends. He was good at that. Rose was already eating out of his hand and he'd make sure her father's life was easier from now on.

He'd really fallen on his feet, so to speak, this time, he thought, as he eased apart their sweating bodies.

Chapter 14

'It must be dinner time by now,' Sarah muttered.

It was nearing the end of Sarah's first day and Matron had moved her to inside the wash house to tackle the worst of the stained washing that had been soaking in hot soda. Her aching back screamed as the bent over a deep vat of cooling water and pounded heavy, soggy calico on a washboard. She had thought that nothing could be worse than scrubbing floors at Meadow Hall. But this was. The clothes had been heavily soiled and the smell of the privy wafted up even after soaking. She needed soap to lighten her load.

At least she had warmed up. She wiped the sweat off her forehead with the back of her wrist and looked around at the other women. Maggie was standing at the next vat, twisting and turning the soaking sheets with a wooden dolly. Her cheeks were pink from the heat of effort and Sarah felt hers must be the same. She straightened up carefully to stretch her back.

The cavernous room was full of steam from coppers and tubs, and above her head wooden racks and rope lines of rinsed linen dripped onto her head. She noticed for the first time that all the other women bent to their tasks were older, some considerably so. She consoled herself with the thought that younger, stronger women were easier to place and surely, *surely,* she would be out of here soon.

Matron was nowhere in sight and Sarah put down her scrubbing brush. 'Why don't we use soap?' she asked Maggie.

'We do but Matron keeps it under lock and key because she has to buy it and labour comes free in the workhouse. I've got a piece in my pocket, though. We'll share it, if you like.'

Sarah blew out her cheeks. 'Oh, thank you. Is there as much washing as this every day?'

'Wait 'til you see how many we are at dinner now. And then there's the menfolk on the other side, and the children upstairs. Whole families come in nowadays. Poor souls can't even afford enough bread to eat. Haven't you heard about the price of corn?'

Sarah had. Harvests of crops and potatoes had failed, and people were starving to death in Ireland. A door open and closed and a murmur of 'she's back' went around the steaming tubs. Maggie showed her the piece of soap in her pocket and winked.

'Where did you get it from?' Sarah whispered.

'Mrs Turnbull has soap and I cut a bit off hers when she's not looking.'

'Well, some of these stains'll never come out. Can't you put some on my board?'

'Go on then.' Maggie leaned over Sarah's board and rubbed the small bar up and down the ridged wooden surface. As she did so, the soap slipped from her reddened fingers and plopped into the water.

'Oh no!' Maggie breathed.

'I'll get it for you.' Sarah pushed her rolled-up sleeves higher, stood on tiptoe and reached down into the tub, but her arms were not long enough to reach the bottom. Hastily she grabbed at a pair of wooden tongs hooked over the edge and swished them around. She thought she had located it and desperately tried to pick it up, but it slipped from the tongs and all she retrieved was a bundle of soaking bedsheets.

'Let me have a go,' Maggie urged. 'Quick, she's coming over here.'

As Sarah shook off the linen and handed the tongs over to her, Matron loomed between them.

'What is going on here?'

'Nothing, Matron,' Sarah answered.

'Then why are you gossiping instead of working?'

'I was showing her how best to scrub, Matron,' Maggie answered.

'And what are you doing here? I put you over there.' Matron peered into Sarah's vat. 'Is that soap on your washboard?'

No one answered her. She raised her voice. 'Well, where is it?'

'I – I,' Maggie stuttered. Sarah kicked her gently but she was too late. Maggie went on, 'I had some left over from the shirts, matron.'

'I took it off her,' Sarah added. 'The sheets weren't coming clean. I thought—'

'*Thought?* You *thought?* You aren't here to think, Meadow, you are here to mend your ways. The doctor is right about you. You are a troublemaker. Give me the soap this instant.'

'I can't—' Sarah began.

Maggie gave her a gentle nudge and shook her head slightly.

'You will give me the soap this minute,' Matron ordered.

'I – I've dropped it,' Sarah continued.

'Pick it up, then.' Matron spoke slowly and deliberately and Sarah could tell that she was very angry.

'In the tub,' Sarah added.

'My good soap is in this tub? How dare you be so wasteful? Your wilful actions are to blame for this.' Matron's voice had risen to a shrill cry. 'You will learn discipline, Meadow.' She tipped back her head as though speaking to the racks of washing on the ceiling. 'Fetch me the cane!'

There was a still silence for what seemed like an age until Matron opened her mouth again. 'I said—,' She stopped as there was a scurrying behind her and a light cane appeared from nowhere. She whipped it across the air showing how flexible it was.

Sarah swallowed and wondered where Matron would apply her punishment.

'Hold out your hands!'

Slowly she lifted her arms, dreading what was to come. Mrs Watson had cuffed her round the head frequently but never used a cane.

'Palms up!'

Sarah turned her wrists, exposing reddened skin, soft from scrubbing, and she flinched as the cane seared across her raw flesh, not once but five times. The pain throbbed as Matron barked, 'Get back to work, all of you.' She marched out, her boots ringing on the stone floor.

Maggie looked contrite but did not utter a word and scurried back to her own tasks. No one spoke or even looked at Sarah. There were raised wheals on her palms where the cane had struck and tiny spots of blood welled along the swelling. She tried to curl her fingers but they refused to move. She gazed at her hands, quelling her mounting anger at such a barbarous punishment for simply dropping the soap.

But this was not Meadow Hall, where supplies were always plentiful even if they were never paid for. This was the workhouse where thrift was a virtue and wastefulness was wicked. She looked at the cooling vat of dingy water and equally dingy sheets that she must pound on the rubbing board to clean. She would have more tomorrow. It came in every day, an endless task to occupy the unfortunate women who were selected for the laundry. It was, Sarah realised, her fate unless she could do something to escape.

A loud voice murmured, 'Get on with it, Meadow.'

She didn't know who said it, but she guessed it was Mrs Turnbull. She glanced around. All the women had their heads bowed, intent on their work. Carefully, she put her stinging hands in the water. The soda magnified her pain so much that she had to press her lips together hard and flare her nostrils to stop herself crying out. She forced her failing fingers to gather up the sodden linen. There were tears in her eyes, but a determination was setting behind them. She had to get out of here. She didn't know how yet, but she would. And the first thing she would do would be to get her revenge on Aidan for bringing her here. She didn't know how she would do that either, but she'd think of something.

At dinner time she filed across the yard with the other women and climbed a flight of stone steps between bare brick walls to the day room where she collected a bowl of soup and a piece of bread that was the main meal of the day. Everyone was hungry.

'Is there any more bread?' Sarah asked Maggie.

'There's never enough to go round as flour is dear to buy. It's not so bad on the days we get meat in the broth.'

'What days are they?'

'Sundays, Tuesdays, Thursdays and Saturdays.'

'Tomorrow, then?'

'We sometimes have dripping at tea-time.'

Sarah thought of the plentiful food at Meadow Hall. 'I used to have bread and dripping for breakfast.'

'We only ever get gruel in the morning here. It's too thin for my liking but at least it's hot.'

It won't have molasses in it either, Sarah reflected, as she remembered her time in the stables. The horses at Meadow Hall were better fed than workhouse inmates.

After dinner they had half an hour of fresh air in the recreation yard at the front of the workhouse where most of the time was spent queuing for the privy in the corner.

Maggie stood beside her. 'I'm sorry about your hands, Sarah,' she said. 'It was good of you to take the blame like that.'

'It was my fault, asking you for soap. I didn't know Matron was so mean.' But I should have realised, she thought.

'I wish I'd had your courage,' Maggie responded.

'It hasn't got me very far though, has it? Why is the Matron so bad-tempered all the time?'

175

'She never has enough of us to do everything.'

Sarah yawned. 'What time's tea? I'm ready for my bed. Will I have to share one with a loony?'

'They'll be in another dormitory. I'll ask if you can share with me, if you want.'

'Matron won't let me. She doesn't like me.'

'I'll say I don't mind.'

'Ta. I'm ever so hungry.'

'We all are. Don't try and take more than they give you or else you'll make some real enemies in here.'

It seemed to Sarah that it didn't matter what she did she'd make enemies, so why bother? Give a dog a bad name and it'll turn into one. Life couldn't get any worse for her so she may as well make the best of if by fair means or foul.

And it seemed to her that foul means got the best results.

'Can you see that new lad anywhere, Jed?'

Daniel Thorpe wanted more men like Aidan Beckwith and Jed; hard working and tough, but they had to be reliable too. With increased demands for his steel and the new railways taking the Sheffield tools made from it across the country, and even across the world, he was hard pressed to keep up supply. He had the bank of crucible furnaces, but he needed more men to increase his output; strong men, like Aidan Beckwith.

'I can't say that I do, Mr Thorpe.'

'Pity. I thought he was the reliable sort.'

It was a fine morning but clouds were blocking the sunrise and there was a promise of rain to come. A bargeman was already stripping off an oiled canvas covering on his vessel. 'We need to get an early start before the weather turns,' Jed suggested. 'The three of us can do it.'

Daniel agreed. This bargeman was a trusted waterman for his valuable cargo and Daniel wanted it in Tinsley dock before night-fall. As the daylight strengthened, the three men worked together silently to unload the heavy ingots of crucible steel into the hold of the barge. After an hour the bargeman straightened to remove his cap and wipe his brow. 'There's summat in the water up by the crane,' he observed.

'I'd best tell the lock-keeper. He won't want it jamming the gates,' Jed answered.

'Aye. It's caught up on a rope but best heave it out.'

'What is it?' Daniel asked.

'I can't rightly say.' The bargeman grimaced. 'It's not a – it's not a body, is it?'

'I'll take a look.' Daniel put down his load of ingots and walked towards the floating bundle. Dear Lord, it was! There was a body floating in the canal. 'Jed! Over here! Quickly, man!'

The younger man sprinted over. 'Ugh. May the Heavens preserve us! Is he dead?'

'It looks like it. The rope's keeping him afloat. Give me a hand to haul him out.'

The two men laid flat on their stomachs to heave the sodden heap out of the water and between them rolled the body onto its back on the towpath. Dirty, gritty water streamed everywhere.

'Who it is, Mr Thorpe?'

'No idea. He's probably a drunk who fell in and couldn't climb out again.'

Jed wiped away pieces of twig and leaves. 'There's bruising on his face. He must have hit something on the way in.' He examined the sodden clothing and squeezed out some of the moisture. 'Do you know, sir, I think it's that Beckwith man. The one you took on yesterday. The jacket's his, I'm sure.'

'He didn't seem like the hard-drinking sort.'

'No, but he had to go over Mosbrough way for lodgings. He could have fallen in with a bad crowd.'

'Are you sure it's him?'

'Well, his face has had a battering from summat but the size of him looks the same. Big fellow, he was.'

Daniel gazed at the bruised and swollen face and, as he did, he detected a tiny movement of the lips. 'He's not dead, Jed! He's trying to say something. Is he breathing?'

Jed put his face against the man's mouth. 'I think he is. Only just, though.'

'You'd best fetch a horse and cart. Run up to the works and bring the supervisor and one of his early-shift men back with you. Quick as you can. We have to get him indoors.' He knelt down beside the still, sodden figure and said, 'Don't try to talk. You're in safe hands now. Just hang on, fellow. Don't give up.'

The man was freezing cold but he was breathing. Daniel wondered how long he had been in the water. He took off his own coat and waistcoat and laid them over Aidan's chest, examining his face closely.

The bargeman did the same. 'Do you know him?'

Daniel nodded. 'He did a day's work for me yesterday. His name is Aidan Beckwith.'

Aidan's lips moved again and he groaned.

'He's in a bad way,' the bargeman commented.

Jed returned within the hour and between them they lifted Aidan gently onto the cart and covered him with a horse blanket. He groaned some more as he was moved.

Daniel left the bargeman to finish loading his precious ingots. He turned to Jed. 'Let's take him home. As soon as we get there, fetch my horse from the stable and ride over to Fordham for the surgeon. Tell him it's urgent.'

'What about getting this fellow in the house, Mr Thorpe?'

Daniel hesitated. 'My furnace-men will help. Give me the reins.'

Chapter 15

Sarah surveyed the back yard of the workhouse. The gates were high wooden structures, with iron spikes on the top, that opened only to admit carrier carts and supplies. The wash house occupied most of the rear wall and its doors were always locked when they went in for tea at the end of the day.

All the other walls were too high to scale without a ladder, but the wash house wasn't and it had drainpipes and water butts to collect rainwater, just as the stables had at Meadow Hall. If she climbed on one of those she could reach the eaves, clamber over the roof and drop down the other side. She'd be free!

But she couldn't do it in daylight and everyone was locked in at night. She needed to hide somewhere at teatime so she'd be locked out of the main building. But where? There was nothing in the yard except the lines of washing and the pump, and – yes, that was it; she could empty one of the butts and hide in there until nightfall. Maggie would make an excuse for her if she was missed and Matron had so much to do she couldn't check on everybody. After dark, she could climb out and escape.

She chose an old butt in the shadiest corner and kicked at the rotten wood at the bottom of the barrel until the wood finally gave way and the water slowly drained away. It was already dusk when the tea bell clanged, and everyone rushed to finish their tasks. Sarah slipped outside and crouched in the shadows behind the butt. No one dallied crossing the yard. Matron was last. She locked the door and hurried off for her glass of ale with the master. Sarah glanced up at the rows of dark windows across the yard before sliding off the wooden lid and diving head first into the empty butt. Had she seen a glow, a movement at one of the third-floor windows or was it her imagination?

The butt wasn't totally empty. There was a good two inches of rainwater swilling around the bottom. She landed on her hands and brought her feet down quickly so she could turn and draw back the wooden lid. The cold water soaked into her boots making her shiver. It was worth it! Tonight she would be free!

Her body was stiff with cold and fear as she crouched in the puddle waiting for total silence and darkness. And when the night bell rang no one came to look for her. She'd done it! The lid clattered to the ground as she slid it away to climb out. It was harder than she thought as there was nowhere to put her feet and she had to heave herself up with numbed arms until she could get her chest over the edge, then a knee and then pull herself over the edge.

There were dim lights at some of the windows, which made it harder to see outside in the dark. Hurriedly she replaced the lid and clambered on top of it to grasp the iron guttering than ran along the front of the laundry roof. She had to lay spread-eagle on the slates to stop herself falling, and her wet boots slipped as she tried to push herself up towards the ridge.

Her heart was pounding as she reached the top and peered over the other side. Freedom! She glanced back. Surely someone had seen her by now? She hoped not. Days were long in the workhouse for inmates and wardens alike; the hard wooden benches and small fireplaces offered little comfort but they beckoned by nightfall.

On the other side it was a long way down from the roof;

higher than the stable window at Meadow Hall. But there was no going back for her now. She slithered carefully down the slates, dislodging one that fell with a crash onto the stones below. The ground sloped away making her drop look even further. She was shaking with anxiety. She had to go on; but she couldn't jump, though. Hang from the edge and just let go? But there was no iron gutter to cling to on this side. She inched along to where the laundry building joined a higher wall and reached over twisting herself so she could grip the top with her hands.

Her arms were stretching out of their sockets. Her fingers were slipping and she could no longer grip the stone. She closed her eyes and slid rapidly down the wall, landing heavily and painfully on the stony ground.

Her breath came in sharply as pain shot through her ankle. She rolled over and sat up, leaning forward to nurse her injury. All the use had gone out of her foot and she sat biting her lips to stop herself from crying out until, gradually, the tenderness eased. She unlaced her boot and eased her swollen ankle from its restrictions. She had not broken a bone, merely turned it as she fell. But it would slow down her escape. She had, at the very least, to be away from town by daylight. Painfully, she pulled her boot over her puffy ankle and struggled to her feet. It was downhill and through scrubland to the navigation.

Lord, what would she do then? She had no money or friends and couldn't even stand at a scullery sink to work. But she wasn't going back. Not now. The bridleway came from round the front of the workhouse and led into town. A footpath veered off through the brambles and shrubs that would give her cover when dawn broke. Cold and wet, she set off slowly towards the waterway.

It was not far before she had to stop and rest her foot. She pushed her hands up the sleeves of her gown to keep them warm, closed her eyes and wished away the ache. The next thing she knew she was being crudely awakened.

'Get up, Meadow. Think you can run off with workhouse clothes on your back, do you?'

'That's stealing, that is.'

Two men took hold of her arms and yanked her, still half asleep, to her feet.

'It's that new inmate, the young trollop. My wife says she's been at it since she was a nipper.'

In the moonlight she recognised the master, with a sinking heart. The younger man was his nephew who served as his clerk in the workhouse office.

'We don't want more of her sort down by the canal, do we, Uncle?'

'Spreading disease through our young men, no, we do not.'

'You'll have to tell Aunty to keep a closer eye on her in future.'

'Oh, she will. Don't you worry, she will after this escape. Mark my words.'

Bleary-eyed, Sarah couldn't think where she was at first. She was rigid with cold but as soon as she moved, her ankle hurt and then, as the pain jarred up her leg, she was wide awake. How long had she slept? she wondered. Not long, she thought, for the sky was still black.

'Come on, now. On your feet. Frame yourself, Meadow.'

'I can't,' she squeaked. 'I can't stand. Honest. I've hurt my foot.'

'That'll teach you to run away then, won't it?' Between them they half-dragged her through the undergrowth and back to the footpath.

'No! Please don't take me back. I can work. I can earn a living.'

'Yes, and we all know how,' the younger man said.

'By lying on your back. Or more like up against the iron-works wall, with your sort. Filthy little whore.'

Sarah seethed with anger. How dare they pass judgement on her like this? She closed her eyes and tried not to think about the pain in her ankle. She had not been mistaken about a movement at the third-floor window. Someone had seen her climb into the water butt and had told on her. Mrs Turnbull, she reckoned; a spiteful telltale. What a horrible place the workhouse was.

She remembered what Mrs Watson's had said. *It's meant to be.*

So you work hard to stay out of it. Or something similar to that, she thought angrily. Well, she didn't want to be here so why wouldn't they let her go? She knew the answer, right enough. It was because that vile doctor had told lies about her. Why? What was she to him? She thought of his creepy hands probing her private areas. Just because she was a workhouse inmate didn't mean he could do that to her!

But who would believe her if she told on him. No one. She was labelled as a moral defective and she had no idea how to shake that off. Depressed by this realisation and worn out by her night's ordeal, she had no fight left in her when she was pushed through the rear gate and into the main building; this time she was taken down flights of stone steps and along a dark, dank underground corridor that linked the male and female quarters.

'Let's see if a week in here will bring you to your senses,' the master said, shoving her into a small room.

The clanging of the door rang in her ears for several minutes and then there was silence. It hung like a damp, black fog in the small cell. But the silence wasn't total. She heard and recognised the scratching of rats and, as her eyes got used to the darkness, she saw them, moving furtively around the wet stone floor. Saliva ran into her mouth and she swallowed.

Forest creatures on a bracken bed she had tolerated; they seemed like her friends. But rats were different. They carried disease, and at Meadow Hall the stables lad wouldn't have them near the horses; they spooked them and ate their mash. She remembered how the lads used to bait the rats in an empty stall, gather with spades and shovels and corner them. Then they'd close the door and beat them to a bloody pulpy mess that was swept out with the straw and burned.

Sarah had not even a stick to fend them off; only a stone bed built against the wall with a dank mattress and blanket. There was a bucket for her privy that she could smell from where she was standing. Angrily, she flared her nostrils and shouted at the sweating stone walls. *'This is your fault, Aidan! I'll never forgive you*

183

for bringing me here. I'll get you back for this, if it's the last thing I do!'

Aidan had drifted in and out of consciousness. He couldn't move and had no feeling in his limbs but he had known that he had to stay alive in the water until morning, when someone would find him. As the warmth returned to his body, so did the hurt, especially when they, whoever they were, moved him. He was on a cart and every jolt of the wheels sent more pain searing through him. Only when he knew he was safe did he allow himself to slip into a welcome total blackness.

After he came too, he couldn't see very clearly but he was in a bed and a young woman was sitting in a chair watching him. His head throbbed, his chest hurt and his eyelids felt like lead as he prised them fully open. He moved his lips but no sound came out. The woman seemed alarmed. She leapt to her feet and went out of the door, calling for help.

He felt cold in spite of a large fire burning in the grate and the down-filled quilt covering the bedding. He was sore all over, but at least he could feel his feet now, and he tried in vain to wriggle his toes. An older man came into the room. He carried a leather bag and he set it down on the dresser, opened it and took out his instruments.

He was a doctor. Thank the Lord; a doctor.

'Well, young man, you've had quite a battle.'

A battle? 'What happened to me?' he croaked.

'You've been fighting for your life. But you have a strong constitution and you are mending. So it is not your fight for life I was referring to. It was the fight you had with the other man.'

'What other man?'

'You don't remember?'

Aidan frowned. His mind was blank. He could not remember anything! Fear and alarm leapt into his eyes.

The doctor's face was expressionless. He raised his voice, slightly. 'Emma, would you ask Liddy to come in here?'

A few minutes later a young girl sidled into the chamber. 'Stand by me where he can see you,' the doctor said.

Aidan tried to smile at her. She was very pretty.

'Have you seen her before?' the doctor asked.

'No.'

'You have!' the girl responded indignantly. 'I filled your canteen from the spring when you were unloading coal from the barges!'

Aidan's eyes were blank.

'You don't remember?' the doctor asked.

Aidan moved his head painfully from side to side.

'Tell me your name, son.'

He racked his brain. 'I can't!' Painfully, he tried to lever himself to a sitting position. 'I don't know who I am!'

'Try and keep calm. You've had blows to your head and a severe shock to your body. But I am told that you were seen to be young and strong before your injuries, and capable of doing a man's work.'

'Do you know me, sir?'

'I do not. You did a day's labouring for Mr Thorpe and were on your way to lodgings.'

'Mr Thorpe? Who is Mr Thorpe?'

'He runs the Bowes Iron and Steel Works. Liddy is his younger sister.'

'Does Mr Thorpe know what happened to me?'

'We believe you were set upon and beaten.'

'Do you know why, sir?'

'I do not. You had only one day's pay about your person. I was hoping you might enlighten us.'

'Does Mr Thorpe know my name?'

'Beckwith. Aidan Beckwith.'

Yes, Aidan sounded right to him. His head seemed to swim around the room. 'Where's my father?' he asked. He had a father. He knew he had a father.

The doctor looked relieved. 'You remember something at least. Good. If we can locate your father he will be able to help you

185

further. Don't ask yourself too many questions. Rest and take nourishment and with God's grace your past will come back to you. Do not try and force it until your mind is ready.'

'Where am I, sir?'

'You're in the home of Mr Thorpe, adjacent to his iron and steel works. One of his labourers recognised your clothes.'

Aidan frowned, trying to force himself to remember until his head throbbed.

'You'll stay here until your injuries are healed. I'm told that you presented yourself as a level-headed personable fellow. Follow my orders and you will regain your strength.'

'What are my injuries, sir?'

'You have cracked bones, bruising and bleeding all over your body. I have stemmed the bleeding and your bruises are fading. It is your head and chest that give me most concern.'

'What did they do to me?'

'No one witnessed the attack on you but you have been in a deep faint for several days. It is the body's way of healing itself and I have kept you so with medicines for even longer.'

'I feel very drowsy.'

'I have given you laudanum. You will find that without it every breath you take will hurt until your ribs mend. I shall reduce your dose as they heal.'

'But my head – I do not know who I am.'

'It is essential you remain calm. You are talking sensibly and that is a good sign. Can you see me clearly?'

Aidan blinked. 'Yes, sir.'

The doctor held up his hand and curled his index finger under his thumb. 'How many fingers am I holding up?'

'Three.'

'Are you sure about that?

'Yes, sir.'

'Good. That is enough talking for now. Your nose was broken and I have straightened it as best I could but you may find you look different after this.'

He couldn't think what he looked like. Who is Aidan Beckwith? Again he tried to sit up and the dull ache all over him suddenly flared into something worse. He stifled a cry of pain.

'You'll hurt much more when the laudanum wears off. I've left you a dose to help you through the night. I'll be in to see you in the morning. Be prepared for a long journey to recovery, Mr Beckwith.'

Aidan closed his eyes. His brain was fuddled and all he wanted to do was go back to sleep. He heard voices murmuring in the background as he let himself drift off. A doctor? Staying in a home that belonged to the owner of an iron and steel works? Did he have money to pay for all this? The doctor had said he had only one day's pay on him. His father once paid money to a doctor. Yes, his father had money. Where was his father? *He wasn't here any more.* But something else had happened. He had a feeling there was something more important that he needed to remember. A sense of urgency overtook him. He racked his mind trying to force himself to think of it. A pair of hazel eyes under auburn hair. A splinter of light pierced his memory as he sank into a drug-induced slumber.

PART TWO

Chapter 16

It was well into spring before Aidan was strong enough to mount a horse. While he was recovering, parts of his memory had returned and he was anxious to encourage it further. He had been able to tell the doctor that his father had died. 'We had a wagon,' he'd added.

'You have a horse?'

Aidan's mind had been blank for a moment. Then he'd remembered trees; the clearing; the rocky stream and the cave. 'We lived in a wood,' he'd said slowly.

'Was your father a woodcutter?'

'He died in the wagon and I took him on our horse to a village church.'

'You're sure about that.'

'I buried him in a churchyard – somewhere.' He had racked his brain until it ached.

'If you can remember anything about the village or the woods, we may be able to find your family.'

'I have a family?'

'Many young men leave their loved ones to seek work in the town. Anything familiar will help you to remember. Also, your mother will want to know that you are safe.'

'My mother is dead.' Aidan had said it with such certainty that he knew it must be true.

The doctor had seemed satisfied with this response. Aidan's body had mended and the laudanum was reduced. The young woman, whose name was Emma, continued to care for him, bringing clean linen and regular trays of nourishment. She told him she was Daniel Thorpe's sister and she helped Mrs Thorpe with making gowns for the gentry.

'Your brother and his wife have been very generous towards me.'

'They're like that with everybody, even their servants. You don't know how lucky you were to be found by our Danny.'

Danny? Dan? He knew a Dan from somewhere; but where? 'The doctor told me I'm well enough to ride,' he said. He was desperate to jog his memory further and asked Emma about the villages surrounding the town.

'Swinbrough is the biggest.'

'This one had a wooded hillside behind it and – and a house, a big house at the bottom of the hill.'

'We've got big houses all over here, where the gentry live.'

'Can you tell me their names?'

'Well, Swinbrough Hall and Fitzkeppel Hall have been here for years, my father says. Then there's High House up by the moor and yon side of town is Meadow Hall. That's empty again I hear—'

Meadow Hall? Meadow Hall had a ring about it. Had he heard of it before? 'Does the village at Meadow Hall have a church?'

'Every village has a church.'

'Is it far? I'd like to go there.'

Mr Thorpe lent him his wife's mare. The horse needed an outing as Mrs Thorpe had been unwell for several days now and had not been able to ride. Emma had told Aidan she didn't think the illness was serious.

The bridleway was easy enough to follow and soon he spied Meadow Hall church spire above the trees. Aidan's memories, though, were more elusive. Sometimes he thought he recognised a cottage or a face, but when he tried to dredge up a name, it flitted away and left him with an unfathomable black hole inside his head. The sexton in the churchyard knew of a Beckwith buried there and Aidan stood in front of the simple wooden cross for a long time waiting for a memory to surface.

He moved on to the Hall. Emma had told him it was empty; again, she'd said. His gentle mount picked its way carefully over the debris in the stable yard. He gazed from horseback at the dovecote. The door was repaired and recently painted. It hadn't always been like that, he thought. How did he know? He'd been here before, and he looked around for a gap in the garden wall expecting to see – to see whom? His eyes travelled over the tree-tops to the crest of the hill. A wagon, a clearing near a rocky stream, flashes of memory continued to torment him. He turned the horse's head towards the well-worn track through the trees.

Aidan slid down from the saddle exhausted, his mind in turmoil. He knew where he was. The empty wagon had gone right over and a wheel was missing but he remembered the spot and – and – he twisted his body round and around – his fire pit. Yes, there it was, away from the trees, as the thin soil gave way to rocky ground by the stream. He unhooked his canteen from the saddle and made his way down to the water. He tipped away the canteen contents and refilled it from the clear spring water, drank thirstily and lay back on the cold, flat rock.

Then he went back to the fire pit and bent down to run his fingers over the blackened stones. He closed his eyes, squeezing his eyes shut, trying to remember. There had been others; a fellow who played the tin whistle and – and the boy; the skinny urchin who had stared at him across the clearing as he worked at his anvil. Where was his anvil? He remembered now that he was a blacksmith, like his father before him.

Clouds covering the sun thickened and the light dimmed. In the gathering gloom his memory jolted. It wasn't a boy. It was a girl and the other fellow had tried to take her virtue. He stared at the splintered wagon and remembered. In spite of the cool shade he became hot.

They'd had a fight. *They had a fight.* Is this where he had been injured? If so, how did he get in to the canal? He forced his brain to think until his head pounded. He'd won this fight on the forest floor. He'd won the girl. So where was she? And how had he come to be in town? His head was spinning and he felt faint. He took bread and cheese from his saddlebag and sat on a boulder to eat, concentrating on the fire pit. She didn't like the heat. He remembered she couldn't take the sun either. She had pale skin that freckled in the sun; and auburn hair. Dear Lord, where was she?

He had been found in the canal after the Lady Day market. What had happened last Michaelmas and Christmas? Images jumbled around inside his head until he could no longer think straight. He led his horse to the stream to drink. After a rest, listening to the soothing sounds of the water running over stones, he felt better. He had remembered more in the last few hours than in all the weeks since his injuries.

On his way back he picked some woodland flowers, laid a posy at the foot of the wooden cross in the churchyard and promised a proper headstone when he could earn the money to pay for it. He was in a huge amount of debt to the Thorpes, which he must repay as soon as possible. The village was quiet as he rode through, although when he passed the farrier's he heard the clang of metal on metal and the hiss of steam as hot iron hit cold water He knew now that all he needed in order to repay the Thorpes was a good fire, bellows and an anvil. Gently, he spurred his horse towards town. He wanted to make a start straightaway.

Aidan was exhausted when he reached Bowes works. The evening air was chilly and a clear sky promised a night frost. He shivered, and tethered the mare instead of stabling her straightaway. The doctor's horse was there, too. He went in the back door and through the scullery but stopped as he heard raised voices in the kitchen. Mr Thorpe and Emma were arguing. He decided not to embarrass them by interrupting but was forced to stand and listen.

'I have to pay him,' Mr Thorpe insisted. 'I asked him to treat the lad.'

'I know. But the doctor will wait for his money and we need every penny more than ever now.'

'We've been in dire straits before. We'll manage.'

'Well, Mariah won't be able to visit her customers for orders.'

'Can you not go instead?'

'I haven't got Mariah's eye. I cannot sketch ideas and I do not know how to cut fabric to flatter her ladies. Besides, I am already too busy helping to run this house. Although, if the doctor had a wife I would suggest we make her a gown.'

'He doesn't take payment in kind any more. He wants money like the rest of us. I'll just have to get it for him.'

'From where, Daniel?'

'*I'll find it.* Now stop worrying. Why is the doctor taking so long with Mariah?'

Aidan waited before he entered the kitchen. Emma was tending a small pan over the range.

'Aidan! You look exhausted. Come and sit by the fire.'

'I'm cold, that's all.'

'Have some broth.'

'Thanks.' He sat at the table and noticed a piece of paper, official looking with an engraved heading in large script. It was a bill for payment, from the doctor. 'Is that for me?' he asked.

Daniel snatched it up. 'He's here to see Mariah.'

'He came to present his bill,' Emma argued. 'I asked him see Mariah.'

'Is Mrs Thorpe ill, sir?' Aidan asked.

'It's nothing,' Emma replied.

Mr Thorpe slid the doctor's bill into his waistcoat pocket.

'Forgive me, sir, if the doctor's bill is for my treatments then I should pay it.'

'And where are you going to find the money?' Emma asked.

'Emma!' Mr Thorpe exclaimed.

'But your sister is right, sir. I must find a way to pay my debts. My strength is returning and I have a proposition for you.'

Daniel Thorpe raised his eyebrows. 'I'm listening.'

'I've jogged a few memories today, sir, and remember now that my talent is for working iron. I have noticed an old forge in the corner of your ironworks that no one seems to use.'

'The yard hasn't had its own smithy since before my time here. It has been used for storage but the roof needs mending.'

'I can repair it and get it going again.'

'You can remember how to work iron?'

Aidan nodded.

Daniel frowned. 'I don't have enough to do in my yard to warrant my own blacksmith.'

'I want to rent the forge from you, sir.'

'Well, there's always plenty of smithy work in this town. We'll have a look at it tomorrow.'

'Thank you, sir.' Aidan held out his hand. 'Will you let me have the bill now?'

Mr Thorpe took it out of his pocket and gave it to him as the doctor came into the kitchen.

'Your wife is well, Daniel,' he said. 'Her symptoms are nothing that I should not expect from a woman in her condition.'

Mr Thorpe and Emma beamed at each other and Aidan realised the nature of Mrs Thorpe's indisposition. She was with child. He stood up and said, 'Congratulations, sir. You are a lucky man.'

'I know.' Mr Thorpe said smiling and, now visibly more relaxed, he disappeared out of the kitchen.

The doctor turned to Aidan. 'Mr Beckwith! Good evening to you. How pleasing it is to see you up and about; and riding too, I hear.'

'Yes, sir. I've been over to Meadow Hall Woods, stirring my memory today. It's odd, though. I can remember some things I did before I came into town for Lady Day, but absolutely nothing of what happened here. I'm told I was in the market the day before I worked for Mr Thorpe but my mind is totally blank. It's as though those last two days before the accident did not exist.'

The doctor gave him a long steady look. 'Well, I've done all I can for you. If your mind has blocked out those hours then it does not want you to recall them. Whatever happened was too much of a jolt to your system so it's best to not try and remember. Let it go. It is likely to be another great shock to you if it comes back. You have made a good recovery so far. Thank the Lord for that, Mr Beckwith, and move forward with your life.'

'Yes, I believe you are right. I have forgotten for a reason. I shall shortly be working again and shall pay your bill as soon as I can.' He glanced at Emma. 'But how I shall ever repay the Thorpes, I'll never know.'

'Oh, there'll be something you can do for them one day, I expect.'

'I hope so.' Aidan stretched out his hand. 'Thank you for everything, sir.'

The doctor grasped his hand firmly. 'It's what I do. It's my vocation. Find yours, Mr Beckwith, and you will have a happy life.'

Aidan nodded. 'I shall.' He was confident he had set himself on the right track already.

'Goodnight then.'

'I'll come outside with you. I have to stable Mrs Thorpe's horse.'

Emma still had a frown on her face when Aidan returned to the kitchen.

'I shall repay you all,' he promised her.

'I worry for them both,' she replied. 'They work so hard to pay their dues to the bank.'

'I know. I shall make it up to them. But I have a favour to ask you, if I may.'

'Of course, if I can.'

'The doctor says I may never remember the two days in town before my injuries. But I feel here –' he banged his fist against his chest '– that I must try. I want to know what happened, however shocking it may be,'

'The doctor has advised you it is best to let it go, Aidan.'

'It is not the doctor who has lost two days of his life. Why do I have this constant aching, this yearning to recall them? They were – are – important days to me; part of me. I—' he shook his head. 'I do not feel whole without them. Can you understand that?'

'I'm afraid I can't. Oh, Aidan, do not torment yourself in this way. You have made such a good recovery so far. You have work, a home and friends who care for you. Please heed the doctor's words. Look to your future, not your past.'

'You will not help me to remember?'

Emma frowned. 'I want to because I am your friend. But it may do you more harm than good and that stops me.'

'Please, Emma. You know this town and I have no one else to turn to.'

Emma chewed on her lip and frowned. 'I do not want to do anything that will cause you distress. However, when I visit the market, I shall make enquiries about that day. If I find out anything that will help then, rest assured, I shall tell you.'

'Thank you. You are a true friend. One name is all I need. Someone I can speak to myself.'

He saw, though, that Emma's frown had deepened.

Chapter 17

Spring brought warmth to the workhouse yard, if not to the icy water that Sarah lifted every day at the pump. Matron had made her life worse than ever after she came out of the punishment cell, giving her the cold outdoor jobs or the worst of the mucky laundry to scrub. As she lifted the heavy wet sheets to peg out in the weak sunshine Sarah glanced across at the forbidding height of the main building and – she shivered at the memory – the tiny window just above ground level. She had been out for a month now and never wanted to go back.

'Here, let me help with those.' Maggie took one end of the sheet and hoisted it onto the line.

'Thanks.' Sarah could manage; her time at Meadow Hall had given her a resilience that was useful in the workhouse, but she enjoyed the company. Her wary eyes darted around. 'Where's Matron?'

'Indoors. The doctor's here so we shan't see her until he's gone.'

Maggie had been Sarah's salvation during her time in the punishment cell. The small high window had iron bars instead of glass and Maggie loitered by it to chat and pass down morsels of bread and cheese when the women came out after dinner or tea.

'I'm sorry about the schoolroom windows,' Sarah said. The master had put lime-wash on them so the children could not look into the yard.

'Me too,' Maggie replied.

Sarah lifted her skirt to reach into her petticoat pocket. 'Look, your Josie did this for you.' She handed her a piece of calico with a few words on it sewn in dark thread.

Maggie's face lit up. 'Oh, it's lovely! How did you get hold of it?'

'Miss Green brings the children down to the privy when I'm emptying the slop buckets. She lets me take them upstairs again. If Matron's not about I stay and help with the little ones.'

'But how did you know who was my Josie?'

'I asked the older ones, and she made this for you in her sewing lessons. They said she was very good with a needle.'

Maggie beamed. 'I know. She takes after me.'

'What does it say?

'Oh, can't you——? I'm sorry, I didn't realise you couldn't read. It says "I love you" and then her name.' Maggie gazed at the scrap of fabric. 'Oh, thank you so much. I hope you don't get into trouble for it.'

'I don't care if I do. I reckon I've had the worst the work-house can throw at me and survived that well enough. Even if Miss Green knows, I don't think she'd tell on me. She really has her hands full in the schoolroom and I watch the little ones for her while she sets work for the others.' Sarah gazed at the lime-washed windows on the third floor. 'I wish I could have lessons.'

Maggie looked sympathetic. 'You're too old now. Most work-house girls of your age have gone into service.'

'Then why haven't I?'

'I expect they're not sure that you'll behave yourself. You're a hard worker, too, so Matron will want to keep you here for herself.'

Sarah sighed. 'I didn't do myself any good trying to escape, did I?'

'I thought you were very brave. But Matron said you were punished because the master caught you in the cellars with a dosser.'

'Why would he say that about me?'

'He didn't want the guardians to know you had escaped. He would have been in trouble himself for that.'

'Miss Green knows the truth. I told her when she came to check on me in the punishment cell.' The schoolteacher's pale face, surrounded by her dark plaited hair, was one of the few that came to peer at her through the grid in her cell door. On her last visit Miss Green had said, 'You have to mend your ways, Meadow.' Another face appeared once; it was that dreadful doctor and he just stared at her.

'*Meadow!*' The master's voice rang across the yard. '*Over here. Now.*'

'Dear Heaven, what does *he* want you for?' Maggie exclaimed. 'Hurry, dear, and don't make any more enemies!'

Sarah dropped her pegs in the washing basket and ran over to the main block.

The master escorted Sarah down the corridor to the schoolroom. 'We'll see if you've learned your lesson,' he said, opening the door. 'The doctor knows all about your sort so you do as he says.'

'Not him, sir! Please don't leave me with him!'

'Will you do as you're told?' He pushed her into the schoolroom where the doctor was waiting for her.

The room was laid out as normal with low benches and nothing much else except a washstand, a teacher's desk, chair and a bookcase. 'Where's Miss Green?' Sarah asked.

The doctor strolled over to the door and turned the key, then took off his long jacket and laid it carefully on a bench. His dark waistcoat contrasted starkly with the white of his shirt. 'How many dossers did you give favours to in the cellar before the master caught you?' he asked as he pulled out Miss Green's chair and sat down.

'I never gave none,' she protested. 'He lied.'

'Come and stand in front of me,' he snapped. 'What am I to say about you to the guardians?'

'You can tell them that I'm not a moral defective, for a start.'

'Don't be insolent, child!'

'I'm not a child.'

'Indeed you are not. You are well grown and versed in the ways of the world. Now do as I say and stand in front of me.'

'Why?'

'Who are you to question me?' he snapped and then, softening his tone, added, 'You will do as I say. And if you do I'll tell the master that you have reformed your ways.'

'That would be a lie for I was not sinful to begin with and you know that.'

'You will be wise not to argue with me, Meadow. Step closer and show me your hands.'

Cautiously she obeyed, displaying her reddened arms and hands; they were always sore from working in the wash house.

'Do you want Matron to keep you in the laundry?'

'I don't mind,' she muttered. At least she had a friend there in Maggie.

This made him angry. 'I can also send you to the punishment cell for another week if you have not reformed!'

Sarah stared at the floor and pressed her lips together to avoid retaliating.

'Well? Have you reformed?'

She remembered what Maggie had said about not making enemies and answered, 'Yes, sir.'

'Would you like to be moved from the wash house?'

'Yes, sir.' She thought that was what he wanted to hear.

'You must convince me.' He said it in such a soft insinuating way that she looked up quickly. 'You must be a good girl for me,' he added. He was leering at her in the same manner as those drunken gentleman in the Jackson house and she did not mistake his meaning.

202

She said, 'I am very good at lighting fires, sir.'

'Do not play fast and loose with me,' he snapped. 'Come over here and do as I say.'

'I don't have to! I'll tell on you. I'll tell Matron.'

'Do you think she will believe you?'

Sarah knew she wouldn't. Matron was silly about the doctor, treating him as some sort of idol when he was the most despicable creature Sarah had ever known.

He sneered at her. 'She will believe me when I tell her you are beyond salvation and that I recommend two weeks in the punishment cell for wilful lying.'

'I haven't lied to you!'

'You haven't been nice to me.'

She felt trapped by this evil man. But she couldn't give in to him. She wouldn't. 'I – don't know what you want,' she said at last.

'Oh, I think you do. What did the dossers ask you do? Come and kneel by my chair and show me.'

She froze to the spot and shook her head.

'Do as I say!'

'No, sir, I won't. I didn't do anything like that with them. I never met no dossers in the cellars.'

'Then I must tell the master how you persist in your lies.'

'The master is a liar as well.'

'How dare you speak ill of your betters!'

'Because I know what he said isn't true!'

The doctor glared at her and said very slowly. 'You will obey me, Meadow, and come here.'

'I won't.'

'Then you will be in the punishment cell again.'

'I'd rather have rats crawling over me than your creepy hands.'

'By God, you are an impudent wench. You will do as I say.' He got up, took hold of her arm and flung her across a bench.

She scrambled to her feet and staggered, shocked and alarmed, as he swiftly unbuttoned his waistcoat.

'There is only one kind of lesson your sort understands,' he growled.

'If you touch me again like you did before, I'll scream. I will! I'll scream the place down.'

'And I'll have you in a straitjacket in the asylum if you do! See if you like it there!'

Horrified, Sarah backed away from him and lowered her voice. 'You wouldn't do such a cruel thing.' He glared at her and, frightened, she added, 'Would you?'

'Not if you're nice to me.'

She stared at him. He meant what he said. He was an evil man; wicked and completely without feeling, except for his own comforts. How could such a despicable person administer to the sick? But this was the workhouse and nothing surprised her anymore. Perhaps, he had disgraced himself in polite society and been forced to bury himself in the workhouse of a growing industrial town. It was the only explanation she could think of.

There was no point in telling Matron, or indeed anyone else about him, for everyone believed him when he said she was a moral defective. The master and his nephew, too, had already formed a bad opinion of her based on her supposed immoral ways. No one would listen to her, and if they did they would say she was telling lies. If she wanted to improve her situation there was nothing she could do except . . . she swallowed slowly . . . except do as he asked.

Dear Lord, was this how women obtained favours in here? It wasn't right. She could understand a pecking order in the wash house, for that was no different from Meadow Hall. But this – this! It was no better than the Jackson whorehouse. She wondered if the master knew about the doctor and hoped not. Surely he would not condone such behaviour?

The doctor sat down in his chair and searched under his waistcoat for the buttons of his trousers. 'Kneel down in front of me,' he ordered.

Sarah's heart thumped as she took very tiny steps towards him.

Her mind was racing but she could think of nothing to avoid doing as he asked that would not make her situation worse. She certainly didn't want to end up in the asylum!

He let out a sigh as the opening in his trousers fell apart. She was drawn by curiosity to look. In all the months she had lived with Aidan and Danby she had hardly more than glimpsed their private parts. But when Danby had been drunk last Christmas she had felt him against her, hard and probing. There was nothing hard and probing about what she saw when the doctor pushed down his under-drawers.

'Come now, I shan't bite you.' Then he laughed, he actually laughed, and added, 'As long as you don't bite me.' When he lifted his flabby thing out of his trousers, she was reminded of the fat sea worms in the wagon timbers that Danby had spoken of. 'Hurry up, child, I haven't got all day. Put your apron over my lap first.' He leaned back his head, closed his eyes and fondled himself.

He really thought she knew what to do! She stood between his splayed legs and looked down at this gross brown maggot in disbelief. Is this what it was all about between men and women? All the tales she had overheard from the maids at Meadow Hall? Anyway, wasn't he supposed to put it inside her? How could he do that if she was kneeling down? And then she remembered something he'd said when she first arrived here; something that had puzzled her then and now became clear. *Did he put it in your mouth, he'd asked.* Was that what he wanted her to do? Put that smelly fat worm in her mouth?

An involuntary shudder of nausea racked her body and vomit rose in her gullet. It burned the back of her throat and made her cough. She tried to suppress it but the image in her mind of what she had to do with something she thought of as repulsive made her feel so sick to her stomach that she couldn't stop herself. She gagged and retched as her innards revolted and her meagre stomach contents spewed out of her mouth, over his open trousers and exposed flesh.

'What the—?' He gasped, then yelled and leapt out of the chair knocking her off balance. 'You – you disgusting little witch!' His chair tipped back and fell. Sarah retched again and a thin slime dribbled from her mouth and fell on the wooden floorboards. She clutched at a corner of the bookcase, pulling it forward so that it toppled, spilling books into her vomit. The doctor grabbed at a cloth from the washstand and rubbed frantically at himself as there was a sharp rapping on the door.

'Is anything the matter in there? I heard raised voices and someone falling.' It was Miss Green. She rattled the knob on the locked door. 'Is anyone hurt? Let me in!'

'Go away!' The doctor's voice was hoarse.

'No, I won't. What's going on in there? Meadow? What are you doing?'

Sarah felt ill. There was not much in her stomach to bring up and the horrid acid taste in her throat made her feel worse. Her insides continued to revolt as the image of an enormous swollen maggot wriggling in her mouth became fixed in her mind. She gagged again. Her knees sagged and she sank to the floor, leaning on the fallen bookcase.

Miss Green continued to rattle the door knob. 'Open up at once or I shall fetch the master.'

The doctor's boots squeaked as he crossed the room and turned the key in the lock, removing himself quickly to look out of the window. 'Take her to the punishment cell, Miss Green. She is beyond any treatment I can give her and I can recommend only the asylum for this one.'

Sarah choked as she tried to voice her protest.

Miss Green marched into the room. 'What has she done?'

'She has attempted to seduce me in the crudest of manners. She is nothing more than a common whore.'

Sarah tried to scramble to her feet. 'I'm not! It's you! You're an evil man. You should be asking what he has done to me!' she spluttered.

'Take her away this instant,' the doctor commanded.

'But look at her, sir!' Miss Green demanded. 'She is sick.'

'She is a wicked girl and her illness is feigned.'

'Is this true, Meadow? Did you make yourself vomit?'

'No, Miss Green. He did it. He made me spew all over him.'

'You see how she lies? She is beyond my help and I shall recommend the guardians remove her to the asylum.'

'Oh, please don't let him do that. It wasn't me, it was him; he asked me to do things to him.'

The doctor gave an exasperated cry. 'Get her out of my sight.'

'Stay where you are, Meadow,' Miss Green responded. 'This is my schoolroom and the doctor is going.'

'What do you propose to do about my clothes? I cannot leave with the stink of vomit about my person.'

'I am sure Matron will tend to your needs more than adequately, sir.'

Surprised by this exchange, Sarah looked up. Miss Green was standing face to face with the doctor, glaring at him. His eyes were as dark as a thundering sky and Sarah thought he might strike the teacher. But he didn't.

'Hand me my hat,' he barked. 'I have had enough of the work-house for one day.' He already had on his long coat and was doing up the buttons. 'The master will hear of your meddling before I depart,' he added.

Miss Green closed the door to prevent the doctor leaving and stood with her back to it. 'No, he won't.' She sounded very determined and, intrigued, Sarah forgot her discomfort. 'If he does,' Miss Green went on, 'I shall initiate enquires into your background.'

'The devil you will! My past is no concern of yours.'

'The guardians will be very interested,' she answered evenly.

'I supplied them with the required testimonials.'

'Then I shall simply ask the master if he has verified them.'

'You will do no such thing!' The doctor glared at Miss Green.

She did not flinch. 'Very well; I shall keep silent if you will recommend to the master that Meadow is removed from the laundry to my schoolroom.'

207

'I shall not! She is wicked and wilful. She should be in an asylum.'

Miss Green stared at him, cold-eyed. 'Which infirmary in London did you say employed you?' she asked.

The doctor did not reply. He picked up his fine leather bag and stood square in front of her and demanded, 'Get out of my way.'

Miss Green stepped aside and opened the door for him. As she did so she said, 'If Meadow is not moved within the week, I shall ask my questions. Good day to you, sir.' She watched him stride down the corridor before she closed the schoolroom door.

'Thank you, miss,' Sarah said.

'There'll be time for thanks later,' Miss Green responded briskly. 'Are you still feeling poorly?'

'No, miss. Not now he's gone.'

'What did he do to you?'

'Nothing; he asked me to . . . Oh, it was horrible. It made me retch just to think about it.'

Miss Green stared at her. 'It was the doctor who made you vomit?'

Sarah nodded wordlessly and turned her tearful face towards the schoolteacher. She saw Miss Green stretch out her hand. The teacher's eyes softened. At last, Sarah thought, here was someone who understood how vile the doctor was!

Sarah took hold of the older woman's hand and felt a reassuring squeeze. She had a friend, an ally against him.

Miss Green was looking at her seriously. 'What did he ask you to do?'

'He wanted me to – to, well I don't really know, but he had his trousers open and – and – it was so – so foul.'

'And did you do what he asked?'

'I couldn't, miss. Just the thought of it made me feel sick.'

Miss Green lowered her voice. 'You – you do not care to – to give pleasure to men in that way?'

Sarah shuddered and shook her head.

208

'But you came here from the streets. You have done these things before.'

'I haven't! It's a lie. Honest, miss. My friend wouldn't let anybody touch me.'

'He kept you for himself?'

Her mouth turned down as she was reminded of Aidan's betrayal. 'No, he wanted me to stay a maid.'

'He said you were a moral defective.'

'*He didn't!* That doctor lied about me. I've never been with a man like – like that.'

'Not even the man who brought you here?'

'I hate him.'

'You hate the man who looked after you? Did he ask you to do things to him as well?'

'Not in the way you think.'

'Did he ever put his arms around you?'

'Once.' She remembered when that was all she ever wanted him to do.

'But did you desire him? Did you want him to kiss you?'

Yes, I did, she thought, and then I would have let him do more than kiss me, but not any more. She had respected and admired him and he had betrayed her. She would never forgive him for that. Never.

'No,' she replied.

'Do you not wish for a man to hold you in that way?'

Sarah thought of the men she had known in her life. The male servants at Meadow Hall who made fun of her; Danby who had tried to force himself on her and really frightened her; those horrible, slavering gentlemen at Jackson's house; and now this doctor who was supposed to be a gentleman. He knew she was a maid and had taken pleasure in humiliating her.

'No, miss,' she replied. 'I hate them all.'

Miss Green squeezed her fingers again. 'You have a very pretty face. Men will always seek to use you so.'

'Even gentlemen like the doctor?'

'Especially gentlemen like him.'

'Well, I don't believe he's a proper gentleman.'

'He is not a proper doctor either. He's a charlatan and he has lied about his previous life.'

'What's a charlatan, miss?'

'Someone who is not what he says he is and is intent on deception.'

'Oh, he's that, right enough. It's a pity Matron doesn't realise it.'

Miss Green raised her eyebrows. 'She is a foolish woman. You are wise beyond your years. Now, rinse your face at the wash-stand while I fetch a bucket of water for you to clean up this mess. You've ruined these books, you know.'

'I'm sorry, miss. I'll get the water for you.'

'No, I should have to go with you anyway to unlock the doors.'

Very few inmates were allowed into the central block which housed the schoolroom as the master's office was located nearby. Sarah made a start on the books, wiping them carefully and wishing she could read the words. The teacher soon returned with fresh water and Sarah set about scrubbing the floor.

Miss Green sat on one of the children's benches and watched her. 'That's enough, Meadow,' she said. 'You don't have to do everywhere. Sit here beside me. Why do you think you are here?'

'The doctor wanted to see me after my punishment.'

'I wished to interview you, too. I have observed you at your tasks and at leisure and I think you would be of great use to me.'

Sarah was wary, wondering what she had in mind. 'I've not had no learning, Miss Green.'

'Yes, that is obvious. But I have seen you helping the little ones and I am in desperate need of some assistance.

Sarah eyes widened. 'Me? Help you here? Matron would never let me do that.'

'It is the master who makes the decisions. He has asked the guardians for a pupil teacher but they do not have any spare funds. Although you have much to learn, you have sympathy with the children.'

'I remember what I felt like as a little girl without a mother or father.'

Miss Green took hold of her hand. 'If the master agrees, I shall be responsible for you.'

Sarah's eyes lit up and she smiled. 'Could I really work up here?'

'I hope so. Would you like to?'

'Oh yes, Miss Green.'

The teacher's plain serious face broke into a rare smile. 'I have already asked the master.'

'If he says yes, will you learn me to read, miss?'

'I teach and you learn,' Miss Green replied.

'You will? Oh thank you, miss.'

The teacher put her head on one side and squeezed her hand. 'I mean, I don't learn you to read, I teach you. You should ask, "Will I teach you to read" not "will I learn you to read".'

Sarah couldn't see what difference it made and responded eagerly, 'You will, though, won't you, miss?'

'We shall see.' Miss Green trailed her hand along Sarah's arm.

Sarah blinked, surprised by such friendliness in the workhouse. Suddenly Miss Green snatched her hand away and said, 'I can hear the children coming up the stairs. Stand over there and be quiet.'

Matron followed the silent children into the schoolroom. She looked flustered and snapped at Sarah, 'Who said you could come up here.'

'The doctor asked to see her privately, ma'am,' Miss Green answered.

'Yes, well, he has to report on her to the guardians as she is a minor as well as a moral defective. I'll take her now. She has plenty to do in the wash house.'

'Would you speak to the master about her first?'

Matron made an exasperated noise in her throat. 'Why is there

211

all this fuss over one little trollop?' Sarah looked at the floor-boards to avoid Matron's eyes as she went on, 'She's been more trouble since she arrived than all the others put together.'

Miss Green was not deterred. 'I believe the doctor has a different course of action in mind for her future. He is such a clever gentleman.'

Matron's eyes softened for a second. 'Oh yes, I know.'

'He will appreciate your support for his recommendation. I know how much he values your opinions.'

'Really? Do you think so?'

'Oh, I do. You will be the doctor's ally in this matter. He is with the master now, ma'am.'

'But I must take Meadow downstairs first,' Matron responded irritably.

'I'll keep her secure in my schoolroom.'

The Matron hesitated. 'Oh, very well,' she decided and hurried away.

Miss Green heaved a sigh. 'Meadow, stand over by the window and stop the little ones from rubbing the lime-wash off the glass.'

'They only want to see their mothers,' Sarah responded.

'Meadow?' Miss Green's tone was enough for Sarah to obey and she occupied the children by silently pulling faces at them and putting her fingers to her lips when they were in danger of giggling too loudly. She was listening to Miss Green teach letters to the older ones and she wondered how to spell 'charlatan'.

The lesson was interrupted by a woman from the kitchen who spoke quietly to the teacher. Miss Green told her charges to copy passages from books that she handed out, one between two, and then, leaving the woman in charge, said 'Come with me, Meadow.'

'Where are we going?' Sarah asked.

Miss Green glared at her, so she followed her down the corridor without another word.

'Straighten your cap and apron.' The teacher knocked on the master's door and entered. After a second's hesitation, Sarah went after her.

So this is where he is when he stands in the bay window and watches us in the recreation yard, she reflected. It was a square room with furniture similar to the master's at Meadow Hall. A shelf held a row of ledgers with the year printed on the spine in red: 1838, 1839, right up to last year; 1844 when Sarah was fifteen. The master sat in a round-backed chair at a big wooden desk. In the room there was also a dining table with chairs, a sideboard and a washstand, too, with drying towels hanging each side and a decorated china ewer and bowl.

'Well, Meadow. Have you learned your lesson?'

'Yes, sir.'

'That remains to be seen. The doctor has advised that you are removed from the laundry to the schoolroom,' he said.

Dear Lord, Sarah thought. The teacher was right about the doctor! He must have something to hide!

'I found this surprising, Miss Green,' the master went on, 'but he told me of a charitable foundation in London where women are taken off the streets and taught how to read and write so they can earn their living in a different way.'

'I have read of their successes in the news sheets, sir.'

He shook his head. 'This one is far too old to learn.'

'Let me try. If older women have learned then—'

'Matron wants her in the wash house.'

'You are the master, sir,' Miss Green reminded him.

He stood up and placed his hands on his desk. 'Indeed I am and I am the one who has to answer to the guardians. They require two things above all else from the inmates; hard work and piety. She has shown neither.'

'But if the doctor believes that she is able, I am sure Mr Parrish will approve. He is advanced in his thinking on these matters.'

'Mr Parrish is not the only guardian I have to please. I cannot have a moral defective, in the schoolroom.'

'But her punishment has done its job, master, and she has promised to mend her ways. Mr Parrish may ask to visit the schoolroom when the guardians meet. He will be pleased to know of your – your progressive ideas.'

Sarah noticed the master thinking about this. Finally, he sniffed audibly and said, 'You'd better be right about this one.'

'Then you will move her?'

He dismissed Miss Green with a flick of his hand. 'Take her with you and send in my nephew. I don't want to hear any more about her.'

'Thank you, sir.'

Miss Green moved quickly. She took Sarah's hand and opened the door.

'You won't let that doctor near me again, will you?' Sarah asked as Miss Green ushered her into the corridor.

'No. He'll move on now I've found out about him.'

'Oh, good. I don't know how to thank you for this.'

Miss Green squeezed her hand again and smiled. 'Do not let me down.'

Chapter 18

'They've wiped the lime-wash off again, Miss Green.'

The children had clattered down the stone stairs and Sarah was tidying the schoolroom. She stared out of the window at the washerwomen pegging out bed sheets in the yard below. She was grateful for being moved and didn't mind being nursemaid to the little ones, but she had been here a few weeks now and Miss Green had not mentioned teaching her to read. Sarah wondered if Miss Green had changed her mind.

'Again?' Miss Green responded. 'I suppose we could ask the master for shutters on the lower windows.'

'They won't be able to see to read or sew, miss.'

'Did you see who did it?'

'They all have a go as they line up for dinner. They pretend to stumble and rub their arm and shoulders on the glass.'

'Is there any way we can stop them?'

'They only want to see their mothers. Why doesn't the master let them?'

'It distracts them from their learning,' Miss Green replied.

'But they can't even have their dinners together!'

'I agree it does seem harsh. But some will leave their mothers for good very soon.'

'Well, I never had no mother,' Sarah stated. 'But if I had and I knew I was going away I'd want to see her as much as I could before I went.'

Miss Green stared into space for moment. 'I never knew my mother either. I have asked the master if the children and mothers may take recreation together on Sunday afternoons but he declined.' She collected her thoughts and added, 'Is that laundry in the corner?'

'Yes. Three of the new ones have wet themselves already today.'

'Did their mothers not teach them to use a privy?'

'Not when they have half a dozen others crying at their skirts,' Sarah replied.

Miss Green sighed, 'I suppose not. We'll have to take them down more often. I am so pleased to have your help.'

'I'm glad to be here, Miss Green.' Sarah liked the teacher very much but she did blow hot and cold with her. One day she'd be really friendly and warm and the next she'd be as strict as Matron. It was as though she wanted to take back any show of friendship, if that's what it had been. Or perhaps she was worried that Sarah might take advantage of her and let her down. This made Sarah more determined to please her. 'I can do much more to help you if you learn me—'

'*Teach,* Meadow. I shan't tell you again.'

'Sorry, miss. If you teach me my letters, I could read them stories.'

'This is the workhouse, not some royal nursery.'

'Bible stories, I mean.'

Miss Green sat down in her high-back chair and sighed. 'Be patient, Meadow. The only time I have is when the children are in bed. As soon as the evenings are light enough to see without candles we can make a start.' She smiled at her and said softly. 'I do look forward to that.' Then she jumped to her feet and said, 'Now stop dawdling. You should be in the day room helping with dinner.'

* * *

As the days lengthened the weather became warmer. Miss Green found time at the end of her day to return to the schoolroom for Sarah's lessons. At first Miss Green sat at her desk and Sarah worked on her slate from the children's bench. Once she had started to learn she was surprised at how much she enjoyed it and now easily it came to her.

One evening Miss Green said, 'Come and stand by my desk, Meadow.'

Sarah got up with her slate.

Miss Green took it from her and put it aside. 'I want you to read to me. You have learned well. Your number work is exceptional and I am proud of your progress.'

'Thank you, miss.'

Her teacher smiled. 'You have exceeded my expectations and I shall be able to write a good report for the guardians.'

'Will I be able to stay with you in the schoolroom?'

'Would you like to?'

'Yes, miss.' Sarah picked up a book from the desk. 'Is this the one you wish me to read?' She opened it at the beginning.

Miss Green took it from her hands. 'I have changed my mind. Tonight we shall talk. Will you sit in my visitor's chair?'

Sarah settled in the only upholstered chair in the room and asked, 'What do you want to talk about?'

'You and me, Meadow. But I shall call you Sarah now we are alone. And you may call me Henrietta.'

Sarah didn't want to. She preferred Miss Green. 'That's a name for a gentlewoman,' she said.

'I used to be a governess for a titled family.'

'You were a governess for the gentry, and now you're a teacher in the workhouse! What happened to you?'

'I was considered suitable for the gentry because I was something called a ward in chancery until I became of age.'

'What's one of them when it's at home?'

'An orphan, a bastard, a child that no one wants.' She said it lightly, but with a frown and Sarah was shocked that she did not seem to mind talking about it.

Sarah said, 'I'm an orphan, too. I'm not a wicked person, though, and I didn't do those things the doctor said. But the master believed him. I've never been with a man, honest.'

'I believe you.'

'Do you?'

'Yes, I recognised a kindred spirit; a child who has been unjustly accused and with no one to care for her, but one with strength and determination, nonetheless.'

Sarah felt a pang of sadness. She'd thought that Aidan had cared for her once, but she'd been wrong. 'Did no one care for you, miss?'

'I was a special kind of orphan. I do not know who my parents were but one of them at least must have had means to pay for my upbringing.'

'Did no one tell you who they were?'

'No one knew, not even the lawyers who held the means to pay for my education.'

'I never knew my parents neither. I wonder what is worse: knowing your parents and not being able to be with them, like in here, or never knowing who they are, only that they did not want you.'

'You are perceptive, Sarah.'

It sounded strange being called Sarah again after so long. 'What did you do wrong?' she queried.

'I was employed as a governess and the mistress of the house took an unusual interest in me. She said she loved me and showed me what my true feelings were.'

'The *mistress* loved you?'

'They called it unnatural but it did not seem so to me at the time.'

Sarah began to feel uncomfortable. It seemed unnatural to her and she didn't know what to say.

'Have you ever felt the same, Sarah?'

'No! Where did you get that idea from?'

'You told me as much after you were alone in here with the doctor. At least you said the sight of a man's private parts made you vomit.'

'But that was because it reminded me of – of an overgrown maggot and I thought he wanted me to put it in my mouth.'

'It wasn't because he was a man?'

'Well, yes, because he was that particular man. He was vile and the very thought of him makes me want to vomit even now. But—,' She remembered the warm summer in the woods with Aidan and how she had wanted him, body and soul, as a man. 'But – I did – I once thought I cared deeply for a man – until he betrayed me.'

A haunted expression filled Miss Green's eyes. 'I – I am mistaken about you. You must not tell anyone here what I have just told you. Promise me you won't.'

The sadness in her voice made Sarah want to weep. 'Of course I promise. I would not want to harm anyone who has helped me as you have. What happened to you when you were a governess?' she asked.

'The master found us together. He – he sent my beloved mistress to an asylum.'

'Oh, poor thing; I suppose he thought she was mad. What happened to you?'

'I was dismissed, of course, without a reference. I obtained another post eventually in a charity school. It ran out of money and closed, so I applied for the position here where no one knows of my past.'

'Did you never wish for a gentleman sweetheart when you were young?' Sarah asked gently.

Miss Green attempted to compose herself. 'Do you think I have not battled against my passion? No. You are too young to know what love is.'

'Love? I do not think love exists. No one has ever shown me any love. I know only of betrayal.'

'Love does exist and it is real. Have you never felt desire for anyone?'

Sarah remembered her desire for Aidan to hold her and kiss her. She believed she would have given herself to him if he had returned her passion, she answered, 'Only in the way of fornication; surely that is not love.'

'It is part of love and may be how it starts. But love is more. It is a burning, lasting need to be with someone, to want to care for them and protect them, and yes, to join your body with theirs.'

Sarah shook her head. 'Then I do not wish to love anyone in that way, or any way. I am glad I do not have a sweetheart, or indeed a family, for I have seen how love can tear people apart when it is not fulfilled. The workhouse denies it for mothers and their children. This is a cruel place.' There was sadness in Miss Green's eyes and, impulsively, Sarah took her hand to comfort her. 'You have been kind towards me. You were the only one who believed me rather than the doctor's lies and I shall never forget that, Miss Green. I shall always be grateful to you.'

Miss Green clutched her fingers. 'It will be enough for me to see you leave this place with a vocation. The workhouse has treated you badly and I shall make sure that you gain from your learning. Even if I can never leave this place, you must.'

'But how? The master still considers me to be a moral defective.'

'Then you must show him you have reformed and how clever you have become. You may help me with the schoolroom records and ledgers.'

Sarah's eyes shone. 'Do you think I am ready for that?'

'Of course you are. I shall show you what to do and you will be as good as any clerk!'

Sarah didn't believe she could do such complicated sums at first. But as the weeks rolled by she realised that bookwork wasn't such a mystery after all and, before long, Sarah was writing all Miss Green's reports and accounts for the master and guardians.

An approaching guardians' meeting was creating quite a flurry of work in the third-floor office of the workhouse as everyone knew Mr Parrish, who was chairman, checked every last detail and Miss Green trusted only Sarah to help compile all the necessary paperwork.

'Mr Parrish was a poorhouse boy himself years ago,' Miss Green explained to Sarah, 'and has worked hard all his life. He owns the glassworks in town.'

'He must be very rich.'

'If he is, it does not show. He is a Methodist and gives much of his wealth away to chapel missions. It was Mr Parrish who insisted on a school for workhouse children. He reads all my reports and has an eagle eye for detail.'

It was evening and the children were settled in their dormitories. Sarah was sitting by the window going over the schoolroom's costing for a second time when the door burst open.

'Oh, there you are!' It was the master's nephew carrying an armful of heavy books. 'Uncle hasn't time to check my figures before I write the reports for the guardians. Will you do them for me, Miss Green?' He dropped the ledgers untidily on a bench.

Miss Green sighed and answered, 'You have left it rather late, young man.'

'Well, I do all my uncle's bookkeeping now. I am to attend the meetings with him in future.'

'Then you had best be sure your accounts are accurate.'

'I know.' He groaned. 'And I have to write the order of business before tomorrow.'

'Leave them with me,' Miss Green responded. 'I'll take them back to the master.'

The master's nephew left speedily without as much as a thank you.

'What are they?' Sarah queried, closing her own record book.

'They're the workhouse records. Every penny must be accounted for. That's why the master has his nephew to help.

Well, you'll have to assist me, Sarah, or I shall be here all night. Draw the table to the window and fetch the candles.'

There was a month of entries and Sarah noted with interest how the money was spent. She noted, also, several errors in the page totals making some expenses appear higher than they were. 'He's put some figures in the wrong column and been very careless with adding up,' she commented. 'I'll get pen and ink to make the changes.'

'No, better not,' Miss Green warned. 'The master does not like crossings-out in his ledgers. I'll tell him where the discrepancies are. His reports will be accurate. But he will have to pray that Mr Parrish doesn't ask to inspect the ledgers for he will spot them too and that will mean trouble.'

'Well, tell his nephew to do his figures in pencil next time; or at least before we've checked them for him.'

'I don't think the master will allow that.'

'Then let me do them for him,' she suggested eagerly.

'He most certainly won't allow that. Be patient, Sarah. I am doing my best for you but in the master's eyes you are still a moral defective and not to be trusted.'

Sarah bit back a response. Was she to be labelled as such for ever? How would she ever get out of the workhouse if Miss Green could not persuade the master to change his mind about her? Dear Heaven, would she be here for ever?

Chapter 19

Not long afterwards, they were in the middle of morning school when the door to the schoolroom opened unexpectedly and the master stood on the threshold.

'On your feet.' Miss Green clapped her hands and forty children stood to attention. Sarah hurried around the little ones pulling them to their feet. Within a minute Sarah could have heard a pin drop and the master stepped into the schoolroom.

'Take them all outside,' he ordered.

'But it's raining, sir.'

'The schoolroom is out of bounds for the remainder of the day.'

'Very well, master,' Miss Green answered and added, 'Meadow, take them to the dormitory for their cloaks. Hurry!'

Sarah shepherded the class along the corridor and up two flights of stairs. Miss Green took away her older pupils for nature study in the workhouse garden, leaving Sarah to cope with the little ones. It took her half an hour to make sure they were wearing shawls under their cloaks before she led them down the stone steps to the yard. As she passed the schoolroom floor she saw what the fuss was about and eavesdropped on the conversation. The master was talking to an artisan about replacing the glass in the schoolroom window. She hoped it was not to be wooden panels; they were so dark and gloomy.

'We're using flawed window glass, sir,' she heard. 'It lets in the light but you can't see through it.'

'Excellent. Carry on.' The master stood outside his office to observe the activity.

Poor children, Sarah thought. Now they would never see their mothers. 'Hurry along,' she chivvied. 'Catch up the others.'

'We can't.'

'Why not?'

'There's a man coming up the steps. He's carrying summat.'

'Outta t'way, you lot!'

The children clattered back to the first-floor landing and crushed Sarah against the wall. They huddled together as the man carried the new glass wrapped in sacking down the corridor to the schoolroom. Sarah stared in amazement. It was Danby. Danby was here in the workhouse carrying building materials. She did not know whether to be pleased or angry; pleased to see a familiar face from her past, but angry – very angry – that he had deserted her so readily.

Why hadn't he come looking for her? They were going to go off together before that – that *treacherous* Aidan had brought her here! Had he forgotten about her so quickly? *As soon as another pretty girl comes along.* Aidan had said that about Danby, and she reckoned it was true. He was as guilty as Aidan and she wanted to march up to him and thump him for deserting her so quickly. Did he never wonder what had happened to her?

As she gazed at him, trying to quell her anger, she could see that he had grown even more attractive, with his piercing blue eyes and shock of curling fair hair. He was a little taller, definitely broader across the shoulders, and clean too. His working clothes were tidy and fitted him well. He must have a proper position somewhere! They were good friends once; perhaps he could help her to get out of here. She pushed her anger to one side.

'Danby!' she called. 'It's me! Sarah!'

He turned his head briefly and she saw a flash of recognition that quickly died.

'Danby?' she repeated, but he had disappeared into the school-room and she set off after him.

'Do you know that man?' the master demanded.

Sarah's features froze and she remembered what the matron had said to Aidan when he left her here. *You don't want to be associated with women like her.* Was that why Danby had not acknowledged her? If he was delivering goods to the workhouse he must be in a trusted position and she had better not mess things up for him; not when she wanted his help.

'No, master,' she replied. 'It was my mistake. I thought he was somebody else.'

'Well get these children out of the way and look sharp about it.'

Sarah ushered them down the stairs in front of her. At the bottom she said to the eldest. 'If Miss Green asks, tell her I've gone back for my shawl.' She hurried back up the steps and heard Danby talking with the other man.

'You make a start on taking out the old windows; I'll go down for the rest of the glass.'

'Right you are, sir.'

The artisan called Danby 'sir'! Swiftly Sarah turned to hide in the stairwell.

Danby's boots rang on the stone steps. She put her finger to her lips and fell into step beside him until they were out of earshot.

'So you're still here.'

'You knew where I was?' Her eyes widened and she reigned in her bubbling anger.

He grimaced. 'That workhouse gown doesn't do much for you.'

As though she had a choice! 'It's as awful to wear as it is to look at. When I think about that lovely soft gown I had off the market I want to weep. This is a dreadful place.'

225

'You don't have to tell me. I was brought up in a workhouse. Why haven't they found you a position?'

'I don't think the master has even tried yet.'

'Well, I never wanted you to come here.'

'So why didn't you come back for me?' She pursed her lips.

'It was Aidan's idea.' He shrugged.

'I know and I hate him for it. Where is he?'

'I've no idea. He disappeared after that set-to at Jackson's house. Maybe he's gone back to the East Riding.'

'Is that where he's from?'

'Didn't you know?'

'Why should I? You were wrong about us two. He never really showed any interest in me last summer.' She stopped and took hold of his arm. 'Danby, can you help me to get out of here.'

'What do you mean?'

'Tell the guardians you're my brother and then they'll have to let me go. We could go round the taverns like you planned.'

'I'm not doing that now. I've got proper work with the glass-works.'

'Have you? What, with wages every week?'

'Aye. I'm going to lodge with the carter at his house.'

'Could I stay there, too?'

'Not from the workhouse, you can't. His missus is respectable.'

Danby didn't want to help her at all and she felt depressed. 'Is she pretty?' she asked.

He grinned at her. 'Not as pretty as you, Sam.'

'Don't call me that.'

'Why not? You could be, let me think, how about Samantha?'

'I prefer Sarah, nobody calls me Sam now. Oh, Danby, please help me. I've got no one else to turn to.'

'I don't know what I can do. I can't look after you and you're only fifteen. You have to have an indenture from a sponsor to be let out.'

'Don't you know anybody? What about the carter? He must know someone. You could make enquiries for me.'

'It doesn't happen like that. The guardians arrange everything.'

'How do you know?'

'I told you, I was brought up in a place like this. Besides, I work for Mr Parrish.'

'Do you? He's one of our guardians!'

'I know, and he owns the glassworks. He's important and I'm not going to get on the wrong side of him, so keep away from me.'

'Oh please, Danby. I have to get out of here somehow. Can't you do anything?' She reached the bottom of the steps and stopped suddenly. 'You'd better stay here while I join the children and don't even glance at me if other folk are around else I'll get the blame.'

He looked surprised. 'Why's that then?'

'The master says I'm a moral defective and will revert to my former ways.'

'And you want me to help you find a place to go? You don't ask much do you?'

'Please, Danby.' She turned her wide beseeching eyes on him. 'There is no one else.'

He shook his head. 'I can't let on I knew you before you were in here. I'd be tarred by the same brush and kicked out of my lodgings.'

'But you have to! You're my only chance.'

He shook his head emphatically and went through a passage to the back yard. Sarah was seething with anger. Did all that friendship and sharing in the woods count for nothing? Seemingly not, but despite her fury she had to turn her attention to the crowd of young children whining to go inside out of the rain.

But meeting him had stirred her memories of Aidan too. She tried not to think of him because it hurt so much to remember how he had betrayed her. It always made her weep and she had to swallow hard to suppress her tears. She had wanted to stay with Aidan for ever and he had just wanted rid of her. Even now, after all this time, she had to stifle a sob. How could he have done it to her? Aidan was a *good* man; worth ten of Danby any day. If he had been fitting glass today, he wouldn't have spurned her as Danby did, would he? She let out an exasperated gasp. He wouldn't! She was sure of it. He would have tried to help her. So why had he not come back for her as he promised?

Chapter 20

'No, I don't want to leave you, Rose, and I shan't. I promise.'
Danby kissed her luscious mouth. He had called in to see her as
he took the cart back from the workhouse. His blood was up
after seeing Sarah. It still rankled that Aidan had stopped him
going off with her, even though he hadn't particularly wanted
her. Well, he would have had her if she offered, but she was
nowhere near as desirable as his Rose.

'But father cannot manage the barrels on his own any
more.'

'Sweetheart, he has to take on a lad; a youngster who does
not mind working for the price of a meal.'

'You get more than your food from me and you know it!'

'Which is why you will always be my love.' He smiled.

'Always?'

'I won't abandon you, but I will not stay here as his unpaid
servant when I can have regular work at the glassworks and proper
lodgings in town.'

'Yes, and it's all thanks to me! I introduced you to that carter
when he came in on a Saturday night.'

Danby put his arms around Rose's ample form and thought

how much he would miss their nightly couplings. 'I'll come over as often as I can. Let me get settled in first.'

'You'll meet someone else.'

'No, I won't. There's no other girl for me.' He bent his head to kiss the mounds of her bosom swelling out of her bodice, and pushed his face into their softness.

'Then stay.'

'I can't. Your father's already listening to the gossip about us.'

'But he believes me when I say I keep the door locked against you.'

'He's not daft. He'll come downstairs one night and kill me.'

'Not if you told him we were getting wed. I'll ask father to clear out an upstairs room for us.'

'Steady on, lass. What would we live on?'

'You don't need money to live here.'

'And have your father push me around like he does you? I'd be the one to kill him, then.' His hands roamed all over her body and she squirmed closer to him, murmuring appreciatively. By God, he was going to miss her. 'I'll call in when I can for a pint or two.'

'But when can we – you know – when can we do it?'

'I'll find a way. I don't want to go without any more than you do. I'll come back later.'

She smiled up at him and he covered her mouth with his, pressing his tongue against hers and feeling his desire rising. He pulled himself away. Doing it two or three times a night didn't matter in an alehouse when he didn't stir until the middle of the morning. But if he had to be up at five or six o'clock for his new job, he'd have to spend his nights away from Rose and her appetite. And he was quite excited about working at the glassworks. He'd been introduced to the owner who had put him on the payroll. Trade was expanding and they needed men with a bit of common sense about them to transport their goods.

Besides, he reckoned he'd be more comfortable lodging with the carter and his family. They lived in a better part of town. He thought that, having a regular wage, he might go to night school at the Mechanics Institute to better himself, and no one would question a drink with his fellow scholars afterwards. But he didn't want to give up Rose. He liked her too much.

Later that evening, Danby jumped down from the cart, shouted 'goodnight' to the carter and doubled back to see Rose. His groin stirred in anticipation and he quickened his step.

Her father was a fat old boozer now and took too much of his own drink. Rose had taken to adding a tincture to his ale so that he slept soundly enough for them to use her bedroom.

The alehouse was shut and the window curtains were closed. He hurried round the back. The kitchen was in darkness but candles burned all around. The still mound of Rose's father was laid out on the kitchen table and Rose was sitting staring at the dying fire in the grate.

'Oh, Danby, thank goodness you're here. I don't know what to do.' Rose fell against him, weeping into his waistcoat. 'He's dead. My father is dead. He just keeled over after his dinner.'

'My poor lass. You should have sent me a note to the glass-works.'

'You're here now. Hold me, Danby. Please.'

He did as she asked and eventually her wailing quietened.

'I need you more than ever now,' she whispered. She stroked the front of his trousers and he resisted a groan. He couldn't do it here, not with the dead body of her father laid out on the kitchen table! But Rose seemed more hungry than usual for his attentions and when her hands and mouth went to work on him, his body never let him down.

'Oughtn't we to wait?' he glanced sideways at the body, 'until after the burial.'

'I can't,' she replied and he allowed her to lead him upstairs.

It was the same as the first time with her – she couldn't get enough of him. She got up to fetch ale, bread and cheese when they had finished.

231

'You didn't put a sponge in,' he commented.

'I didn't expect you. But everything will change now father has gone, won't it?'

'How do you mean?

'We can marry, of course. There's nothing to stop us.'

'Hey, wait a minute. Where will we live?'

'Here. This place belongs to me now.'

'You mean your father left it to you?'

'That's right. I've waited long enough for the old tyrant to go.'

'You're not thinking of running it on your own, are you?'

'Didn't you hear what I said? There'll be two of us so there's nothing to stop us getting wed.'

'But there is! Mr Parrish is a chapel-goer and he's teetotal. He'll get rid of me if I marry a woman who's an alehouse keeper. He'll not stand for it.'

'So? You can come here.'

Danby did not answer for a long time. He wanted Rose but he didn't want to live in this grubby little alehouse on the rough side of town. He preferred his comfortable lodgings and his regular wage from Mr Parrish. He watched Rose's face getting angrier and angrier at his silence

'You think I'm not good enough for you now you've got a respectable job. You're as bad as that old bugger laid out downstairs. He used me as his domestic slave and you – you just used me for – for this!'

She took hold of his flaccid cock and gave it a yank.

'Get off, you witch. That hurt.'

'It was meant to!'

'Well, I seem to remember it was you who came to me for it first.'

'Aye, but you kept coming back for more. And it wasn't the board and lodging you came for. You can't go without it, can you? Well, if you don't wed me you're going to have to. Or pay one of the tavern women and see how you like what they'll give you as well as your oats.'

232

He knew what she meant. 'Don't be like that, Rose. I'm in the same noose as you were with your father. I have to toe the line with Mr Parrish. He's a Methodist and they don't hold with ale and spirits. We'll just have to wait a bit. He's an old man and once he's dead and gone it won't matter about your alehouse.'

She calmed and he was relieved. He didn't want to lose her and it wasn't only their couplings that he craved. He was really fond of her and he couldn't do without her now.

'Did I really hurt you?' she said in a small voice.

'Yes,' he replied. 'I hope you haven't done any damage.'

'Oh!' Rose sounded alarmed.

'You'd better see, hadn't you?' He lay back on the pillows and placed his hands behind his head. 'Go on then.'

She kissed him briefly and then moved her mouth to his most sensitive area where her lips and tongue worked their magic on him. Oh dear Lord. What bliss, he thought. He gazed at their shadows on the ceiling and closed his eyes. When he was ready, she turned and lowered herself over him, sitting astride his body. She moved on top of him, riding him like a horse, and he gave himself up to the unbelievable thrill. Dear God, she was wonderful. This was better than ever with her. She finished before him, cried out his name then stayed there, over him, still moving and panting until he pulsed inside her. He let out a long sighing groan, smiled in the darkness and opened his eyes. Her head was flung back, her arms hung loosely behind her body, so her beautiful, plump and drooping breasts were thrusting towards him. He placed his hands over them, lifted his strong back off the mattress and buried his face in them. She was his own special woman and he wanted to keep it that way.

'Are you coming in for dinner, Aidan?'

'I'll be right with you, Mr Thorpe.'

Aidan gripped his tongs and plunged a red-hot curl of wrought iron into the water. The steam and sizzle were satisfying. He enjoyed working in his forge and had nearly finished the railings.

He caught up with his landlord and they entered the kitchen together.

'My word, that smells good.'

Emma looked up from the cooking range. 'I've put clean water in the scullery. It's just the three of us in here. Mariah and Sarah are busy in the workroom. I'll take them a tray.'

Sarah? Every time Aidan heard the name, he thought it sounded familiar. But he did not know this Sarah and she had never met him before. 'I am pleased that Mrs Thorpe is well,' he commented as he washed black smuts from his face. 'You will be wanting my chamber for a nursery soon. I shall look for lodgings close by.'

Mr Thorpe handed him a drying cloth. 'I have another solution. My stable lad lives with his family and the coachman's quarters over the horses is empty. It's yours if you are interested.'

'I most certainly am, sir.'

'Have a look at it sometime. It might need a repair here and there.'

'Thank you, Mr Thorpe.'

Their dinner of mutton stew and dumplings followed by gooseberry pie was soon over and Mr Thorpe took a can of tea with him back to his furnaces. Aidan and Emma shared a pot at the table.

'Any news from the marketplace?' he asked.

'Are you sure this is wise, Aidan?'

'I've made a full recovery.' Physically, he thought. Why do I feel that a part of me is still missing?

'An ironmonger in town thinks you went into his shop with samples of hinges. He said they were good quality so it could well have been you.'

'Where is he situated?'

'On Bridgegate, just down from the market.'

'I'll go and talk to him. Thank you, Emma.'

'There's something else.'

'Yes?' he pressed eagerly.

Emma took a deep breath. 'Aidan, this may stir painful

memories. You do not know what happened, only that you were almost killed. I don't wish to make you unhappy.'

'Tell me, Emma. I beg you.'

'Very well. You were looking for a place; a domestic position for your – your sister.'

'I was?'

'The ironmonger's daughter had need of a servant for the house and you were going to take her along later. You never went back with her, though.'

'I didn't think I had a sister,' he said.

'That's what I thought. You remembered your parents so I feel sure you would have some memory of a sister.'

Aidan frowned and shook his head.

'Perhaps she was your sweetheart?'

Aidan was aware that his heart started to beat faster and he felt hot. She was the girl in the woods? If he had brought her into town, where was she now? Something dreadful had happened to her; something so awful that his mind would not let him recall it. His eyes lost their focus as he desperately, *desperately,* tried to remember.

'Aidan? What's wrong? *Aidan!* Are you ill?'

Emma had half risen to her feet before Aidan refocused on her face. He wiped his forehead with the back of his hand and felt the sweat clinging to his skin.

'I'm – I'm – I don't know.'

'I think you are. The doctor warned you about this. Really, Aidan, I don't think you should continue this – this pursuit for those lost days.'

'*Where is she?*'

'Aidan, please listen to me. If she were – if she were still here and – and you were dear to her, she would be searching for you.'

'Yes! Yes, she would!' Her name is Sarah, he thought suddenly. I am sure of it. 'Is anyone looking for me?'

'Not as far as I know,' Emma replied.

He tried to calm his anxiety. Emma was a sensible, kind young

235

woman and he did not want to alarm her in any way. 'I'll speak to the ironmonger myself.'

'Aidan, please don't seek out trouble. You really oughtn't to be asking questions about a girl who – who might be, well, just a girl from the streets.'

'Very well,' he agreed uneasily. 'I'll do as you ask.' Emma and her family had been so kind and generous to him it would be ill-mannered of him to cause them further worry. 'I'll try to leave those days behind me and accept that they have disappeared from my life.'

Emma looked relieved, and Aidan headed back to his anvil.

He had the makings of a good business in the forge. It would take all his time and effort to make it sound. He resolved to throw himself into his work and try to forget about the past, at least for now. But, underneath, the questions continued to nag him. Why had Sarah not come looking for him? What had happened to her? Why did he still feel like there was something important that he couldn't recall? For a second he thought he remembered – a fleeting image that flitted away as soon as it arrived. His frustration was worse as he could no longer share it with Emma. He sighed and picked up his hammer trying to lose himself in work.

Chapter 21

Summer, 1848

'I have asked the master if you may wait on the guardians' meeting.'

'Instead of the master's nephew?'

'As well as him, my dear. They are to discuss your progress. You have worked in the schoolroom and the master's office for three years now and grown into a clever, confident young woman.'

'Thank you.'

Sarah had benefitted from Miss Green's devotion. Although she was still in the workhouse, she was now employed solely in the schoolroom, which meant she answered directly to the master and was spared Matron's venom and spite. As for Miss Green, she, unlike matron, accepted her role in life stoically and Sarah admired her fortitude. She had nurtured and protected Sarah, giving her tuition and guidance that allowed Sarah's talent for numbers to flourish.

'I do not think the master could hold his meetings without your help, Miss Green.'

'Well, his nephew has not shown much promise for the future.'

'He does his best.' Sarah thought that he lacked concentration.

'There will be meat and drink for the guardians as Mr Parrish is saying farewell to workhouse duties. He is of advancing years and his glassworks is thriving so he must give up one or the other. I heard a rumour that he needs a clerk.'

'Perhaps the master's nephew will go with him?'

'Mr Parrish is more likely to take a favoured inmate. He was a poorhouse child himself, in the days before we had workhouses, and believes in rewarding those who work hard to help themselves.'

'That will be good news for one of the boys from the school.' Sarah had long since stopped asking if she might obtain an indenture and leave. Miss Green relied on her for many teaching and clerical tasks and in this respect she was no different from Matron. Sarah glanced at her skirts. 'I shall have to sponge this gown if I am to wait on gentlemen.'

'I have a gown you may wear. It is plain and serviceable, but I have linen collar and cuffs for Sundays and you may wear them for the meeting.'

'I wish my sewing talents were equal to my clerical skills.'

'They are satisfactory. You cannot excel at everything!' Miss Green laughed.

The gown was dark grey, as dowdy as her workhouse brown, but Sarah worked on it with Miss Green's guidance until it fitted well. The linen, though cream with age, was good quality and it laundered well. She polished her boots until they shone.

The little ones were settled early as they were promised stories from the older children and, if no sounds came from the dormitory, biscuits as well.

'Where do the biscuits come from?'

'Mr Parrish sent them for the schoolroom; and joints of boiled bacon for the kitchen.'

'That is very generous of him.' Sarah felt excited about meeting them kindly benefactor.

The meeting room was grand compared with the rest of the workhouse and lay immediately behind the entrance lobby. It had a large fireplace with a wooden surround and the fire was lit early. In the centre of the room was a long polished table and matching chairs with wooden arms and upholstered seats were arranged around it. A light supper was laid out on a sideboard.

'Look at all that!' Sarah was astounded. The guardians' supper was a feast: ham, butter and cheese, enough loaves of fresh-baked bread for everyone to eat their fill, lettuce hearts and radishes. Sarah had not seen so much appetising food since her days at Meadow Hall.

'Hush, Sarah. Mr Parrish has provided the feast for his farewell. It is what the guardians are used to eating in their own homes. Do not forget that they give their time freely for the benefit of the workhouse.'

A harassed Matron brought in ewers of ale and a large dish of summerberry fruits on a tray. She took one look at Sarah and barked, 'What are you doing in here dressed like that? Don't you dare touch any of this or I'll have your hide.'

'She won't.' Miss Green stepped forward from the shadows.

'I didn't see you there, Miss Green,' Matron said.

'The master gave his permission for Meadow to help with preparations for the guardians' meeting. He is to show them how successful we have been with a moral defective.'

It still wounded Sarah to be so described, but she did not protest. She realised that the worse she had appeared to be when she came in, the better the job Miss Green had done with her. And she was determined to impress the guardians. She was eighteen now and wanted a position. She had copied out the order of business for the master and laid the beautifully scripted sheets of paper around the table exactly as Miss Green had shown her.

The master arrived next and demanded, 'Where are the costings?'

'Your nephew will bring them down when he has finished,' Sarah answered.

'That boy!' Matron hissed. 'He's too slow to carry a cold dinner.'

Sarah silently agreed, but concentrated on her task. Miss Green had turned her attention to pouring glasses of sherry wine and Matron was distracted by the sounds of horses and carriages from outside. As the gentlemen arrived, the master met them in the lobby and Matron took their hats and coats.

Miss Green gave Sarah the wooden tray of sherry wine to offer the men when they entered the meeting room. She kept her eyes down as instructed. One or two of the gentleman took a second glance at her and said, 'Thank you, my dear,' but most immersed themselves in conversation with their fellow guardians straightaway. Mr Parrish was last to arrive. Sarah was surprised by his small stature and advancing years. He was wrinkled and bent and needed one of his coachmen to assist him from his carriage. At least she supposed he was a coachman until the gentlemen parted and she saw who it was.

Danby was helping Mr Parrish to his chair at the head of the table. She was astounded. He must be well acquainted with the chairman of the guardians to be assisting him in such a personal manner. Danby was certainly more than just an artisan now! He wore a long tailored jacket and highly polished boots; had he been working for Mr Parrish since she had last seen him? Surely he could have done something – anything – to offer her some hope of release? Danby knew from his own experiences what workhouse life was like and she was still furious with him for ignoring her plight three years ago. He was as treacherous as Aidan in that respect. The very thought of Aidan's betrayal made her shake with anger and her fingers clenched the rim of the tray so tightly her knuckles went white.

Danby saw her and frowned. Then he gave a small shake of his head and looked away, busying himself with settling Mr Parrish in his chair. He left the room without a backward glance at her. Dear Lord, he had not given her a second thought since she had last seen him and, even now, had no wish to acknowledge her. If her future were not so dependent on her good behaviour in the meeting she would have thrown the tray of wine glasses after him!

She inhaled deeply, a ruse Miss Green had taught her in order to control her temper, and took her tray of sherry wine over to Mr Parrish. He declined with a brief smile. His face was lined and it obviously pained him to move but his eyes were bright and alert.

'Meadow!' Miss Green whispered. 'Pay attention. The master's nephew is here with the costings. Help him put them out.'

Sarah took the thick sheets of paper and laid one carefully underneath each order of business. As she did so, she cast her eyes over the contents, mentally noting the items and amounts the master had spent. When she got to the last place around the table, she ran her index finger down the column of figures and said, without thinking, 'It's wrong.'

Not everyone heard her, but those standing nearby, including the master, did. His face set in anger. 'Be quiet,' he snapped. 'Miss Green, you can take Meadow outside now.'

Puzzled, Sarah repeated, 'But it *is* wrong, sir.'

Mr Parrish heard her and picked up his copy, scanning it briefly. 'Come here and show me, miss,' he said.

Sarah thought at first he meant Miss Green and looked at her. But she nodded at Sarah and tipped her head in Mr Parrish's direction, signalling to her to obey.

'It's this column here, sir,' Sarah explained. 'The total shouldn't be as high as that.'

'You have learned number?'

'Yes, sir. Miss Green taught me.'

'What is your name, miss?'

'Meadow, sir.'

'Ah yes. We are to discuss your future today.' Mr Parrish took out his pince-nez spectacles and examined the figures. 'It appears very orderly to me. How can you be sure?'

'Well, if you add up the pounds roughly in your head it can't come to that much at the bottom, it just can't.'

'You have an eye for detail.' He ran his thumbnail down the column. 'You are correct. Can you show me where the error lies?'

Sarah scanned the list again. 'Oh, yes. It's there, sir.' She pointed to an item from the butcher. 'That figure has been entered in the wrong columns. Look, sir, those meat bones at sixpence each should come to two pounds, two shillings and sixpence, but it's been added in as twenty-two pounds and six shillings.'

Mr Parrish turned to the master. 'What do you say, sir?'

Sarah hardly dared look up as a silence surrounded her. The gentlemen had stopped talking and moved to their places around the table. One or two were looking at their papers.

The master's face slowly turned a dark, angry red. His wife and nephew slid out of the door and Miss Green put down the tray she was carrying.

'Well?'

'I – I – it appears that there has been an error in the copying, sir.'

'In the copying, you say?'

'I am quite sure it is the copying, sir.'

'In that case, your bought ledger will be correct. Would you kindly fetch it for my inspection?'

The master's eyes widened. 'You want to see it now, Mr Parrish?'

'I believe I must, sir. I have called this meeting to ensure work-house affairs are in order before I retire and I do not wish to leave inaccurate records.' When the master did not move, he added, 'Bring it to me at once, please.'

The master's agitation worsened. 'Rest assured, sir, that I shall punish my clerk severely for his mistake.'

'The ledger,' Mr Parrish repeated.

Sarah stood very still as the door slammed shut behind the master and the sound of raised voices came back through the woodwork.

'Take your seats, gentlemen. Whilst we wait, shall we deal with item nine? Miss Green, tell us about the progress you have made with this particular inmate?'

The master was away for a long time, giving the guardians ample time to question Sarah closely about her remorse for the

242

past, and her learning. Miss Green had schooled her well and she responded in a modest manner. One of the guardians asked her what she would do if she were released. She replied, 'I should like to give service to others.'

'I sincerely hope, by that, you mean to your husband and children.'

'No, sir, for I do not expect to be so blessed. I mean that I wish for gainful employment.'

The guardians murmured to each other and she strained her ears to hear. Miss Green added, 'Meadow has been very useful to me in the schoolroom.'

Mr Parrish shook his head. 'The guardians cannot recommend her for a position as a pupil teacher.'

'She has demonstrated excellent ability with record keeping, sir.'

'Is she as good with letters as she is with numbers?'

'Yes, sir.'

'And her behaviour is exemplary at all times?'

'Yes, sir.'

'Very well, Miss Green. You may take her away now. And find the master; tell him to hurry up.'

Miss Green chivvied Sarah out of the door. 'Go and inspect the dormitories.'

'But what will happen to me now? Will they let me go?'

'The children, Sarah,' Miss Green repeated, and Sarah hurried away.

She had checked on every child, many of whom were still awake and delayed her progress with chatter, when one of the matron's kitchen maids came clattering up the stone steps and panted, 'The master wants you downstairs.'

A summons to see the master usually meant chastisement, and alarmed, Sarah returned slowly to the meeting room. Miss Green was waiting for her.

'Mr Parrish wishes to talk to you. Listen carefully to what he says to you.' Miss Green tidied Sarah's appearance and added, 'Do not look so worried. He is a kind gentleman.' Miss Green opened the door and propelled Sarah into the room.

Mr Parrish looked up as she entered. 'Come and stand by me, Miss Meadow.'

Miss Meadow? She obeyed, not daring to look at the number of eyes staring at her.

'I have read all your reports and discussed them with my fellow guardians. You were a wild, ill-used child when you arrived, and you did not respond to discipline. We thought we would not be able to tame you. However, you have, we are agreed, shown exceptional progress during your time with Miss Green and there is no doubt that you have an aptitude for detailed record keeping.'

Was this Sarah Meadow that he was referring too? She had always done her best for Miss Green, but her teacher had never given such praise. Sarah glanced at her, standing inconspicuously by the door. She had a satisfied, indeed almost smug, look on her face.

Mr Parrish continued. 'Your early behaviour has cautioned me that the guardians would be taking too much of a risk to ask anyone to sponsor you for a position. But, faced with the evidence of your ability, I am persuaded otherwise. However, I should not wish to impose a risk on our workhouse benefactors and, for that reason, I shall offer you a position myself.' His sharp eyes roved around the serious gentlemen seated at the table. 'Indeed, if guardians are not willing to take on children from the work-house, then how can we ask our sponsors to do the same?'

Sarah glanced at the other guardians; some were frowning and shaking their heads. They did not all agree with Mr Parrish.

He returned his attention to her. 'I need a clerk for my glass-works. Normally, I should consider one of the older, more able boys, but Miss Green assures me you are capable of the task and I respect her judgement. I shall continue as your guardian until you are one and twenty. Until then, you will work for me and I will provide lodgings in my home.'

Sarah hardly dared to believe what she was hearing. 'I – I am

244

to leave the workhouse?' she breathed. A jumble of emotions tumbled through her. Happiness, apprehension, even momentary fear and – and gratitude. Miss Green had done it! She had found a way out for her! Sarah wanted to rush over to the door and hug her. Instead she stood rigidly by Mr Parrish's chair trying desperately to stop her body shaking with sheer excitement.

'Th – thank you, sir,' she mumbled at last. 'I shall not let you down.'

'You will be letting Miss Green down as well if you do.'

The room seemed to blur around her. She couldn't think straight. She was leaving! When? When was she going? How would she get there? Her mouth opened but no sounds came out. Miss Green came forward and took one of her hands and lead her out of the room.

In the corridor her teacher calmed her down. She grasped both her hands and said, 'This is your chance, Sarah, an opportunity to make something of yourself.'

Dazed, Sarah answered, 'I can't believe it after all these years. I thought I was here for ever.'

'You have a kind and tolerant benefactor. He is firm but he is fair. Do not forget that you still have much to learn about the world.'

Miss Green's words brought Sarah back to earth. What was it like outside the workhouse? The regime had been harsh but, latterly, it had been a shield from the dangers that had once threatened her. A shiver of fear ran down her back as she wondered just exactly what was waiting for her out there.

Chapter 22

'Look at Matron,' Sarah whispered. 'She is still furious with me.'

'The master shouts at her all the time. He is out of favour with the guardians because they believe he was cooking the books,' Miss Green said. 'Remember that, Sarah. Do not bite the hand that feeds you.'

'No, Miss Green.'

The wind whipped across the laundry yard reminding Sarah of that first day when she worked the pump until she was exhausted. She shivered and pulled up her cloak hood. It had been a long month since the guardians' meeting; weeks of constant fretting that Mr Parrish might change his mind about employing her. None of Miss Green's assurances persuaded her otherwise until today when she packed a small box of belongings and said goodbye to the children. Despite Sarah's good fortune, it had been a wrench to leave Maggie's children, especially Josie, and she had shed more tears when she told Maggie she was going.

Matron unlocked the door and they went in out of the cold. The workhouse reception room hadn't changed and Sarah shivered as she remembered Aidan pushing her through the door and the evil so-called doctor who had fled the workhouse within a week of Miss Green's challenge. But most of all, when she thought about it, she recalled the sick emptiness she had felt at Aidan's betrayal.

Why, oh why did it still hurt to think of him? She had accepted long ago that he had not cared for her; that he must have left the Riding for a new life without her. He was probably miles away in the East Riding, wed to a pretty girl from a respectable family, and that notion punctured her joy at leaving the workhouse. She had been a foolish girl to imagine a future with him. Well, she was no longer that wayward child; she was a woman with the ability and confidence to show the world her mettle.

This was a new beginning for Sarah Meadow. She had learned much more than letters and numbers from Miss Green. She had learned that she did not have to marry to stay out of the workhouse; she could earn a living and survive as a spinster. It seemed to her that being a spinster with her own, albeit modest, means was a much more attractive future than finding a sweetheart and risking his betrayal.

'Hurry up, Meadow,' Matron called.

It was time for her final goodbyes and she felt Miss Green's hand creep into hers. How would she have survived Matron's unjust harshness without Miss Green's patronage? She owed everything to her and words of thanks did not seem enough. She wanted to hug her, but such shows of affection were not commonplace in the workhouse.

'Goodbye, Sarah,' Miss Green whispered. 'Go forward to your future.'

'I don't know how to thank you.'

'You have done that already by your determination.'

Sarah noticed tears glistening in Miss Green's eyes as the older woman turned away and she did not let go of Sarah's hand. Sarah's impulsive nature may have been tamed, but it was still a part of her and she gave in to it now. She placed her arms around Miss Green and embraced her forcefully. 'Goodbye, Miss Green. Thank you for all you've done for me.'

The words seemed inadequate but Sarah meant them with all her heart and Miss Green knew that for her arms tightened around Sarah's slender body, almost squeezing her breath away. 'Perhaps we shall meet someday in town?' Sarah murmured.

'No, my dear, do not look back. You will become a lady so you must put your years in the workhouse behind you.'

'I'll never forget you.'

'Nor me you, but this must be a final goodbye for us.' Miss Green released her and stepped back.

'I said hurry up, Meadow,' Matron repeated. 'The trap is already here for you. The Lord only knows why Mr Parrish wants to take on the likes of you. He's a *gentleman,* for Heaven's sake.'

Sarah didn't comment. Miss Green had counselled her well. She was leaving the workhouse and its spiteful matron for good. She gave one backward tearful glance at her mentor, picked up her box and stepped through the outer door. Matron slammed it shut behind her. She heard the key turn in the lock. She stood still and inhaled the air of freedom.

Mr Parrish's trap was waiting outside the gates, the driver standing by the horse's head holding its bridle. This carriage was waiting for *her,* to carry Sarah Meadow to her new life. A shiver of apprehension trickled through her. She squared her shoulders and walked purposefully towards her future.

PART THREE

Chapter 23

'Is it far, sir?' she asked as the trap rattled along the track.

'George, miss. You don't call me sir. That's reserved for Mr Parrish and the new gentleman he's taken on for the glassworks.'

'Oh.' She was not the only new employee. But 'gentleman' did not imply a workhouse boy.

'Don't worry, you'll soon settle in. I'm from the workhouse; so is the housekeeper and the maid.'

'Mr Parrish is a very charitable gentleman.'

'Aye, he is that. He looks after you as long as you're loyal to him.'

As they journeyed Sarah recognised some of the town landmarks but there were also lots of change. The new houses on either side of the Mansfield road were not mansions like Meadow Hall, but they were grand; built of stone, they had large gardens at the front and carriage houses at the back. As the trap slowed, Sarah realised that Mr Parrish lived in one of these impressive villas. An outdoor servant opened the gates as they approached. Sarah gazed entranced at the large windows and tall chimneys. This was to be her home. She wondered if she would sleep in the attic as she had at Meadow Hall.

George pulled up the horse as they reached the house, and the front door opened. 'That's Mrs Couzens,' he said. 'She runs the house and she'll show you where to go.'

Sarah climbed down from the trap and dragged out her box.

'Come along in, my dear, and welcome to your new home.' Mrs Couzens held open the wide front door. 'Put down that box of yours and give me your cloak.'

Sarah obeyed, taking in her grand new surroundings. The entrance hall was spacious, panelled and floored in burnished wood. A wide staircase rose from the far end and divided into two, giving a balcony effect to the first-floor landing.

'It's beautiful,' she breathed.

'I'll take you upstairs to change out of those workhouse clothes. When you're ready, come down to the office, that door –' she indicated, '– to meet Mr Parrish.' Mrs Couzens carried Sarah's cloak to a small lobby by the front door.

Sarah bent down to retrieve her box.

'Leave that, miss. Mary will bring it for you.'

'Oh, I can carry it.'

Mrs Couzens gave her a level stare. 'You don't want young Mary to think I have no need of her, do you?'

'No, of course not.' Sarah straightened quickly. 'Where shall I be sleeping?'

'You're on the first floor, same as Mr Parrish and the new gentleman.'

'I shall have a room to myself?'

'You shall. You are family, you see, like the new gentleman.'

'But where is Mr Parrish's own kin?'

'Bless you, miss. He has no one of his own. He had a wife years ago but she passed on having his firstborn. The infant went with her. They say it was after that he turned to his works and his charities. You'll not be lonely, though. Mary will look after you. We have chambers above you. George lives in the carriage house. He's in charge of the garden as well as the horses.'

Sarah remembered how many servants Meadow Hall had had.

This was a smaller establishment but even so there would be a lot of domestic work. 'I expect you will want me to help with your housekeeping.'

'I will not! You are not a servant. We have a girl from the town when we need her, and George has his gardeners. It's not like in the country. Town is full of folk wanting a day's work.'

'You mentioned another gentleman living here?'

'He'll be home for dinner to meet you. I'll leave you to settle in and change.'

Sarah was overwhelmed. She had been the lowest of the low at Meadow Hall and labelled a defective by everyone except Miss Green in the workhouse. Here she was considered to be an equal to the master. Miss Green had told her she would be a lady, so she must rise to it. With a mounting nervous excitement, she followed Mrs Couzens to her chamber.

The bedchamber did nothing to quell the fluttering in her stomach. It was grandly laid out with polished furniture and heavy drapes at the windows, a clothes cupboard, dressing chest and looking glass. There was also a further cheval glass, a day bed with two matching upholstered chairs . . . she sank down in one and gazed around in amazement. This is what money and position bought. She dearly hoped that Mr Parrish would find that she was worth it. She stood up quickly. Of course she was. She must prove that his faith in her was not misplaced. She would show him; with God's will she would show the whole town!

Mary had laid out two gowns on the bed; they were simply cut in a plain brown and a grey. Sarah fingered the material. Although the colours reminded her of workhouse garb, the fabric was soft and flawless and she had three sets of linen collars and cuffs, one edged in lace for Sundays. She sat in front of the looking glass and pulled off her workhouse cotton cap. She had plaited her hair and wound it around her head in the same fashion as Miss Green, giving her a severe, though wholly dependable, appearance. A square of linen pinned over the back of her head eased the severity a little.

She chose the brown gown, which suited her best, and buffed her boots. Miss Meadow, clerk to Mr Parrish, Sarah decided, would be plain, polite and poised at all times. Satisfied with her appearance she took three deep breaths to calm her overactive insides and went downstairs to Mr Parrish's office.

Mr Parrish was sitting at a desk facing a bay window overlooking the back garden. He had pince-nez on his nose and a knitted shawl around his thin shoulders. He laid down his pen and swivelled in his leather chair to greet her.

'Welcome, Miss Meadow. Forgive me if I do not rise. Please be seated at your desk.'

It was ready for her to occupy and was equipped with writing instruments and inkwells and a smaller version of Mr Parrish's leather chair. It was then she noticed the cupboards lining the walls, most with glass fronts, that displayed his ledgers.

He explained about his glassworks' purchases and sales, and correspondence, the glassmakers' guild and his chapel connections. 'I used to walk down to my furnaces every day until recently. With your able assistance I shall run everything from here now. I commence at nine sharp and work until dinner at one o'clock. Then I rest and often go out later on chapel business. Your afternoon here will continue until six. I shall give you small tasks to begin with and you must not be diffident about asking for guidance. My intention is for you to be able to deal with every aspect of my affairs in my absence.'

'May I consult you in the evenings, sir?'

'My strength is waning, Miss Meadow, which is why I also have an assistant at my works. He will join us for dinner. That is when I talk about my business.'

'Yes, sir.'

He picked up a bundle of documents. 'Begin with these.'

Sarah collected the papers and placed them on the tooled-leather top of her desk. It was a beautiful piece of furniture. She smoothed her hand backwards and forwards over the surface as she sat down. She glanced at Mr Parrish who was watching her, gave him a brief smile and settled down to work.

There was a timepiece in the office that chimed the hour as well as every quarter in between, but Sarah quickly forgot the time. She was absorbed by the intricacies of supplies and sales, and calculations for wages. There was indeed a large amount of number work as well as correspondence and she had to concentrate as the processes were unfamiliar. Mr Parrish answered her queries patiently, even when she asked him to repeat his answer. She was vaguely aware of the clang of the dinner bell when Mr Parrish stood up.

'It is time to wash for dinner, Miss Meadow. There will be hot water in your chamber.'

'Thank you, sir.'

Mr Parrish left the room. Sarah finished transferring costings to the ledger and stood up to stretch. Where had the morning gone? From her room she heard men's voices in the hall. Her colleague had arrived as anticipated. Her apprehension bubbled again. He was a gentleman, and she hoped he would consider her a lady. She smoothed down the skirt of her new gown, cleaned the ink from her fingers and tidied her hair before going back to the office.

'In here, you say?' The door opened and the gentleman walked in.

'You!' he exclaimed. 'Mr Parrish told me he was getting someone from the workhouse to do his paperwork. He didn't say it would be a woman.'

'Danby? I was expecting to meet a gentleman.'

'And so you have.' He brushed an imaginary speck of dust from his smartly tailored jacket. 'So don't you go saying otherwise.'

Astounded, Sarah's apprehension turned to disbelief. 'Are you Mr Parrish's assistant at his glassworks?'

'Why shouldn't I be? I worked hard for his carrier and kept his teams working when he was too exhausted to visit his works. I get on as well with him as I do his gaffers.'

'I don't doubt that. But – you a – a gentleman?'

'You're turning yourself into a lady, aren't you? Mind, you look more like one of his chapel matrons got up like that. Still, I suppose you have a reputation to live down.'

'Don't! You know the accusations were not true.'

'I know nothing about you, if anyone asks! And I don't want Mr Parrish to find out that we knew each other in the past. He definitely wouldn't approve of the life I've led.'

'He knows all about mine and is giving me this chance,' she parried.

'Well, he doesn't know about me. As far as he is concerned I come from a respectable farming family and my folks have died.'

'You've lied to him?'

'How else was I to get a decent position? You and me are strangers. Is that understood?'

'Perfectly,' she retaliated irritably. 'It was understood when you turned down my plea for help three years ago!'

'Is it that long since I saw you last? And here we are again, sharing the same camp. A bit different now though, eh?' Danby said with a leer.

Dear Lord, yes, she thought. He was living under the same roof; his bedchamber was along the landing from her. Would he try to take advantage of her as he had on her fifteenth birthday? Surely, in Mr Parrish's house, he would not dare? But he was still the same self-centred Danby. She had a sinking feeling in her heart as well as her stomach. Of course her good fortune couldn't last, but she really didn't care for Danby's deceitful ways and it would be difficult not to show it sometimes. It would be no problem for him, lies rolled off his tongue with ease. He could charm anybody into believing anything.

'What exactly do you do for Mr Parrish?' she asked.

'Distribute samples, collect orders, arrange deliveries; I'm a go-between for the gaffers so he doesn't have to visit the furnaces every day.'

'Where are the furnaces?'

256

'They're down by the navigation; those big cone-shaped structures. It's where I spend most of my days.'

That at least was some consolation, Sarah thought. 'Well, just be sure you keep your distance from me, *Mr Jones*.'

'Have no fear, *Miss Meadow*, I shall.'

His tone confirmed to Sarah that he didn't like the situation any more than she did. The timepiece chimed the hour and they went into the dining room.

Mr Parrish's success was founded on the manufacture of wine glasses, a process requiring skilled teams of glassmakers led by gaffers. Each cone had six teams working around the central furnace and gaffers were paid according to their output. During the summer Danby took Sarah to visit the yard, she was overcome by the heat inside the cone and had to hover near the rear brick wall to watch the men.

'The servitor takes a glob of molten glass from the pot in the furnace and blows a bowl then he hands it to the gaffer who makes and shapes the stem and the foot,' Danby explained. 'He's the one sitting down – that's why the team is called a "chair" – and the others fetch and carry for him. The finished glasses have to be cooled slowly or else they crack; then they go off to engravers for decoration.'

'I see now why we pay the gaffers so much.'

'Too much,' Danby muttered.

'But each is responsible for his team's wages,' Sarah argued.

'Aye and they think they rule the roost.'

Sarah detected a note of derision in Danby's voice and replied, 'Well, they do, don't they?'

He didn't comment further and it was dark inside the cone so Sarah couldn't see his expression. But she recalled his words when, a few months later, he came into Mr Parrish's office before dinner to present a plan for the future.

'Bottle making is where more profit is, sir,' Danby insisted. 'You don't need chairs and the expense of gaffers. Servitors can

257

blow glass into moulds. It's quicker and cheaper and I have a promise of big orders from breweries.'

Mr Parrish was studying Sarah's account books. 'My reputation is built on my loyal chairs, Mr Jones, and my wine glasses fetch a premium price. By its nature, the process is time consuming and expensive.'

'I'm not saying turn all of your manufactory over to this new method. You have two cones and I'll use only one for the bottle-blowers. I can fit all the chairs in the other.'

'I see the sense of it,' he responded. 'Miss Meadow, would you hand me my new shawl.' The garment was as light as cobweb, made on one of the Scotch islands, and had cost a huge amount from a store in Leeds. Sarah knew because she had handled the correspondence and payment. She knew also that customers for wine glasses were few and far between in the Riding and Mr Parrish was having to seek markets further afield. He was a wealthy man but not overly extravagant and he gave much of his gains away to the chapel and other charitable causes.

'A change of this magnitude needs careful consideration,' Mr Parrish went on. 'This kind of manufacturing needs men who labour in a different way from the ones I have now. I don't have to oversee my gaffers, it's their vocation, but that may not be so with the sort of men I shall need for the mass production of bottles.'

Sarah agreed, although she thought of the many less skilled men in town whose wives and families would benefit from regular work. 'But the additional employment is surely welcome, sir, for it will mean more fathers will be able to earn enough to feed their children,' she said. 'And a new product will enhance your business.'

'Yes, indeed, I understand your reasoning. However, it is more responsibility for Mr Jones.'

'Perhaps you could afford another supervisor?' she suggested.

'We don't need one,' Danby argued. 'I know the kind of men we will have to take on. I wouldn't recommend an expansion I could not manage.'

Privately, Sarah wasn't so sure, but kept silent; as did Mr Parrish, who thought for several minutes before deciding, 'Very well. I shall venture into bottle making.'

Danby's plan for expansion had stimulated Sarah's thinking about an idea of her own. Since learning about glassmaking she had conceived a design for a container that was more useful than wine glasses to the households of working folk. Mr Parrish had encouraged her to discuss it with him but she feared the cost of their production using existing methods would prove too expensive for ordinary folk to buy. Danby's comment gave her an idea.

She said, 'Using moulds for my storage jars would bring down the price.'

'What storage jars?' Danby asked.

'I did mention it to you a while ago,' she answered. 'You weren't interested.'

Mr Parrish added, 'Were you not, Mr Jones? The idea was sound.'

'I must have been busy running the factory,' Danby responded. 'Of course I am interested.'

Only because you know Mr Parrish supports the idea, Sarah thought. She hadn't told Danby that before and so he had dismissed her 'silly notion'. She had as little to do with Danby as possible, but acknowledged that he was personable and an asset to Mr Parrish. He had a persuasive way with him and was never short of willing labour and carriers to transport the finished glassware. Glass-blowing was a hot and strenuous occupation and when the gaffers had finished he bought the men welcome ale in a tavern after hours. Mr Parrish did not know about this and he would not have approved.

A month later, Sarah sat writing down a letter dictated by Mr Parrish. When she had finished she said, 'Mr Jones is bringing home samples of the storage jars as soon as they are cooled. I can't wait to see them' she added.

'Yes, he has been invaluable to me in the day-to-day running of my works yard. If only he had a level head on his shoulders,'

Mr Parrish commented. 'If he had your head on his shoulders, Miss Meadow, he could take over the whole manufactory for me.' Mr Parrish was becoming increasingly frail. Sarah heard his chest wheeze as he took in a breath.

Sarah swallowed her response. If only I were a man, she thought, I could take over the whole factory for him.

'I am indeed a lucky gentleman,' he went on. 'I have two new products thanks to you and Mr Jones. You have proved my theory about the importance of education for the young. I do believe with both of you in my glassworks, its future – and that of the workers – will be secure after I am gone.'

'I'm sure it won't be for a long time yet, sir.'

'I hope not.' His chest rattled again. 'I miss the guardians' meetings. But my eyes are tired; they are failing me. You will have to read the newspaper to me again tonight, when you have finished in my office.'

'Of course, Mr Parrish.' It was not a chore for Sarah. He was so patient and tolerant with her she would do anything to ease his ageing faculties. He enjoyed the reports of government affairs and stories from the big cities, and so did she. 'Shall you sit outside for an hour?'

'It is too cold. Give me your arm and take me to the drawing-room window where the sun's rays may warm my thin blood.' When she had settled him by the window, he added, 'I know I keep saying it, but you are such an asset to me, my dear, both you and Mr Danby. Your achievements as workhouse children have given me great satisfaction.'

Sarah wanted to bend over and kiss the top of his head. During the past months she had spent in Mr Parrish's household she had grown genuinely fond of him and he was the only person who made her think there was such a thing as love for another. Oh, it was not the passionate love that Miss Green had talked of. It was more of a respect and devotion that had grown out of her genuine concern for him and his untiring work to do what he could to help those less fortunate than himself.

She said. 'Won't you take your doctor's advice and move to the countryside where the air you breathe will be cleaner and fresher?'

'Perhaps,' he murmured, 'when the new processes are up and running.'

Sarah returned to the office and cleared the papers from his desk. She knew the glassworks business as well as Mr Parrish now, and probably better than Danby. She conceded that Danby got on with the men better than she ever could, although she wondered if his familiarity with them was always wise.

At that moment Danby came into the drawing room carrying a large tray of tea. Mrs Couzens followed with his heavy basket of glass mouldings.

'Mr Parrish, how are you today.' He took the tray over to a table in the bay window. 'Shall we take tea over here today, sir?' He rearranged the furniture so that the sofa faced Mr Parrish's chair.

'Mr Jones?' the housekeeper called. 'Where shall I leave the basket?'

'Over here. Then you can go. Miss Meadow, won't you join us by the window.'

He always does that, she thought. He comes in as though he is in charge and takes over.

'Come and pour our tea, Miss Meadow. Look at these, Mr Parrish.'

Sarah ignored his request and picked up one of the mouldings. They were based on the stoneware jars used for storage and would take the same cork and wax seals. But glass had the advantage over stoneware in that the housekeeper and cook were able to see the contents. Sarah felt excited by this new development. If they manufactured enough to keep the selling price down it was not only the gentry who would buy them! She had been through the finances several times and Mr Parrish didn't need persuading that the investment would be a good one.

Mr Parrish turned to his housekeeper. 'Thank you. Now tell me what you think of this as a storage jar.'

Danby gave a jovial laugh. 'Well, you'll be the only one to use them here,' he said. 'Miss Meadow does not dirty her hands in the kitchen.'

But Mr Parrish did not laugh. He said, 'Miss Meadow has suggested a glass lid sealed by a metal lever similar to that used for carbonated water bottles.'

'Ginger beer stoppers, actually,' Sarah added.

Mr Parrish had the last word. 'I intend to develop her idea and apply for a patent,' he said, and turned to Mrs Couzens for her opinion of the jars.

'It was my idea to use the moulds,' Danby muttered to Sarah.

'But we use moulds for all our bottles and jars now,' she pointed out.

'What do you know about it?'

'Keep your voice down,' Sarah murmured, glancing across to Mr Parrish who was engrossed in conversation with Mrs Couzens.

Danby moved closer to her and whispered, 'I've just about had enough of you wheedling your way into the old man's affections.'

'I am doing no such thing! And don't speak of Mr Parrish in that way.'

'I'll call him what I like. I'm tired of you sitting up here in the office while I graft away down at the factory all day.'

'Oh, grow up will you? He needs us both.'

'No, he doesn't. He never told me he was taking on a clerk. If he had I'd have told him not to. I could have done the ordering and paid the bills without you.' He kept his voice low but he sounded cross. The next minute he had walked away from her, put on his charming airs and had joined in the discussion between Mr Parrish and Mrs Couzens.

Sarah turned away and stared out of the window. Danby's childish outburst had angered her. He had become even more selfish over the years and now compounded it with an arrogant streak. She really wished she didn't have to live under the same roof as him and inhaled deeply to calm herself. It was becoming more and more difficult for her to be civil towards him, but she must make the effort, for Mr Parrish's sake.

Chapter 24

'Take me to the High Street, Aidan,' Mrs Thorpe called from the back of her trap as she retied her bonnet ribbons. 'The market will be over for today.'

It was a fine sunny day with a fresh breeze that took away the smoke from the chimneys of the town's manufactories. Aidan enjoyed the drive. He had shut himself away in his forge for too long. But all the years of sweating at his anvil were beginning to pay off.

A carrier cart making a delivery to the hardware store on Bridgegate delayed his progress and he reined in the docile pony.

'What are they carrying, Aidan?'

He surveyed the wooden crates lined with straw. 'Glass from Parrish's by the look of it.'

'Oh, it will be their new storage jars. I heard they were coming in. Will they be long to unload?'

'I'll try and get round but there's another cart coming the other way, ma'am.' Mrs Thorpe's second child was nearly due and Aidan didn't want to take any risks.

A small crowd had gathered and Aidan saw a notice in the window of the store announcing the arrival of the new glass storage jars. Two men came out of the shop to collect another crate. One of them was familiar. Aidan stared at him, memories rushing into his head. He knew that man. His fair hair and handsome face was a spectre from the past. Who was he? Aidan focused his eyes on him and racked his brain. His name was Dan something . . . yes, Danby, Danby Jones. Aidan remembered him! Danby had been living at the camp in Meadow Hall woods four years ago. He must be nearly twenty years of age by now for Aidan would be two and twenty in the autumn. Judging by Danby's clean smart clothing and the way he was giving the orders, he had done well for himself. The reins slackened in Aidan's fingers and he was aware of his heart beating loudly in his chest.

Aidan rarely spoke of the days he had lost but, alone at night, he often searched his mind for them and the nagging questions remained unanswered. The sudden appearance of Danby brought back his anguish with a rush. He remembered now that they had fought over Sarah. Was she with him now? Is that why she had not come looking for him. Aidan tried to pull himself together. He wanted to dash over and grab Danby, to demand to know where Sarah was. Caution prevailed. Sarah could be his wife and that was why she hadn't come looking for him. The thought hit him like a punch in the stomach.

'I'll make a purchase from the draper while we wait,' Mrs Thorpe decided. 'Can you help me down?'

'I don't think you ought to get out of the trap, ma'am. Tell me what you want and I'll get it.'

'I want to look for myself, Aidan.'

'Wait until we are nearer, ma'am.' But she would have none of it and he realised what Mr Thorpe meant by her determination as she pleaded with him to help her down.

'I'm sorry, Mrs Thorpe, but no.'

'Then I'll just have to get down myself.'

He felt the trap rock and turned round in alarm. She meant it! He jumped down from the driver's seat and raced round to the back in time to help her – he needed to put both his hands around her ample waist to lift her to safety. Her cloak fell back revealing her bulging belly for all to see. Embarrassed for her he pulled the edges of her cloak around her, covering her bulge. It was, he realised, an intimate gesture but necessary, he thought.

Mrs Thorpe did not appear discomforted and seemed amused by the stares from onlookers. 'Thank you, Aidan.' She adjusted her bonnet and added, 'Now give me your arm, please.' He led her carefully across the roadway and into the drapers. The delivery cart was moving away but when Aidan turned he saw Danby was looking back at him. The recognition had been mutual.

He led Mrs Thorpe to a chair by the counter. 'I need something from the hardware shop. I shall be as quick as I can.'

'Take as long as you like,' she replied cheerfully and, beaming at the proprietor, said 'I should like to see your new silks.'

Aidan hurried outside. The cart had disappeared so he headed straight to the ironmonger's to select nails and ask his questions.

'Do you mean the young fellow with fair hair?' Mr Smith answered. 'Yes, I know him; he's Mr Parrish's right-hand man, he is; in charge of orders and deliveries for the glassworks. We don't see much of him in town as a rule.'

'He works at the Parrish glassworks?'

'That's the one.'

'Where does he live?'

'Well, I don't rightly know. I thought he was with Mr Parrish at his big house on the Mansfield road. But there's them that says he has — well now, how shall I put it — he has, what you might call, lodgings on the valley road. You can always find him at the glassworks, though. They say he has the keys to the yard. Now, are you here to buy these nails or not?'

'Nails? Oh, yes, of course. Thank you.'

Mr Smith took payment and handed them over. 'I don't see you in town much these days.'

'I spend most of my time in my forge.' He said, 'Good day,' and left.

When Aidan returned to Mrs Thorpe she had a parcel from

the draper. Aidan carried it out to the trap and helped her aboard. 'Straight home now, do you think?' he said.

She sighed. 'Yes, please. I am quite tired out. Actually, you have gone quite pale yourself, Aidan.'

Later that evening Aidan loitered in the shadows by the glassworks. He waited patiently and, eventually, followed Danby on foot to a small neat house on the valley road. An oil lamp burned behind closed curtains at the front-room window. There was a polished brass knocker on the door and Aidan let it fall twice. The door opened to reveal Danby with his jacket off and his necktie loosened. He was fiddling with his collar button and, when he saw Aidan demanded, 'What do you want?'

Aidan didn't answer at first. He heard the sound of a wailing infant and a woman's voice called, 'Who is it, Danby?'

'Nobody,' he answered over his shoulder.

'I want to talk to you,' Aidan said.

'Well, I don't want to talk to you. I'd forgotten about you until I saw you in town earlier. I have a new life now. What happened to your nose?'

Aidan ignored the question. He was used to its new alignment. 'I'm looking for the girl.'

'What girl?'

'The one we were with in the woods?'

Danby lowered his voice. 'I told you, I want to forget all about that and so does she. You can't come here and start raking up the past like this.'

A door behind him opened and the infant's wailing became louder. The woman asked, 'Who's nobody, then?'

'Is that her?' Aidan tried to see round him but Danby half closed the door and stood in the gap.

'No, it's not!' He hissed. He half turned and raised his voice, 'Go back into the front room, Rose. He's from the works and he's just leaving.' He glared at Aidan. 'Clear off. I don't want to know you.'

267

'If she's not here, where is she?'

'She doesn't want to know you either. Not after you left her in the workhouse.'

'I – I *what?*'

'Don't try and deny it.' Danby lowered his voice again. 'You stay away from me. If you so much as breathe a word to anyone that you've seen me here, I'll kill you! I mean it! You can't push me around any more. I've got friends in this town.'

The door closed firmly in Aidan's face and stayed shut despite his repeated knocking. He turned away reluctantly. *He'd left Sarah in the workhouse?*

He had a rough idea where the workhouse was and hurried back to town to find it. From what Danby has said she was no longer inside but as he gazed up at the austere walls and high forbidding gates the flashes of memory that the doctor and Emma had warned him to ignore finally fell into place. He remembered it all: the rescue from Jackson's clutches; his fear for Sarah's safety and her venom when he left her. With good reason, he thought; but what else could he have done without money or a roof over his head?

He had left her here more than three years ago and did not go back! She would have thought he had deserted her and – and, dear Lord, he had. He fell against the rough stone, beseeching the heavens for forgiveness, and wept. He had promised to return for her and he had not. His legs buckled and he crumpled to the ground, reliving his anxiety at the time, his heart crushing under the weight of his despair.

Danby inhaled deeply. Where the hell had Aidan Beckwith sprung from? He thought he'd gone for good after that risky business with Sarah at the Jackson place. He could do without that kind of danger now. The stories that went round about that mob made your hair curl. He was respectable now. Well, almost.

'Danby!' Rose called. 'Has he gone?'

He went into the front room where Rose was suckling baby

Albert, and bent down to kiss her exposed breast. 'I can't stay long. I'm going to a lecture at the institute.'

'What did that fellow want?'

'It's nothing for you to worry about, my sweet.'

'Well, I do.' Rose's voice trembled. 'When will the ceremony be, Danby?'

'I told you. It's difficult to tell Mr Parrish about you.'

'But you said everything would be fine if I sold the alehouse and moved here. You said you would tell him about us then.'

'How could I? With a babe already sucking at your titty?'

She choked. 'He's your baby too.'

'Aye. But you never asked me if I wanted him, did you? You just stopped using the sponges when your father died.'

Rose's voice went up an octave. 'You don't love him! You don't love me!'

'Of course I do.'

'You said we'd be wed one day,' she whined. 'You said.'

Oh Lord, she was going to start weeping again. He knelt down beside her. 'We shall; when the time is right. You know Mr Parrish is a bible-basher. I'll have to tell him you're a widow.'

'Tell him what you like, but hurry up about it.'

He gazed at his suckling son and stroked Rose's breasts with his knuckles. 'Has he nearly finished?'

'No.'

'How long will he be? I have to be seen at the lecture.'

'Well, go now if that's how you feel.'

'Don't be like that, Rose. You used to want me all the time.'

'I have Albert to look after now.'

'Well, can't you arrange it so he's sleeping when I come round?'

'If we were wed, you would be here all night.'

'You wouldn't want me any more than you do now.'

'I'd still give you what you want, though, wouldn't I? I've never denied you, never.'

That was true, he acknowledged. When she had her bleeding and even when she could hardly stand with her swollen belly, he didn't go without. She did it with her hands and her mouth. She was a good mistress.

'Can't you put him down for a minute?'

'He'll cry. You don't like it when he cries. You'll have to come back later.'

He stood in front of the looking glass over the fireplace to do up his necktie. 'Perhaps I will tonight.'

Danby wasn't even sure Rose had heard him as she transferred Albert to her other breast. It wasn't as though he didn't want to wed her, but he didn't want to risk losing his comfortable income from Mr Parrish, some of which now kept Rose's neat little house going. If he said he was marrying a young widow with an infant, instead of an alehouse keeper's obliging daughter, he might even get a settlement. Mr Parrish had been making suggestions to him about the value of being a family man. He'd have to get Rose to dress a bit more like stuffy Sarah to make the right impression on him.

God, Sarah! He must warn her about Aidan. Neither of them wanted him turning up talking about the past and asking questions. It was dead and buried; and good riddance. He went off to the institute, planning what he would say to Sarah.

Sarah was reading by the light of an oil lamp in the drawing room when Danby came in. The rest of the household had retired an hour ago. She closed her book.

'Was it a good lecture?'

'It was interesting. There's talk of an exhibition in London to show the world our industries.'

'Really? It'll be timely for Mr Parrish's patent jars.' She stood up and yawned. 'Did you lock the front door?'

'Yes. Don't go up just yet. I want to talk to you.'

'Can't it wait? I'm tired.'

'It's not about the glassworks.' Danby paused. 'Aidan Beckwith's turned up. I've seen him in town.'

Sarah sat down with a bump, and a turmoil of emotions

270

threw her composure. 'What in God's name does he want?'

'He's looking for you.'

'Well, he'd better not find me! I shan't be responsible for my actions if he does.'

Danby blinked at her. 'I thought you were sweet on him once.'

'He betrayed me! He betrayed my trust in him.'

'Aye, he thought he knew what was best for you. He was a cocky bugger.'

'I don't want him round here stirring up the past. I want to forget what he did to me.'

'It's that Jackson incident that worries me. If word gets out about our involvement—'

'That was a long time ago, Danby.'

'Folk have long memories in these parts. If Jackson found out I was there when you were snatched, or it was you we stole from him, he'd want his revenge. He has a violent reputation to keep up.'

'What do you mean?'

'He has to show the lowlife in town what happens if they cross him. It's the same with his women. If they try and get away they end up in the canal.'

'Do you think Aidan knows this?'

Danby shrugged. 'No idea.'

'Well, won't he be in danger? Someone should warn him.'

'Why do you care?'

'I don't,' said Sarah uncertainly.

'Well, then. I've already told him to stay away from me. Make sure you do the same.'

'I don't take orders from you, Danby Jones.'

'You know what I mean. We've both got good positions here and we don't want anybody spoiling it for us.'

'Oh, don't worry. Your reputation is safe. I'm the one who was found to be the moral defective.' The injustice of it, she seethed silently. Aidan Beckwith has much to answer for!

'Even so, I don't want him asking me questions,' Danby stressed.

'You sound as though you have something to hide.'

'Me? Lord, no.'

'You're late back from the lecture,' she commented.

'Some of the fellows take a drink at the Red Lion afterwards. That's how I heard about the exhibition.'

Sarah mouth twisted. She knew Danby liked wine and spirits but they were not allowed in Mr Parrish's Methodist household, unless he had important visitors. 'Is that where you saw Aidan?'

'He was in town earlier; with a woman in a trap. She was—' Danby made a curve shape over his belly with his hands.

'She was with child? He has a wife?'

'It seems so. They looked like they had brass.'

'He married well, then.'

'Aye. I don't know why he was asking about you.'

'Perhaps he has a conscience about what he did to me? I most certainly hope so.'

'Well, I made it clear he had to stay away. We've got a good set-up here and we don't want him coming along and rocking the boat.'

It was one thing she and Danby agreed on. But she couldn't help wondering where Aidan had been and what he had been doing in the intervening years. She went into the kitchen to prepare a hot toddy for Mr Parrish's nightcap. Her hands shook as she poured the drink into a cup. The thought of seeing Aidan had unsettled her. Sarah took the hot toddy upstairs to Mr Parrish's chamber.

His wheezy chest had cleared at last and he was sitting up in bed reading a brochure from a London store. 'You are a good, kind lady, Miss Meadow.'

'Thank you, sir. But you know I am not a lady.'

'You will be one day, mark my words.'

She smiled in the lamplight. 'I should have to marry for that and I have vowed never to do so.'

'Then it was a hasty decision, my dear. You must change your mind. You are still young and you are made to have a family.'

272

Sarah blushed slightly. 'I shouldn't wish to leave you, sir.'

He sighed. 'I should not want you to. Your loyalty does you credit. I'm afraid I have been a selfish old man where you are concerned. I have not encouraged you to meet suitable gentleman and as your guardian I should have.'

'No gentleman would wish to court a workhouse defective, even if she had reformed.'

'Come now, Miss Meadow. A true gentleman would look beyond your past and see the capable young woman you have become. I have lived a good deal longer than you and I see the world around me very clearly. Times are changing. We are moving to a new way of life where the entrenched ways of the gentry will be challenged by a new middle class of people. You will be part of that, my dear. Indeed you are a part of it now.' His eyes closed. 'I shall not get up tomorrow. You must bring my office papers to me here, Miss Meadow.'

'Of course, sir,' she answered. 'Goodnight.'

In the privacy of her own bedchamber, she reflected on his words. Being reminded of Aidan's betrayal only served to re-inforce her decision to remain a spinster. But she had to admit that although her life was comfortable enough it was, somehow, lacking. Danby's news of Aidan had unsettled her. Oh, she still hated him with a vengeance for what he did to her, but the image of him with a wife kept pushing to the front of her mind. She felt envious of his wife. And it was not because she was gentry, or more likely this new middling class that Mr Parrish talked of. Aidan's wife was with child and the more Sarah thought about this the more distressed she became.

She tossed and turned, unable to sleep. How dare Aidan Beckwith and his wife cause her so much unhappiness! Dear Lord, she had tried so hard to forget him and the way he had treated her. It was too much for her to bear. She squeezed her eyes tight shut, but the tears pushed through her eyelids.

Chapter 25

It did not take Aidan long to find out that Danby also lived in the Parrish household on the Mansfield road and he called there one evening after following him home. The door was opened by a maid.

'Is Mr Jones expecting you, sir?'

'No, but he'll see me when you tell him who I am.'

'Do you have a card, sir?'

Aidan shook his head wordlessly. 'I am a friend from the institute. My name's Beckwith.'

'One moment, please, sir.' She closed the door in Aidan's face and he waited. After a few minutes he rapped again on the door and stepped back to look for any sign of movement at the windows. He knocked again and the door opened a fraction.

'I said, stay away from me,' Danby hissed. 'Especially stay away from here. This is where I live.'

'But don't you live . . . ?'

Danby glared at him.

'Oh, I see. The woman in the other place, the one with the infant, is your mistress?'

'Be quiet!'

'I shall if you tell me where Sarah is.' He added loudly, 'I have a message for Mr Jones from—' Aidan smirked and whispered, 'What is her name? Oh, never mind.' He raised his voice again, 'I have a message from a house in the valley—' His last words were smothered by Danby's hand over his mouth and his fist in his gut.

Aidan choked at the unexpected pain. His own fists clenched. 'You'd better step outside if that's what you want.'

'I don't think so,' Danby said.

'Come with us, sir. We don't want any trouble here.' George, accompanied by one of his gardeners, came round the side of the house and Aidan felt a strong hand grip each of his arms. Between them they directed him firmly away from the front door and let him go only when he was outside the front gates.

Inside, Mary hovered uncertainly behind Danby as Sarah came down the main staircase with an armful of ledgers. 'What was that commotion?' she asked.

'Nothing,' Danby answered. 'The gates were left open and we had a beggar at the front door.'

'Oh, did you give him a coin?'

'No, I did not.'

'There was a time when you were in similar straitened circumstances and were glad of a little charity.'

'Well, I'm not now.'

'No indeed,' she sighed. 'Mary, would you come with me to the office for a few minutes.'

'Yes, Miss Meadow.' Mary followed Sarah into the dark, wood-lined room and took the ledgers from her to replace on the shelves. Sarah sat down at the large oak desk. 'Shall I turn up the lamp, miss? You don't want to be straining your eyes.'

'Thank you, Mary. I suppose the beggar has left by now. We should have given him some food at least.'

'Oh, he weren't no beggar at the front door, miss. He was clean and had on decent clothes.'

Sarah dipped her pen in the inkwell. 'He was not a beggar, you say?'

'No, miss. Mind you, he didn't have no card neither so I didn't let him in.'

'Did he give his name?'

'Mr Beckwith, miss. He said he was a friend of Mr Jones from the institute but Mr Jones still wouldn't see him.'

The pen slipped from Sarah's fingers and left a blot on the sheet of paper in front of her. 'Did you say Beckwith?'

'Yes, miss.'

'You are sure that was his name?'

'Yes, miss. Are you quite well, miss? Shall I fetch you some tea?'

Sarah composed her features, picked up her pen from the blotter and recharged it with ink. But the notes she was writing blurred before her eyes. What was Aidan doing here? Surely he had no more scores to settle with Danby? It was she who had a score to settle with him. She wanted to hit him for what he had done to her. But she was not a workhouse brat any more. She was Miss Meadow, respected in the town as Mr Parrish's invaluable assistant. Brawling was not the sort of behaviour she could indulge in. But it did not stop her wanting to. Her hand began to shake and another drop of ink sullied the fresh sheet of paper.

'Oh, hell,' she whispered and heard Mary breath in sharply at her language. Mr Parrish prided himself on his God-fearing household and blasphemies were rare. She replaced the pen in its tray and covered her eyes with her hands. 'I am so sorry, Mary. I am not myself. Yes, tea will be most welcome.' As Mary bobbed a curtsey and turned for the door, she called after her, 'Would you tell Mrs Couzens I shall be out this evening?'

A friend from the institute. Resentment and frustration bubbled through her so that when Mary came back with the tea she was pacing the room to release her anger. She had to – had to – what? Talk to him? Ask him why he treated her so cruelly?

As Mary poured the tea Sarah said, 'There's a special concert at the Mechanics Institute tonight. Mr Parrish has given me tickets so why don't you come with me?'

'Oh, could I, miss? I'd like that.'

'See that Mr Parrish is settled for the evening then put on your Sunday gown.' Sarah gulped down her tea then took the stairs two at a time to Danby's chamber. She knocked firmly and called, 'I must speak with you before you leave.'

He came to the door eventually, buttoning on a fresh shirt and tie. 'Come in, Miss Meadow.' He grinned. 'I do believe this is the first time you have called on me in my chamber.' He glanced at the four-poster bed. 'What will the servants say?'

She ignored his innuendo. 'Are you going to the institute?'

'Yes.'

'Will you be meeting your friends?'

'I expect so. The lecture is on – on railway transport.'

'How interesting.' She did not believe he ever went to the institute. He would have known about the concert if he did. She wondered where he did go in the evening.

'I have to keep up with new developments.'

'Who was at the front door earlier?'

He looked down at the buttons on his shirt.

'There was a caller,' she prompted.

'I told you, it was a beggar? I sent him away. Does that offend your charitable nature? Well, it doesn't mine. We oughtn't to be encouraging that sort. Once the word gets round, we'll have every waif and stray at our door.'

'Are you certain it was a beggar?'

He shrugged. 'Judging by the rags on his back.'

He was lying about everything, she thought. Why? Surely he had no grudge against Aidan. They had battled over her in the past but that was years ago and Danby was not interested in her as a woman. She thought he had matured in the intervening years and had his more animal appetites in check. It was one of his redeeming features that enabled her to tolerate living in the same household as him.

'Why the interest?' he added.

'I – I, it may have been someone I knew in the workhouse. I could have helped them.'

'Forget it. You don't want to be reminding folk where we came from. I thought we'd agreed on that.'

'Why do you think he called here?'

'Dear God, Sarah. It was just a beggar.'

She had given him so many chances to tell her. And it wasn't her feelings he was trying to spare. Danby didn't want Aidan around for reasons of his own. He was hiding something.

'I have friends as well as enemies from my past,' she responded.

'And you'd be well advised to forget them all.' He turned back to his looking glass. 'Is that all?'

Sarah watched Danby preening in the mirror. He spent more time on his appearance than she did. But then, she acknowledged, he had to impress customers and she was content to blend into the background in her plain gowns and caps.

Eventually he said, 'If you're so upset by this beggar, why don't you join one of the ladies' welfare groups in town? You're just the kind of do-gooder they welcome.' He continued staring at his image in the glass. 'You even dress like they do.'

She closed the door and went to her own chamber. Danby had meant to be unkind about her appearance, but in some ways she was flattered. It was precisely the image she had set out to portray. Mr Parrish approved, and when she visited lawyers and bankers on his behalf, they treated her with respect. That was worth more to her than any number of admiring glances from men like Danby. She wrapped herself in a warm cloak and went downstairs to join Mary in the hall.

They arrived early and had seats near the front. The room was brightly lit with lamps and candles and the musicians were tuning their instruments as town folk trickled in. As they waited for the room to fill, Sarah read some of the difficult words in the programme for Mary and chatted with her about her Sunday school lessons. The temperature rose and she undid her cloak, letting it fall back over her wooden chair. She twisted to straighten it and glanced around the audience. She recognised a couple of faces from the High Street.

When she caught sight of him she thought she must be dreaming. Before she could react the lights dimmed and the tuneless scales became more melodic. The hum of hushed voices in conversation faded. It was him. There was something different about him, his nose no longer had the fine straight line she had admired, but it was Aidan, she was sure. He was talking in a lively way with folk around him; he seemed happy and relaxed. She turned her head sharply to face the front, her heart thumping strongly in her breast, her body as rigid as the hard wooden chair that supported it.

The musicians must have played tunes, that she knew. But if anyone had asked her she could not tell them which. Even when everyone else had left and the caretaker was turning down lamps and dousing the candle stubs, Sarah sat motionless. Mary noticed her reticence; she stood up and said, 'Will you take my arm, Miss Meadow. I do believe you are not yourself today.'

Earlier, she had wanted to hit him, yet when she saw him, somehow her courage deserted her. There was so much to say about what she had endured because of him and at the same time nothing to say except, 'Is it really you? Are you well?' He appeared to be enjoying his evening out; perhaps his wife had given birth to a healthy infant and he was celebrating with her family.

'We must leave now, miss.' Mary pulled the cloak around Sarah's shoulders.

'Have all the others gone?'

'Every last one. Mr Parrish will be wanting his nightcap, miss.'

'Mr Parrish?' Sarah made an effort to pull herself together.

'Yes, I always take it to him at this hour. We must hurry.'

The manager smiled indulgently as they made their way into the cold night air. 'Quite overcome by the music were you, miss? It always affects me that way. Shall we see you next time?'

'Yes – yes of course.' She stopped. 'May I ask you a question, sir?'

'Of course, miss.'

'There was a party in here, near the back on the right-hand side. Would you know their names? I thought I recognised them.'

'Well, let me see now, the Thorpes were in tonight.'

'Oh, yes, I saw them,' Mary added. 'They were behind us. I know their Liddy from Sunday school and her brother runs the Bowes ironworks.'

'Aye, he does. There was a nasty business with the Bowes family a few years ago, but the young miss got through it when she wed Mr Thorpe.'

'Oh, Miss Meadow, they say she makes the most beautiful gowns you've ever seen.'

'Thorpe, you say?'

'Aye. Nice folk, they are; decent family. Now if you don't mind, miss . . .' He rattled his keys.

Sarah resisted asking more questions. Mr Parrish had accounts at several suppliers in the High Street and she was on speaking terms with the proprietors. If Aidan was living in town and a friend of the Thorpes, it would be easy to find him.

Chapter 26

After seeing Aidan, Sarah's anger had simmered and she could not settle to her work. When Mr Parrish noticed her lack of concentration she decided to do something about it. She must seek out Aidan and confront him. The next night she called at the Thorpes' house after tea on the pretext of an enquiry from Mr Parrish about iron grills in his stables.

'Oh, you need to speak with Mr Beckwith. He's normally at the forge in the yard but he's shut up shop for the day now. An order, you say? Well, he lives over the carriage house. Go down the side of the house and follow the ironworks wall to the bottom of the garden.'

He was washing at the pump by the horse trough, and she stopped abruptly. She was holding on to her anger so tightly that she was afraid of what she might do to him. She stood in the shadow of a tree, hard up against the ironworks wall. Through an open stable door she heard movements and a voice as the carthorses were fed and watered.

Why had she come here? Certainly not to place an order! She was honest enough with herself to admit she wanted to hurt Aidan, and hurt him as much as he had hurt her when he had turned his back on her and forgotten she even existed. And why had he songht out Danby after all this time if not to resurrect more trouble?

At the sight of him, her memories of the way he had left her to the privations of the workhouse flooded back. He was to blame for all that had happened to her in there! His fault! His fault! Her heart began thumping, as it always did when she thought of him. He had dumped her in a place where she was so maligned and pilloried that she had almost believed the lies herself.

A young man came out of the stable and called, 'The horses are secure for the night, Aidan. I'm off home now for me tea.'

Aidan waved and went back to washing his arms and chest in the cold water. He was bigger, broader, probably stronger than she recalled. Her anger bubbled. How could he behave so calmly when she was shaking with rage? She could no longer stifle her anger. It was as though it was yesterday when he walked out on her, leaving her with that spiteful matron and perverted so-called doctor. She ran out from the shadow of the tree with her fists flying. His arms were raised as he rubbed a drying cloth over his wet hair and she set about pummelling his exposed body with all her might.

'What the—'

A strong hand grabbed one of her wrists but that did not stop her thrashing. Her knuckles slipped on his wet skin and she could smell the soap he had used. His muscled body felt cold and hard beneath her hands. She heard him say, 'Stop this. Whoever you are, stop this at once.'

His other hand finally stilled her as his fingers circled her arm and pinned it to her sides. Her bonnet had slipped along with her cotton cap, revealing strands of auburn hair.

She struggled to release herself from his grip. 'Let me go. You deserve this and more for what you did to me!'

'Sarah? Is it really you? I've been looking for you.'

'Aye and well you should! I could be dead from pestilence for all you cared about me!'

He released his hold on her and she resumed her pummelling, aiming blows at his stomach and chest, indeed anywhere she could. This time he did not try and stop her and she rained blows on his wet skin until she was exhausted from the effort. She was breathing sharply in short, shallow snatches and her arms were aching. Involuntary tears pushed out from her eyes and rolled down her nose and cheeks until she was obliged to sniff noisily.

When she dropped her arms he stepped back and sat on the edge of the stone trough staring at her. She fell against him, half sobbing, half shouting, 'Why didn't you come back for me? You promised me!' Her voice fell to a whisper and she repeated, 'You promised me.' And then her sobbing took over, racking her body and draining her strength.

'I know Sarah, I'm so, so sorry.' His arms came around her and held her tightly to his chest, squeezing the breath out of her.

She didn't know how long they sat there, as she sobbed and shuddered in his arms. Her hands and feet grew quite cold. The skin of his naked chest too became roughened with goosebumps but he did not move; except occasionally his hands travelled slowly up and down her arms. Eventually she pushed herself away and straightened. 'Every time I thought of you, I wanted to do that. And now that I have, I feel no better. I'll never forgive you for leaving me in the workhouse. Never.'

He handed her the cloth to wipe her face and stretched to retrieve his thick shirt from the pump handle without taking his eyes off her. He was aware of a mild ache here and there from her punches and reflected that she was as strong now as she had ever been; perhaps even stronger, for she was most certainly lovelier.

How could he have *ever* forgotten such radiance? Her cotton cap and straw bonnet had slipped to show her hair and, pulled away from her features and wound around her head in those intricate plaits, its coppery colour served only to accentuate her beauty. Under her cloak, her gown was buttoned to the neck; and the fact that every inch of her was covered stimulated his desire to explore her. She had grown into a fine, handsome woman and with a shock he realised he wanted her more than ever.

A female voice called down the garden. 'Aidan, your tea's ready.'

He stood up, pulling on his shirt and answered, 'I'll be in later, Emma.' Then he took Sarah's hand, quite gently this time, and said, 'Come inside by the fire. Let me explain.'

'Make excuses, you mean.'

'Give you my reasons and tell you what happened to me.'

'Why? What did happen?'

'I was attacked and injured. Afterwards I couldn't remember anything of those two days in town with you, or indeed any of our time together for several months. I still have no recall of the attack itself.'

He had been injured. It had not occurred to her that he had not returned to her because he *couldn't*; she had thought of him as enduring, immortal even.

He led her into the carriage house, through the tack room and up a winding staircase to the coachman's quarters under the roof tiles. It was sparsely furnished and dark.

'Is this where you live?' she asked.

'Yes. The stable lad goes home at night, so they let me use it.'

Sarah looked around. 'With your wife?'

'My wife?'

'Danby said he saw you with your wife.'

'You have seen him? He told you about me?'

'We live in the same house.'

'So you were there when I called!'

'We work for the same glassmaker.'

'Mr Parrish. Yes, his name was on the carrier. He's well respected in town.'

'He was a guardian at the workhouse. I owe him everything. He took me out and gave me a place.'

'I am pleased you have a comfortable position. It is what I wished for you.'

'Then why—?' she choked. She shook her head unable to finish.

He turned up the lamp. 'I had a plan to get work and lodgings and then offer you marriage. The workhouse would have released you into my care then.'

'You never said anything to me about marriage!'

'Well, I couldn't until I had a job and somewhere to live.'

'By which time you had forgotten about me rotting away in the workhouse and married someone else. Where is she tonight, Aidan?'

'She is not my wife.'

Her eyes narrowed. 'You have not wed her! But Danby said she is with child! What kind of man have you become, Aidan?'

'The lady with me was Mrs Thorpe; my employer's wife.'

'Oh!'

'Oh? Is that all you have to say? You haven't changed much, have you? You were always hasty in your conclusions.'

'I take as I find,' she muttered. She should have said sorry but she was hurting too much.

'Well, you find me in reduced circumstances compared with you and Danby.'

'Tell me what happened.'

He didn't answer her immediately. He stared into space and then said, 'I'll just get some ale from the barrel downstairs. Will you take a glass of sherry with me?'

'Yes. Thank you.'

'Make up the fire while I'm gone, would you?'

She wandered around and finally settled in the only fireside chair in the room. Two hard wooden kitchen chairs stood at a small, deal table which held the oil lamp, and a narrow bed occupied the darkest corner. These were not comfortable circumstances for anyone. But she believed the Thorpes were a respectable family. She watched him take the sherry and wine glass from a cupboard and his movements stirred a long-suppressed desire in the pit of her stomach. How could she hate him and find him attractive at the same time?

He handed her a wine glass and commented. 'You have risen to a very comfortable position in a relatively short time.'

Stung by his implication that her journey had been easy, she retaliated, 'You don't know what I went through in the workhouse!'

'And you don't know what I suffered at the hands of Jackson!' he snapped.

'Jackson? It was me they kidnapped!'

'And me they tried to kill!'

Her eyes rounded. 'Why? How?'

'Two of them hunted me down and beat me up.'

'Is that how you got your new nose?'

His hand covered it for a second. 'I am used to it now.'

She gazed at him. He was still just as handsome to her. She noticed the lines around his eyes and realised that he had had a tough time of things.

'Jackson is not a man you cross,' he went on. 'Everyone in town knows that. I crossed him by taking you away from them and I had to pay. I couldn't even remember who I was when I came round.'

'Oh dear Lord. Then it was my fault!' She was horrified that he had come so close to death on her account.

'No.' He shook his head emphatically.

'Yes, it was! If I hadn't been so wilful and run away from you that day, I wouldn't have been picked up by him.'

'Why did you run away from us?'

'I was so fed up with you and Danby squabbling about me. I was a burden to you both.'

'Not to me! I wanted to take care of you but I don't think Danby did. You'd have been no better off with Danby than you were with the Jacksons.'

'You're wrong. Mr Parrish can't run his glassworks without Danby.'

'Did you say he lives in the same house as you?' Aidan asked, stung by Sarah's defence of Danby

'We don't have much to do with each other. I run Mr Parrish's office at the house and Danby's out all hours getting orders or delivering. In the evening he studies at the Mechanics Institute too. He's turned out quite well, considering he was a workhouse boy from birth.'

Aidan didn't comment and looked thoughtful.

She continued, 'Well, we're all grown up now and have gone our different ways. There is no reason why all of us should not be considered respectable, as long as we can forget our past.'

His eyes flashed. 'Forget it? You wouldn't say that if you knew what it was really like to forget your past!'

'I – I'm sorry, I didn't think.'

'No, you never did.'

Why should it hurt her so when he said such things? She came here hating him and wanting her revenge. At least, that's what she thought. But now when she looked at him she saw everything that had stirred her confusing adolescent desires all those years ago. She took a sip of her sherry. It was good and she missed this small pleasure in the Parrish household. There were many comforts that she had grown used to while Aidan existed in this hayloft. How could she continue to hate the man who had endured so much for her welfare? Perhaps it wasn't hate; more anger and disappointment that had coloured all her other feelings for him.

'What did Jackson do to you?' she whispered.

'Broke my ribs and knocked me senseless then chucked me in the canal to die.'

'Dear Lord, no! He did that because you took me away from him?'

'Yes. And only the Lord knows what he would have done to you if he had got his evil hands on you again. I stick by my actions and would do the same again. You were safer in the work-house.'

'Perhaps,' she commented quietly. 'Earlier on you said you would have married me. Did you really mean that?'

'I see now that it was a foolish notion, for what could I offer you? I had no proper home; not even regular work and no man can take a wife in those circumstances.'

He had truly wished to wed her and her heart was beating faster as she contemplated what might have been.

'I felt responsible for you,' he added. 'But I could not look after you without ruining your reputation.'

Her germinating joy was dashed and broken. 'You would have wed me out of duty? Did you not consider how I might feel about the arrangement?'

He stared at her for a long time. She wished, oh how she wished she could read his thoughts. 'It would not have been a hardship for you,' he said.

'You don't know that.'

After a further pause he added, 'I could have taken you during that summer when we were living in the woods. I knew you were a girl.'

He was right. She had desired him as a woman does a man. She might have gone to him, too, if Danby had not returned. And now? No one apart from Mr Parrish had questioned her continuing unmarried status. She was content with her spinsterhood . . . she thought . . . until now . . . She moved closer to Aidan and murmured, 'Would you really have wed me?'

She noticed his hands clench and his lips move slightly. She lifted her chin a fraction and her pulses quickened. His head lowered towards her. She wanted him to kiss her, to be held in his arms, but after a tantalising second he stepped back and said, 'I was not in a position to offer you marriage. Nor am I now. You are a lady accustomed to the comforts of wealth.'

That would count for nothing if you loved me, she thought. But she said, 'No, I am not nor do I take my position for granted.'

'You are better off than I. Look around you. What have I to

show for the years since then? This one room is hardly an improvement on my wagon.'

She swallowed the thumping on her chest. 'But you have a sponsor and a trade. You have a future, Aidan.'

'I have a future laden with debts. I still owe money to the surgeon and the apothecary, not to mention the Thorpes for all their care and support.' His tension subsided and he added. 'That's unfair; the Thorpes won't take a penny for saving my life and taking me into their home. I have managed to persuade them to agree to some form of payment in kind by way of new fencing around the front of the house, and a new gate through to the works yard. But they could not afford to pay for the doctor's ministration and medicines; they have struggles of their own.'

Sarah knew the cost of the medical men who visited Mr Parrish. She had money. Mr Parrish paid her a generous stipend and she had little to spend it on. 'Will you let me help? It was my fault you were attacked and I have an income.'

He became angry. 'Is that why you think I am telling you this? You believe I came to your house to beg for charity from those in better circumstances? I am explaining why I did not keep my promise to you.'

'And I wish to help because I am, or I used to be, your friend. I came here with vengeance in my heart but I am sorry that I beat you and I am truly sorry for what happened to you because of me.'

'I don't want your pity.'

'I do not pity you.' She glared at him irritably. 'You have grown too proud. And you are not happy.'

'I am content. I have orders to fill and I can pay my rent. Be happy for me.'

But she could not. He had not only changed in his appearance; his outlook was different and she must accept some responsibility for his straitened circumstances. Yet she thought he had seemed more than content with the Thorpes at the musical

289

evening. She stood up to leave and asked, 'Are you bitter about what happened?'

'I am sorry that I let you down. But you have survived well enough and that gives me a little ease.' He followed her down the stairs. 'It is quite dark now. I'll walk with you.'

'There's no need.'

'Yes, there is. I may not be a gentleman but I can behave as one.'

She acquiesced. 'Very well; will you come in to meet Danby?'

'He does not want to see me.' He stopped and turned to face her. 'Do you and he have an understanding?'

'Oh yes.' Her mouth twisted. 'We acknowledge each other as distant cousins might, who have accepted the patronage of an elderly uncle and all that it entails. You would be astonished at how civil our behaviour has become.'

'Yes, I believe I should.'

His tone was mildly scornful and Sarah responded, 'Don't misunderstand me. Both of us shall always be grateful to our benefactor and neither of us would compromise his hospitality by our behaviour in any way.'

'That does not sound like the Sarah I used to know.'

'Why should it? I was a foundling who knew no better. I have had education and example in the workhouse.'

'So there was a silver lining to your black cloud of despair?'

'No thanks to you,' she retaliated. She heard his intake of breath and immediately regretted her response. 'Would you really have come back for me?'

'Yes. But that was then. You do not need me now.'

But I do, she thought. I need you more than ever. Stung by his rejection of her, she said, 'And you have no need of your former friends. You have the Thorpe family, though I suppose you cannot control them in the way you tried with me.'

'Is that what you think? That I wished to control you? I cared only for your well-being. Clearly, you now have others with more wealth and status to fill that role.'

290

'Is there nothing left of our friendship?'

'Friendship? You sought me out in anger.'

'But you understand why, and I have said I am sorry.'

'I am a simple blacksmith and we do not move in the same circles. You converse readily with merchants, lawyers and the town's dignitaries. A friendship with me would be frowned upon by them and be an obstacle to your advancement. You deserve your success and I should only become an embarrassment to you.'

Pained by the implication that she would reject him as he had her, she responded, 'Do you really believe that?'

'I know it. Propriety is everything in this town and I am sure your benefactor has ambitions for you.'

'Well, yes he has,' she agreed reluctantly.

'Then do not let him down. Allow him the privilege of being proud of you.'

She had no answers; only a certain knowledge that she wanted to see him again and a deep hurt at his downright refusal.

'Goodbye, Sarah,' he added.

'Goodbye then.'

Her disappointment, when he walked away, was profound.

Chapter 27

The following day, at the end of her morning's work in the office with Mr Parrish, she tidied away the papers and ledgers and said, 'With the new railway line we can sell more of our glass further afield. A London store has ordered a gross of my new storage jars.'

'They ship to customers in India and the America. So could we, Miss Meadow.'

Her eyes widened. 'But we'd need somewhere in London for warehousing; and a representative.'

He was nodding. 'I have already made enquiries at the guild about agents.'

Many of Mr Parrish's business colleagues called at the house and the drawing room was in frequent use to receive them.

'A few weeks ago, sir, you mentioned improvements to the house and I wondered if you had given the idea more thought?'

'I have and I believe I am too old for the upheaval it will cause, not to mention the smell of oil paint on my chest.'

'I have an idea to improve the outside, sir.'

'You ideas are always worth listening to, Miss Meadow.'

'I have seen a house in town with the most beautiful wrought-iron railings and gates at the front. They enclose a small court-yard and give the house a grand appearance that impresses callers.'

'I already have a full-grown hedge. Why should I replace it?'

'We are an ironworks town and your business colleagues would surely be impressed when they visit.'

'They are made locally?'

'I understand they come from the Bowes yard.'

'Are you sure? Bowes make only steel nowadays.'

'The ironmaster there has reopened his old forge in the yard and rented it to a blacksmith. Do have a look at the railings outside the house next to their yard when you drive by.'

A month later Sarah was walking down the stairs to her break-fast when an excited Mary burst into the hall. 'They're taking out the front hedges, miss!'

'Yes, I know, Mary. We are to have a stone wall built for Mr Parrish's new wrought-iron railings.'

'Well, they have a fine day for it. The sun is already quite hot.'

Sarah went into the front drawing room and watched from the window.

The railings arrived with stone, mortar and two hefty men on a Bowes cart driven by Aidan. He secured the wheel brake and jumped down to inspect the prepared ground. Within minutes they were all at work laying the stone foundations for the iron-work. He was engrossed in his task until suddenly he looked towards the house and saw her staring.

She jumped, not knowing whether to disappear from the window or stay where she was. She opted for the latter, smiled, and raised her arm to acknowledge his presence. His response surprised and irritated her. He did not return her smile. He took off his cap and bowed his head in a stiff, formal greeting that she found hurtful. She hoped he might walk towards the front door then she would open it and speak with him. But he did not move and she let her arm fall slowly. The smile faded from her lips. Aidan turned back to his work and Sarah moved away from the window.

293

Her irritation turned to annoyance and she marched into the kitchen where Mrs Couzens was busy preparing vegetables for dinner. 'Is there lemonade in the pantry?' she asked.

'Fresh made yesterday and stone cold by now. I'll tell Mary to bring it through to you.'

'I thought the men building our new railings might enjoy some.'

'Oh! In that case I'll ask George to take it out.'

'He's busy in the garden. I'll see to it.'

'George will do it, Miss Meadow.'

Sarah simply smiled at Mrs Couzens and set up a tray with stoneware mugs. It was heavy when she had filled them with drink. She picked it up and walked slowly and steadily out of the kitchen around the side of the house until she came to front garden.

'Mr Beckwith,' she called. 'Would your men care for a cold drink?'

They all stopped work and stared at her. Aidan immediately dropped the section of railing he was fixing and came over to take the tray from her. 'Very kind of you, ma'am,' he said.

She maintained her grip on the tray. 'Tell them to come over here for it,' she said. 'And call me Sarah, for heaven's sake.'

'Not in front of my men,' he replied.

But he called over his men and she noticed that he watched her hand out the mugs. She caught his eye and he looked away quickly. He was hot from exertion and she was reminded of the summer in the woods when she had helped him make artefacts to sell in the market. They were happy times, she reflected, and she often remembered them fondly. Perhaps he did, too, for when he turned his gaze back on her she thought she detected a softness in his eyes.

'Shall we sit?' she suggested indicating a nearby garden bench. 'I should like to discuss your progress.'

Aidan remained standing. 'I shall be finished by the end of the day,' he answered.

'Will you come in for tea before you leave?'

His face took on a more serious expression. 'Do not do this, Sarah. You are already raising eyebrows and will be the talk of the taverns tonight if you do not take care.'

She frowned and pursed her lips. Was it so easy for a lady to lose her reputation?

'But you are respectable, Aidan,' she countered.

'I am not your equal.'

George had appeared in the front garden and was collecting the empty mugs from the men. He came over for the tray. 'Excuse me, miss, you're needed indoors.' He nodded briefly to Aidan and added, 'Sir.'

Aidan took his cue. 'Good day, Miss Meadow.' He bowed his head and returned to his task.

Sarah sat alone on the garden bench and fumed. Mrs Couzens must have sent George! She stood up reluctantly and walked slowly towards the side of the house. Just before she turned the corner she took one last lingering look at Aidan. He was staring at her. She wished she had been close enough to see right into his eyes and fathom what he was truly thinking. She went inside in a pensive mood.

Mr Parrish rose early and was at work in the office, bent over his desk by the window, a shawl round his shoulders and his spectacles on his nose.

'How are you today, sir?' Sarah asked. Mr Parrish had recovered from winter bouts of fever with the help of his physician, but, his small, bent body seemed frailer than ever and now he always went up to his chamber to rest every afternoon, sometimes retiring for the remainder of the day.

'You always brighten my day, Miss Meadow, and your presence puts my mind at ease because I know how well you run my office.'

'Thank you, sir.'

'I see you are reducing the profit margin on our patent storage jars.'

Well, he may be old and his body may be weakening but his mind is still sharp, thought Sarah. He had already inspected her calculations. 'It is only for local sales, sir. We are producing too many less-than-perfect jars that I cannot send to London. I am offering them locally but Riding housekeepers need more encouragement than London ones to change their ways so I have lowered the selling price.'

Her explanation must have been satisfactory for he went on, 'Take a look at the news sheet today. Prince Albert's exhibition will go ahead.'

'How exciting! Will you go and see it, sir.'

'A trip to London might see me off for good. I'm barely strong enough to get down to my works yard nowadays.'

'That is nonsense, sir. Your strength will return as soon as the weather warms up.'

'God willing,' he commented. 'However, my frailty should not prevent you from going to London. Would you like to?'

Sarah's eyes shone. 'I should indeed, sir. I could visit our warehouse and meet our agents as well as see the exhibits.'

'Are you not a little nervous about the journey?'

'Well, yes I am,' she admitted. 'London is a long way away and I have never travelled beyond the Riding.'

'Or on the railway train.'

'The railway?' Now Sarah felt really apprehensive. They moved at such high speed. 'Does the railway go all the way?'

'You have to go to Derby first and change to another line for London. But it takes less than a day, you know, instead of three days by post.'

'Truly?' Sarah was impressed but fearful of travelling anywhere so fast.

'You are frowning, Miss Meadow.'

'Well, it's not only the journey, sir. I should have to stay somewhere and be looked after by strangers,'

'Mary will go with you.'

Heavens, thought Sarah, she will be more frightened than I am!

'You will need a new silk gown for evening dinner, too.'

A new gown! Sarah was as excited as any young woman would be about this prospect but realised there would be a good deal of preparation for the trip.

'Oh dear, sir. It does sound a lot of fuss just for me.'

'That is only because it is your first journey to London.' Mr Parrish stretched out a frail hand and laid it over hers. 'You will enjoy the exhibition and benefit so much from the experience. It is time to spread your wings and become accustomed to railway carriages and hotels. I know you will manage quite well for you have never let me down yet.'

Sarah looked at him and smiled. She really was very fond of him. He had been unfailingly kind to her and she had learned so much under his patronage. He was as dear to her as a – as a father, she supposed, although she had never known her own father. But if she had she would have wanted him to be like Mr Parrish.

'Then I should like to go,' she said and was rewarded with a smile. She ought to travel more and find things out for herself instead of relying on Mr Parrish for guidance. And when had Sarah Meadow baulked at the unknown? She began to look forward to the venture.

She glanced at the array of papers on his desk. 'You have been inspecting all our figures this morning.'

'Have you noticed changes in output?'

'I have, sir. I told you that Danby was to reduce bottle output to make the new jars. The blowers use similar methods and moulds.'

'Well, it looks to me as though we've cut down on our wine glasses instead.'

Sarah frowned. 'There may have been a problem with one of the furnaces?'

'Then why didn't Mr Jones tell me?'

'Well, he'll be home for his dinner soon and you can ask him. Are you ready for your tonic, sir?' It smelled like wine to Sarah, but Mr Parrish's physician had recommended it for his digestion.

Sarah went back to the drawing room and glanced out of the window. Aidan and his men were hard at work and she watched him, unnoticed, for several minutes. Whatever he thought about their differences in status, he was the same man who had worked at his anvil in Meadow Hall woods where she had grown to respect and admire him. And she wanted him as a man, she acknowledged to herself with a sigh.

She had come close to making a fool of herself in front of his men, but she had only wished to be near to him for a few moments. And she was sure he had welcomed her presence in spite of his reprimand. She took Mr Parrish's tonic into the office on a tray and tidied the desk while he sipped. It revived him and, as soon as Mary came to tell them dinner was ready, Sarah helped him to his feet and into the dining room next door. Midday dinner was a substantial meal as Mr Parrish ate only a light tea and no supper. It was the time for Sarah and Danby to sit around the table with him and discuss business affairs.

Today they had boiled mutton with vegetables from the garden followed by rhubarb pie. Their fare was plain but always well cooked and Sarah's appetite was good. Danby, too, ate heartily which seemed to please Mr Parrish.

'There was a time when I could eat as much as you young folk,' he said, as Danby carved second helpings of meat. 'I have noticed the wages bill has increased and my coal order is up.'

'Oh, is it?' Danby shrugged.

'Can you tell me why?'

Danby hesitated. 'We have smelted more glass.'

'Then why aren't we selling more tableware? What has happened to the London order?'

There was a silence until Mr Parrish repeated his second question and added, 'It has been shipped, hasn't it?'

'Not yet, sir.'

'Are you telling me it is not on its way to London?'

298

'It isn't ready. I – I had a problem with one of the furnaces.' He took a swallow of water.

Sarah's eyebrows went up. According to returns from the works, they were on full production. 'What kind of problem?' she asked.

'It didn't affect your jars,' he replied with a sneer.

'Well, what did it affect, Mr Jones?' Mr Parrish's tone was sharp.

Sarah looked at Danby's pale face and wondered what he had done. A terrible suspicion crept into her head. She had ordered the raw materials and made out bank drafts for Danby to pay their suppliers. But Danby had not asked her to send invoices for the wine glasses yet. Normally she trusted him because Mr Parrish did, although her own experience told her Danby was not a dependable man. She stared straight into Danby's narrow blue eyes. 'Answer Mr Parrish,' she demanded quietly.

Chapter 28

'They didn't get the wine glasses out on time.'

'They?'

'The gaffers! It was their fault!' Danby protested. 'I don't know who they think they are but they want to run the cones instead of me. I'm not having that. You put me in charge.'

Mr Parrish sat quite still. Sarah said, 'I have not written to advise our London agent of late delivery. I must do that immediately.' Agitated, she rose to leave.

Danby looked troubled and said, 'There's no point,'

'Of course there is. I shall explain about the furnace and give him a new date. Tell me when, Danby.' As a rule, Sarah did not call him that in front of Mr Parrish but she had to make him understand how important this was. She noticed her employer raise his eyebrows, but in a kindly rather than disapproving manner, she thought. However, Danby still didn't reply so she went on, 'Danby, when shall I say?'

'The way the gaffers have acted up it'll be never,' he muttered.

'Do not take this lightly, Mr Jones. You must give a date,' Mr Parrish warned.

'I can't.'

Sarah stayed silent. This was a serious matter. If Danby did not deliver, Mr Parrish would lose his London orders. She knew how much of the bank's money he had invested in setting up the London warehouse. It was essential for him to meet this commitment.

'Of course you can,' Mr Parrish answered quietly. 'When do the gaffers say they will finish the order?'

Danby stood up letting his napkin fall to the floor. 'I'll go and ask them.'

'Don't you know already?'

'I've said I'll find out, haven't I?'

'Do not raise your voice to me, Mr Jones.' Mr Parrish's face was stony.

Danby went out without an apology, which shocked Sarah. Mr Parrish had gone quite pale and she said, 'I'll go after him, sir, and bring back the information I need for the letter.'

'I shall go with you.' He leaned heavily on the arms of his chair and rose awkwardly. 'Ask Mary to fetch my topcoat.'

'It is cold out of doors today, sir, even if you are well-wrapped. I do not want you to catch a chill. I'll ask the gaffers how they are getting on. They know me and have met with me in the furnaces before.'

'I should see for myself.' He staggered and sat down again.

'I shall tell you if there is anything truly amiss, sir.'

'I thank the Lord for you, Miss Meadow.' Mr Parrish closed his eyes.

'You should rest now, sir. Let me help you to the couch.'

As soon as her employer was comfortable by the dining-room fire, Sarah hurried to collect her bonnet and cloak and set off after Danby. When she arrived at the works she was surprised that no smoke billowed from the top of one of the chimneys. As she neared she realised it was the tableware cone. Surely if the fire had cooled, the glass-blowers had finished?

Inside the cavernous building she felt some residual warmth and walked in a circle around the eight melting pots. In the gloom, she detected no gaffers, no glassware, no straw or packing crates; only one lad sitting snoozing against the warm wall next to a broom. Her spirits rose. The order must have been completed and despatched. She walked nearer to a doorway and called, 'You, lad! Come over here to the light.'

'Who says?'

'Miss Meadow.'

He scrambled to his feet and picked up his broom. 'Yes, miss. Sorry, miss, I didn't hear you come in.'

'Where are the gaffers?'

'They've all gone, miss.'

'Thank Heaven! The order is completed after all. Mr Parrish will be so relieved.'

The lad's eyes darted from side to side and he chewed on his lip.

'They have finished, haven't they?' she added slowly.

'You'd better ask Mr Jones, miss.'

'I am asking you. Tell me your name, boy, and which chair you are with.'

'It wasn't my fault, miss! Ask my gaffer!'

'You are here and he is not. Now tell me what you know. Have the wine glasses been packed or not?'

'They never made none.'

Sarah thought she was going to faint. The curved brick walls were spinning around her head. 'None at all?' she whispered. 'What happened?'

The lad looked at his feet. 'I wish you'd ask Mr Jones, miss.'

'I want to hear the chairs' side first, from you.'

He shuffled his feet. 'We haven't had no coal delivered.'

'But I saw for myself that our coal orders were up!'

'Can you do something, miss? We haven't had no wages neither and me mum relies on mine.'

'But surely your gaffer has paid your wages?' Sarah had made out the bank drafts for Danby herself.

'That's what I mean, miss. The gaffers haven't had no wages

and they've all cleared off. Parrish's is not the only glassworks in town, miss.'

Sarah's head spun. She had made out the drafts to Danby so he could draw cash and make the payments. These were substantial amounts of money. What was Danby playing at? Oh dear Lord, this was much worse than Sarah had imagined. 'Where is Mr Jones now?' she demanded.

'I dunno, miss.'

'You must have some idea.'

'He spends a lot o' time wi' the bottle-blowers.'

'Right. You can get off home now.'

'Can you find me summat to do, miss? Me mam needs a wage.'

'Very well. Come with me.'

The bottle furnace was working at full heat and no one noticed them enter the cone. At least one cone was working. The air was stifling and Sarah loosened the fastenings on her cloak.

'You'd best stay well back, miss. I'll see if I can find Mr Jones for you.'

She stood in the shadow of the curved brick walls and watched. The bottle-blowing teams were the least skilled of Mr Parrish's workers but they worked remarkably fast. Sarah marvelled at how they knew exactly how much of the molten glass they needed to produce a bottle of the required thickness. She lost count of the number of cooling moulds accumulating and cluttering their workspace.

The lad came back. 'He says he can't talk to you now and you've got to go back home.'

'Does he indeed? Where exactly is he?'

'He's on t'other side, miss. Best go round t'outside.' She noticed the lad had brightened and he added, 'Shall I come with you, miss?'

'Why not?' she answered and marched away.

Danby was leaning on the wall in the fresh air with a bottle of beer in his hand and as she approached he put it to his lips and drank. A handful of working men she did not recognise were with him, also drinking beer from bottles and standing around a wooden crate from the brewery. If Mr Parrish knew about this he would be furious. As it was he had no idea that one of the cones was out of action.

'Mr Jones, may I speak with you?'

Her request was greeted by degree of jostling and ribbing about his 'lady friend' and she was pleased that he denied that association vehemently. As soon as her name was mentioned they fell quiet. He walked towards her. 'Not here, Sarah, old girl. Didn't the lad say?' His speech was already slurred.

'Yes, he did and I am not your "old girl".'

'And for that I give thanks. Now get off home to your little office. This is no place for a woman.'

'It is no place for drinking either.'

'God, you're as stuffy as the old man.'

'Don't be so disrepectful.'

'This is how I operate. You'd know that if you came down here more often.' He picked up a bottle of ale from the crate and released the wired metal stopper. 'You should try one of these; it might loosen your drawers a bit.'

The silence that followed was palpable. The men stopped their bantering and some were clearly embarrassed. Sarah eyes were sparks of flint. She wanted to hit him; to step forward and slap him hard across his smug, handsome face.

'Oh well, if you don't want it, I'll drink it,' he went on and raised it to his lips.

Swiftly, Sarah stepped forward, reached up and wrenched it from his grasp. She smashed it against the wall and said, 'You've had enough, all of you.' She turned to the workers and added, 'Get back to work, and one of you give this lad something to do. Mr Jones and I have urgent business to discuss.'

The men disappeared into the cone taking the lad with them. Danby's face was like thunder. 'Don't you ever do anything like that in front of my men again!'

'And don't you speak to me like that ever again! When

were you going to tell Mr Parrish about the tableware order?'

'What do you know about them? What has that little rat been saying?'

'Nothing! I can work it out for myself! What else does a cold furnace and no sign of the gaffers mean? Have you any idea how much time and money has gone into setting up this London contract?'

'And have you any idea how much work I do in this hellhole every day, while you swan around preening yourself in the big house up the road!'

'I work hard for Mr Parrish!'

'So do I!'

'He knows that, so why didn't you tell him there was trouble?'

'I did, didn't I?'

'Not until he asked you at dinner today. You should have told him as soon as you knew we wouldn't meet the order. Dear Lord, if we lose it, he'll be bankrupt.'

'Don't talk daft, he's laden with cash. He must be with two cones turning out glass.'

'There isn't much profit on bottles. You have to make hundreds for it to pay.'

'Well, we do.'

'Yes and it keeps us going day to day, but it won't pay the bank without the tableware. We have to get the gaffers back as soon as possible. Why haven't you paid them; or our suppliers? I gave you the drafts.'

'I'll get the money.' he snapped. 'I just need a few more days.'

'What do you mean you'll get it?' she shouted. 'Where is it now?'

'You mind your side of the business and I'll mind mine,' he shouted.

'Money is my side. What have you done with it? I'm not moving until you tell me.'

At first she thought he was going to hit her. But he quietened suddenly and gave her his most charming smile. 'A man has needs.

But you wouldn't know anything about that. I deserve a life away from here. I've earned my fun so just sign me another one of those drafts and I'll pay the suppliers.'

'I don't believe you, Danby Jones! Are you telling me you've spent the gaffers' wages and the coal money on *yourself*? What on earth possessed you?'

'Oh, don't be so stuffy. Find a way to write up the ledger so old Parrish won't ask where it's gone.'

'But there is no more money,' Sarah yelled. 'And there won't be if we can't fulfil the London order.'

'Don't be daft. Old Parrish is rolling in it.'

'*He isn't!* And what if he was? It's his money, not yours. Dear Lord, however shall I tell him?'

'You don't have to; not yet, anyway. Just give me another bank draft.'

'Don't be ridiculous!' She tried to calm herself. 'I'll have to explain somehow.'

'You'll think of something. You're the clever one.'

'Well, I think *you* should tell him. What time will you be home tonight?'

'Late. Tell the old bugger I'm fixing the furnace.'

'Tell him yourself! He's getting the truth from me. I owe him that at least.'

He grabbed hold of the edges of her cloak with both hands and breathed, 'If you lose me my position here I'll make you suffer. One way or another, I'll make you pay. I'll ruin you, so help me. How do you fancy going back to the workhouse after living in the big house?'

'Let go of me, Danby, and don't threaten me.' But she knew how easy it was for a man with Danby's influence and contacts to ruin a woman's life.

'Why not? Isn't that what you're doing to me?' He shoved her away and added, 'Now clear off.'

Sarah walked slowly up the hill to home, her mind wrestling with what she would say to Mr Parrish. He trusted her to be honest with him. He once said her readiness to speak her mind might be her downfall, but he valued it in his clerk. She had to tell him the truth.

He was downstairs in the office, going through papers at this desk. He looked up at her, and she hesitated by the open door. His face was grey; old and wrinkled and ghostly. She pressed her lips together, inhaled deeply and went in.

'Well?'

'I think I should take the letter to London personally, sir. I can get there as quickly as the letter carrier and it is best for – for bad news to be delivered with a – a solution.'

'Then it is as I feared. The order is not ready.'

'It is worse. The furnace is cold and the gaffers have left.'

He sagged in his chair, making him seem even smaller than he was. 'We are down a furnace. Will it take long to repair?'

'The cones are sound. The coal was not delivered and – and the gaffers have not been paid.'

'The money was taken from my bank.' He said it quietly, in a tone as cold as glass.

'Mr Jones can explain, sir.'

'What on earth has he been he playing at? He knows about my London contract.'

'We cannot meet it, sir.'

'What? Call for my carriage. I shall go and see for myself.'

He placed his hands on the desk and pushed himself to his feet. At first Sarah thought he was simply too weak and she darted forward to help but he slumped back and his head lolled to one side. He was trying to speak to her but she could not make out his words and saliva was collecting around his lips. His eyes were wide and terrified. Dear Lord, he was having some kind of seizure!

She raced to the door and called, 'Mary! Mrs Couzens! Come quickly.' She waited until she heard the kitchen door open and ran back to Mr Parrish, calling over her shoulder, 'Mary, run for the doctor, as fast as you can. Tell him it's urgent. Mrs Couzens, help me with Mr Parrish. What do I do?'

307

Mr Parrish quietened and his eyes closed. His limbs were limp but he was still breathing. 'We should get him to bed,' Mrs Couzens said. He was in a deep faint. They made him as comfortable as they could in the chair and dragged it between them to the bottom of the stairs.

'I'll fetch George to carry him,' Mrs Couzens said. She returned with him through the kitchen at the same time as Mary arrived at the front door accompanied by Mr Parrish's physician. They were all out of breath from running.

Mr Parrish's servants moved away as the doctor opened his bag and examined his patient with a grave expression on his face. Finally, he straightened. 'I am sorry to have to tell you that Mr Parrish has gone.'

Sarah gave a half laugh in her throat. 'No, he hasn't. You've made a mistake. He was well at dinner time. It's only his legs that have failed him. His mind is perfect, so you must be wrong.' Her eyes were already filling with tears and she started towards him.

The doctor caught her arm. 'He is dead, Miss Meadow.'

Chapter 29

'He can't be.' Sarah tore herself free and ran over to Mr Parrish's still form. She placed her hands on his frail shoulders. 'Wake up, sir. It's me. Miss Meadow.' He did not move and she twisted her head, wild-eyed, to plead for more help. 'Do something!' she cried.

'It's no use, miss. He's gone.' The doctor signalled to Mary to help Sarah. Mrs Couzens and George exchanged sympathetic frowns.

'He was quite old, miss,' Mary said, taking her hand.

'But he was *well*,' Sarah anguished. 'He was. He can't have gone. He can't leave me; not yet.' Her tears were flowing freely as she refused to release her hold on his shoulders. 'He's been like a father to me since I came here. He believed in me; gave me a home and security. He respected me when others didn't. I won't let him go. I won't.'

'You have to, miss. It is his time,' Mary said.

The doctor added, 'In a gentleman of his years, Miss Meadow, this kind of seizure is not uncommon.'

But Sarah could not be consoled and slumped to the floor, weeping profusely. The doctor fetched a chair from by the wall, placed it beside her and helped her to her feet. He continued in his low, gentle voice. 'It can be brought on easily by anxiety or bad news.'

Sarah felt the blood drain from her face. 'Then it was my fault. I told him. It was me.'

'No, my dear, you're not to blame for it might have happened at any time. Now sit down, you have had a shock yourself.' He looked at the other servants. 'Bring her some brandy, please.'

Sarah stared wide-eyed across the hall. She had let him down. If she hadn't told Mr Parrish the truth he would be alive still. And now, the only person who valued her and seemed to understand her was dead. But she had had to speak. He expected honesty from her and she had had to tell him. He would have been angry with her if she had not told him the truth. His glass-works was in a mess and Danby had said nothing.

Danby! This was all down to Danby and his constant reassurance that all was well. All was not well and now Mr Parrish was dead because of it. It was all Danby's fault! He was as much, if not more, to blame as she was. He had deliberately kept important information from Mr Parrish and from her. They could not meet the bank payments without the London contract and had probably lost it for ever.

The front door opened and Danby walked through it. He stopped in the open doorway and smiled his charming smile at them all. How dare he, she fumed; how dare he come home with a smile on his face when he knew of the troubles at the works?

Her fists were clenching by her side as she stood up angrily. 'It's your fault! Everything is your fault. You should have told him sooner that you were in trouble. I could have written to London, travelled there to talk to them!' She stopped for breath but had not finished. 'Why didn't you tell me?' she cried. 'You left it too late. Mr Parrish knew it would mean the end! He knew!'

She was hardly aware of what she was saying. There were people around her, pushing her onto a chair and pressing a glass of brandy to her lips. She could not stop her tears and wiped her face with the heel of her hand.

'Take her upstairs, Mary,' Mrs Couzens said. 'I'll ask the doctor to leave her a powder when he finished talking to Mr Jones.'

Sarah swallowed the rest of her brandy. Danby appeared surprised as the doctor told him the distressing news, but when he walked past her she detected the faint hint of smirk around his lips. She did not think it was possible to hate him even more, but she did. He seemed pleased that Mr Parrish had died. She supposed it was because he had got away with his dishonest thieving without chastisement or any loss of his position.

The doctor said, 'Go to your chamber, Miss Meadow, and take my sedative. I'll inform Mr Parrish's lawyer. I am so sorry, indeed there are many folk in this town who will be sorry about his passing.'

Sarah stood at the bottom of the stairs and watched as Danby saw the doctor out of the front door. As she climbed the stairs she heard Danby say to George, 'Fetch the carriage round for me, Georgie, I'm off out again.'

'At this hour, sir?'

'I'll drive it myself.'

'I was about to shut up the horses.'

'Just fetch it, there's a good fellow.'

'If you wish, sir.'

'You can lock the door after me, Mrs Couzens,' he called over his shoulder as he left, and she realised that he planned to stay out all night.

The sedative made Sarah sleep heavily for a few hours. It was dark when she woke and she listened for the chimes of the church clock in town. Three o'clock. She could not believe that Mr Parrish had gone, and she lay awake forcing back tears. It was nobody's fault, the doctor had said, anything could have brought on the seizure. She tossed and turned for two hours then rose, heavy-eyed, and went down to the kitchen to light the fire in the range.

The kettle was boiling when Mrs Couzens came in at six. 'I thought it was you I heard moving about. Is Mary not down yet?'

'Let her sleep in this once. I'm making tea. Sit and drink it with me.'

'What'll happen to us, Miss Meadow?'

Sarah remembered the same question asked in a similar situation years ago at Meadow Hall. Were the next few years of her life to be as eventful as the ones after then? She thought fondly of her time with Aidan in the woods and bitterly of the years that followed in the workhouse. She prayed that they would all be spared that fate this time.

'We'll be looked after, I'm sure,' she replied, forcing a weak smile.

George came in from the back garden and Mrs Couzens stood up. 'I'd better get on with Mr Jones's breakfast.'

'Finish your tea, lass,' George said. 'He never came back with the horse and carriage last night.'

'I hope he hasn't had an accident with them,' Mrs Couzens commented.

'Nay, he'll have drunk too much and stayed over with some crony from the institute.'

Sarah agreed that this was the most likely explanation, and when Mary joined them around the kitchen table they made another pot of tea.

George commented, 'He used to say to me, "Always look after the pennies and the pounds'll take care of themselves".'

'Aye, he could be right frugal at times, considering he was so rich.'

'Well, he wasn't that rich,' Sarah corrected. 'I mean, a lot of money came in, but a lot went out as well and it didn't always balance. When he did have any spare he gave it away to the chapel and his charities.

'He won't have forgotten us, though?'

'Don't worry, Mary. I'm sure none of us will have to go back to the workhouse.' But Sarah wasn't as certain as she sounded.

'I reckon Mr Jones will be in charge now, don't you, miss?'

'I suppose so.' She tried to hide her concern. Danby was not as worried about the future of the glassworks as she was. 'Wherever he was last night, I expect he'll be at the yard this morning.' She stood up and smoothed down her skirt. 'I ought to go and talk to him. There are important things to discuss.'

'Have you got a mourning gown, miss?' Mrs Couzens asked.

Sarah blinked and shook her head. She was known in the town and would be expected to be dressed appropriately.

'You can't go down there without showing respect.'

'No, of course not. Mary, I'll write you a note to take to Mrs Thorpe after breakfast.'

'George, get your black armband on and bring in your Sunday best suit; it'll need sponging and pressing for the funeral.' Mrs Couzens stood up. 'Now, shall I do some breakfast for us?'

Sarah spent the morning making sure that the glassworks invoices and ledgers were in perfect order and that Mr Parrish's desk was polished and tidy. She arranged his writing tray and blotter, sat down in his old chair and gave in to another weep. Danby sent a message from town saying that he would be bringing Mr Parrish's lawyer with him for dinner, and to open a bottle of wine from the supply kept for visitors. She went upstairs to put on her darkest day gown, re-pin her hair and dress it with a little black lace borrowed from Mrs Couzens.

The lawyer, Mr Withers, had visited before and he was acquainted with Mr Parrish's household. He was always soberly dressed in a dark suit of clothes. Danby, more stylishly turned out, had purchased an armband and necktie, both in black silk. Sarah greeted them in the hall and Mr Withers took her hand and offered condolences. But she noticed that he was scrutin- ising every inch of her attire and was glad she had observed the proprieties of mourning as best she could. As well as grieving for Mr Parrish, she was aware that she was very much alone for she knew that Danby could not be relied upon for any kind of support to help her through. His own interests always came first. She went into the dining room feeling anxious and tense.

After Mary had cleared the soup, Mr Withers broke the strained silence around the table. 'It is not normally my practice to speak of the will before the funeral. But Mr Parrish has left important matters of business which affect others in the town and I believe it is my duty to inform you of his wishes.' He paused before adding, 'You are indeed the most fortunate of young people.'

Sarah blinked. What on earth did he mean? She cast a puzzled glance at Danby who smiled broadly and asked, 'What's he left us, then?'

'You may not be quite so pleased when you realise that your good fortune comes with responsibility. Mr Parrish invested recently in a planned overseas expansion and he wished for that to continue.'

Sarah's heart missed a beat. She wondered if Mr Withers knew as much as she did about the extent of that expansion. She asked, 'Have you spoken with his banker, sir?'

'I meet with him this afternoon, Miss Meadow. Mr Parrish always spoke highly of your skill with figures as well as words. Would you care to accompany me?'

'I should be the one to go with you, surely?' Danby responded. 'I run the works.'

'Indeed you do, Mr Jones. But do you have an understanding of its financial commitments?'

'Of course I do! I pay the men's wages, don't I?'

Sarah almost exploded. She clenched her fists to control her anger and said tightly, 'After I have calculated their earnings.' Then she added, 'My mourning gown is not ready, Mr Withers, so I should not venture out yet.'

'I shall go alone today,' Mr Withers decided.

'I don't see—' Danby began.

'Ah, here is the beef,' Sarah interrupted. 'Would you carve, Danby?'

He took up the knife and sharpened it briskly on the steel, then pierced the juicy roast with the fork. When everyone's plate was full of meat and vegetables, Mr Withers continued, 'Mr Parrish asked me to redraft his will after his negotiations for the London warehouse. He was aware that the next few years would be critical for his glassworks, and he needed to be sure its future – and yours – would be secure. He did this for the benefit of his workers as well as your good selves.'

'Who has he left it to, then?' Danby pressed. 'Are you going to tell us or not?'

Mr Withers poured gravy over his meat. 'You need to know now that both of you are trustees as well as myself. Therefore, we are responsible for the glassworks until probate is granted and then ownership will be transferred.'

'Are we paid for doing that?' Danby queried.

'I am,' he replied. 'You are not.'

'That's not—'

Sarah interrupted him. 'Oh, do be quiet, Danby, and let Mr Withers speak.'

The lawyer acknowledged her interruption with a grateful nod. 'I shall run it until the legalities are complete. And then it will belong to you. He has left it to you both in gratitude for your hard work and loyalty to him.'

A whoop of triumph escaped from Danby's throat and in his excitement he knocked over a wine glass half full of claret. Costly red liquid spread over the polished mahogany wood. He snatched his white napkin from his lap and stemmed the flow.

'Do take care, sir!' Mr Withers exclaimed. His mouth turned down in distaste. 'Mr Jones, please remember I am here because of Mr Parrish's death.'

Sarah's eyes focused on the red stain spreading through the linen. She could hardly believe her ears. Mr Parrish had left his beloved glassworks to them! He must have held them both in a

315

very high regard. But how awful for him to know, in his dying moments, his life's work was in danger of collapse. She frowned at Danby. Mr Withers had mentioned responsibility. It's time Danby realised just how precarious his inheritance was. She opened her mouth to speak.

Mr Withers raised a hand to silence her and added, 'There are conditions.'

Sarah closed her mouth.

'You will have equal shares but a covenant will not allow you to dispose of your share unless it is to the other one.'

'So I could have your half, Sarah?'

'If you could afford to buy it,' she responded.

Mr Withers looked from one to the other. 'Mr Parrish wanted most of all to ensure continuity of ownership. He had faith in and respect for families, and loyalty was paramount to him, as I am sure you are aware. Although neither of you are related to Mr Parrish, he regarded both of you as family. He informed me that you have shared his home amicably for several years; that you are civil with each other and towards the servants. You will, of course have to live somewhere; both of you.'

'Don't tell me he's left us this house as well.' Danby refilled his own wine glass then offered more claret to Mr Withers, who declined curtly.

Mr Withers went on, 'In essence, yes. Although there is one more condition.' Again he looked from Sarah to Danby. 'Mr Parrish was not a gentleman to show his emotions but he told me that his household had come alive in recent years with young people living in it. However, he was particularly concerned that Miss Meadow's devotion to her work for him had impacted on her opportunities for marriage, and that spinsterhood is a precarious state. He observed that you valued each other's contribution to the glassworks and – well.' He stopped to take a deep breath. 'Mr Parrish wished to secure your future, Miss Meadow, so he stipulated that you and Mr Jones must marry each other in order to inherit. You will become the foundations of a dynasty, and ownership of the house will then pass to your eldest child.'

There was stunned silence. Danby and Sarah looked across the table at each other, horror clear on their faces, united in their astonishment.

'No.' Sarah's voice was strained. 'He – he,' she croaked. Her throat closed. She was so shocked that she couldn't get the words out of her mouth. She remembered fleeting strands of conversations with Mr Parrish when he had expressed his guilt at her unmarried status. But she had told him she was content to be a spinster, and, although she knew it was not a desirable state for a woman, she had meant it at the time.

Her heart began to thump. She had questioned that contentment lately, because she *had* indulged in dreams of marriage. But they had never, ever, included Danby. He was the last person she wanted as a husband. It was Aidan who constantly intruded into her thoughts. It was the memory of their happy times living in the woods that beckoned her back to him. She couldn't marry Danby – she couldn't marry anyone – when it was Aidan that she dreamed of.

Sarah could not think clearly and became agitated. She was vaguely aware that Mr Withers, having delivered his shattering news, excused himself and left for the bank. She hardly remembered his parting words. After she had seen him out, she glanced in the looking glass by the front door and saw her frowning face, paler than usual. She could not believe this was happening to her.

Mary emerged from the dining room carrying plates and spoons. Sarah pulled herself together and asked her to bring coffee to the table immediately. Mary hurried away.

Danby, too, seemed lost for words. He had gone quite white, clearly as shocked as she was. He paced about the dining room barely concealing his anger. 'He can't do that.'

'What can't he do? Leave the factory to us?'

'Don't be clever with me. He can't insist that we marry.'

'No, he can't. But you heard Mr Withers. We forfeit the

inheritance if we don't. Anyway there may not be any factory to inherit after your spending fiasco.'

'He must have something stashed away.'

'He hasn't! The bank will foreclose and the glassworks will be bankrupted. All Mr Parrish's work will have been in vain.'

'Mine too,' he muttered. 'I'm not giving up everything I've been slaving at for all these years, bowing and scraping to that old bugger to stay in his favour. I deserve that factory.'

'Danby! Whole families will starve if the factory closes down.'

'I don't care! He's still trying to run our lives, even from the grave.'

'Well, I'm not surprised. He was a respectable, pious man and wanted the same for us. Our marriage would mean we can stay living in this house.'

'So you are willing to go ahead with his wishes?'

'I didn't say that.'

'No, you didn't, because you don't want to marry me any more than I want to marry you.'

She agreed with him about that and said, 'We'll have to leave if we don't.'

He didn't appear to hear her. 'God this is a mess! Just as I thought everything was working out for us.'

'Us?'

He shrugged. 'Y'know; the glassworks.'

But it wasn't working out at present, she thought with a frown. 'Are you going back this afternoon? You should make sure the remaining cone stays open.'

'Don't you tell me what to do! Look, I'll move out for a few days. I wouldn't want to tarnish your reputation now the old boy has gone.'

Sarah was surprised he had any concern for her. 'Where will you go?'

'I have friends in town. But don't you forget this is my house as much as yours.' He finished his coffee and left the room.

Sarah let out a depressed sigh. She couldn't imagine anything worse than having Danby as a husband, let alone being forced to marry without love, or even affection. She despised him after what he had done to the glassworks. He was greedy and selfish and hid it from others with a veneer of practised charm. And what on earth was Mr Parrish thinking of, expecting her to marry Danby? Had their pact of civility given him a mistaken belief that they had a regard for each other? Nothing could be further from the truth. Perhaps they should have argued more in front of him, but it was too late now. If they did not marry she wondered what the alternative was for the glassworks and the men who laboured there.

'Thank you for coming over, Miss Meadow. Mrs Thorpe has taken her infant to visit his grandfather who is not at all well, and I am left in charge of the workroom.'

Sarah followed Emma Thorpe upstairs to the fitting room. 'It is civil of you to accommodate me at such short notice. I have had no need of mourning clothes until now.'

'I am so very sorry for your loss.'

'Thank you. I was Mr Parrish's clerk but he was as dear as family to me.' Her tears threatened again. She had never felt more alone; except perhaps as a girl hiding in the stables of an empty mansion.

Emma smiled sympathetically and said briskly, 'We have cut a day gown in wool and another in silk with a matching cape for afternoons.'

Emma and her assistant worked silently around her, pinning and measuring to ensure that the fit would be perfect. Sarah stared out of the window over the garden to the wrought-iron gate in the brick wall that led to the works yard next door. Sounds of metal ringing on metal came from the forge.

'Mr Beckwith is hard at work, I hear,' she commented. He had been her salvation at Meadow Hall when she had no one to turn to, and he had left her the pigeons. She recalled that simple act of kindness. It was long ago but she remembered it clearly.

'Indeed he is,' Emma replied. 'He has three journeymen now and has used up all of my brother's spare storage sheds. It is my opinion that he works too hard, though.'

It is his way, she thought. He is strong. He is clever and determined and . . . She dare not even think of how much she cared for him. He had shown very clearly that she should not consider him as a sweetheart. She answered truthfully, 'He deserves his success.' For a few seconds she wondered if his status had changed enough for him to think again about their differences and asked, 'Where does he reside these days?'

'Oh, he is still occupying our carriage house.'

'Surely he can afford to rent a house?'

'He is looking for premises first, to expand his forge.'

'Near to the canal, I suppose, like everyone else.'

'Or the railway; his vision goes beyond the South Riding.'

'And rightly so. The railings he made for Mr Parrish are constantly admired by visitors.'

'I'm sure he would be pleased to hear that, Miss Meadow. Indeed, your testimonial for his work would be a welcome addition to his brochure.'

'Then I shall call on him at his forge.' She said it without thinking but she meant it. She had to see him whether he agreed to it or not. If Emma disapproved she didn't show it and continued silently with her task.

Aidan had three blacksmiths and two lads busy in his forge. He was bent over an anvil, sweaty and sooty as he worked a strip of red-hot iron into an intricate curve. Heat radiated out as far as the open doorway and the noise of hammers on metal was deafening. Sarah watched him silently for several minutes, marvelling at his skill. Eventually he dipped his finished work into the water butt, making it hiss and sizzle as it cooled. He took it over to his colleague and it was then that he noticed her.

'Sarah?' He looked surprised, then glanced at his men and added hastily, 'Miss Meadow, please take care. The sparks are dangerous.'

'May I speak with you?' She gave a slight smile.

He put down his tongs and came over. They moved outside to the sunshine. She thought he seemed pleased to see and her heart swelled a little. But it was short-lived for he stood a yard way from her and looked at her with a frown.

'I read about Mr Parrish. I am so sorry,' he said. 'I know how fond you were of him.'

'Thank you. It happened so very suddenly. One minute he was fine and the next he – he had gone. I had not time to prepare myself for – for losing him.'

'It does not make any difference. My father was dying for six months and it was still a shock to me when he passed on.'

Has he changed, she wondered? He is being kind to me because I am bereaved. She tried to read the sentiment in his sooty face and judged that his distant manner and reserve were still there.

He went on, 'It is very hard to bear when you lose someone you love and even harder if you have no one else.'

He did understand how she felt! He knew how alone she was. He seemed to be searching behind her eyes when he said, 'You are very unhappy.'

She nodded and a tear threatened. She blinked it back. His dirty greasy clothes were covered with a scarred leather apron and his exposed arms were blackened by smuts.

'How is Danby taking it?' he asked.

She was brought back to earth by the mention of Danby. She hated the way his existence was governing her life and answered, 'I don't think he cared much for Mr Parrish. He seems more interested in what he has to gain.'

Aidan ignored the barb. 'I saw in the newspaper that Mr Parrish had set up a London base.'

She nodded, not wishing to go into detail, and they stared silently at each other.

One of Aidan's men called, 'Mr Beckwith! Can you take a look at this?'

He turned and acknowledged him but seemed reluctant to move away from her.

'I should leave you to your work,' she said.

'Not yet,' he replied. 'Tell me why you are here.'

She bit on her lower lip. The truth would be that she needed to see him. But she had a reason and had almost forgotten about it. 'Emma told me you were expanding your markets and would appreciate a testimonial from Parrish's.'

'I should indeed; how thoughtful of you.'

'Will you call at the house to collect it?'

His eyes widened marginally. 'Is that wise? You are a single lady of some wealth and I am an unmarried man. You may send it across with a servant.'

'Perhaps you can advise me what to write?'

'Then it's hardly valid.'

'Please. Mr Parrish was always my guiding hand and I miss him.'

Aidan was persuaded. 'Well I suppose it would be acceptable if Danby were present—'

'He won't be. He's staying with friends.'

Aidan frowned. 'He has left you alone at a time like this?'

'I have the servants. Once the funeral is over I shall receive visitors. Come for tea on Sunday afternoon. Please.'

'Very well.'

Her heart lifted. At last she had something to look forward to. 'Thank you.'

The call from inside the forge sounded more urgent and Aidan bowed his head formally. 'Will you excuse me? I have an urgent commission to complete.'

'Of course. Tell me about it on Sunday.'

'Oh, Miss Meadow, black is very becoming for your colouring. I've never seen anyone look so beautiful in mourning.'

'Do you think so, Mary? I think it makes me look too pale.' Sarah pinched at her cheeks to redden them. The silk skirts of her afternoon dress swished as she moved away from her looking glass.

'Delicate, miss; like a piece of fragile china.'

'Has Mr Withers arrived?'

'He is with Mr Jones in the drawing room. I gave the fire a good fettle, like you asked.'

Sarah went downstairs and heard Danby's raised voice before she opened the door.

'You can't insist. The old boy's dead, for God's sake. What does it matter to him now?

The lawyer's face was stony but he smiled when he saw Sarah. 'Miss Meadow.' He walked over to her and took her hand. 'How are you?'

'I am well, thank you, sir.'

Danby continued his angry tirade. 'Tell him, Sarah. Tell him you don't want to marry any more than I do.'

'Shall we sit?' Sarah suggested. 'I should like to know if there is an alternative.'

The lawyer waited until they were comfortable before he spoke. But he did not answer her query. 'You might be able to keep one of the cones in production,' he said. 'You are committed to the London warehouse lease which you may be able to sell but interest on the bank loan is already mounting. You will not be able to clear the debt without using your income from bottle production. But you are each able in your own way and together there is a chance to save the bottle furnace.'

'I'll do that, then,' Danby said, 'as long as we don't have to marry.'

'Mr Parrish's wishes are clear. You cannot inherit the glass-works unless you marry.'

'Won't it all belong to me then, anyway?' Danby asked.

'Miss Meadow's half is protected by the terms of the will.'

Sarah raised her eyebrows. 'He really wanted me to own half of it?'

'He did.'

'Marriage is a big step, sir,' Sarah responded. 'What will happen to the glassworks if we refuse to marry?'

'It will be sold and the profits, if there are any, divided between his charities. After speaking with the bank, it is my opinion that there will be very little gain for anyone if we sell now.'

'But surely the cones can be sold as a going concern and people will keep their jobs,' Sarah pressed.

'Unlikely. The furnaces are old. Mr Parrish's strength was in his gaffers. Rival glassworks have already taken them on. It is likely that they will also buy the cones, shut them down and lay off the men. They'll take the customers then sell off the land.'

'We can't let that happen!' Sarah protested. 'Whole families will be in the workhouse!'

'I'm afraid so, Miss Meadow. The town's dignitaries will not thank you for allowing the glassworks to close.'

'And I could not allow anyone that fate,' Sarah murmured. 'I cannot take action that will throw men out of work.'

'What about this house?' Danby interrupted. 'Can we sell it?'

'No. It's in trust for – well, for your firstborn when you marry.'

'But you are the trustee, sir,' Sarah said. 'Would you allow a mortgage against it to keep the glassworks open?'

'I don't see why not. If we can show that it would benefit the child's future.'

'Then we have our answer. We raise capital on the assets of the trust to get the glassworks back into profit.'

'And marry,' Mr Withers reminded her.

'Do we have to marry each other?' Sarah asked.

'Should one of you marry someone else, the trust will be wound up and everything sold for the benefit of Mr Parrish's named charities.'

'Well, could we both live here if we don't marry?'

'That is precisely what Mr Parrish wanted to avoid. If you are not man and wife within six months, the same thing will happen. You will have to vacate and go your separate ways.'

'With nothing!' Danby scorned.

'With experience enough to obtain another position, sir,' the lawyer pointed out. He heaved a sigh. 'You know, the gentry have

324

contracted marriages of convenience for the sake of their lands and estates for generations. This is no different. Industrialists see the sense of it to keep their manufactories solvent.'

'But it would have to be a proper marriage!' Sarah protested. 'Mr Parrish expects us to have a child!'

Danby added. 'What happens if we marry and don't have offspring?'

'I should advise you to adopt, otherwise the house would revert to charity.'

Suddenly, Danby appeared less angry and more interested. 'The gentry do that right enough. They take on a distant relative as their own child and leave their estates to him. Could we do that?'

'There is nothing in the will to prevent it. He wanted you to own and run his glassworks and pass it on as he has done.'

Sarah noticed a smile play around Danby lips. He saw that as a possibility. Indeed, so did she; a marriage on paper meant they kept the glassworks and the house, she would have an independent income as Mr Parrish wished and, well it was easy, they simply adopted a baby; an orphan who would otherwise have a miserable existence in the workhouse. It *was* an option for them.

She wasn't sure how she would live in the same house as Danby without Mr Parrish's sobering influence on him. But her office was here and Danby spent much of his time in town at the glassworks or the institute, perhaps it could work.

Danby's eyes were gleaming. 'I should need a woman living in to look after the child as Sarah will have her glassworks responsibilities.'

'Aren't you getting ahead of yourself, Danby? I haven't said I will marry you yet.'

He shrugged. 'Think of it as another contract for the glassworks. You'll see the sense of it then.'

She hated to agree with him, but she did. 'It is the only way forward,' she said slowly.

* * *

325

Sarah was accustomed to sleepless nights. Mrs Couzens said it was a symptom of her bereavement. But her anxiety that night was of a different nature. If she went ahead and married Danby then she had to give up all hope of ever having a happy marriage. But what hope had she anyway? At least marriage to Danby meant the glassworks would be rescued and Mr Parrish's wishes fulfilled. The men's livelihoods would be secured and their families saved from the shame and degradation of the workhouse. Her happiness was of little consequence in comparison with that of so many families.

And why should Sarah Meadow have any expectation of future happiness? She had had more than her share of good fortune already in her short life, so it was right that she concern herself with the benefits of others.

But she despaired that marriage to Danby would bring an end to all her hopes and dreams, and her heart was heavy. Aidan was the only man she had ever, would ever, consider as a husband and just thinking about a future with him was a futile waste of time.

She did love Aidan. She was certain of that. She desired him; she dreamed of his body next to hers, caressing her, loving her and – and oh such joy if he were Danby and they were obliged to marry and have a child. She believed he would welcome her then as his bride. His determination to protect her reputation and position in town would not matter then. However, it was a foolish notion and in the darkness of the night she accepted this and wept.

Chapter 30

Sarah smoothed down her silk skirts and opened the front door. 'Come in, Aidan.'

'Good afternoon, Sarah.' His eyes roamed all over her. 'You look very well in black. Are you in good health?'

'Thank you, yes; are you?'

'Champion.' He glanced beyond her into the dark hall. 'No housemaid to let in your callers?'

'I am perfectly capable of doing it myself.'

He smiled. 'Indeed you are.'

But Sarah wasn't as self-assured as she sounded. She had been nervous since dinner, afraid that he might not visit and even more afraid that he would. Now that he was here she wanted to wrap her arms around him and lay her head on his chest.

'You look quite the gentleman with your tall hat and black cane. Shall I take them for you; and your topcoat?'

He shrugged out of his new outdoor coat with its fashionable shoulder cape and Sarah placed them on the stand in the hall. 'I have a good fire in the drawing room and Mary will bring tea in half an hour.' She stared at him. 'Oh, Aidan, I am so pleased to see you.'

'I came to collect my testimonial,' he reminded her.

'It is there waiting for you on the side table.'

He put his head on one side. 'So you did not need my help after all?'

'Are you not happy also for us to meet?'

'What exactly do you want from me. Sarah?'

'I – I should like your friendship.'

'In spite of our differences, you will always have that.'

'Then let us sit by the fire, toast pikelets and talk.' She led the way into the drawing room. 'Tell me about your new commission.'

'You will hardly believe this but it is for Meadow Hall. The new owners are rebuilding the boundary walls and wish for a grand pair of entrance gates. I believe you started a fashion when you persuaded Mr Parrish to order his.'

She shook her head. 'Not me. You did that by giving Mrs Thorpe's residence a new frontage. Now everyone wants wrought-iron railings and ornate gates with their initials entwined in the centre. You are so clever.'

'I have found premises to expand my forge, too. It needs reno-vation but the bank will advance me the cost.'

'Oh, do be careful, Aidan! Mr Parrish did something similar and – and it, well, he has left debts.'

'Has he? I didn't know,' he answered. 'Are the glassworks safe?'

'I – I hope so. I am not certain what will happen.'

'Will you have to move?'

'I may stay here for as long as I live.'

'That was generous of Mr Parrish. He must have thought very highly of you.'

She nodded. 'Danby, too.'

'Danby? Is he back now?'

'No. He spends hardly any of his time here these days. In fact, he moved out the day Mr Parrish died; he's staying in town with a friend. I was surprised because I know how much he likes this house. He said it would preserve my reputation.'

Sarah saw a frown crease Aidan's brow and he said, 'He told you that, did he?'

'It was kind of him, don't you think? He doesn't usually think of others so readily.'

'No.'

'You have given heavy inflection to such a small word. Can you not try to put your differences with Danby behind you?'

'Have you?'

'Come now, Aidan. We are adults; we must take a mature attitude to each other now. I have forgiven you for what you did to me, you must put the past behind you also.'

'It is not the past that concerns me. It is the present. How much do you know about his friend?'

'He is from the institute.'

'He?'

'Danby has a friend he meets with at the institute.'

'And stays with him at his home?'

'Well, I don't know whom he visits. Perhaps there are several?'

'Or just the one?'

'Really, Aidan, do not be so hard on him. Mr Parrish was an exacting taskmaster. I believe that is why Danby has been more cheerful since he passed on. I was upset about this at first but I am sure Danby has his reasons.'

'Oh, he has those, right enough.'

'Why do you say that?'

The drawing-room door opened and Danby was forgotten as Mary carried in a large tray. 'I've made the tea,' she said, 'and the kettle's bubbling on the range if you want a top up.'

'Did you bring the toasting fork?' Sarah asked. 'Oh yes, I see it. Off you go, then, to see your friends. Be back by nine.'

'Oh, I will, miss. George and Mrs Couzens are collecting me in the trap. It's ever so nice of you to let them lend it.'

'Borrow it, Mary,' she corrected with a smile.

'Yes, thank you, miss. We all get more time to talk when we

don't have to walk there and back.' Mary scurried out of the room.

Sarah poured tea into china cups. Then she took the plate of pikelets and slid forward to her knees on the rug. 'Do you like them toasted?'

'Do I!' Aidan responded. He took up the long brass fork from the tray. 'I'll toast and you butter.'

It was fun sitting on the rug before the fire, as though they were living in the woods again. Sarah still thought they had been the happiest of times for her, but this afternoon she was experiencing a similar contentment. Her nervousness had vanished and she felt at ease with Aidan. It was as though the difficult years between them had evaporated. They knelt in the heat of a glowing fire, ate and drank as friends again and she was happy.

He twisted to reach for the napkins on the tray. 'You have butter on your chin, madam,' he said with mock formality and added, 'Don't let it drip and stain your gown.'

'No, sir, that would never do for a lady, but I am more concerned about this expensive Eastern rug,' she responded, and they laughed. She wiped away the butter aware of a sudden stillness between them.

'I wish I were a gentleman living in a fine house like this,' he said quietly. 'I should be able to offer you a home.'

'But I—' She stopped. She was going to say she had no need of a home until she remembered it was their difference in status that troubled him and she did not wish to spoil their afternoon. She replied, 'You have always been a gentleman to me, Aidan.'

'But I do not have a home like this, so please don't mock me, even in humour.'

'I don't. I mean it. Your behaviour towards me has never been other than that of a gentleman.'

'And where has it got me? Perhaps if I had been more like—' He stopped.

She frowned. She hoped he was not going to compare himself

330

with Danby. She placed a finger across his lips to silence him. 'If you were any different, you would not be my Aidan.'

'Your Aidan?'

She looked down, embarrassed. 'I'm sorry. I meant that you do not need a fine house to be my friend.'

'I want to be more than your friend, Sarah.'

In the silence that followed she could hear the clock ticking in the hall. The pulse in her temple began to throb. 'You are. You must know that. You have always had a special place in my heart.'

'Had?'

'Please don't fence words with me, Aidan. Do you not know I have loved you since our summer in the woods? That love has been tested to destruction but it has survived.'

He moved towards her. 'Since we met again I have watched you command respect in this town and felt proud of your achievement. But I have an ache in my heart when I see you enjoying you illustrious life with increasing confidence.'

'Aidan, I would have moved into the carriage house with you if you had given me an inkling of hope that you cared for me in that way. You pushed me away. You shunned me. I was hurt.'

'I had no wish to hurt you and for that I am sorry. But I know the hardship you have suffered and I cannot, indeed will not, allow you to endure that again.'

'It is not a hardship for me to be loved by you!'

'Poverty is a hardship that can destroy the strongest of affections.'

'You are wrong! You are the man I love and will continue to love, whatever happens in the future.'

'I – I should like your future to be with me.'

I want my future to be with you, too, she thought. She leaned forward to wipe a speck of butter from his lips. He took the napkin from her and held her hand, lifting it to his lips. He kissed the back of her hand with such tenderness that her heart melted as swiftly as the butter before a fire. She raised her head. Her hazel-brown eyes were serious. How could he not know that her body yearned for his? She opened her mouth to his and he needed no further invitation.

Yet, he seemed afraid to hold her; it was as though she would break in two if he did. His arms encircled her gently and he kissed her lightly, and it was the most wonderful feeling in the world. His lips brushed hers, and she closed her eyes to the joy of his nearness. Her hands crept around his waist to roam his broad, straight back. She wanted to remove his jacket, to undo the buttons and push it from his shoulders so that she could feel the strength of his body; a body that she wanted to be closer to hers. But still she feared he would resist and she hesitated.

He was aware of her uncertainty for she felt his lips cease moving against hers as he whispered, 'I should stop this now.'

'Please don't.'

Already she was trembling with anticipation and his arms tightened around her. His mouth explored hers with an increasing passion that swelled her heart. She responded with a release of desire that excited and frightened her at the same time. She had believed for so long that this moment would never happen that she hardly knew what to do. But she was in no doubt that he did, as his kiss strengthened and deepened with a hungry need that matched her own.

They fell sideways on the rug, but their mouths did not part. His hands were touching the silk of her gown; her waist, her hips, her bosom, and then her throat and neck. He stroked her neatly dressed hair and she felt the pins loosen and fall. Her instinct was to shake her head and let her curls fall free about her shoulders. When his lips moved to nibble at her ear and then kiss her throat she could bear it no longer and her fingers fumbled with the fastenings on his coat.

His strong hands stilled hers and he murmured, 'I love you dearly, Sarah. But we should cease this madness before we regret it.'

'I should never regret it. I want you and I have already waited too long.'

He stifled a groan in his throat. 'Do not encourage me so. I shall not be able to stop.'

'I don't want you to. I want you to be mine, all of you, joined to me so we are as one. Tell me you want the same.'

'You know I do.'

'Then let us not waste this chance we have. Love me, Aidan, and let me love you in return.'

'You are testing my resolve to breaking point, but I cannot let you do this.' He pushed himself away from her and sat up. 'You are used to the services of a housekeeper and maid. You cannot want a future living above a carriage house with me.'

She rolled onto her knees. The heat from the fire radiated onto her face but a cold draught penetrated her heart. 'Yes, I can. I want to be with you,' she breathed.

'And I you.'

'Then why should we not be together now?'

'You are so headstrong, Sarah. I must marry you first.'

She was stunned into silence. She listened to the hissing fire and watched the flames licking around the logs. Was he saying that he wanted to marry her after all; that their differences no longer counted?

He continued, 'Will you marry me?'

The joy of becoming Aidan's wife was too overwhelming for her to contemplate and she pushed the notion away, aware of a withering sensation in her heart. 'I can't,' she replied.

'Can't?' He inhaled sharply. 'But your circumstances have changed. Townfolk will understand that, now you are left without a patron, you need a husband.'

'It's not that, I am expected to marry soon.'

'Then why do you hesitate?'

She couldn't say it. She couldn't tell him and ruin this beautiful love between them. She formed the words in her head but they stuck in her throat and she was aware of a rising tension in his eyes as she remained silent.

'I'm not wealthy enough for you, am I? You are expected to

333

take someone established in the town, who can offer you a home as grand as this?' He stood up and pulled her to her feet.

'It's not the house. Well, yes it is. . .' she began. Yet still she could not say it.

'Stop speaking to me in riddles, Sarah. You have just offered me your virtue, at least I presume you are a maid, so have the courtesy to be honest with me.'

Her eyes were filling with tears. She swallowed hard. 'Please don't be angry with me,' she said in a small voice. 'I have no choice.'

He indicated to her to sit and followed suit, demanding, 'No choice in what?'

'No choice in who I marry!' she shouted. The echo of her voice rang in the silent room. Her lips trembled and tears spilled out of her eyes onto her flushed cheeks.

The silence lengthened as Aidan absorbed her outburst. 'You are already betrothed,' he said at last. 'Did Mr Parrish promise you to someone before he died? Please tell me that it is not true.'

'It is. I have to marry him.'

His shoulders sagged. 'You offered yourself to me knowing this.' He stifled a strangled cry. 'You said you loved me. Sarah, how could you do this to me?' He inhaled raggedly and turned away from her.

'It's not what I want,' she sobbed. 'I want you; only you.'

'But you have agreed to the marriage?'

Her tears were choking her and she could not say the word. He twisted and demanded, 'Well, have you?'

She swallowed and nodded.

Aidan stood up and walked to the door. 'Will he come after me and kill me for my behaviour this afternoon? I should if I were him.'

Her hands clutched at her throat. 'Dear Lord, no. I shall not tell him.'

'Dishonesty is no way to start your married life, but I suppose I should be grateful. Who is he?'

'I am to marry Danby.'

She heard his sharp intake of breath. 'No! It is surely a lie! You cannot marry him!'

'I have to. I am bound by my duty to secure the future of the glassworks.'

'Your duty?' This seemed to calm him and his anger quelled to a more sympathetic concern. 'Does it have to be him? You know the type of man he is.'

'Oh, I know his faults well enough.'

'You do? And you are still prepared to be his wife? What has happened to you, Sarah?'

'I grew up. Please, Aidan, don't resurrect rivalries from the past. I am not the child you lived with in the woods.'

'Sarah, listen to me. He will never be a gentleman; he will never be your equal.'

'He is accepted in polite society and . . .' She could not go on.

'But he will only bring you heartache. Oh, Sarah, do not do this foolish deed. He can never make you happy.'

'Happy? What is happy? I shall be comfortable and gainfully occupied by the glassworks. I shall be content.'

'You will be content? You cannot settle for a lifetime of contentment! You must not marry him.'

'I have promised.'

He looked so hurt she regretted telling him.

'Then I see that you must,' he said.

She hid her shaking hands in the folds of black silk and whispered, 'I am sorry. I ought to have told you before. Perhaps you should leave now.'

If only she had known earlier that Aidan loved her, if only he had not been so proud . . . But it was too late now. She had made her decision and said she would marry Danby. Mr Withers, the labourers in the glassworks, the house servants, not to mention Danby and his ambitions, everyone depended on her to keep her word.

Chapter 31

'When, Danby, when?' Rose pressed.

'Soon, my love, I promise you.'

'But it's over a month since the old man died and you said we would be wed by now!'

'These things take time.'

'What things?'

'Affairs of business. Everything is tied up in the glassworks. It's something called probate. I have to do what it says or I don't get my share.'

'Well, what about my share? Your boy needs his father every day; not just when the fancy takes you.'

'It's not like that, Rose. I come here as often as I can, but I can't have any gossip about me. You know what folk are like.'

'No, I don't. Not any more. I've been living out here alone since my dad passed on.'

'Don't you like it here?'

'Yes, but I want to be with you. You said you'd wed me as soon as the old man died.'

'Yes, but his will has changed everything. I told you it would.'

'Not between us, though! You do still love me, don't you?'

'Of course I do. And we will be together soon. You and little Albert will be able to come and live with me in the big house in town.'

'You mean we are getting wed? Oh when, Danby, tell me when.'

'Calm down, my love. Sit down and listen to me. You have to be patient, because we can't get wed just yet.'

'Why can't we, if I'm coming to live with you?'

'Because – because – oh hell.' He had to tell her and there was no way to soften the blow. 'I've got to marry someone else.'

She sat so still that he thought she had not heard him. Then she whispered, 'You're lying to me. You have to be.'

'I wish I was. But you have to understand that I'm doing it for you and Albert. I don't want to but it's the only way to keep my position at the glassworks. I'll be the owner of half of it. Think of that, Rose.'

She hadn't moved in inch, not even blinked or swallowed. 'When?' she demanded.

'When what?'

'*When will you marry her, you oaf?*'

'Soon.'

She screamed; a loud piercing squeal at the top of her voice, followed by a stream of invective that would have made a workhouse dosser blush. He tried to take her in his arms to comfort her but she pushed him away, picked up a heavy pottery mug and threw it at his head. It glanced off the side of his cheek and he winced. I suppose I deserve that, he thought.

'How long have I waited for the old man to die? *You promised me!*'

'But I don't love her, Rose,' he protested. 'I don't even like her. It's you I love, you know that, and I am doing this for you and Albert.'

'Get out of my sight, Danby. I never want to see you again.'

'You don't mean that.'

'Just go, will you.'

He went through to the back kitchen, took out his hip flask and drank. Then he returned to the front room. She was sitting by the fire with a scowl furrowing her brow.

'After I'm wed, I'll get out of it somehow, Rose,' he said from the doorway.

'How are you going to do that? Murder your wife?'

'Don't be stupid, love. She doesn't want to be married any more than me. Once we've met the terms of the will we'll go our separate ways and I can be with you.'

'But I won't be married to you!' she cried. 'What about little Albert?'

'Little Albert is the reason why you have to come and live with me in town. The glassworks is in trouble and I can't give you any more money to live here. I won't desert you, Rose. I love my son. I'm going to adopt him as my heir.'

'What about her?'

'She won't care. It's just that we have to have a child if we are to stay in the house and I already have one.'

'So she'll be his mother?'

'Only on a piece of paper. You are his mother and you'll look after him just as you do now.'

'And the three of us will be living in the same house?'

'It's a big house and I've got servants.'

'You're insane! I'm not doing that, not for you nor anybody. She's not having him. Albert's mine and he's staying mine until you marry me.'

'But the house won't be his if I don't adopt him.'

'Well, you'll have to think of another way around the will, won't you?'

Damn it, Danby thought. She wasn't going along with his plan. What on earth could he do? But Danby Jones had been in tight corners before and had always found a road out, even if this was a stickier fix than any before. He wasn't bothered about the glassworks; only the money and a future for the three of them. He'd have to think hard this time.

'I shall, my sweet,' he replied firmly. 'I shall.'

Sarah stood at Mrs Thorpe's front door and admired the decorative railings. The ironwork twisted and turned in a repeated pattern and she followed the intricate detail, trailing her fingers through it, admiring the combination of strength and beauty. Aidan had made these, she thought miserably.

Emma opened the door. 'Welcome, Miss Meadow. You really didn't have to come here. We would have brought the gown to your home.'

Sarah shrugged and stepped inside.

'Forgive me, miss, but you are quite pale this morning.'

Sarah gave her a weak smile.

Emma looked closely at Sarah's face. 'Are you ill, Miss Meadow? You do not look yourself.'

Sarah handed over her cloak and gloves silently and waited to be led upstairs to Mariah Thorpe's fitting room. Her lilac silk wedding gown was waiting on the mannequin. Sarah glanced at it, sighed and sat on the velvet-covered couch. She wished she hadn't come. She didn't want to wear it. She didn't want to be married next week.

Mariah Thorpe came into the room. 'Good morning, Miss Meadow. How kind of you to call. I do so like to make sure my wedding gowns are perfect before I fit them on the day.'

Sarah managed a small smile and brief nod. It was a beautiful gown and Mrs Thorpe had worked hard on it. She stood up and noticed Mrs Thorpe glance over her and frown.

'You are thinner, madam,' she said. 'I need to measure you again.' She went out of the room for her notebook.

Sarah covered her eyes with her hand. She wasn't surprised she was thinner. Mrs Couzens had become quite cross with her for not eating. But she had no appetite. Nor had she any energy these days. Alone, she wandered over to the window. It overlooked the garden. Through the fruit trees she could see the carriage house and her features twisted in misery. It was a mistake to call here and she ought to leave immediately. She went over to the door. Mrs Thorpe had left it slightly ajar and she stopped short as she heard voices outside.

'She looks as though she hasn't slept for a month!'

'I know. When I let her in I thought she was ill.'

'Perhaps she didn't take breakfast? Go and prepare something, Emma, and I'll bring her down to the morning room.'

'What about the fitting?'

'We'll have to make any final adjustments on the morning of her wedding. I'll just take her measurements for now.'

Sarah stepped back as the door opened wider. 'I – I've just remembered another appointment,' she began.

'Will you stay for a drink of tea?'

Sarah shook her head. The closeness to Aidan only increased her distress and there was no going back from her marriage to Danby now.

Mrs Thorpe took her downstairs. 'You look quite tired out, Miss Meadow. Shall I send for your carriage?' she asked.

'I can walk.'

'Would you consider calling the apothecary? Marriage is a big occasion for any woman and he can give you something to help you through it.'

'I am quite well, Mrs Thorpe. Good day to you.' Sarah turned away, thankful to be leaving.

As soon as she reached home, Sarah retreated to her chamber and wept.

'Aren't you just a little bit excited, miss? I can't wait to see your gown in the morning.'

'It is not so long since Mr Parrish passed on, Mary.'

'But it's what he wanted, isn't it? You and Mr Jones wed?'

Sarah turned away with a grimace and caught a glimpse of herself in her looking glass. Hollow-eyed and pale, she would be glad when the ceremony was over and done with. 'Is your own gown ready for tomorrow?' she asked.

Mary jumped. 'Oh! Mrs Couzens said she'd go with me to the draper for lace when she had finished in the kitchen.'

'You are leaving it very late. It is growing dark already.'

'What about your hair, Miss Meadow?'

'Off you go. Ask George to take you down in the trap.'

'Thank you, miss.'

Sarah unpinned her hair and sat alone in her chamber watching the darkening sky through her window. She heard the trap rattle down the drive and stood up to watch. At least the servants seemed happy for her. She took off her day gown and corset and prepared for bed, reflecting that tomorrow night she would be Mrs Jones. Her only consolation was that Mr Parrish's loyal workers and their families would be safe from the workhouse.

She liked to watch the evening traffic on the Mansfield road. It was a busy evening and there were many carriages rushing by; lots of people too, she noticed, hurried up the hill in the gathering gloom. One figure in particular was familiar and her heart seemed to leap into her throat. It must be Aidan! No one else possessed his height and stride. She moved behind the drapes and heard the front gate open and close.

What did he want? Her heart began to thump as the door knocker rose and fell. Hastily she pulled a dressing robe over her chemise and drawers and ran in stockinged feet down the wide wooden stairs. Mrs Couzens had lit lamps in the hall before she left. She drew back the bolt, opened the door a fraction and peered around the edge.

'What are you doing here?' Sarah asked anxiously.

'I – I heard you were ill.'

'No. I'm well,' she replied. But she was shivering.

'Emma said you were not. Are you cold?'

She pulled her robe closer. She wasn't cold, she was – she was fearful that someone might see him. 'You shouldn't be here, Aidan.'

'I know.' His voice was a groan. 'Forgive me, Sarah, I had to see you. I am going mad with worry about you.'

'I am alone in the house. I can't let you in.'

'Please; for a few minutes only. I beg of you. I've tried to stay away and I cannot.'

'Aidan, I am to be married tomorrow.'

'And I am leaving tonight. We shall not see each other again.'

'No!'

He pushed at the door and stepped inside. 'Emma is right. You're thinner; paler too. Oh, my dearest, sweetest Sarah, what are you doing to yourself?' He kicked the door shut behind her and took her in his arms, holding her close and caressing her long, loosened hair. Through her thin cotton garments she could feel the roughness and chill of his outdoor clothes and smell the soap on the skin of his face as he lowered his mouth to kiss her.

The deep satisfaction of his lips on hers evaporated any last vestige of her resistance. To be held and cherished one last time by the man she loved awakened such a strong need in her that she almost fainted with desire. Her body yielded its softness to his urgent embrace as his lips travelled from her mouth to her eyes to her throat and neck. Her insides were melting for him.

'I know we can never be together,' he murmured. 'But it does not stop me loving you.'

'Nor I you. I want you so much, it hurts.'

He tightened his grip on her, almost squeezing the breath out of her body.

'Let me go,' she breathed. 'We shall not have this chance again. Come with me now.'

He released her. She turned and fled up the stairs, pausing only at the top to see him shed his topcoat and follow her, taking the steps two at a time. He had discarded his jacket on the floor of her bedchamber when he kissed her again. Her whole body tingled with a yearning she had not known before. The fire was low and the air was chilly but it was of no consequence for a passion burned within her that threatened to consume them both and she dared not watch him undress. He kissed the nape of her neck as he approached her to remove her robe. She leaned backwards and his arms crept around her waist. It was then that she felt his love for her, his insistent hardness, and she thrilled at the anticipation.

She had thought to keep on her chemise and drawers but Aidan slipped them from her before she could protest. Not that she would have; she was honest enough with herself to know she wanted this as much as he did. His eyes gleamed in the twilight. 'You are sure about this?' he asked quietly.

'Never more sure,' she replied, and drew back the bed covers. She smiled over her shoulder. 'It will be cold in here, but not for long.'

He slid past her and between the sheets, drawing her body on top of his and rubbing the skin of her back and bottom to warm them. He kissed her again and she began the most wonderful journey of her life.

The moon rose as they loved, casting a silvery light through the window. When they were exhausted and spent he climbed, naked, out of bed to throw logs on the embers in the hearth.

'I love you, Sarah,' he said. 'Come away with me. Marry me instead.'

If only he knew how much she wanted that, and the temptation threatened to overwhelm her. Eventually she said, 'You know I cannot.'

He sighed heavily. 'I do understand. But I fear for your happiness.'

Her heart twisted in her breast as she realised their shared passion could never be repeated. 'Love is a luxury, Aidan. I am not accustomed to luxury so I shall not suffer. We have stolen this interlude together and now we must forget each other. It is as well that you are moving away.' It was a cruel thing to say but she knew she could not survive her marriage to Danby if Aidan stayed close by.

'It is a necessity. I cannot see you wed to another and live in the same town.'

She heard voices through the window and George opening the gates. 'Dear Lord, the servants are back!'

343

She pulled on her nightgown as he hastily gathered his clothes. 'You have time enough. They will go down to the carriage house first and walk back to the kitchen. Go out of the front.'

He dressed quickly and she watched him with increasing sadness. He crossed to the bed and gave her one last kiss. 'Goodbye, my love.'

'Wh – where will you go?' she asked with tears in her eyes.

'Birmingham.'

'So far away,' she whispered. 'Good luck.' He would not need it, she thought. He would be successful wherever he went.

He closed the door quietly behind him. She listened to his boots clattering down the stairs and the front door open and close. She strained her ears for the clang of the wrought-iron gate; his gate. He may be gone from her life for ever, but she would never forget him. There were mementos of him all around. She lay on her back and ran her hands backwards and forwards over the linen sheet covering her soft feather mattress. She would always have *this* memory of him. No one could take that away from her. She curled into a ball on her side, letting her tears flow, reliving those precious hours until she drifted into sleep.

Chapter 32

During the weeks before her marriage, the servants had put Sarah's unhappy countenance down to grief compounded by worry about the precarious state of the glassworks' finances. But the morning after Aidan's visit Mary noticed Sarah's glowing cheeks and shining eyes.

'Oh, miss, you look better this morning. I've brought you hot water to wash and tea as you asked. Mrs Thorpe is here already with your wedding gown.'

'Tell her to come up in thirty minutes.' Sarah felt refreshed. She had slept well and a glance in the looking glass told her that Mary was right. She wondered how long her sense of well being would last – it was already ebbing away as the despair of what she was about to do overtook her. Mary came back to lace her corset and dress her hair. Mariah Thorpe joined them to help drape Sarah's slender frame in petticoats and silk. It was a modestly cut gown with a high neckline, long sleeves and few adornments, but it fitted beautifully.

'I had to guess the measurement of your thinner waist,' Mariah commented as she finished an adjustment to the shoulders. 'Sit down while I button on your boots.'

They were the softest, lightest kid. Sarah remembered a time long ago when she had had to button on Mrs Watson's boots at Meadow Hall. 'I'll do them,' she said.

'No, you won't, miss,' Mary responded. 'You have to sit still while I pin your headdress.'

A circle of violets nestled where once Sarah had worn her plaits, and a short lilac veil covered her hair. When her dressers were satisfied they allowed her to stand in front of the cheval glass. She hardly recognised herself and acknowledged that Mariah had made her look very handsome. If only . . . if only she were marrying . . . She pulled herself together and tried to smile. 'Thank you, Mrs Thorpe. Will you change your mind and come to the chapel?'

'It is a ruling of mine, ma'am. I never attend the ceremonies of brides I have dressed. It is your gown now. Wear it with pride.'

Sarah felt wretched. She wished she could.

Mrs Couzens tapped on the door and called, 'The carriage is ready, miss, and Mr Withers is here.'

Slowly, she went downstairs to the hall where Mr Withers offered her his arm. When they were settled in the carriage he said, 'Do not be so nervous, my dear. You will be a wealthy woman and my good lady will give you all the guidance you need for your married life. Do try to smile. You are very pretty when you smile.'

The chapel was quiet, less than a dozen people including her own household and some of Danby's business associates attended the blessing. Danby was waiting restlessly at the front with a friend. She had seen little of him during the weeks before her marriage. Faced with his presence as she walked towards the chaplain she hesitated. This was a mistake! She couldn't do this.

But she couldn't let everyone down. Mr Withers gave her arm a gentle tug and she forced herself to put one foot in front of the other. She stood stony-faced by Danby's side. When he turned to her she could smell the spirits he had drunk, and he stumbled over his vows. But the simple chapel ceremony was soon over and they were riding silently together in the carriage to their marital home.

Mrs Couzens had prepared a wedding breakfast in the dining room and Sarah went through to the kitchen to thank her. As she returned to the hall, she heard a local brewery owner utter her name and recognised Danby's voice in response. She lingered at the other side of the open door and listened.

'This is a good day for you, young fellow. The storage jar patent alone will make you a rich man eventually.'

'Mr Parrish left it to Sarah in his will.'

'It is of no matter. You are in charge now and once she has a trio of little ones around her skirts she'll lose interest in the glass-works. She will be happy to sign anything you put in front of her.'

'I'm not so sure. She has a strong will.'

'My advice is to keep her busy in the bedroom and nursery.'

'But we only have to have one child to secure the inheritance.'

'You need several heirs, just to be sure.'

'Well, we have talked of adoption.'

'Adoption? She's pretty enough for you, isn't she?'

'I suppose so.'

'You are, forgive me, healthy in that respect?'

'Of course. I just wish she — she was someone else.'

The brewery owner laughed. 'I see. We all think that of our wives at some time. Once she has a growing family she won't want you near her. Then you can look elsewhere. But make sure she has five or six infants first.'

She heard Danby return the laugh and said, 'I'll do what I can.'

Sarah's jaw dropped. She hoped he had not changed his mind about the nature of their marriage. However, later when she had retired and was in her nightclothes she heard Danby's heavy

347

footfall on the landing outside her chamber. Dear Lord, she hoped he would not come in!

He tapped lightly on her door and she feigned sleep. A more insistent rapping followed. 'Who is it?' she called softly.

'Danby. I'm coming in.' He opened the door before she could respond, walked over to the bed and placed a lamp on her bedside cabinet. More surprisingly, he was in his riding clothes.

'I'd rather you waited to be invited.'

'I'm your husband, aren't I?'

Her hand went to her throat in a gesture of defence. She hoped he was not going to insist on consummating their marriage. They had agreed not to, hadn't they? But Danby was not a man to trust to keep his word. She swallowed. 'What do you want?'

'Well, not my conjugal rights, that's for sure.'

Relief flooded through her. 'Then can it not wait until morning?'

'No, it can't. We have to talk.'

She shuffled up the bed. The fire had gone out long ago and the air was chilly despite her long-sleeved nightgown. 'Pass me my shawl.'

He reached over to the chair for it and threw it at her. 'I don't like this marriage any more than you do. But we've got the glass-works and you have to make sure we hang on to it.'

'Well, you have to make sure you don't lose any more skilled men to our rivals.'

'I'll open up the other cone to make more of the storage jars.'

'It will still be risky. The London end is draining our resources.'

'Then you have to do something about it!'

'I am fully aware of that, Danby! Is that all you want to say?'

'No. We need a child to secure the house as soon as possible.'

She clutched her shawl more tightly around her and said, 'We have agreed to adopt, haven't we?'

'Yes.'

She began to relax. 'We'll take a child from the workhouse and—'

'I've already found one.'

'You have?'

'A – a friend of mine has died and – and left a widow with no money and a child – a boy – to bring up. She could come and live here and look after the child for you.'

'I was looking forward to caring for the child myself.'

'You have the glassworks to keep you busy. You'll need a nurse-maid. Who better than the child's own mother?'

'Will she agree, do you think?'

'Leave that to me.'

Sarah nodded. It seemed a perfect solution. 'There is one other thing. People will talk. They may guess the truth about not consummating our marriage. It isn't legal if we don't.'

'Just say you're barren. We'll have to wait to establish that, before we officially adopt. But if the child and his mother are already part of our household, it'll seem quite natural.'

'Do you mean you want us to take in this child and his mother immediately?'

'Yes. Have you any objection?'

Sarah paused. This was all very sudden but she couldn't deny a home for the woman and her child. 'Not if the mother is willing.'

'That's settled then.' Danby picked up the lamp and left her chamber without even saying goodnight.

She heard him ride out a few minutes later and wondered where he was going. She didn't think he would tell her if she asked. Marriage had made no difference to their relationship and for that she was thankful, but the Danby she had known in Meadow Hall woods would have used her for his own satis-faction, regardless of any agreement they had. She knew he had never felt any genuine affection for her; not then, not now. Perhaps he had feelings for someone else, someone he visited regularly when he said he was at the institute. It would explain how he had spent Mr Parrish's money in the first place. She missed her benefactor, and Danby would always be a thorn in her side. If only she had Aidan to turn to. But she had closed that door for ever. Alone in the house, Sarah felt the cold draught of a long and lonely life ahead.

Chapter 33

Married life for Sarah was hardly any different from being a spinster. She continued to deal with administration for the glassworks, and visited Mr Withers once a week to report on progress. It was a struggle to reopen the second cone as it meant borrowing more from the bankers, but she had the security of her patent and a growing reputation for business dealings. Danby seemed to avoid her, a state of affairs that she welcomed for she had a more pressing concern to deal with.

They had been married less than three months when Danby appeared in the breakfast room. She had not slept well and would have preferred to eat alone as she normally did. 'You are early this morning,' she commented.

He helped himself to hot food from the sideboard. 'I want to talk to you.'

'Is there is a problem at the glassworks?'

'No. The second cone is in production.' He sat down with his plate and the sight of devilled kidneys and bacon made her feel quite queasy. 'Pour me some tea,' he ordered.

Sarah had not been well in the mornings for a few weeks but had kept it to herself for she was aware of the most likely reason

351

for her morning sickness. Feeling out of sorts, she objected to Danby's tone and answered, 'The pot is nearer to you.'

He shook his head impatiently. 'You see, that's the trouble here. It's not the glassworks. It's you.'

'I beg your pardon?'

'You're supposed to be my wife and you don't even pour my tea.'

'You are perfectly capable of doing it for yourself and I am not your servant.'

'You wouldn't stay for long if you were.'

Sarah heaved a sigh. 'What is it you wish to say to me?'

He waved his fork around. 'I want to talk about this marriage; this arrangement with the house. It's not working out the way I planned.'

Not for me either, she thought, and wondered if today was when she should tell him her news. 'You haven't given it much time yet.'

'I've already given it too much and I want to be free of you. And sometimes I want to be free of this town and its petty restrictions too.'

For a moment Sarah magined her life without Danby and welcomed the idea as well.

'The woman with the child is unhappy about adoption,' Danby said.

Sarah was relieved by this, and not surprised. She remembered the anguish of the mothers in the workhouse whose children were given up to the guardians and she had no desire to cause unnecessary suffering. 'I can understand her concerns and we should respect her wishes. We shall easily – that is, we can find another child.'

'No, we can't. I want that boy.'

'Why? What is so special about him?'

'I – I promised his – his father I would look after him.'

She approved of Danby's loyalty to his late friend but sympa-thised more with the mother's dilemma. 'We cannot force a mother to give up her son.'

352

'She won't have to if you leave. My friend has a small house that you can use. It's not far and you can have the trap for travelling to the glassworks.'

Sarah was astounded. 'You are quite stupid sometimes, Danby. How would that look to folk in town?'

'She has no desire to lose her son to you. If you do not live here, her anxiety will be less.'

'And you want me to move out so that this woman and her child can move in as – as servants? Really, Danby, you have the most outrageous ideas.'

'I don't care what you think. The child is more important to me than you and I want him here. So you must leave.'

'And break the terms of the will?'

'I'll find a way round it—'

'Stop this at once, Danby. I am not going anywhere.'

He glared at her across the breakfast table. 'You will do as I say. I am master in this house.'

She stared at him in disbelief. 'Our marriage is a business agreement. We are partners.'

'We have equal shares in the glassworks, I grant you, but that is only because the old man put your half in a trust for you. Otherwise it would all be mine by rights as I'm your husband.'

'Yes. I think Mr Parrish knew very well what he was doing. He was forward in his ideas. We have a woman reigning over the country now, Danby.'

'But not over this house. Do you understand? I say what goes on in this household and I want you out.'

Sarah thought of the child growing within her, Aidan's child, and it gave her a more steely resolve to stay. 'Don't be ridiculous. This is my home. Besides, we are supposed to be a devoted husband and wife.'

'And nothing could be further from the truth! I can't stick it any longer. We'll live apart. The gentry do it all the time.'

'We are not gentry and I am as much entitled to be here as you are. If you don't like it, you go and live in this other house!'

'You are my wife and you will obey me.'

'Or else what?' she scorned. 'I will not be pushed out of my position here so that you can run things exactly as you wish. Under the terms of Mr Parrish's will, I have the same rights as you.'

'Neither of us have any rights to this house if we don't have an heir. I have one and I will have him here with his mother.'

'You have an heir?' The implication of what he had said made her catch her breath and a cold hand clutched at her heart. Surely the woman's child could not be his? Surely he had not lain with his sick friend's wife? 'An heir?' she repeated. 'Are you telling me the woman's child is yours?'

'You may as well know. My son's mother is not a widow. But for old Parrish's will and you, she would be my wife.'

He had a mistress with a child. Why had this not occurred to her before? She recalled Aidan's warning about Danby. Men talked while they laboured and in the taverns afterwards. He probably knew about Danby's mistress and child. As she absorbed the implication of Danby's words she realised with a sickening heart that Aidan had thought she had known about Danby's mistress when he had tried to persuade her not to marry him.

Her heart began to race. She ran her hands quickly over her stomach and she thought of her own infant's future.

'Your son cannot be your heir unless you adopt him,' she pointed out.

'Good God, woman! That is what I am trying to achieve.'

'But there is no need! Yes, you are master in this house and may stride around giving orders. But you also have responsibilities to your wife and they are so much greater when she becomes a mother.'

'Stop preaching to me. I had enough of that from the old man.'

'We shall have an infant of our own.'

'No, we shall not! I've told you. I'm not doing that with you.'

'You don't have to, Danby. The deed is already done.' She paused and looked directly into his eyes. 'I am with child!'

Poleaxed. She had heard the term and now saw what it meant. The colour drained from Danby's face and he sagged forward against the table.

'You can't be! We haven't—'

She pushed back her chair and smoothed her skirts over the slight swell of her stomach. The bulge was little more than usual but his jaw dropped open as he stared.

'It's not mine,' he whispered. '*You whore.*'

She ignored his insult and said brightly, 'My child will be born in wedlock. We have no need of adoption now, do we?' Her smile faltered as she saw his face darken and she realised the extent of his anger.

'You scheming, manipulative witch!' he shouted. 'Did you know about Rose all the time? Is this your idea of a sick revenge? You deliberately became with child to spite me?'

'No, but considering how much you have lied and deceived Mr Parrish and me, I think there is a kind of justice here.'

'Whose is it?'

She stayed silent.

'Well? I am your husband; I have a right to know.'

'And I am your wife and I had a right to know you have a mistress with a child!'

'I won't have your offspring take precedence over my son. I'll make it known it is not mine; I'll disown the bastard.'

'And I shall inform the lawyers that you were not willing to consummate our marriage. I shall get it annulled and you'll lose everything.'

'So will you.'

For the first time Sarah realised that she had something much more important to care about than her status and wealth. She was proud to be with child and even prouder that it was Aidan's, although she realised that her child's father must remain her secret for ever. She could weather a slur on her own reputation; the

355

workhouse had prepared her well for that. But she was not prepared for her child to suffer so, for them both to end up in the workhouse. Her child would be respectable and would be regarded as the rightful heir that her benefactor had wished for. She would not lose everything now.

She did not regret her brief interlude of passion with Aidan. If truth be told she had been thrilled when she had first realised she was to bear his child; his secret child. For a moment she felt a pang of conscience that her child would never know his father, but she had long since suppressed her desire to write to Aidan – she was not prepared to risk tarnishing his name. He may be far away, but Beckwith's Forge still thrived in town under his foreman.

The child was her secret and hers alone to guard. She was prepared to go to any lengths to keep it so. She had so much to give this child and she was determined to cherish it with the love she'd never had. She had forfeited Aidan's love by marrying Danby and she regretted that with all heart. But she carried a part of him with her. It was a kind of compensation and it was enough.

'Our marriage is a mistake anyway,' she responded. 'Neither of us wanted it.'

'I want this house.'

'Well, it will belong to my child, conceived within matrimony, as Mr Parrish intended. Or, our marriage will be annulled and everything we have both worked for will be taken from us.' And if that happens I shall still have my child, she thought; Aidan's child. I shall be happy.

They sat in silence until she asked, 'What is your son's name?'

'Albert.'

Sarah racked her brain. Surely there was some way of escaping the mess they were in; a way out for both of them? 'I can support my child without the help of a husband and it would not be considered totally unacceptable for me to live alone,' she said. 'But you would have a difficult time of it in the Riding if you lived openly with your mistress and child. Rose and Albert would be pilloried by our small society. Is that what you want for them?'

'I want them with me, sharing my wealth.'

'Does it have to be here in the Riding?'

Danby looked at her. 'If only I had means I would leave this country and its hidebound ways and seek my fortune elsewhere. I've been thinking about it for a long time.'

'You are prepared to move overseas?'

'I am for Rose and Albert. But I'll not go empty-handed. I want my share.'

'We can't do that. The will—'

'The will! The lawyers! Damn them all! It's our fortune now and we can do what we like with it!'

'You can only sell your half to me and I have no capital to buy it.' She inhaled suddenly. 'But I do have the patent. The revenue is keeping our London warehouse going.'

'I'll have that,' Danby snapped. 'I'll go if you sign it over to me.'

'The glassworks will be bankrupt!'

'Then close them down, for God's sake. You'll have some capital from selling off the land.'

'What about the men who work there?'

'Do it, Sarah,' Danby urged. 'It's the only way out for us. I'll leave you and the Riding. Dear God, I'll leave this country if I can take the patent with me.'

She did not want to risk the glassworks but she could think of no other way out. She and Danby would at least be rid of each other, and she may be able to take on a partner to make sure Mr Parrish's business continued. She'd be able to keep one of the cones going surely . . . ? 'It will take months to set up. You know how long these things take.'

Danby appeared satisfied with her response. 'I need a year at least, anyway. We'll do everything through the London lawyer. It'll make sense to him. Prince Albert's Great Exhibition is next summer and there will be so much going on in London, our paltry business will be of little interest. We'll take chambers at the hotel old Parrish used. I'll disappear during our visit.'

'Disappear? Where will you go?'

'It doesn't matter. What you don't know you can't divulge. You can declare me dead after seven years.'

'Seven years.' she breathed. Then she would be truly free of him!

'I want the patent and all the bank reserves,' he demanded. 'That's my price. Take it or leave it.'

She nodded slowly. There was no other answer.

Chapter 34

1851

In London, Sarah was overwhelmed by the hoards of people. It was busier than market day at home, and carriages clattered about dangerously, turning everywhere and blocking the roadways. People shouted at each other instead of talking.

Mary was wide-eyed. 'I've never seen so many grand ladies and gentlemen out and about.'

'Me neither. The back streets are the same as at home though; dirty and smelly, and with a lot more poor people than we have.'

'It's too noisy, as well, and the carriages go so fast. I really shouldn't like to live here all the time.'

The smell of horse droppings made Sarah's eyes water and she turned her infant daughter's face into her skirts. She was nearly a year old, toddling and talking well enough to be a demanding child. She handed her to Mary and said, 'Take Belinda inside quickly. I'll make sure our luggage comes off.'

The hotel had provided a carriage to collect them from the station. Danby had travelled down several days earlier and Sarah expected him to be waiting for them in the foyer.

'Is Mr Jones in his suite?' Sarah asked at the reception desk.

The clerk looked at the room keys. 'His key is here so he must be out, madam.'

She had to breathe deeply to quell her anxiety. The long journey had been exhausting but she was resolved to maintain her composure.

She said, 'Perhaps he is as the Exhibition. Have you visited it yourself yet?'

'I've not had a day to myself for nigh on two months, madam.'

Sarah remained calm until she was safely in her suite, when her brow furrowed and she twisted a handkerchief in her fingers. The hotel was a grand house with a fine entrance hall and wide staircase that reminded her of Meadow Hall. Mr Parrish had used a suite of rooms on the first floor, which Danby had reserved for them. It had a comfortable sitting room and large gracious bedchamber. Mary occupied the smaller bedchamber, which the hotel had furnished as a nursery. She was sitting in a nursing chair, cradling Belinda in her arms.

Sarah's face softened. Having Belinda was the most wonderful experience for Sarah and, whatever happened, she would always love her. However, she worried about who would take care of her child if anything happened to her and was grateful for Mary's devotion. 'Have we got everything we need for her?' she asked.

'Yes, ma'am. The hotel has a baby carriage to hire for when we go to the Exhibition,' Mary answered as she placed Belinda carefully in the crib. 'Shall I unpack for you and fetch hot water?'

'You have enough to do already; and a chambermaid will bring water for us to wash.' Sarah looked down at her clothes. 'My beautiful travelling outfit is so dusty. Railway trains are indeed fast but the smoke from the engine gets everywhere.'

'Well, it was too hectic for me, ma'am.'

'Are you not thrilled to be in London, Mary?'

'More frightened, ma'am. You hear such stories.'

'You're quite safe here.' Sarah smiled. 'Go downstairs for your supper. There is really no need to worry.'

The worry is all mine, she thought. But I have agreed to the

360

plan and will carry it through. Danby had been in London for several weeks now and she was becoming increasingly concerned about the viability of the glassworks. She had, ostensibly, sold her patent to an Australian gentleman and lodged the proceeds in a London bank. The account was held jointly with Danby and she had added the glassworks bank reserves as he requested. It would be left to her to wind up the warehouse lease with as little damage as possible

She took off her travelling coat and hat and went through to the large bedchamber. It was very tidy and she noted the couch as well as the large bed that Danby had been using. Her portmanteau was placed on a luggage stand and she searched for her key. She took out her dinner gown from its folds of calico and opened the clothes cupboard. A few of Danby's clothes remained. She looked in the drawers and they also contained a few items of clothing; nothing new or especially stylish, but definitely his. It was all her husband had left for her. Danby had already gone.

She had expected to see him one last time in the hotel but, clearly, he had other ideas. Her heart began to pound and she sat down on the couch. He had really done it. She had not asked him questions because she did not want to know the answers; and it was best for Belinda's sake if she didn't. But she guessed what he had done. If she went to her London banker she would find her account emptied by a single banker's draft and somewhere further down the Thames was a ship waiting to sail to Australia with a gentleman, his wife and son as passengers; and her patent in his pocket.

She breathed very deeply. She must be calm. She knew what she had to do, but now she was faced with it her courage was failing. She went back to Belinda, picked her up and hugged her closely. She was beautiful, she was hers, and Sarah loved her more than anything else in the world. She had agreed to Danby's plan for Belinda's future. But she fretted about her own part in the deception and what would happen if anyone found out. Belinda was heavy to hold in her arms but she clasped her tightly until Mary returned.

'Stay with her, Mary. Mr Jones isn't here and I must ask the staff if they have seen him.' Sarah said anxiously.

'Of course, ma'am.'

Sarah hurried downstairs to reception. Although it was summer the late hour meant that darkness had fallen and it was right that she should express concern. 'My husband has not returned yet,' she said.

'He will be waiting for a hire carriage, ma'am. They are in short supply at this hour.'

'But he said he would be here to meet me. Something must have happened to him!' Sarah's anxiety was genuine, though it was not because of her disquiet about Danby. He could take care of himself.

The gentleman at reception tried to pacify her. 'I'm sure that is not so, madam,'

'You don't know that. He could have been set upon by ruffians and be dying by the highway.'

The hotel manager appeared by her side. 'Come and sit in the foyer, Mrs Jones. A brandy will calm your nerves.' He clicked his fingers at the bellboy.

Sarah would not be pacified. 'Would you have me wait here all night? He could be anywhere and I must find him before it's too late.' She hurried to the hotel entrance, followed closely by the manager. 'Come back, ma'am, you do not want to be out there alone.'

She shrugged off his restraining hand. 'I must find a constable to look for him.'

'Very well, Mrs Jones, I shall send for the constable.'

Satisfied, Sarah allowed herself to be led back inside.

The constable was patient and paternal. He listened to her worries and reassured her that he had no report of the dead body of a gentleman and that he was sure Mr Jones was in good health. He explained that it was too soon to report her husband as a missing person but he noted down Danby's description and advised Sarah to retire to her chamber for the night.

Sarah tossed and turned all night. What would happen to her if anyone discovered that she was involved Danby's disappearance? She awoke more tired than the she had been the night before but nonetheless ordered a hire carriage to take herself, Mary and Belinda to the Exhibition in Hyde Park as planned. She was so nervous and apprehensive that she was convinced she would not enjoy anything. But when she saw the huge structure in front of her she was quite overcome by its splendour.

She gazed in wonder at the vast expanse of glass and ironwork. She understood now why it was called the Crystal Palace. And inside, there was gallery upon gallery of exhibits, thousands of them, from strange exotic animals to huge machines and displays of art from times gone by. It was wondrous. Sarah took Belinda from her small carriage and held her in her arms so that she could point out and talk to her about these splendours.

She adored these precious moments with her daughter. Belinda had Aidan's dark hair and his nose, at least how it was before it was broken. But she had her mother's large wide eyes; except that they were an unusual colour, not brown or grey; more green, Sarah thought. Sarah grew hot inside the glass and reluctantly returned Belinda to the baby carriage. She sent Mary for flavoured ices that were for sale.

When Mary came back her eyes were shining. 'You'll never guess, ma'am, but there's a whole group of folk here from town. They travelled together and are staying in lodgings. The institute did it all for them; railway tickets and everything. Look, there they are; over by the door.'

Sarah glanced up from talking to Belinda. She recognised one or two faces and – and another, standing to one side, with writing paper and pencil in his hand and his head tipped back. He was concentrating on the intricate roof structures of this massive glasshouse.

Dear Lord, he was here! Aidan was at the exhibition! She

stared, open mouthed as he sketched. He hadn't changed much but he was clean-shaven, exposing his handsome features, and his dark hair was tamed with macassar. As she gazed at him her eyes lost their focus, her pulses began to pound in her temple and she grew even hotter. She thought they had parted for ever on the night before her marriage. But oh, how she had longed to see him again since then! She must talk to him this minute . . .

'Aidan!' She said his name without thinking. He heard and looked around but two ladies walking past in their huge crinolines and elaborate hats blocked his view.

'Mary, give Belinda her ice for me.' She hurried over to him, her mind racing frantically to think of what she would say.

'Aidan?'

He glanced up from his notes and sketches. 'Sarah!' He put his pencil behind his ear and pushed the notes in his pocket. 'Sarah? This is a surprise.' He meant it. In fact it was a shock to him to see her. He noticed immediately that she was more beautiful than ever; mature, poised and confident except – except her eyes were tired. As he looked at her he felt again that intense desire for her that had caused him to leave town when she married. He tried to remain cool and detached but couldn't disguise his pleasure at seeing her again. He asked politely, 'Are you enjoying the Exhibition?'

Sarah composed herself. 'I am, thank you. It's wonderful, isn't it?' She paused, searched his sombre face and asked, 'How are you?' She really did want to know.

'I'm very well. And you?' He paused significantly before adding. 'You have a child now, haven't you; a little girl. Is she well?'

'You know about her?'

'Daniel Thorpe travels to Birmingham occasionally and brings the Riding newspapers for me. I saw the announcement.'

'Belinda is over there with Mary.'

He leaned to one side to get a better view and stared at her for a long time. 'She has dark hair,' he commented. 'Danby is a lucky fellow.' He looked around. 'Where is he?'

364

'I – he – he left early.' Not quite a lie, she thought, but not quite the truth. How shall I get through this? She so much wanted to tell Aidan everything. He would understand, she was sure, but was it fair to involve him in her deceptions? 'Are you staying in London for long?' she asked.

'Another night only.'

'May we – may we meet?'

'I don't think so, Sarah.'

'But I must see you. Come to my hotel this evening.'

'I don't think Danby will welcome me.'

'He's not there. I told you; he left.' In spite of the flavoured ice, she became hotter.

Aidan frowned. 'You seem anxious, Sarah. Is something amiss?'

She looked away.

'Where has Danby gone?' he pressed.

'I don't know. Truly I don't.'

'But I understood he had reformed when you had your child? The house where his – his mistress lived has been sold. Daniel said she has left town.' Suddenly his hand was under her chin, turning her to face him, and his eyes were on hers, searching for an answer. 'He hasn't gone after her, has he?'

She didn't answer. It was the truth and she could not say it; not yet. 'I – I have to talk to you, Aidan. Please say we can we meet?'

He lowered his voice. 'You are still his wife, Sarah. You must observe propriety or you will be the damned one instead of him.'

'My daughter and my maid are with me.'

'Even so . . .'

'I must speak with you, Aidan,' she responded desperately.

He glanced at members of the institute party who were taking an interest in this exchange.

Sarah whispered, 'They do not know that Danby has left me.'

His brow furrowed, his eyes darkened and his expression became unreadable. 'Very well,' he agreed at last. 'Where are you staying?'

As soon as she had handed him the hotel card Mary wheeled

the baby carriage towards her and said, 'There's a circus in the middle part, madam. Shall I take Belinda? They've got this man who walks across a rope high up in the roof; it's ever so exciting and it's starting in a minute.'

'You go on ahead and I'll catch you up.' When Mary was out of earshot she said, 'Promise me you'll call, Aidan.'

He nodded, but he was frowning as she hurried after Belinda.

Later, tense and tired, she walked with Belinda through Hyde Park to admire the fountains which rivalled the Exhibition itself for magnificence. It was cooler by the water and she relaxed, taking Belinda out of her baby carriage to exercise her little legs. She was still worried about the glassworks closing now she had lost her patent. And if anyone found out about Belinda's real father, she would lose the house as security too. But, somehow, none of this mattered at the moment. Aidan was in London and coming to see her tonight.

Sarah took Belinda straight upstairs to put her to bed. Poor mite, she was exhausted from all the excitement. Mary was at an open-air concert with the folk she had met at the Exhibition. Sarah washed, changed into her Indian muslin summer gown and cape, and re-dressed her hair. But nothing would quell the flutterings in her stomach and she paced around her sitting room wondering when Aidan would arrive to see her. She jumped, literally, when a bellboy knocked on her door to give her Aidan's card. Aidan was waiting in the foyer. After a few deep breaths and one last look in the glass she picked up her parasol and went downstairs.

He stood up as she approached, although he didn't smile. He gave her a stiff old-fashioned bow of his head and said, 'You look delightful.'

'Thank you. My gown is one of Mrs Thorpe's.' Sarah sat in the middle of the couch to accommodate her full skirts and Aidan chose a fireside chair. He wore a fashionably long jacket with a silk necktie and boots that looked new. Her heart was doing somersaults and she tried to formulate her words.

'Grand living seems to suit you, Sarah. Do you enjoy it?'

'It is more comfortable than being a washerwoman in the workhouse.' She changed the subject abruptly. 'The hotel has a pleasant garden with a shrubbery. Shall we walk?'

'What is it you wish to say to me?' he asked as he got up.

She waited until they were strolling among the flowerbeds before answering, 'Danby has disappeared from the hotel.'

'He has? I expect he'll be back. You know what he's like.'

'I have asked the constables to search for him.'

'Dear Lord! There must be a million people in London at present.'

Sarah chewed on her lip and nodded. 'He is not coming back.'

'I see,' Aidan responded thoughtfully. 'You mean he has left you. Well, I know it wasn't a marriage made in heaven but he wouldn't give up the glassworks, surely?'

When she did not answer, he prompted, 'Would he?'

'You've no idea how much he disliked me. He wanted me to leave and I wouldn't.'

'So he has cut and run instead? Well, that's true to form for him. But, if I know Danby, he hasn't gone for nothing.'

'I have given him my patent and the bank reserves.'

'Are you mad, Sarah? Have you risked the glassworks?'

'I hope not, although I could lose my home.'

It was quiet in the setting sun as they wandered through the gardens. Sarah wondered how much more to tell him. She wanted him to know everything, yet it didn't seem fair to involve him in her deception. She felt the tension stretch between them and said softly, 'It was worth it to be rid of him.'

'Oh, Sarah!' he breathed. 'Do not torture me with thoughts of your freedom. You will still be his wife.'

'Not if they cannot find him. After seven years he will be presumed dead and I shall be free of him forever.'

'Seven years? I can't wait seven years for you!'

She stopped stock still on the path.

He covered his face with his hands. 'I shouldn't have said that.

367

But when I saw you at the Exhibition with Belinda I envied Danby so much that it hurt. I imagined him dead, killed off in some freak accident in the glassworks; I wanted you to be free so that I could offer marriage to you.'

'You would marry me?'

'If only that were possible, Sarah! In all the times I have been apart from you I have never stopped loving you.'

A frisson of delight shivered through her skin. 'Nor I you.'

They stared at each other in silence for a few moments until Aidan said, 'Come over here, by the shrubbery.' He took her hand and pulled her after him.

In the cool quiet shade, she used her parasol to shield her head and shoulders from the pathway. He lifted her chin gently with his finger and kissed her mouth deeply and passionately. She clung to him, willing his lips to linger on hers for ever. They let go of each other eventually only so that they could breathe.

'Let's go upstairs to my chamber in the hotel,' she whispered.

He groaned and shook his head, 'It's too risky. What about your reputation? Word will get out, you'll be scandalised in the Riding and I cannot let that happen. Oh God, what am I going to do for seven years.'

Well, I'm not waiting that long for you either, Sarah thought. You are the man I want to spend the rest of my life with.

She had known his love and could no longer live without him. We have to find a way to be together, she thought.

Aidan left London the following day and returned to the South Riding to discuss a new venture with Daniel Thorpe. He would still be in town, he told her, when she returned with Belinda. The hotel manager, convinced by Sarah's obvious anxiety agreed with her that something sinister had happened to her husband, and called in the constable again who made copious notes and assured her they would 'explore all possibilities'.

The policeman smiled benignly, thinking that these young women from the provinces do get worked up. He'd bet his week's wages her husband had simply gone off with a business associate to enjoy the pleasures London had to offer a young blade with money in his pocket.

'In the meantime, madam, you must cease your worrying and go shopping. All the ladies go to Bond Street,' he said.

As ordered, Sarah spent a couple of days visiting Bond Street stores and the Tower of London. A few days before she was due to leave London she returned to the hotel to find the uniformed constable waiting for her. 'Mrs Jones,' he said, gesturing towards a couch. 'Will you sit down?'

She looked at his serious face. 'What is it? Have you found my husband?'

'Please sit down, madam.'

'No. Tell me what's happened.'

'My task is not a pleasant one. We have recovered a body that has been in the Thames for a day or so. I should like you to accompany me to the mortuary.'

'Mortuary?' Dear Lord, no. But it can't be him, she thought, because he's on his way to Australia.

'I'd like you to come with me for identification purposes, madam. The age, height and build fit the description you gave us.'

She had no choice and followed the policeman outside into the waiting carriage.

'He was a victim of a criminal act of violence and we have not been able to identify him,' the constable explained as they rode. 'He was hit over the head, robbed of all possessions and thrown in the river. Please prepare yourself, ma'am, for it is not a pretty sight. I should not ask you, but we have exhausted all other lines of enquiry.'

The mortuary was a cold cavernous chamber in the basement of a hospital. It had tiled walls and floors and the constable led Sarah to an alcove where the body was laid out on a table. It was covered by sheeting. The constable showed her a pile of clothing. They could have belonged to Danby. They were good

369

quality, of a stylish cut and he had, no doubt, purchased new garments while he was in the capital.

The mortuary attendant, wearing a large rubber apron, drew back the sheet. She gagged, choked and put her hand to her mouth, unable to speak. The face was a pallid grey, the colour of washed chitterlings on the butcher's slab, and shedding fragments of white skin were clinging to the cheeks and forehead. It could be anybody, she thought, but the hair was fair like Danby's. She staggered and turned away and the constable placed his hand on her arm. 'I know it is hard for you, ma'am, but do you recognise anything about him?'

'May I sit down?'

'Take your time, Mrs Jones. Would you care for a glass of water?'

'Thank you, yes.'

If only I could be sure, she thought. If only it were him I should be free to marry Aidan. Belinda would have her father and I – I should be truly happy. A vision swam before her eyes. She was walking through a wood holding one of Belinda's hand and Aidan was beside her, clasping Belinda's other hand, smiling first at her and then at their daughter. They were together, they were a family, they were happy.

It would be so easy to just say this was Danby lying cold on the marble slab, but what if someone found out she had lied and they sent her to gaol? What would happen to her beloved Belinda? She would have to reveal her secret then and tell Aidan the truth. How she ached to shed her burden of secrecy and do that. She sipped the water and tried to compose herself.

'Madam?' The attendant waited patiently for her to stand up.

She swallowed the vomit rising in her throat as he pulled the sheet down further. 'This might help,' he said. 'Would you look at this mark, madam?'

It was a small strawberry birthmark, quite low down on his abdomen. Only a wife or lover would have seen it. Did Danby have such a mark? She had no idea. It wasn't Danby anyway; the shape of the jaw wasn't his. Besides, she was sure he was on the high seas with his mistress, and her patent.

'Is this your husband, Mrs Jones?' the policeman asked.

This was her chance for happiness. She couldn't let it slip away. She swallowed again and found her voice at last. 'Yes. That's him,' she whispered.

'Thank you, madam. Please come this way.'

It was well past tea time when Sarah, with Mary and Belinda, arrived at the train station in Mosbrough. It had been a long dusty journey from London back to the Riding but, as it was summer, not yet dark.

Sarah talked softly to Belinda for a few minutes while George collected their luggage and loaded it into her carriage. She kissed her infant daughter and handed her to Mary. 'You go with her in the carriage and put her to bed for me tonight. I shall walk home.'

'You're not walking alone are you, ma'am?' Mary protested.

She shook her head. 'I am meeting a friend,' she replied cheerfully and patted the document in her skirt pocket.

He was here. She knew he would be and, as soon as she saw him, she was certain she had done the right thing, however much he would, no doubt, disapprove. She would never love anyone as much as she loved Aidan. It was an enduring love that had been strained and tested to breaking point. But the underlying bond between them had not broken; perhaps it had been fractured by their actions in the past but it had grown back stronger than before and she was reminded of that strength when she saw him waiting for her in the shadow of the station building.

He wore a flamboyant necktie with his fashionable new jacket. She wanted him to wrap his arms around her and kiss her but knew he would not. Not yet anyway. There would be time enough for each other in the future and because of that she was more at ease in his presence. He took her hand, though, and kissed it lovingly, glancing at her with hungry eyes.

371

'I have good news for your glassworks,' he said. 'The whole town is talking of the Exhibition and every prosperous shopkeeper and manufacturer will want his own Crystal Palace after this summer.'

'Tell me more as we walk.' She smiled.

'If your cones have the capacity to provide window glass, my forge will fashion iron frameworks and between us we shall make a conservatory for every household that can afford one.'

Sarah let out a huge sigh. 'Oh, yes. What a wonderful idea. The glassworks and labourers will be safe. It has been a huge worry for me since Mr Parrish died.' She took a breath. 'I have news for you, too.'

'Good news, I hope.'

'See for yourself.' She took the document from her pocket and handed it to him.

He unfolded it. His eyes darted across the paper and he frowned. 'This is dated only a few days ago.'

'They found a body in the Thames.'

'And it was Danby?'

'That paper says it was, doesn't it?'

'What have you done, Sarah?' Aidan said with a frown.

'I've made it possible for us to be together. Aren't you pleased?'

'You told them the body was Danby? Were you absolutely sure?'

She gave a tiny shake of her head. 'It wasn't him.'

'You are quite mad. What if someone else claims him?'

'The constable said he'd tried. I was his last option. Anyway, with this hot weather, I had to arrange to bury him quickly in London.'

'You shouldn't have lied to the police, Sarah.'

She saw the pain in his face and whispered, 'I'm sorry. Please don't hate me now that I can put everything right between us. After a period of mourning I shall be able to receive you in my house. You – you did say that you would offer me marriage if he were dead.'

'But this – this would be bigamy.' Aidan's face was severe and she became anxious that she had gone too far by drawing him into her deceit.

'No, it won't! That piece of paper says it won't be. No one will ever know. Danby won't come back. He hates this town and he's got what he wanted.'

'And have you, Sarah?'

'I shall have when we marry.'

'I haven't asked you yet.' He frowned at her again and shook his head as though in despair.

Please Lord, she prayed, don't let him change his mind. Not now.

He went on, 'If I did marry you I should be turning you into a criminal.'

They had reached the bridge over the navigation and she heard the water splashing against the stone arches below. Soon they would be approaching the town shops where lamps were glowing and they would be noticed together. She stopped and took both his hands so that she could look directly at him. 'I've done that already by my actions. Is it why you hesitate? Or is it because you still believe you are not my equal because you do not have wealth and status. I thought you were wrong before and think you are wrong now.'

'Perhaps I am. But I am thinking only of you.'

Her heart turned over. 'Life has changed for both of us, Aidan,' she said. 'You have premises in Birmingham and the Riding. You dress and behave as a gentleman. I know what I have done is wicked but I had my reasons.' She faltered and swallowed before going on, 'I did not do it just for myself. I – I have a daughter who needs a father.'

His face softened. 'Yes, I have seen how much you cherish her and she is a delightful child. But you compound your sin by depriving her of her father for ever. Did you think of that in your scheming, Sarah?'

Sarah was hurt by his response. He did not understand. How

could he when he did not know the truth about Belinda. 'I did it for her,' she whispered. She ought to tell him now but she feared he might despise her even more.

'Danby is a fool,' Aidan said. 'He had a beautiful, intelligent wife and an adorable daughter. I know you two didn't get on, but how could he leave behind such a treasure as Belinda?'

'Because . . . because . . .' She couldn't say the words.

'Poor child,' Aidan went on. 'She has a loving mother but she will never know her father.'

She will if you marry me, Sarah beseeched silently. She said quietly, 'Belinda needs her father. So do I.' Her eyes were wide and shiny with tears as she silently pleaded with him to understand – and to forgive.

Aidan didn't respond for a few moments. She feared that she had said too much and shocked him. She turned away to walk on but he pulled her back and demanded, 'What do you mean?'

Sarah sighed heavily. 'Everything was so complicated after Mr Parrish died. I did what I did because I know what it's like to be destitute and I couldn't let down the glassworkers. And then – later – I wanted to protect my child from poverty.'

'Will you explain to me what you are talking about?'

'I'll try.'

The evening breezes whipped up dust and debris as Sarah and Aidan progressed through the town's streets. Shopkeepers were closing their doors and putting up their window shutters.

'Tell me everything, Sarah.'

So she did; about the will, the marriage, the inheritance for her firstborn, but she still couldn't tell Aidan that he was the father of her child. She finished, 'In the end I did it for Belinda. She was all I had and I wanted the best for her.'

Aidan's face was grim. 'You drove a hard bargain but I suppose Danby deserved it after the double life he'd been living. He must have loved his mistress and son very much. Although I am still shocked he gave up his daughter. I should have found that impossible.'

I have to tell him now, she thought. Her heart began to thump and when she tried to speak her lips were trembling. 'She – she is not his daughter. She – she is—'

'Not his?'

The corners of Aidan's mouth turned down, whether in query or distaste she could not tell. Sarah found the trembling spreading through her arms and legs. She forced herself to go on. 'Belinda is your daughter.'

'*My* daughter?'

'She is your child, Aidan. I have never told a living soul until now.'

His eyes searched hers for a moment. 'Belinda is mine? Truly?' Then his face darkened. 'But you were married to Danby. How can you be so sure?'

'I was never a wife to Danby in that respect.'

It was as she feared. He was angry and his voice rose. 'Why didn't you tell me? Dear Lord, Sarah, you bore my child and never told me!' His eyes flashed and he clenched and unclenched his fists by his sides. 'I had a daughter – have a daughter.' He shook his head as though lost for words. 'You should have told me!'

'Please don't be angry with me. I did what I did for Belinda's future.' Sarah was close to tears. Dear Heaven, this was all going wrong!

'Did Danby know?' Aidan demanded.

'Not that she was yours; only that she was not his. He didn't want me any more than I wanted him.' She pressed her lips together to stop them trembling. Now was not the time to be weak. 'I wanted you and I wanted Belinda,' she insisted.

Her words seemed to calm him. 'I have always wanted you,' he said, 'even after you were married.'

She added firmly, for good measure, 'It wasn't a proper marriage.'

His anger faded. He stopped in the middle of the street, wrapped

375

his arms around her and hugged her close to his body. 'Ours will be, though, won't it?' he said.

'Yes, it will.'

His eyes shone as he smiled at her and said, 'I can hardly believe this is happening and I shall waste no more time.' Without further thought he bent his head to kiss her and she met his searching lips and tongue with a matching passion of her own. When he paused for breath she straightened her bonnet and murmured, 'People are looking at us.'

'It's dark, they will not recognise us.'

She didn't agree but said, 'Even so, we are not betrothed.'

'Then you will allow me to rectify that?' He stepped back and dropped to one knee on the dusty ground. 'Sarah, I love you to distraction. Will you do me the honour of becoming my wife?'

She smiled and thought of how much she loved him. 'Of course I will.'

'Now we are betrothed, I may kiss you to my heart's content.'

'And mine.'

A Note on Inspiration

By Catherine King

The Orphan Child is my fifth nineteenth-century saga located in South Yorkshire and neighbouring areas. When I look back, I realise that I didn't choose this setting. It chose me. I was racking my brain for something different to write about and quite by chance attended a local history exhibition in Rotherham, the town where I was born and went to school. Until then, history had meant the kings and queens of England, although I had vague recollections of lessons about Gladstone and Disraeli. As I progressed around the tables and talked to local enthusiasts, I realised that 'something different' was staring me in the face.

At the same time, I was researching my family history and it became clear that Yorkshire coal, iron and steel were in my blood. But there were other trades, notably tailoring, and a 'woodman with nine acres', who appeared to be a patriarch for three generations. These were real people who worked through and survived hardship and rapid change during their lives, and who inspire the characters in my books. I was, however, a little disappointed to find no evidence of a major scandal and only two illegitimate births. I'm sure my family had its share of wrong-doers and villains, but their stories didn't make the newspapers at the time.

Fortunately, there are enough records and reports of others to inspire me!

The Orphan Child, like my other books, is set in the early Victorian period, which was a time of immense economic and social change in rural and urban England. Coal-fired steam power led to increased mechanisation of many agricultural and manu-facturing processes. Constructing the new machines meant bigger demands on furnaces and forges, and South Yorkshire was no exception. Railways to transport raw materials and manufactured products were spreading across the country, further increasing the appetite for coal, iron and steel.

Earlier in the nineteenth-century, wealth had been created by providing cannon for Lord Wellington's army fighting Bonaparte in Europe. But after the Battle of Waterloo, when the war came to an end, premises were abandoned and men laid off until the Industrial Revolution really took off and resurrected demands. In South Yorkshire, manufacturing partnerships formed to make new fortunes, and dissolved just as readily when the fortunes were lost. They were numerous reasons for failure including inad-equate funding or expertise, plain bad luck or ill health or, of course, profits frittered away on drinking and gambling. These Victorian vices were not burdened by any allegiance to class and the rich were as susceptible as the poor.

I think it is reading about disaster and failure that gives me my best inspiration. What was it like to be thrown out of the only home you had known without a penny to your name, even if you were just a servant? What choices would you have when there was no safety net in the form of welfare? This is where I started with *The Orphan Child*. I wanted to explore how three young people from varying backgrounds would survive being on their own and how the experiences might affect them as they matured.

In this book there are no direct comparisons of the charac-ters with my ancestors. However, one of my great-grandfathers came from 'Thomas Hardy country' in the South of England.

The census shows him unemployed in a family of agricultural labourers until he set off on his own to make his fortune in the industrial north. He headed for the north-east Yorkshire town of Middlesbrough and set up as a coal-dealer. By the end of the Victorian era he was an established coal merchant with a prestigious address in the town. It is his courage and determination that I wished to capture in my book. If you are a Toogood living in the Middlesbrough area you may be a distant cousin of mine!

The industrial revolution was just as hungry for people as it was for coal and iron. But mines, mills and manufactories needed skill as well as muscle, especially engineers and mechanics. They learned their trades by working alongside more experienced colleagues and by attending the Mechanics Institutes that were set up in most towns and cities. These establishments were the community centres of the era and often a meeting place for working men, especially if they had no money for the ale house. Many of these buildings still exist and are in use to this day. I only have to stand and stare at the one in Wentworth, near Rotherham, to imagine the comings and goings when there were no cars, pavements or street lights, for an idea to form in my head.

In *The Orphan Child* one fortune is lost on horses and another one is made with a furnace, this time to smelt glass rather than iron or steel, but still needing fuel from the coal field that lies underneath most of South Yorkshire.

We have a saying in the North of England, which I'm sure my great-grandfather must have heard in Hardy's Wessex. It goes, 'where's there's muck there's brass' (muck meaning coal and brass meaning money) and in my nineteenth-century South Riding, it is true. However, in my story I take this a step further, for where there is money there is vice. Despite the constant struggles of municipal authorities, vice in its various guises, thrived, making any vulnerable person a prey to its greed. Neither Sarah nor Aidan nor Danby in my book are immune to its effects and each has to deal with it in his or her own way.

On a brighter note, one of the enduring features of towns all over the world is the market place. Rotherham was granted its charter centuries ago and the market remains an important aspect of the town's culture. As a child in school, my first 'composition' that my teacher read out to the whole class was written about going to town on market day with my mother. The impression on me must have run deep, for a market appears regularly in my books and it is frequently the scene of significant events. I adore markets. Of course the ones nowadays are not the same as they used to be, revolving, as they were, around livestock. But the traditions of selling local produce and providing entertainment have survived, and long may they continue. Sarah, my orphan child of the title, experiences the good and the bad of market day and grows up quite a lot during her visits.

Of course, the dreaded workhouse, set up by the municipal authority to 'deal with the poor', provided the setting for a significant part of the book. When I visited one that is now a museum, the guide told me that Henry VIII was to blame for the establishment of workhouses. His reasoning was that when King Henry crushed the monasteries, he removed the only facility that considered it a duty to take in and care for the poor and needy. So these unfortunate souls had nowhere to go and became an increasing problem until the workhouse provided a solution.

At the time it was a generally considered that if a poor man was hale and hearty then he was poor through his own fault and if he learned discipline and hard work, his difficulty would go away. Life in the workhouse was made as unattractive as possible so that it was everyone's last resort in a crisis. If a family was unfortunate enough to end up there, then it was split up and parents lost their children, who became wards of the workhouse Guardians. Sometimes the children were lucky and the workhouse had a school log before municipal education was compulsory.

Workhouses also provided overnight accommodation for the many itinerants wandering nineteenth-century England, specifically to keep them off the streets. These men and women were always made to work for their B&B and were known as 'dossers'. The dossers themselves shared their accumulated knowledge of the best and worst of the workhouses they'd visited.

There were others, too, who had to be kept off the streets as well to protect society at large. These were mainly women and labelled 'morally defective'. In my researches I could not find an incident of a man labelled as such. However, going into the workhouse was always considered a stigma. A friend of mine remembers her great-aunt who flatly refused to attend hospital, despite her doctor's pleading because it was located on the site of the old workhouse. Memories are long in Yorkshire!

Like any new enterprise, workhouses took several years before best practice was established and some suffered crime and corruption from the staff, let alone the inmates. After my visit to a workhouse museum I came away with numerous ideas of ways to challenge poor Sarah when she was eventually admitted.

One of the reasons the glass furnaces flourished in Victorian England was the fact that breweries prospered. Outbreaks of cholera made people wary of drinking water. Ale was a safer choice, and working long days in hot furnaces and forges gave a man a thirst. Of course, barrels were still the most popular means of transporting ale to the inns and taverns, but as soon as secure stoppers were mass produced the popularity of bottles for all kinds of liquid contents soared.

Victorian England was a time of novelty and invention. Her Majesty ruled over an empire and one small country seemed to lead the world in engineering and technology. This national prosperity was demonstrated by the staging of the Great Exhibition in the middle of the century. It was huge. Housed in the largest glass house ever known, designed by Joseph Paxton, it covered acres of Hyde Park in London and contained everything from enormous machinery to high wire acrobats and exotic animals from all corners of the world.

Iron, steel and glass made the Great Exhibition possible, and iron, steel and glass made my fictional South Riding thrive. These industries provided employment and wealth for the people in my book, so it seemed a fitting setting to draw my story to a close.

I always enjoy the research for my books whether it is my own family or the history of a location. But the most exciting part is when I write the story. I don't have too many fixed ideas about what will happen as I'd rather wait and see. All the factual information goes into my head and I never know how it is going to come out as fiction until I sit down at my lap-top and type. As far as I'm concerned, it's sheer magic!

Best wishes
Catherine

WOMEN OF IRON

Catherine King

For Sale: One child, six months old. Lissie.

The seller: Grace Beighton watched the baby's mother die. Only she knows who the real father is.

The buyer: Luther Dearne has made a fortune with the wealthy iron masters of Yorkshire. Corrupt, powerful, apparently above the law, he has everything he could possibly want – except children. Now he can buy one of those, too.

A story of loves lost and found, of sexual exploitation, deceit, greed and murder, *Women of Iron* is a spellbinding saga in which only the toughest survive.

978 0 7515 3907 3

SILK AND STEEL

Catherine King

Revenge
Mariah Bowes thinks that being alone and penniless is the worst thing that can happen to her, but then she becomes the victim of a horrifying act of revenge.

Deception
Daniel Thorpe is consumed with guilt. He couldn't have imagined the terrible consequences of his affair with the beautiful Lily. Will he ever convince Mariah to trust him again?

Secrets
But for Mariah there are further truths to uncover. Not least the awful secret that her father, Ezekiel Bowes, successful iron master and respectable member of the community, is determined to keep in the dark.

Silk and Steel, Catherine King's second Yorkshire novel, is a powerful tale of one woman's fight for survival.

978 0 7515 3908 0

WITHOUT A MOTHER'S LOVE

Catherine King

Abandoned. Olivia Copley is an orphan. Sent to live with her uncle, the ruthless mine owner Hesley Mexton, she soon discovers that a house ruled by men can not only be desperate: it can be cruel.

Humiliated. A new governess, Harriet Trent, offers Olivia a glimpse of hope. But Harriet's past is full of secrets and, alone and without protection, Olivia realises that Hesley Mexton will take full advantage of her vulnerability – despite her governess's protests.

Determined. Starved of love, Harriet and Olivia form a close bond. But, when forced to fight for their freedom, will find the courage to defy the man that seeks to hold them captive?

978 0 7515 4131 1

A MOTHER'S SACRIFICE

Catherine King

Destitute
Quinta Haig is struggling to make ends meet. The small
Yorkshire farm she shares with her ailing mother is run down
but, even at fifteen, Quinta is prepared to do almost anything
to survive.

Coveted
Noah Bilton, a wealthy neighbour, has designs on their land
as well as on the two Haig women. He offers an uneasy
solution to keep them out of the workhouse and is flatly
refused – but Noah is determined to take what he wants by
fair means or foul.

Deserted
Finding love against all odds, Quinta is abandoned at her
most vulnerable. Filled with a steely determination to survive,
she has yet to realize just how much she must sacrifice . . .

978 0 7515 4132 8

Other bestselling titles available by mail:

☐ Women of Iron	Catherine King	£6.99
☐ Silk and Steel	Catherine King	£6.99
☐ Without a Mother's Love	Catherine King	£6.99
☐ A Mother's Sacrifice	Catherine King	£6.50

The prices shown above are correct at time of going to press. However, the publishers reserve the right to increase prices on covers from those previously advertised, without further notice.

───────────────── sphere ─────────────────

Please allow for postage and packing: **Free UK delivery.**
Europe; add 25% of retail price; Rest of World; 45% of retail price.

To order any of the above or any other Sphere titles, please call our credit card orderline or fill in this coupon and send/fax it to:

Sphere, P.O. Box 121, Kettering, Northants NN14 4ZQ
Fax: 01832 733076   Tel: 01832 737526
Email: aspenhouse@FSBDial.co.uk

☐ I enclose a UK bank cheque made payable to Sphere for £ . . . .
☐ Please charge £ . . . . . . to my Visa, Delta, Maestro.

Expiry Date ☐☐☐☐   Maestro Issue No. ☐☐

NAME (BLOCK LETTERS please) . . . .

ADDRESS . . . .

. . . .

. . . .

Postcode . . . . Telephone . . . .

Signature . . . .

Please allow 28 days for delivery within the UK. Offer subject to price and availability.